Other Books in the Analog Anthology Series Edited by Stanley Schmidt

WRITERS' CHOICE
VOLUME II

ANTHOLOGY #8

WRITERS' CHOICE
VOLUME II

Edited by
Stanley Schmidt

Davis Publications, Inc.
380 Lexington Avenue, New York, N.Y. 10017

COPYRIGHT NOTICES AND ACKNOWLEDGMENTS

Grateful acknowledgment is hereby made for permission to reprint the following:

Breeds There a Man . . . ? by Isaac Asimov; copyright 1951 by Isaac Asimov, renewed; reprinted by permission of the author.

To Be Continued by Robert Silverberg; © 1956 by Street & Smith Publications, Inc., renewed 1984 by Davis Publications, Inc.; reprinted by permission of the author.

The End of Summer by Algis Budrys; copyright 1954 by Street & Smith Publications, Inc., renewed 1982 by Davis Publications, Inc.; reprinted by permission of the author.

Won't You Walk— by Theodore Sturgeon; © 1955 by Theodore Sturgeon, renewed; reprinted by permission of Kirby McCauley, Ltd.

Operation Syndrome by Frank Herbert; copyright 1954 by Street & Smith Publications, Inc., renewed 1982 by Davis Publications, Inc.; reprinted by permission of Kirby McCauley Ltd.

The Bright Illusion by C. L. Moore; copyright 1934 by Street & Smith Publications, Inc., renewed; re-printed by permission of Don Congdon Associates, Inc.

The Mechanic by Hal Clement; copyright © 1966 by Hal Clement; reprinted by permission of the author.

A Small Kindness by Ben Bova; © 1983 by Davis Publications, Inc.; reprinted by permission of the author.

The Unreachable Stars by Stanley Schmidt; copyright © 1971 by The Conde Nast Publications, Inc.; reprinted by permission of Scott Meredith Literary Agency, Inc.

Rescue Squad by Katherine MacLean; formerly titled "Fear Hound"; copyright © 1968 by Katherine MacLean; reprinted by permission of the author.

Gulf by Robert A. Heinlein; copyright 1949 by Robert A. Heinlein, renewed, reprinted by permission of Spectrum Literary Agency.

CONTENTS

INTRODUCTION

by Stanley Schmidt

Approximately a year ago the editors and publishers of *Analog Science Fiction/Science Fact* produced an anthology called *Analog: Writers' Choice*. The title could, I suppose, be construed as a *double entendre*. *Analog*, formerly known as *Astounding*, has long been the first choice of many top writers as the showplace for their best science fiction. And the stories in that book were the authors' own choices from among those they had written for this highly regarded magazine.

Readers enjoyed *Writers' Choice*, but they must have shared my frustration at being able to include only a few of their favorite writers. There were many more who obviously belonged in such a book, by virtue of popularity or prolific output or some other special importance in the history of *Astounding/Analog*, but I only had so many pages at my disposal. Putting together a book with a fixed number of pages is something like assembling a jigsaw puzzle. The pieces will only go together in certain ways, and if the pieces you have don't all fit, you may have a few left over.

That (along with a few other routine problems such as some writers' being unavailable when we tried to contact them) is what happened to *Writers' Choice*. It was obvious from the start that it would take more than one book to come close to giving a just representation, and I said in the Introduction to the first *Writers' Choice* that there would probably be at least one more.

This is it: *Writers' Choice, Volume II*. Not "second choices," by any means, but simply more of the first choices which wouldn't fit between one set of covers. The writers represented this time include both of the living past or present editors of *Analog* (with stories originally bought by their predecessor, John W. Campbell), as well as nine others whose names are all well known and instantly identified with highly entertaining, thought-provoking science fiction. Each has prefaced his story with a few words about his choice.

Of course, such a selection will never be really complete. There are many other writers who have left a trail of memorable work in *Analog*s but have yet to find their way into these anthologies. To them I say only, "Sorry; no slight intended. Maybe later." And, of course, there are those "new" writers who have started blazing such a trail but have not yet been working long enough to produce a large body of work or become firmly established in many people's memories. But they will. *Analog* is a living, growing magazine. It has always published not only first-rank established writers, but the most promising new talent. Many, if not all, of the writers in this book first attracted readers' attention in the pages of *Astounding/Analog*, and I have not the slightest doubt that many of the newcomers appearing there now will be just as well known and widely admired a few years hence.

But to see what *they* are doing, you will have to go to the current issues of *Analog* itself, whether via newsstand or subscription. I hope you will enjoy this book enough to make you want to do just that. ■

Joel Davis, President and Publisher; **Leonard F. Pinto,** Vice President & General Manager; **Carole Dolph Gross,** Vice President, Marketing & Editorial; **Leonard H. Habas,** Vice President, Circulation; **Fred Edinger,** Vice President, Finance.

Stanley Schmidt, Editor; **Shelley Frier,** Editorial Assistant; **Ralph Rubino,** Corporate Art Director; **Gerard Hawkins,** Associate Art Director; **Terri Czeczko,** Art Editor; **Carl Bartee,** Director of Manufacturing; **Carole Dixon,** Production Manager; **Iris Temple,** Director, Subsidiary Rights; **Barbara Bazyn,** Manager, Contracts & Permissions; **Michael Dillon,** Circulation Director, Retail Marketing; **Kathy Tully-Cestaro,** Circulation Manager/Subscriptions; **Paul Pearson,** Newsstand Operations Manager; **Irene Bozoki,** Classified Advertising Director; **William F. Battista,** Advertising Director (NEW YORK: 212-557-9100; CHICAGO: 312-346-0712; LOS ANGELES: 213-795-3114)

BREEDS THERE A MAN . . . ?

Isaac Asimov

In the years immediately following the nuclear bombing of Hiroshima and Nagasaki, there was a virtual avalanche of stories of nuclear doom. (Some even appeared before the bombing.)

I tended to avoid that because I saw at once that it would be overdone. It was also my feeling that science fiction stories tied too closely to the concerns of today tended to become quickly outdated and to show no ability to endure. Consequently I scorned what I called "tomorrow fiction" and concentrated on backgrounds sufficiently far in the future to seem reasonably fresh to later generations of readers.

However, it is difficult for me to follow my own rules always. For one thing, I sometimes forget them in the excitement of an idea, and, for another, there comes a time when the breaking of a rule becomes a challenge. Maybe "tomorrow fiction" is a bad idea as a rule (goes the rumination within my mind) but I'll bet I can write a good one. —So I try to do it.

So here is my nuclear doom story except that, being me, I avert it—but bring in a worse and subtler doom.

Oh, one thing. I don't like to have my characters all bear bland Anglo-Saxon names, so I began the story with a strongly ethnic one. I decided to make up a name that sounded Polish and produced Mankiewicz out of my imagination. I was very proud of it until I found out it was a perfectly common Polish name, though I could swear I had never heard it until after *I wrote this story.*

—Isaac Asimov

POLICE SERGEANT MANKIEWICZ was on the telephone and he wasn't enjoying it. His conversation was sounding like a one-sided view of a firecracker.

He was saying, "That's right! He came in here and said, 'Put me in jail, because I want to kill myself.'

"I can't help that. Those were his exact words.

". . . I can't help that. Those were exact words. It sounds crazy to me, too.

". . . Look, mister, the guy answers the description. You asked me for information and I'm giving it to you.

". . . He has exactly that scar on his right cheek and he said his name was John Smith. He didn't say it was Doctor anything-at-all.

". . . Well, sure it's a phony. Nobody is named John Smith. Not in a police station, anyway.

". . . He's in jail now.

". . . Yes, I mean it.

". . . Resisting an officer; assault and battery; malicious mischief. That's three counts.

". . . I don't care who he is.

". . . All right. I'll hold on."

He looked up at Officer Brown and put his hand over the mouthpiece of the phone. It was a ham of a hand that nearly swallowed up the phone altogether. His blunt-featured face was ruddy and streaming under a thatch of pale-yellow hair.

He said, "Trouble! Nothing but trouble at a precinct station. I'd rather be pounding a beat any day."

"Who's on the phone?" asked Brown. He had just come in and didn't really care. He thought Mankiewicz would look better on a suburban beat, too.

"Oak Ridge. Long Distance. A guy called Grant. Head of somethingological division, and now he's getting somebody else at seventy-five cents a min . . . Hello!"

Mankiewicz got a new grip on the phone and held himself down.

"Look," he said, "let me go through this from the beginning. I want you to get it straight and then if you don't like it, you can send someone down here. The guy doesn't want a lawyer. He claims he just wants to stay in jail and, brother, that's all right with me.

"Well, will you listen? He came in yesterday, walked right up to me, and said, 'Officer, I want you to put me in jail because I want to kill myself.' So I said, 'Mister, I'm sorry you want to kill yourself. Don't do it, because if you do, you'll regret it the rest of your life.'

". . . I *am* serious. I'm just telling you what I said. I'm not saying it was a funny joke, but I've got my own troubles here, if you know what I mean. Do you think all I've got to do here is to listen to cranks who walk in and—

". . . Give me a chance, will you?" I said, 'I can't put you in jail for wanting to kill yourself. That's no crime.' And he said, 'But I don't want to die.' So I said,

'Look, bud, get out of here.' I mean if a guy wants to commit suicide, all right, and if he doesn't want to, all right, but I don't want him weeping on my shoulder.

". . . I'm *getting* on with it. So he said to me, 'If I commit a crime, will you put me in jail?' I said, 'If you're caught and if someone files a charge and you can't put up bail, we will. Now beat it.' So he picked up the inkwell on my desk and before I could stop him, he turned it upside down on the open police blotter.

". . . That's right! Why do you think we have 'malicious mischief' tabbed on him? The ink ran down all over my pants.

". . . Yes, assault and battery, too! I came hopping down to shake a little sense into him, and he kicked me in the shins and handed me one in the eye.

". . . I'm not making this up. You want to come down here and look at my face?

". . . He'll be up in court one of these days. About Thursday, maybe.

". . . Ninety days is the least he'll get, unless the psychos say otherwise. I think he belongs in the loony-bin myself.

". . . Officially, he's John Smith. That's the only name he'll give.

". . . No, sir, he doesn't get released without the proper legal steps.

". . . OK, you do that, if you want to, bud! I just do my job here."

He banged the phone into its cradle, glowered at it, then picked it up and began dialing. He said, "Gianetti?" got the proper answer and began talking.

"What's the A.E.C.? I've been talking to some Joe on the phone and he says—

". . . No, I'm not kidding, lunk-head. If I were kidding, I'd put up a sign. What's the alphabet soup?"

He listened, said, "Thanks" in a small voice, and hung up again.

He had lost some of his color. "That second guy was the head of the Atomic Energy Commission," he said to Brown. "They must have switched me from Oak Ridge to Washington."

Brown lounged to his feet, "Maybe the F.B.I. is after this John Smith guy. Maybe he's one of these here scientists." He felt moved to philosophy. "They ought to keep atomic secrets away from those guys. Things were OK as long as General Groves was the only fella who knew about the atom bomb. Once they cut in these here scientists on it, though—"

"Ah, shut up," snarled Mankiewicz.

Dr. Oswald Grant kept his eyes fixed on the white line that marked the highway and handled the car as though it were an enemy of his. He always did. He was tall and knobby with a withdrawn expression stamped on his face. His knees crowded the wheel, and his knuckles whitened whenever he made a turn.

Inspector Darrity sat beside him with his legs crossed so that the sole of his left shoe came up hard against the door. It would leave a sandy mark when he took it away. He tossed a nut-brown penknife from hand to hand. Earlier, he had unsheathed

Isaac Asimov

its wicked, gleaming blade and scraped casually at his nails as they drove, but a sudden swerve had nearly cost him a finger and he desisted.

He said, "What do you know about this Ralson?"

Dr. Grant took his eyes from the road momentarily, then returned them. He said, uneasily, "I've known him since he took his doctorate at Princeton. He's a very brilliant man."

"Yes? Brilliant, huh? Why is it that all you scientific men describe one another as 'brilliant'? Aren't there any mediocre ones?"

"Many. I'm one of them. But Ralson isn't. You ask anyone. Ask Oppenheimer. Ask Bush. He was the youngest observer at Alamo-gordo."

"O.K. He was brilliant. What about his private life?"

Grant waited. "I wouldn't know."

"You know him since Princeton. How many years is that?"

They had been scouring north along the highway from Washington for two hours with scarcely a word between them. Now Grant felt the atmosphere change and the grip of the law on his coat collar.

"He got it in '43."

"You've known him eight years then."

"That's right."

"And you don't know about his private life?"

"A man's life is his own, Inspector. He wasn't very sociable. A great many of the men are like that. They work under pressure and when they're off the job, they're not interested in continuing the lab acquaintanceships."

"Did he belong to any organizations that you know of?"

"No."

The inspector said, "Did he every say anything to you that might indicate he was disloyal?"

Grant shouted, "No!" and there was silence for a while.

Then Darrity said, "How important is Ralson in atomic research?"

Grant hunched over the wheel and said, "As important as any one man can be. I grant you that no one is indispensable, but Ralson has always seemed to be rather unique. He has the engineering mentality."

"What does that mean?"

"He isn't much of a mathematician himself, but he can work out the gadgets that put someone else's math into life. There's no one like him when it comes to that. Time and again, Inspector, we've had a problem to lick and no time to lick it in. There were nothing but blank minds all around until he put some thought into it and said, 'Why don't you try so-and-so?' Then he'd go away. He wouldn't even be interested enough to see if it worked. But it always did. Always! Maybe we would have got it ourselves eventually, but it might have taken months of additional time. I don't know how he does it. It's no use asking him either. He just looks at you and says, 'It was obvious,' and walks away. Of course, once he's shown us how to do it, it *is* obvious.''

The inspector let him have his say out. When no more came, he said, "Would you say he was queer, mentally? Erratic, you know.''

"When a person is a genius, you wouldn't expect him to be normal, would you?''

"Maybe not. But just how abnormal was this particular genius?''

"He never talked, particularly. Sometimes, he wouldn't work.''

"Stayed at home and went fishing instead?''

"No. He came to the labs all right; but he would just sit at his desk. Sometimes that would go on for weeks. Wouldn't answer you, or even look at you, when you spoke to him.''

"Did he ever actually leave work altogether?''

"Before now, you mean? Never!''

"Did he ever claim he wanted to commit suicide? Ever say he wouldn't feel safe except in jail?''

"No.''

"You're sure this John Smith is Ralson?''

"I'm almost positive. He has a chemical burn on his right cheek that can't be mistaken.''

"OK. That's that, then I'll speak to him and see what he sounds like.''

The silence fell for good this time. Dr. Grant followed the snaking line as Inspector Darrity tossed the penknife in low arcs from hand to hand.

The warden listened to the call-box and looked up at his visitors. "We can have him brought up here, Inspector, regardless.''

"No,'' Dr. Grant shook his head. "Let's go to him.''

Darrity said, "Is that normal for Ralson, Dr. Grant? Would you expect him to attack a guard trying to take him out of a prison cell?''

Grant said, "I can't say.''

The warden spread a calloused palm. His thick nose twitched a little. "We haven't tried to do anything about him so far because of the telegram from Washington, but, frankly, he doesn't belong here. I'll be glad to have him taken off my hands.''

"We'll see him in his cell,'' said Darrity.

They went down the hard, bar-lined corridor. Empty, incurious eyes watched their passing.

Dr. Grant felt his flesh crawl. "Has he been kept *here* all the time?''

Darrity did not answer.

The guard, pacing before them, stopped. "That is the cell.''

Darrity said, "Is that Dr. Ralson?''

Dr. Grant looked silently at the figure upon the cot. The man had been lying down when they first reached the cell, but now he had risen to one elbow and seemed to be trying to shrink into the wall. His hair was sandy and thin, his figure slight, his eyes blank and china-blue. On his right cheek there was a raised pink patch that trailed off like a tadpole.

Dr. Grant said, "That's Ralson."

The guard opened the door and stepped inside, but Inspector Darrity sent him out again with a gesture. Ralson watched them mutely. He had drawn both feet up to the cot and was pushing backwards. His Adam's apple bobbled as he swallowed.

Darrity said quietly, "Dr. Elwood Ralson?"

"What do you want?" The voice was a surprising baritone.

"Would you come with us, please? We have some questions we would like to ask you."

"No! Leave me alone!"

"Dr. Ralson," said Grant, "I've been sent here to ask you to come back to work."

Ralson looked at the scientist and there was a momentary glint of something other than fear in his eyes. He said, "Hello, Grant." He got off his cot. "Listen, I've been trying to have them put me into a padded cell. Can't you make them do that for me? You know me, Grant. I wouldn't ask for something I didn't feel was necessary. Help me. I can't stand the hard walls. It makes me want to . . . bash—" He brought the flat of his palm thudding down against the hard, dull-gray concrete behind his cot.

Darrity looked thoughtful. He brought out his penknife and unbent the gleaming blade. Carefully, he scraped at his thumbnail, and said, "Would you like to see a doctor?"

But Ralson didn't answer that. He followed the gleam of metal and his lips parted and grew wet. His breath became ragged and harsh.

He said, "Put that away!"

Darrity paused, "Put what away?"

"The knife. Don't hold it in front of me. I can't stand looking at it."

Darrity said, "Why not?" He held it out. "Anything wrong with it? It's a good knife."

Ralson lunged. Darrity stepped back and his left hand came down on the other's wrist. He lifted the knife high in the air. "What's the matter, Ralson? What are you after?"

Grant cried a protest but Darrity waved him away.

Darrity said, "What do you want, Ralson?"

Ralson tried to reach upward, and bent under the other's appalling grip. He gasped, "Give me the knife."

"Why, Ralson? What do you want to do with it?"

"Please. I've got to—" He was pleading. "I've got to stop living."

"You want to die?"

"No. But I must."

Darrity shoved. Ralson flailed backward and tumbled into his cot, so that it squeaked noisily. Slowly, Darrity bent the blade of his penknife into its sheath and put it away. Ralson covered his face. His shoulders were shaking but otherwise he did not move.

There was the sound of shouting from the corridor, as the other prisoners reacted to the noise issuing from Ralson's cell. The guard came hurrying down, yelling, "Quiet!" as he went.

Darrity looked up. "It's all right, guard."

He was wiping his hands upon a large white handkerchief. "I think we'll get a doctor for him."

Dr. Gottfried Blaustein was small and dark and spoke with a trace of an Austrian accent. He needed only a small goatee to be the layman's caricature of a psychiatrist. But he was clean-shaven, and very carefully dressed. He watched Grant carefully, assessing him, blocking in certain observations and deductions. He did this automatically, now, with everyone he met.

He said, "You give me a sort of picture. You describe a man of great talent, perhaps even genius. You tell me he has always been uncomfortable with people; that he has never fitted in with his laboratory environment, even though it was there that he met the greatest of success. Is there another environment to which he has fitted himself?"

"I don't understand."

"It is not given to all of us to be so fortunate as to find a congenial type of company at the place or in the field where we find it necessary to make a living. Often, one compensates by playing an instrument, or going hiking, or joining some club. In other words, one creates a new type of society, when not working, in which one can feel more at home. It need not have the slightest connection with what one's ordinary occupation is. It is an escape, and not necessarily an unhealthy one." He smiled and added, "Myself, I collect stamps. I am an active member of the American Society of Philatelists."

Grant shook his head. "I don't know what he did outside working hours. I doubt that he did anything like what you've mentioned."

"Um-m-m. Well, that would be sad. Relaxation and enjoyment are wherever you find them; but you must find them somewhere, no?"

"Have you spoken to Dr. Ralson, yet?"

"About his problems? No."

"Aren't you going to?"

"Oh, yes. But he has been here only a week. One must give him a chance to recover. He was in a highly excited state when he first came here. It was almost a delirium. Let him rest and become accustomed to the new environment. I will question him, then."

"Will you be able to get him back to work?"

Blaustein smiled. "How should I know? I don't even know what his sickness is."

Isaac Asimov

"Couldn't you at least get rid of the worst of it; this suicidal obsession of his, and take care of the rest of the cure while he's at work?"

"Perhaps. I couldn't even venture an opinion so far without several interviews."

"How long do you suppose it will all take?"

"In these matters, Dr. Grant, nobody can say."

Grant brought his hands together in a sharp slap. "Do what seems best then. But this is more important than you know."

"Perhaps. But you may be able to help me, Dr. Grant."

"How?"

"Can you get me certain information which may be classified as top secret?"

"What kind of information?"

"I would like to know the suicide rate, since 1945, among nuclear scientists. Also, how many have left their jobs to go into other types of scientific work, or to leave science altogether."

"Is this in connection with Ralson?"

"Don't you think it might be an occupational disease, this terrible unhappiness of his?"

"Well—a good many have left their jobs, naturally."

"Why naturally, Dr. Grant?"

"You must know how it is, Dr. Blaustein. The atmosphere in modern atomic research is one of great pressure and red tape. You work with the government; you work with military men. You can't talk about your work; you have to be careful what you say. Naturally, if you get a chance at a job in a university, where you can fix your own hours, do your own work, write papers that don't have to be submitted to the A.E.C., attend conventions that aren't held behind locked doors, you take it."

"And abandon your field of specialty forever."

"There are always non-military applications. Of course, there was one man who did leave for another reason. He told me once he couldn't sleep nights. He said he'd hear one hundred thousand screams coming from Hiroshima, when he put the lights out. The last I heard of him he was a clerk in a haberdashery."

"And do you ever hear a few screams yourself?"

Grant nodded. "It isn't a nice feeling to know that even a little of the responsibility of atomic destruction might be your own."

"How did Ralson feel?"

"He never spoke of anything like that."

"In other words, if he felt it, he never even had the safety-valve effect of letting off steam to the rest of you."

"I guess he hadn't."

"Yet nuclear research must be done, no?"

"I'll say."

"What would you do, Dr. Grant, if you felt you *had* to do something that you *couldn't* do."

Grant shrugged. "I don't know."

"Some people kill themselves."

"You mean that's what has Ralson down."

"I don't know. I do not know. I will speak to Dr. Ralson this evening. I can promise nothing, of course, but I will let you know whatever I can."

Grant rose. "Thanks, Doctor. I'll try to get the information you want."

Elwood Ralson's appearance had improved in the week he had been at Dr. Blaustein's sanitarium. His face had filled out and some of the restlessness had gone out of him. He was tieless and beltless. His shoes were without laces.

Blaustein said, "How do you feel, Dr. Ralson?"

"Rested."

"You have been treated well?"

"No complaints, Doctor."

Blaustein's hand fumbled for the letter-opener with which it was his habit to play during moments of abstraction, but his fingers met nothing. It had been put away, of course, with anything else possessing a sharp edge. There was nothing on his desk, now, but papers.

He said, "Sit down, Dr. Ralson. How do your symptoms progress?"

"You mean, do I have what you would call a suicidal impulse? Yes. It gets worse or better, depending on my thoughts, I think. But it's always with me. There is nothing you can do to help."

"Perhaps you are right. There are often things I cannot help. But I would like to know as much as I can about you. You are an important man—"

Ralson snorted.

"You do not consider that to be so?" asked Blaustein.

"No, I don't. There are no important men, any more than there are important individual bacteria."

"I don't understand."

"I don't expect you to."

"And yet it seems to me that behind your statement there must have been much thought. It would certainly be of the greatest interest to have you tell me some of this thought."

For the first time, Ralson smiled. It was not a pleasant smile. His nostrils were white. He said, "It is amusing to watch you, Doctor. You go about your business so conscientiously. You must listen to me, mustn't you, with just that air of phony interest and unctuous sympathy. I can tell you the most ridiculous things and still be sure of an audience, can't I?"

"Don't you think my interest can be real, even granted that it is professional, too?"

"No, I don't."

"Why not?"

"I'm not interested in discussing it."

"Would you rather return to your room?"

"If you don't mind. No!" His voice had suddenly suffused with fury as he stood up, then almost immediately sat down again. "Why shouldn't I use you? I don't like to talk to people. They're stupid. They don't see things. They stare at the obvious for hours and it means nothing to them. If I spoke to them, they wouldn't understand; they'd lose patience; they'd laugh. Whereas you must listen. It's your job. You can't interrupt to tell me I'm mad, even though you may think so."

"I'd be glad to listen to whatever you would like to tell me."

Ralson drew a deep breath. "I've known something for a year now, that very few people know. Maybe it's something no *live* person knows. Do you know that human cultural advances come in spurts? Over a space of two generations in a city containing thirty thousand free men, enough literary and artistic genius of the first rank arose to supply a nation of millions for a century under ordinary circumstances. I'm referring to the Athens of Pericles.

"There are other examples. There is the Florence of the Medicis, the England of Elizabeth, the Spain of the Cordovan Emirs. There was the spasm of social reformers among the Israelites of the Eighth and Seventh centuries before Christ. Do you know what I mean?"

Blaustein nodded. "I see that history is a subject that interests you."

"Why not? I suppose there's nothing that says I must restrict myself to nuclear cross-sections and wave mechanics."

"Nothing at all. Please proceed."

"At first, I thought I could learn more of the true inwardness of historical cycles by consulting a specialist. I had some conferences with a professional historian. A waste of time!"

"What was his name; the professional historian?"

"Does it matter?"

"Perhaps not, if you would rather consider it confidential. What did he tell you?"

"He said I was wrong; that history only appeared to go in spasms. He said that after closer studies the great civilizations of Egypt and Sumeria did not arise suddenly or out of nothing, but upon the basis of a long-developing sub-civilization that was already sophisticated in its arts. He said that Periclean Athens built upon a pre-Periclean Athens of lower accomplishments, without which the age of Pericles could not have been.

"I asked why was there not a post-Periclean Athens of higher accomplishments still, and he told me that Athens was ruined by a plague and by a long war with Sparta. I asked about other cultural spurts and each time it was a war that ended it, or, in some cases, even accompanied it. He was like all the rest. The truth was there; he had only to bend and pick it up; but he didn't."

Ralson stared at the floor, and said in a tired voice, "They come to me in the laboratory sometimes, Doctor. They say, 'how the devil are we going to get rid of the such-and-such effect that is ruining all our measurements, Ralson?' They show me the instruments and the wiring diagrams and I say, 'It's staring at you. Why don't you do so-and-so? A child could tell you that.' Then I walk away because I can't endure the slow puzzling of their stupid faces. Later, they come to me and say, 'It worked, Ralson. How did you figure it out?' I can't explain to them, Doctor; it would be like explaining that water is wet. And I couldn't explain to the historian. And I can't explain to you. It's a waste of time."

"Would you like to go back to your room?"

"Yes."

Blaustein sat and wondered for many minutes after Ralson had been escorted out of his office. His fingers found their way automatically into the upper right drawer of his desk and lifted out the letter-opener. He twiddled it in his fingers.

Finally, he lifted the telephone and dialed the unlisted number he had been given.

He said, "This is Blaustein. There is a professional historian who was consulted by Dr. Ralson some time in the past, probably a bit over a year ago. I don't know his name. I don't even know if he was connected with a university. If you could find him, I would like to see him."

Thaddeus Milton, Ph.D., blinked thoughtfully at Blaustein and brushed his hand through his iron-gray hair. He said, "They came to me and I said that I had indeed met this man. However, I have had very little connection with him. None, in fact, beyond a few conversations of a professional nature."

"How did he come to you?"

"He wrote me a letter; why me, rather than someone else, I do not know. A series of articles written by myself had appeared in one of the semi-learned journals of semi-popular appeal about that time. It may have attracted his attention."

"I see. With what general topic were the articles concerned?"

"They were a consideration of the validity of the cyclic approach to history. That is, whether one can really say that a particular civilization must follow laws of growth and decline in any matter analogous to those involving individuals."

"I have read Toynbee, Dr. Milton."

"Well, then, you know what I mean."

Blaustein said, "And when Dr. Ralson consulted you, was it with reference to this cyclic approach to history?"

"U-m-m-m. In a way, I suppose. Of course, the man is not an historian and some of his notions about cultural trends are rather dramatic and . . . what shall I say . . . tabloidish. Pardon me, Doctor, if I ask a question which may be improper. Is Dr. Ralson one of your patients?"

"Dr. Ralson is not well and is in my care. This, and all else we say here, is confidential, of course."

"Quite. I understand that. However, your answer explains something to me. Some of his ideas almost verged on the irrational. He was always worried, it seemed to me, about the connection between what he called 'cultural spurts' and calamities of one sort or another. Now such connections have been noted frequently. The time of a nation's greatest vitality may come at a time of great national insecurity. The Netherlands is a good case in point. Her great artists, statesmen, and explorers belong to the early 17th century at the time when she was locked in a death struggle with the greatest European power of the time, Spain. When at the point of destruction at home, she was building an empire in the Far East and had secured footholds on the northern coast of South America, the southern tip of Africa, and the Hudson Valley of North America. Her fleets fought England to a standstill. And then, once her political safety was assured, she declined.

"Well, as I say, that is not unusual. Groups, like individuals, will rise to strange heights in answer to a challenge, and vegetate in the absence of a challenge. Where Dr. Ralson left the paths of sanity, however, was in insisting that such a view amounted to confusing cause and effect. He declared that it was not times of war and danger that stimulated 'cultural spurts,' but rather vice versa. He claimed that each time a group of men showed too much vitality and ability, a war became necessary to destroy the possibility of their further development."

"I see," said Blaustein.

"I rather laughed at him, I am afraid. It may be that that was why he did not keep the last appointment we made. Just toward the end of the last conference he asked me, in the most intense fashion imaginable, whether I did not think it queer that such an improbable species as man was dominant on Earth, when all he had in his favor was intelligence. There I laughed aloud. Perhaps I should not have, poor fellow."

"It was a natural reaction," said Blaustein, "but I must take no more of your time. You have been most helpful."

They shook hands, and Thaddeus Milton took his leave.

"Well," said Darrity, "there are your figures on the recent suicides among scientific personnel. Get any deductions out of it?"

"I should be asking you that," said Blaustein, gently. "The FBI must have investigated thoroughly."

"You can bet the national debt on that. They *are* suicides. There's no mistake about it. There have been people checking on it in another department. The rate is about four times above normal, taking age, social status, economic class into consideration."

"What about British scientists?"

"Just about the same."

"And the Soviet Union?"

"Who can tell?" The investigator leaned forward. "Doc, you don't think the Soviets have some sort of ray that can make people want to commit suicide, do you? It's sort of suspicious that men in atomic research are the only ones affected."

"Is it? Perhaps not. Nuclear physicists may have peculiar strains imposed upon them. It is difficult to tell without thorough study."

"You mean complexes might be coming through?" asked Darrity, warily.

Blaustein made a face. "Psychiatry is becoming too popular. Everybody talks of complexes and neuroses and psychoses and compulsions and what-not. One man's guilt complex is another man's good night's sleep. If I could talk to each one of the men who committed suicide, maybe I could know something."

"You're talking to Ralson."

"Yes, I'm talking to Ralson."

"Has *he* got a guilt complex?"

"Not particularly. He has a background out of which it would not surprise me if he obtained a morbid concern with death. When he was twelve he saw his mother die under the wheels of an automobile. His father died slowly of cancer. Yet the effect of those experiences on his present troubles is not clear."

Darrity picked up his hat. "Well, I wish you'd get a move on, Doc. There's something big on, bigger than the H-Bomb. I don't know how anything *can* be bigger than that, but it is."

Ralson insisted on standing. "I had a bad night last night, Doctor."

"I hope," said Blaustein, "these conferences are not disturbing you."

"Well, maybe they are. They have me thinking on the subject again. It makes things bad, when I do that. How do you imagine it feels being part of a bacterial culture, Doctor?"

"I had never thought of that. To a bacterium, it probably feels quite normal."

Ralson did not hear. He said, slowly, "A culture in which intelligence is being studied. We study all sorts of things as far as their genetic relationships are concerned. We take fruit flies and cross red eyes and white eyes to see what happens. We don't care anything about red eyes and white eyes, but we try to gather from them certain basic genetic principles. You see what I mean?"

"Certainly."

"Even in humans, we can follow various physical characteristics. There are the Hapsburg lips, and the hemophilia that started with Queen Victoria and cropped up in her descendants among the Spanish and Russian royal families. We can even follow feeble-mindedness in the Jukeses and Kallikaks. You learn about it in high-school biology. But you can't breed human beings the way you do fruit flies. Humans live too long. It would take centuries to draw conclusions. It's a pity we don't have a special race of men that reproduce at weekly intervals, eh?''

He waited for an answer, but Blaustein only smiled.

Ralson said, "Only that's exactly what we would be for another group of beings whose life span might be thousands of years. To them, we would reproduce rapidly enough. We would be short-lived creatures and they could study the genetics of such things as musical aptitude, scientific intelligence, and so on. Not that those things would interest them as such, any more than the white eyes of the fruit fly interest us as white eyes.''

"This is a very interesting notion," said Blaustein.

"It is not simply a notion. It is true. To me, it is obvious, and I don't care how it seems to you. Look around you. Look at the planet, Earth. What kind of a ridiculous animal are we to be lords of the world after the dinosaurs had failed? Sure, we're intelligent, but what's intelligence? We think it is important because we have it. If the Tyrannosaurus could have picked out the one quality that he thought would ensure species domination, it would be size and strength. And he would make a better case for it. He lasted longer than we're likely to.

"Intelligence in itself isn't much as far as survival values are concerned. The elephant makes out very poorly indeed when compared to the sparrow even though he is much more intelligent. The dog does well, under man's protection, but not as well as the housefly against whom every human hand is raised. Or take the primates as a group. The small ones cower before their enemies; the large ones have always been remarkably unsuccessful in doing more than barely holding their own. The baboons do the best and that is because of their canines, not their brains.''

A light film of perspiration covered Ralson's forehead. "And one can see that man has been tailored, made to careful specifications for those things that study us. Generally, the primate is short-lived. Naturally, the larger ones live longer, which is a fairly general rule in animal life. Yet the human being has a life span twice as long as any of the other great apes; considerably longer even than the gorilla that outweighs him. We mature later. It's as though we've been carefully bred to live a little longer so that our life cycle might be of a more convenient length.''

He jumped to his feet, shaking his fists above his head. "A thousand years is a day—''

Blaustein punched a button hastily.

For a moment, Ralson struggled against the white-coated orderly who entered, and then he allowed himself to be led away.

Blaustein looked after him, shook his head, and picked up the telephone.

He got Darrity. "Inspector, you may as well know that this may take a long time.''

He listened and shook his head. "I know. I don't minimize the urgency.''

The voice in the receiver was tinny and harsh. "Doctor, you *are* minimizing it. I'll send Dr. Grant to you. He'll explain the situation to you.''

Dr. Grant asked how Ralson was, then asked somewhat wistfully if he could see him. Blaustein shook his head gently.

Grant said, "I've been directed to explain the current situation in atomic research to you."

"So that I will understand, no?"

"I hope so. It's a measure of desperation. I'll have to remind you—"

"Not to breathe a word of it. Yes, I know. This insecurity on the part of you people is a very bad symptom. You must know these things cannot be hidden."

"You live with secrecy. It's contagious."

"Exactly. What is the current secret?"

"There is . . . or, at least, there might be a defense against the atomic bomb."

"And that is a secret? It would be better if it were shouted to all the people of the world instantly."

"For heaven's sake, no. Listen to me, Dr. Blaustein. It's only on paper so far. It's at the E equals mc square stage, almost. It may not be practical. It would be bad to raise hopes we would have to disappoint. On the other hand, if it were known that we *almost* had a defense, there *might* be a desire to start and win a war before the defense were completely developed."

"That I don't believe. Wars are not started; they happen. But, nevertheless, I distract you. What is the nature of this defense, or have you told me as much as you dare?"

"No, I can go as far as I like; as far as is necessary to convince you we have to have Ralson—and fast!"

"Well, then tell me, and I, too, will know secrets. I'll feel like a member of the Cabinet."

"You'll know more than most. Look, Dr. Blaustein, let me explain it in lay language. So far, military advances have been made fairly equally in both offensive and defensive weapons. Once before there seemed to be a definite and permanent tipping of all warfare in the direction of the offense, and that was with the invention of gunpowder. But the defense caught up. The medieval man-in-tank-on-treads, and the stone castle became the concrete pillbox. The same thing, you see, except that everything has been boosted several orders of magnitude."

"Very good. You make it clear. But with the atomic bomb comes more orders of magnitude, no? You must go past concrete and steel for protection."

"Right. Only we can't just make thicker and thicker walls. We've run out of materials that are strong enough. So we must abandon materials altogether. If the atom attacks, we must let the atom defend. We will use energy itself; a force field."

"And what," asked Blaustein, gently, "is a force field?"

"I wish I could tell you. Right now, it's an equation on paper. Energy can be so channeled as to create a wall of matterless inertia, theoretically. In practice, we don't know how to do it."

"It would be a wall you could not go through, is that it? Even for atoms?"

"Even for atom bombs. The only limit on its strength would be the amount of energy we could pour into it. It could even theoretically be made to be impermeable to radiation. The gamma rays would bounce off it. What we're dreaming of is a screen that would be in permanent place about cities; at minimum strength, using practically no energy. It could then be triggered to maximum intensity in a fraction of a milli-second at the impingement of short-wave radiation; say, the amount raidating from a mass of plutonium large enough to be an atomic warhead. All this is theoretically possible."

"And why must you have Ralson?"

"Because he is the only one who can reduce it to practice, if it can be made practical at all, quickly enough. Every minute counts these days. You know what the inter-national situation is. Atomic defense *must* arrive before atomic war."

"You are so sure of Ralson?"

"I am as sure of him as I can be of anything. The man is amazing, Dr. Blaustein. He is always right. Nobody in the field knows how he does it."

"A sort of intuition, no?" The psychiatrist looked disturbed. "A kind of reasoning that goes beyond ordinary human capacities. Is that it?"

"I make no pretense of knowing what it is."

"Let me speak to him once more then. I will let you know."

"Good." Grant rose to leave; then, as if in afterthought, he said, "I might say, Doctor, that if you don't do something, the Commission plans to take Dr. Ralson out of your hands."

"And try another psychiatrist? If they wish to do that, of course, I will not stand in their way. It is my opinion, however, that no reputable practitioner will pretend there is a rapid cure."

"We may not intend further mental treatment. He may simply be returned to work."

"That, Dr. Grant, I will fight. You will get nothing out of him. It will be his death."

"We get nothing out of him anyway."

"This way there is at least a chance, no?"

"I hope so. And by the way, please don't mention the fact that I said anything about taking Ralson away."

"I will not, and I thank you for the warning. Good-bye, Dr. Grant."

"I made a fool of myself last time, didn't I, Doctor?" said Ralson. He was frowning.

"You mean you don't believe what you said then?"

"*I do!*" Ralson's slight form trembled with the intensity of his affirmation.

He rushed to the window, and Blaustein swiveled in his chair to keep him in view. There were bars in the window. He couldn't jump. The glass was unbreakable.

Twilight was ending, and the stars were beginning to come out. Ralson stared at them in fascination, then he turned to Blaustein and flung a finger outward. "Every single one of them is an incubator. They maintain temperatures at the desired point. Different experiments; different temperatures. And the planets that circle them are just huge cultures, containing different nutrient mixtures and different life forms. The experimenters are economical, too—whatever and whoever they are. They've cultured many types of life forms in this particular test tube. Dinosaurs in a moist, tropical age and ourselves among the glaciers. They turn the sun up and down and we try to work out the physics of it. Physics!" He drew his lips back in a snarl.

"Surely," said Dr. Blaustein, "it is not impossible that the sun can be turned up and down at will."

"Why not? It's just like a heating element in an oven. You think bacteria know what it is that works the heat that reaches them? Who knows? Maybe they evolve theories, too. Maybe they have their cosmogonies about cosmic catastrophes, in which clashing light-bulbs create strings of Petri dishes. Maybe they think there must be some beneficent creator that supplies them with food and warmth and says to them, 'Be fruitful and multiply!'

"We breed like them, not knowing why. We obey the so-called laws of nature which are only our interpretation of the not-understood forces imposed upon us.

"And now they've got the biggest experiment of any yet on their hands. It's been going on for two hundred years. They decided to develop a strain for mechanical aptitude in England in the seventeen hundreds, I imagine. We call it the Industrial Revolution. It began with steam, went on to electricity, then atoms. It was an interesting experiment, but they took their chances on letting it spread. Which is why they'll have to be very drastic indeed in ending it."

Blaustein said, "And how would they plan to end it? Do you have any idea about that?"

"You ask *me* how they plan to end it. You can look about the world today and still ask what is likely to bring our technological age to an end. All the Earth fears an atomic war and would do anything to avoid it; yet all the Earth fears that an atomic war is inevitable."

"In other words, the experimenters will arrange an atom war whether we want it or not, to kill off the technological era we are in, and to start fresh. That is it, no?"

"Yes. It's logical. When we sterilize an instrument, do the germs know where the killing heat comes from? Or what has brought it about? There is some way the experimenters can raise the heat of our emotions; some way they can handle us that passes our understanding."

"Tell me," said Blaustein, "is that why you want to die? Because you think the destruction of civilization is coming and can't be stopped?"

Ralson said, "I *don't* want to die. It's just that I must." His eyes were tortured. "Doctor, if you had a culture of germs that were highly dangerous and that you had to keep under absolute control, might you not have an agar medium impregnated with, say, penicillin, in a circle at a certain distance from the center of inoculation? Any germs spreading out too far from that center would die. You would have nothing against the particular germs who were killed; you might not even know that any germs had spread that far in the first place. It would be purely automatic.

"Doctor, there is a penicillin ring about our intellects. When we stray too far; when we penetrate the true meaning of our own existence, we have reached into the penicillin and we must die. It works slowly—but it's hard to stay alive."

He smiled briefly and sadly. Then he said, "May I go back to my room now, Doctor?"

Dr. Blaustein went to Ralson's room about noon the next day. It was a small room and featureless. The walls were gray with padding. Two small windows were high up and could not be reached. The mattress lay directly on the padded floor. There was nothing of metal in the room; nothing that could be utilized in tearing life from body. Even Ralson's nails were clipped short.

Ralson sat up. "Hello!"

"Hello, Dr. Ralson. May I speak to you?"

"Here? There isn't any seat I can offer you."

"It is all right. I'll stand. I have a sitting job and it is good for my sitting-down place that I should stand sometimes. Dr. Ralson, I have thought all night of what you told me yesterday and in the days before."

"And now you are going to apply treatment to rid me of what you think are delusions."

"No. It is just that I wish to ask questions and perhaps to point out some consequences of your theories which . . . you will forgive me? . . . you may not have thought of."

"Oh?"

"You see, Dr. Ralson, since you have explained your theories, I, too, know what you know. Yet I have no feeling about suicide."

"Belief is more than something intellectual, Doctor. You'd have to believe this with all your insides, which you don't."

"Do you not think perhaps it is rather a phenomenon of adaptation?"

"How do you mean?"

"You are not really a biologist, Dr. Ralson. And although you are very brilliant indeed in physics, you do not think of everything with respect to these bacterial cultures you use as analogies. You know that it is possible to breed bacterial strains that are resistant to pencillin or to almost any bacterial poison."

"Well?"

"The experimenters who breed us have been working with humanity for many generations, no? And this particular strain which they have been culturing for two centuries shows no signs of dying out spontaneously. Rather, it is a vigorous strain and a very infective one. Older high-culture strains were confined to single cities or to small areas and lasted only a generation or two. This one is spreading throughout the world. It is a *very* infective strain. Do you not think it may have developed penicillin immunity? In other words, the methods the experimenters use to wipe out the culture may not work too well any more, no?"

Ralson shook his head. "It's working on me."

"You are perhaps non-resistant. Or you have stumbled into a very high concentration of penicillin indeed. Consider all the people who have been trying to outlaw atomic warfare and to establish some form of world government and lasting peace. The effort has risen in recent years, without too awful results."

"It isn't stopping the atomic war that's coming."

"No, but maybe only a little more effort is all that is required. The peace-advocates do not kill themselves. More and more humans are immune to the experimenters. Do you know what they are doing in the laboratory?"

"I don't want to know."

"You *must* know. They are trying to invent a force field that will stop the atom bomb. Dr. Ralson, if I am culturing a virulent and pathological bacterium, then, even with all precautions, it may sometimes happen that I will start a plague. We may be bacteria to them, but we are dangerous to them, also, or they wouldn't wipe us out so carefully after each experiment.

"They are not quick, no? To them a thousand years is as a day, no? By the time they realize we are out of the culture, past the penicillin, it will be too late for them to stop us. They have brought us to the atom, and if we can only prevent ourselves from using it upon one another, we may turn out to be too much even for the experimenters."

Ralson rose to his feet. Small though he was, he was an inch and a half taller than Blaustein. "They are really working on a force field?"

"They are trying to. But they need you."

"No. I can't."

"They must have you in order that you might see what is so obvious to you. It is not obvious to them. Remember, it is your help, or else—defeat of man by the experimenters."

Ralson took a few rapid steps away, staring into the blank, padded wall. He muttered, "But there must be that defeat. If they build a force field, it will mean death for all of them before it can be completed."

"Some or all of them may be immune, no? And in any case, it will be death for them anyhow. They are trying."

Ralson said, "I'll try to help them."

"Do you still want to kill yourself?"

"Yes."

"But you'll try not to, no?"

"I'll *try* not to, Doctor." His lip quivered. "I'll have to be watched."

Blaustein climbed the stairs and presented his pass to the guard in the lobby. He had already been inspected at the outer gate, but he, his pass, and its signature were now scrutinized once again. After a moment, the guard retired to his little booth and made a phone call. The answer satisfied him. Blaustein took a seat and, in half a minute, was up again, shaking hands with Dr. Grant.

"The President of the United States would have trouble getting in here, no?" said Blaustein.

The lanky physicist smiled. "You're right, if he came without warning."

They took an elevator which traveled twelve floors. The office to which Grant led the way had windows in three directions. It was soundproofed and air-conditioned. Its walnut furniture was in a state of high polish.

Blaustein said, "My goodness. It is like the office of the chairman of a board of directors. Science is becoming big business."

Grant looked embarrassed. "Yes, I know, but government money flows easily and it is difficult to persuade a congressman that your work is important unless he can see, smell, and touch the surface shine."

Blaustein sat down and felt the upholstered seat give way slowly. He said, "Dr. Elwood Ralson has agreed to return to work."

"Wonderful. I was hoping you would say that. I was hoping that was why you wanted to see me." As though inspired by the news, Grant offered the psychiatrist a cigar, which was refused.

"However," said Blaustein, "he remains a very sick man. He will have to be treated carefully and with insight."

"Of course. Naturally."

"It's not quite as simple as you may think. I want to tell you something of Ralson's problems, so that you will really understand how delicate the situation is."

He went on talking and Grant listened first in concern, and then in astonishment. "But then the man is out of his head, Dr. Blaustein. He'll be of no use to us. He's crazy."

Blaustein shrugged. "It depends on how you define 'crazy.' It's a bad word; don't use it. He has delusions, certainly. Whether they will affect his peculiar talents one cannot know."

"But surely no sane man could possibly—"

"Please. Please. Let us not launch into long discussions on psychiatric definitions of sanity and so on. The man has delusions and, ordinarily, I would dismiss them from all consideration. It is just that I have been given to understand that the man's particular ability lies in his manner of proceeding to the solution of a problem by what seems to be outside ordinary reason. That is so, no?"

"Yes. That *must* be admitted."

"And other scientists here?"

"How can you and I judge then as to the worth of one of his conclusions. Let me ask you, do *you* have suicidal impulses lately?"

"I don't think so."

"No, of course not."

"I would suggest, however, that while research on the force field proceeds, the scientists concerned be watched here and at home. It might even be a good enough idea that they should not go home. Offices like these could be arranged to be a small dormitory—"

"Sleep at work. You would never get them to agree."

"Oh, yes. If you do not tell them the real reason but say it is for security purposes, they will agree. 'Security purposes' is a wonderful phrase these days, no? Ralson must be watched more than anyone."

"Of course."

"But all this is minor. It is something to be done to satisfy my conscience in case Ralson's theories are correct. Actually, I don't believe them. They *are* delusions, but once that is granted, it is necessary to ask what the causes of those delusions are. What is it in Ralson's mind, in his background, in his life that makes it so necessary for him to have these particular delusions? One cannot answer that simply. It may well take years of constant psychoanalysis to discover the answer. And until the answer is discovered, he will not be cured.

"But, meanwhile, we can perhaps make intelligent guesses. He has had an unhappy childhood, which, in one way or another, has brought him face to face with death in very unpleasant fashion. In addition, he has never been able to form associations with other children, or, as he grew older, with other men. He was always impatient with their slower forms of reasoning. Whatever difference there is between his mind and that of others, it has built a wall between him and society as strong as the force field you are trying to design. For similar reasons, he has been unable to enjoy a normal sex life. He has never married; he has had no sweethearts.

"It is easy to see that he could easily compensate to himself for this failure to be accepted by his social milieu by taking refuge in the thought that other human beings are inferior to himself. Which is, of course, true, as far as mentality is concerned. There are, of course, many, many facets to the human personality and in not all of them is he superior. No one is. Others, then, who are more prone to see merely what is inferior, just as he himself is, would not accept his affected pre-eminence of position. They would think him queer, even laughable, which would make it even more important to Ralson to prove how miserable and inferior the human species was. How could he better do that than to show that mankind was simply a form of bacteria to other superior creatures which experiment upon them. And then his impulses to suicide would be a wild desire to break away completely from being a man at all; to stop this identification with the miserable species he has created in his mind. You see?"

Grant nodded. "Poor guy."

"Yes, it is a pity. Had he been properly taken care of in childhood— Well, it is best for Dr. Ralson that he have no contact with any of the other men here. He is too sick to be trusted with them. You, yourself, must arrange to be the only man who will see him or speak to him. Dr. Ralson has agreed to that. He apparently thinks you are not as stupid as some of the others."

Grant smiled faintly. "That is agreeable to me."

"You will, of course, be careful. I would not discuss anything with him but his work. If he should volunteer information about his theories, which I doubt, confine yourself to something noncommittal, and leave. And at all times, keep away anything that is sharp and pointed. Do not let him reach a window. Try to have his hands kept in view. You understand. I leave my patient in your care, Dr. Grant."

"I will do my best, Dr. Blaustein."

For two months, Ralson lived in a corner of Grant's office, and Grant lived with him. Gridwork had been built up before the windows, wooden furniture was removed and upholstered sofas brought in. Ralson did his thinking on the couch and his calculating on a desk pad atop a hassock.

The "Do Not Enter" was a permanent fixture outside the office. Meals were left outside. The adjoining men's room was marked off for private use and the door between it and the office removed. Grant switched to an electric razor. He made certain that Ralson took sleeping pills each night and waited till the other slept before sleeping himself.

And always reports were brought to Ralson. He read them while Grant watched and tried to seem not to watch.

Then Ralson would let them drop and stare at the ceiling, with one hand shading his eyes.

"Anything?" asked Grant.

Ralson shook his head from side to side.

Grant said, "Look, I'll clear the building during the swing shift. It's important that you see some of the experimental jigs we've been setting up."

They did so, wandering through the lighted, empty buildings like drifting ghosts, hand in hand. Always hand in hand. Grant's grip was tight. But after each trip, Ralson would still shake his head from side to side.

Half a dozen times he would begin writing; each time there would be a few scrawls and then he would kick the hassock over on its side.

Until, finally, he began writing once again and covered half a page rapidly. Automatically, Grant approached. Ralson looked up, covering the sheet of paper with a trembling hand.

He said, "Call Blaustein."

"What?"

"I said, call Blaustein. Get him here. Now!"

Grant moved to the telephone.

Ralson was writing rapidly now, stopping only to brush wildly at his forehead with the back of a hand. It came away wet.

He looked up and his voice was cracked, "Is he coming?"

Grant looked worried. "He isn't at his office."

"Get him at his home. Get him wherever he is. *Use* that telephone. Don't play with it."

Grant used it; and Ralson pulled another sheet toward himself.

Five minutes later, Grant said, "He's coming. What's wrong? You're looking sick."

Ralson could speak only thickly, "No time— Can't talk—"

He was writing, scribbling, scrawling, shakily diagramming. It was as though he were driving his hands, fighting it.

"Dictate!" urged Grant. "I'll write."

Ralson shook him off. His words were unintelligible. He held his wrist with his other hand, shoving it as though it were a piece of wood, and then he collapsed over the papers.

Grant edged them out from under and laid Ralson down on the couch. He hovered over him restlessly and hopelessly until Blaustein arrived.

Blaustein took one look. "What happened?"

Grant said, "I think he's alive," but by that time Blaustein had verified that for himself, and Grant told him what had happened.

Blaustein used a hypodermic and they waited. Ralson's eyes were blank when they opened. He moaned.

Blaustein leaned close. "Ralson."

Ralson's hands reached out blindly and clutched at the psychiatrist. "Doc. Take me back."

"I will. Now. It is that you have the force field worked out, no?"

"It's on the papers. Grant, it's on the papers."

Grant had them and was leafing through them dubiously. Ralson said, weakly, "It's not *all* there. It's all I can write. You'll *have* to make it out of that. Take me back, Doc!"

"Wait," said Grant. He whispered urgently to Blaustein, "Can't you leave him here till we test this thing? I can't make out what most of this is. The writing is illegible. Ask him what makes him think this will work."

"Ask *him?*" said Blaustein, gently. "Isn't he the one who always knows?"

"Ask me, anyway," said Ralson, overhearing from where he lay on the couch. His eyes were suddenly wide and blazing.

They turned to him.

He said, "*They* don't want a force field. *They!* The experimenters! As long as I had no true grasp, things remained as they were. But I hadn't followed up that thought—*that* thought which is there in the papers—I hadn't followed it up for thirty seconds before I felt . . . I felt— Doctor—"

Blaustein said, "What is it?"

Ralson was whispering again, "I'm deeper in the penicillin. I could feel myself plunging in and in, the further I went with that. I've never been in . . . so deep. That's how I knew I was right. Take me away."

Blaustein straightened. "I'll have to take him away, Grant. There's no alternative. If you can make out what he's written, that's it. If you can't make it out, I can't help you. That man can do no more work in his field without dying, do you understand?"

"But," said Grant, "he's dying of something imaginary."

"All right. Say that he is. But he will be really dead just the same, no?"

Ralson was unconscious again and heard nothing of this. Grant looked at him somberly, then said, "Well, take him away, then."

Ten of the top men at the Institute watched glumly as slide after slide filled the illuminated screen. Grant faced them, expression hard and frowning.

He said, "I think the idea is simple enough. You're mathematicians and you're engineers. The scrawl may seem illegible, but it was done with meaning behind it. That meaning must somehow remain in the writing, distorted though it is. The first page is clear enough. It should be a good lead. Each one of you will look at every page over and over again. You're going to put down every possible version of each page as it seems it might be. You will work independently. I want no consultations."

One of them said, "How do you know it means *anything*, Grant?"

"Because those are Ralson's notes."

"*Ralson!* I thought he was—"

"You thought he was sick," said Grant. He had to shout over the rising hum of conversation. "I know. He is. That's the writing of a man who was nearly dead. It's all we'll ever get from Ralson, any more. Somewhere in that scrawl is the answer to the force field problem. If we can't find it, we may have to spend ten years looking for it elsewhere."

They bent to their work. The night passed. Two nights passed. Three nights—

Grant looked at the results. He shook his head. "I'll take your word for it that it is all self-consistent. I can't say I understand it."

Lowe, who, in the absence of Ralson, would readily have been rated the best nuclear engineer at the Institute, shrugged, "It's not exactly clear to me. If it works, he hasn't explained why."

"He has no time to explain. Can you build the generator as he describes it?"

"I could try."

"Would you look at all the other versions of the pages?"

"The others are definitely not self-consistent."

"Would you double-check?"

"Sure."

"And could you start construction anyway?"

"I'll get the shop started. But I tell you frankly that I'm pessimistic."

"I know. So am I."

The thing grew. Hal Ross, Senior Mechanic, was put in charge of the actual construction, and he stopped sleeping. At any hour of the day or night, he could be found at it, scratching his bald head.

He asked questions only once, "What is it, Dr. Lowe? Never saw anything like it? What's it supposed to do?"

Lowe said, "You know where you are, Ross. You know we don't ask questions here. Don't ask again."

Ross did not ask again. He was known to dislike the structure that was being built. He called it ugly and unnatural. But he stayed at it.

Blaustein called one day.

Grant said, "How's Ralson?"

"Not good. He wants to attend the testing of the Field Projector he designed."

Grant hesitated, "I suppose we should. It's his after all."

"I would have to come with him."

Grant looked unhappier. "It might be dangerous, you know. Even in a pilot test, we'd be playing with tremendous energies."

Blaustein said, "No more dangerous for us than for you."

"Very well. The list of observers will have to be cleared through the Commission and the FBI, but I'll put you in."

Blaustein looked about him. The field projector squatted in the very center of the huge testing laboratory, but all else had been cleared. There was no visible connection with the plutonium pile which served as energy-source, but from what the psychiatrist heard in scraps about him—he knew better than to ask Ralson—the connection was from beneath.

At first, the observers had circled the machine, talking in incomprehensibles, but they were drifting away now. The gallery was filling up. There were at least three men in generals' uniforms on the other side, and a real coterie of lower-scale military. Blaustein chose an unoccupied portion of the railing; for Ralson's sake, most of all.

He said, "Do you still think you would like to stay?"

It was warm enough within the laboratory, but Ralson was in his coat, with his collar turned up. It made little difference, Blaustein felt. He doubted that any of Ralson's former acquaintances would now recognize him.

Isaac Asimov

Ralson said, "I'll stay."

Blaustein was pleased. He wanted to see the test. He turned again at a new voice. "Hello, Dr. Blaustein."

For a minute, Blaustein did not place him, then he said, "Ah, Inspector Darrity. What are you doing here?"

"Just what you would suppose." He indicated the watchers. "There isn't any way you can weed them out so that you can be sure there won't be any mistakes. I once stood as near to Klaus Fuchs as I am standing to you." He tossed his pocketknife into the air and retrieved it with a dexterous motion.

"Ah, yes. Where shall one find perfect security? What man can trust even his own unconscious? And you will now stand near to me, no?"

"Might as well." Darrity smiled. "You were very anxious to get in here, weren't you?"

"Not for myself, Inspector. And would you put away the knife, please."

Darrity turned in surprise in the direction of Balustein's gentle head-gesture. He put his knife away and looked at Blaustein's companion for the second time. He whistled softly.

He said, "Hello, Dr. Ralson."

Ralson croaked, "Hello."

Blaustein was not surprised at Darrity's reaction. Ralson had lost twenty pounds since returning to the sanitarium. His face was yellow and wrinkled; the face of a man who had suddenly become sixty.

Blaustein said, "Will the test be starting soon?"

Darrity said, "It looks as if they're starting now."

He turned and leaned on the rail. Blaustein took Ralson's elbow and began leading him away, but Darrity said, softly, "Stay here, Doc. I don't want you wandering about."

Blaustein looked across the laboratory. Men were standing about with the uncomfortable air of having turned half to stone. He could recognize Grant, tall and gaunt, moving his hand slowly to light a cigarette, then changing his mind and putting lighter and cigarette in his pocket. The young men at the control panels waited tensely.

Then there was a low humming and the faint smell of ozone filled the air.

Ralson said harshly, "Look!"

Blaustein and Darrity looked along the pointing finger. The projector seemed to flicker. It was as though there were heated air rising between it and them. An iron ball came swinging down pendulum fashion and passed through the flickering area.

"It slowed up, no?" said Blaustein, excitedly.

Ralson nodded. "They're measuring the height of rise on the other side to calculate the loss of momentum. Fools! I *said* it would work." He was speaking with obvious difficulty.

Blaustein said, "Just watch, Dr. Ralson. I would not allow myself to grow needlessly excited."

The pendulum was stopped in its swinging, drawn up. The flickering about the projector became a little more intense and the iron sphere arched down once again.

Over and over again, and each time the sphere's motion was slowed with more of a jerk. It made a clearly audible sound as it struck the flicker. And eventually, it *bounced*. First, soggily, as though it hit putty, and then ringingly, as though it hit steel, so that the noise filled the place.

They drew back the pendulum bob and used it no longer. The projector could hardly be seen behind the haze that surrounded it.

Grant gave an order and the odor of ozone was suddenly sharp and pungent. There was a cry from the assembled observers; each one exclaiming to his neighbor. A dozen fingers were pointing.

Blaustein leaned over the railing, as excited as the rest. Where the projector had been, there was now only a huge semi-globular mirror. It was perfectly and beautifully clear. He could see himself in it, a small man standing on a small balcony that curved up on each side. He could see the fluorescent lights reflected in spots of glowing illumination. It was wonderfully sharp.

He was shouting, "Look, Ralson. It is reflecting energy. It is reflecting light waves like a mirror. Ralson—"

He turned, "Ralson! Inspector, where is Ralson?"

"What?" Darrity whirled. "I haven't seen him."

He looked about, wildly. "Well, he won't get away. No way of getting out of here now. You take the other side." And then he clapped hand to thigh, fumbled for a moment in his pocket, and said, "My knife is gone."

Blaustein found him. He was inside the small office belonging to Hal Ross. It led off the balcony, but under the circumstances, of course, it had been deserted. Ross himself was not even an observer. A senior mechanic need not observe. But his office would do very well for the final end of the long fight against suicide.

Blaustein stood in the doorway for a sick moment, then turned. He caught Darrity's eye as the latter emerged from a similar office a hundred feet down the balcony. He beckoned, and Darrity came at a run.

Dr. Grant was trembling with excitement. He had taken two puffs at each of two cigarettes and trodden each underfoot thereafter. He was fumbling with the third now.

He was saying, "This is better than any of us could possibly have hoped. We'll have the gun-fire test tomorrow. I'm sure of the result now, but we've planned it; we'll go through with it. We'll skip the small arms and start with the bazooka levels. Or maybe not. It might be necessary to construct a special testing structure to take care of the ricocheting problem."

He discarded his third cigarette.

A general said, "We'd have to try a literal atom-bombing, of course."

"Naturally. Arrangements have already been made to build a mock-city at Eniwetok. We could build a generator on the spot and drop the bomb. There'd be animals inside."

"And you really think the field in full power would hold the bomb?"

"It's not just that, General. There'd be no noticeable field when the bomb is dropped. The radiation of the plutonium would have to energize the field before explosion. As we did here in the last step. That's the essence of it all."

"You know," said a Princeton professor, "I see disadvantages, too. When the field is on full, anything it protects is in total darkness, as far as the sun is concerned. Besides that, it strikes me that the enemy can adopt the practice of dropping harmless radioactive missiles to set off the field at frequent intervals. It would have nuisance value and be a considerable drain on our pile as well."

"Nuisances," said Grant, "can be survived. These difficulties will be met eventually, I'm sure, now that the main problem has been solved."

The British observer had worked his way toward Grant and was shaking hands. He said, "I feel better about London already. I cannot help but wish your government would allow me to see the complete plans. What I have seen strikes me as completely ingenious. It seems obvious now, of course, but how did anyone ever come to think of it?"

Grant smiled, "That question has been asked before with reference to Dr. Ralson's devices—"

He turned at the touch of a hand upon his shoulder. "Dr. Blaustein! I had nearly forgotten. Here, I want to talk to you."

He dragged the small psychiatrist to one side and hissed in his ear, "Listen, can you persuade Ralson to be introduced to these people? This is his triumph."

Blaustein said, "Ralson is dead."

"*What!*"

"Can you leave these people for a time?"

"Yes . . . yes— Gentlemen, you will excuse me for a few minutes?"

He hurried off with Blaustein.

The Federal men had already taken over. Unobtrusively, they barred the doorway to Ross's office. Outside there were the milling crowd discussing the answer to Alamogordo that they had just witnessed. Inside, unknown to them, was the death of the answerer. The G-man barrier divided to allow Grant and Blaustein to enter. It closed behind them again.

For a moment, Grant raised the sheet. He said, "He looks peaceful."

"I would say—happy," said Blaustein.

Darrity said, colorlessly, "The suicide weapon was my own knife. It was my negligence; it will be reported as such."

"No, no," said Blaustein, "that would be useless. He was my patient and I am responsible. In any case, he would not have lived another week. Since he invented the projector, he was a dying man."

Grant said, "How much of this has to be placed in the Federal files? Can't we forget all about his madness?"

"I'm afraid not, Dr. Grant," said Darrity.

"I have told him the whole story," said Blaustein, sadly.

Grant looked from one to the other. "I'll speak to the Director. I'll go to the President, if necessary. I don't see that there need be any mention of suicide or of madness. He'll get full publicity as inventor of the field projector. It's the least we can do for him." His teeth were gritting.

Blaustein said, "He left a note."

"A note?"

Darrity handed him a sheet of paper and said, "Suicides almost always do. This is one reason the doctor told me about what really killed Ralson."

The note was addressed to Blaustein and it went:

"The projector works; I knew it would. The bargain is done. You've got it and you don't need me any more. So I'll go. You needn't worry about the human race, Doc. You were right. They've bred us too long; they've taken too many chances. We're out of the culture now and they won't be able to stop us. I know. That's all I can say. I know."

He had signed his name quickly and then underneath there was one scrawled line, and it said:

"Provided enough men are penicillin-resistant."

Grant made a motion to crumple the paper, but Darrity held out a quick hand.

"For the record, Doctor," he said.

Grant gave it to him and said, "Poor Ralson! He died believing all that trash."

Blaustein nodded. "So he did. Ralson will be given a great funeral, I suppose, and the fact of his invention will be publicized without the madness and the suicide. But the government men will remain interested in his mad theories. They may not be so mad, no, Mr. Darrity?"

"That's ridiculous, Doctor," said Grant. "There isn't a scientist on the job who has shown the least uneasiness about it at all."

"Tell him, Mr. Darrity," said Blaustein.

Darrity said, "There has been another suicide. No, no, none of the scientists. No one with a degree. It happened this morning, and we investigated because we thought it might have some connection with today's test. There didn't seem any, and we were going to keep it quiet till the test was over. Only now there seems to be a connection.

"The man who died was just a guy with a wife and three kids. No reason to die. No history of mental illness. He threw himself under a car. We have witnesses, and it's certain he did it on purpose. He didn't die right away and they got a doctor to

Isaac Asimov

him. He was horribly mangled, but his last words were, 'I feel much better now' and he died.''

"But who was he?" cried Grant.

"Hal Ross. The guy who actually built the projector. The guy whose office this is."

Blaustein walked to the window. The evening sky was darkening into starriness.

He said, "The man knew nothing about Ralson's views. He had never spoken to Ralson, Mr. Darrity tells me. Scientists are probably resistant as a whole. They must be or they are quickly driven out of the profession. Ralson was an exception, a penicillin-sensitive who insisted on remaining. You see what happened to him. But what about the others; those who have remained in walks of life where there is no constant weeding out of the sensitive ones. How much of humanity *is* penicillin-resistant?"

"You *believe* Ralson," asked Grant in horror.

"I don't really know."

Blaustein looked at the stars.

Incubators? ∎

TO BE CONTINUED
Robert Silverberg

It was October of 1955. I was twenty years old and had already sold a couple of dozen science-fiction stories, and even a novel. But I didn't think of myself as a Real Pro, because I hadn't sold a story to John W. Campbell, Jr., who to me was the arbiter of true science fiction. What other people's magazines printed might be SF, or it might be only a clever imitation; but JWC's Astounding *was the true scripture, and nobody could call himself a science fiction writer who hadn't sold him one.*

Oh, actually I had *sold him one: two, in fact, the first two Bel-rogas stories in what would become the book* The Shrouded Planet. *But those were collaborations with Randall Garrett, and Garrett was an* Astounding *contributor from way back. Though my contributions to those stories had been far from insignificant, I couldn't help thinking that I had hitchhiked my way into the magazine on Garrett's shoulders.*

But then I wrote ''To Be Continued,'' after some plot discussion with Garrett, and I took it to Campbell, and he bought it that day or the next. It was my first solo sale to Astounding. *And I confess I wandered around in a daze most of that evening. I was twenty years old, and I had sold a story to Campbell all by myself. What worlds were left to conquer now? I was at the summit of my career!*

—Robert Silverberg

GAIUS TITUS MENENIUS sat thoughtfully in his oddly-decorated apartment on Park Avenue, staring at the envelope that had just arrived. He contemplated it for a moment, noting with amusement that he was actually somewhat perturbed over the possible nature of its contents.

After a moment he elbowed up from the red contour-chair and crossed the room in three bounds. Still holding the envelope, he eased himself down on the long green couch near the wall, and, extending himself full-length, slit the envelope open with a neat flick of his fingernail. The medical report was within, as he had expected.

"Dear Mr. Riswell," it read. "I am herewith enclosing a copy of the laboratory report concerning your examination last week. I am pleased to report that our findings are positive—emphatically so. In view of our conversation, I am sure this finding will be extremely pleasing to you and, of course, to your wife. Sincerely, F. D. Rowcliff, M.D."

Menenius read the letter through once again, examined the enclosed report, and allowed his face to open in a wide grin. It was almost an anti-climax, after all these centuries. He couldn't bring himself to become very excited over it—not any more. He stood up and stretched happily. "Well, Mr. Riswell," he said to himself, "I think this calls for a drink. In fact a night on the town." He chose a smart dinner jacket from his wardrobe and moved toward the door. It swung open at his approach. He went out into the corridor and disappeared into the elevator, whistling gaily, his mind full of new plans and new thoughts.

It was a fine feeling. After two thousand years of waiting, he had finally achieved his maturity. He could have a son. At last!

"Good afternoon, Mr. Schuyler," said the barman. "Will it be the usual sir?"

"Martini, of course," said W. M. Schuyler IV, seating himself casually on the padded stool in front of the bar.

Behind the projected personality of W. M. Schuyler IV, Gaius Titus smiled, mentally. W. M. Schuyler *always* drank Martinis. And they had pretty well better be dry—very dry.

The baroque strains of a Vivaldi violin concerto sang softly in the background. Schuyler watched the TV accompaniment—a dancing swirl of colors that moved with the music.

"Good afternoon, Miss Vanderpool," he heard the barman say. "An Old Fashioned?"

Schuyler took another sip of his Martini and looked up. The girl had appeared suddenly and had taken the seat next to him, looking her usual cool self.

"Sharon!" he said, putting just the right amount of exclamation point after it.

She turned to look at him and smiled, disclosing a brilliantly white array of perfect teeth. "Bill! I didn't notice you! How long have you been here?"

"Just arrived," Schuyler told her. "Just about a minute ago."

To Be Continued

The barman put her drink down in front of her. She took a long sip without removing her eyes from him. Schuyler met her glance, and behind his eyes Gaius Titus was coldly appraising her in a new light.

He had met her in Kavanaugh's a month before, and he had readily enough added her to the string. Why not? She was young, pretty, intelligent, and made a pleasant companion. There had been others like her—a thousand others, two thousand, five thousand. One gets to meet quite a few in two millennia.

Only now Gaius Titus was finally mature, and had different needs. The string of girls to which Sharon belonged was going to be cut.

He wanted a wife.

"How's the lackey of Wall Street?" Sharon asked. "Still coining money faster than you know how to spend it?"

"I'll leave that for you to decide," he said. He signaled for two more drinks. "Care to take in a concert tonight, perchance? The Bach Group's giving a benefit this evening, you know, and I'm told there still are a few hundred-dollar seats left—"

There, Gaius Titus thought. The bait has been cast. She ought to respond.

She whistled, a long, low, sophisticated whistle. "I'd venture that business is fairly good, then," she said. Her eyes fell. "But I don't want to let you go to all that expense on my account, Bill."

"It's nothing," Schuyler insisted, while Gaius Titus continued to weigh her in the balance. "They're doing the Fourth Brandenburg, and Renoli's playing the Goldberg Variations. How about?"

She met his gaze evenly. "Sorry, Bill. I have something else on for the evening." Her tone left no doubt in Schuyler's mind that there was little point pressing the discussion any further. Gaius Titus felt a sharp pang of disappointment.

Schuyler lifted his hand, palm forward. "Say no more! I should have known you'd be booked up for tonight already." He paused. "What about tomorrow?" he said after a moment. "There's a reading of Webster's 'Duchess of Malfi' down at the Dramatist's League. It's been one of my favorite plays for a long time."

Silently smiling, he waited for her reply. The Webster was, indeed, a long-time favorite. Gaius Titus recalled having attended one of its first performances, during his short employ in the court of James I. During the next three and a half centuries, he had formed a sentimental attachment for the creaky old melodrama.

"Not tomorrow either," Sharon said. "Some other night, Bill."

"All right," he said. "Some other night."

He reached out a hand and put it over hers, and they fell silent, listening to the Vivaldi in the background. He contemplated her high, sharp cheekbones in the purple halflight, wondering if she could be the one to bear the child he had waited for so long.

She had parried all his thrusts in a fashion that surprised him. She was not at all impressed by his display of wealth and culture. Titus reflected sadly that, perhaps, his Schuyler facet had been inadequate for her.

No, he thought, rejecting the idea. The haunting slow movement of the Vivaldi faded to its end and a lively allegro took its place. No; he had had too much experience in calculating personality-facets to fit the individual to have erred. He was certain that W. M. Schuyler IV was capable of handling Sharon.

For the first few hundred years of his unexpectedly long life, Gaius Titus had been forced to adopt the practice of turning on and off different personalities as a matter of mere survival. Things had been easy for a while after the fall of Rome, but with the coming of the Middle Ages he had needed all his skill to keep from running afoul of the superstitious. He had carefully built up a series of masks, of false fronts, as a survival mechanism.

How many times had he heard someone tell him, in jest, "You ought to be on the stage?" It struck home. He *was* on the stage. He was a man of many roles. Somewhere, beneath it all, was the unalterable personality of Gaius Titus Menenius, *cives Romanus*, casting the shadows that were his many masks. But Gaius Titus was far below the surface—the surface which, at the moment, was W. M. Schuyler IV; which had been Preston Riswell the week before, when he had visited the doctor for that fateful examination; which could be Leslie MacGregor or Sam Spielman or Phil Carlson tomorrow, depending on where Gaius Titus was, in what circumstances, and talking to whom. There was only one person he did not dare to be, and that was himself.

He wasn't immortal; he knew that. But he was *relatively* immortal. His life-span was tremendously decelerated, and it had taken him two thousand years to become, physically, a fertile adult. His span was roughly a hundred times that of a normal man's. And, according to what he had learned in the last century, his longevity should be transmittable genetically. All he needed now was someone to transmit it to.

Was it dominant? That he didn't know. That was the gamble he'd be making. He wondered what it would be like to watch his children and his children's children shrivel with age. Not pleasant, he thought.

The conversation with Sharon lagged; it was obvious that something was wrong with his Schuyler facet, at least so far as she was concerned, though he was unable to see where the trouble lay. After a few more minutes of disjointed chatter, she excused herself and left the bar. He watched her go. She had eluded him neatly. Where to next?

He thought he knew.

The East End bar was far downtown and not very reputable. Gaius Titus pushed through the revolving door and headed for the counter.

"Hi, Sam. Howsa boy?" the bartender said.

"Let's have a beer, Jerry." The bartender shoved a beer out toward the short, swarthy man in the leather jacket.

To Be Continued

"Things all right?"

"Can't complain, Jerry. How's business?" Sam Spielman asked, as he lifted the beer to his mouth.

"It's lousy."

"It figures," Sam said. "Why don't you put in automatics? They're getting all the business now."

"Sure, Sam, sure. And where do I get the dough? That's twenty." He took the coins Sam dropped on the bar and grinned. "At least you can afford beer."

"You know me, Jerry," Sam said. "My credit's good."

Jerry nodded. "Good enough." He punched the coins into the register. "Ginger was looking for you, by the way. What you got against the gal?"

"Against her? Nothin'. What do y'mean?" Sam pushed out his beer shell for a refill.

"She's got a hooker out for you—you know that, don't you?" Jerry was grinning.

Gaius Titus thought: *She's not very bright, but she might very well serve my purpose. She has other characteristics worth transmitting.*

"Hi, Sammy."

He turned to look at her. "Hi, Ginger," he said. "How's the gal?"

"Not bad, honey." But she didn't look it. She looked as though she'd been dragged through the mill. Her blonde hair was disarranged, her blouse was wrinkled, and, as usual, her teeth were discolored by the lipstick that had rubbed off on them.

"I love you, Sammy," she said softly.

"I love you, too," Sam said. He meant it.

Gaius Titus thought sourly: *But how many of her characteristics would I not want to transmit. Still, she'll do. I guess. She's a solid girl.*

"Sam," she said, interrupting the flow of his thoughts, "why don't you come around more often? I miss you."

"Look, Ginger baby," Sam said. "Remember, I've got a long haul to pull. If I marry you, you gotta understand that I don't get here often. I gotta drive a truck. You might not see me more than once or twice a week."

Titus rubbed his forehead. He wasn't quite sure, after all, that the girl was worthwhile. She had spunk, all right, but was she worthy of fostering a race of immortals?

He didn't get a chance to find out. "Married?" The blonde's voice sounded incredulous. "Who the devil wants to get married? You've got me on the wrong track, Sam. I don't want to get myself tied down."

"Sure, honey, sure," he said. "But I thought—"

Ginger stood up. "You think anything you please, Sam. Anything you please. But not marriage."

She stared at him hard for a moment, and walked off. Sam looked after her morosely.

Gaius Titus grinned behind the Sam Spielman mask. She wasn't the girl either.

Two thousand years of life had taught him that women were unpredictable, and he wasn't altogether surprised at her reaction to his proposal.

But he was disturbed over this second failure of the evening nevertheless. Was his judgment that far off? Perhaps, he thought, he was losing the vital ability of personality projection. He didn't like that idea.

For hours, Gaius Titus walked the streets of New York.

New York. Sure it was new. So was Old York, in England. Menenius had seen both of them grow from tiny villages to towns to cities to metropoli.

Metropoli. That was Greek. It had taken him twelve years to learn Greek. He hadn't rushed it.

Twelve years. And he still wasn't an adult. He could remember when the Emperor had seen the sign in the sky: *In hoc signo vinces*. And, at the age of four hundred and sixty-two, he'd still been too young to enter the service of the Empire.

Gaius Titus Menenius, Citizen of Rome. When he had been a child, he had thought Rome would last forever. But it hadn't; Rome had fallen. Egypt, which he had long thought of as an empire which would last forever, had gone even more quickly. It had died and putrified and sloughed off into the Great River which carries all life off into death.

Over the years and the centuries, races and peoples and nations had come and gone. And their passing had had no effect at all on Gaius Titus.

He was walking north. He turned left on Market Street, away from the Manhattan Bridge. Suddenly, he was tired of walking. He hailed a passing taxi.

He gave the cabby his address on Park Avenue and leaned back against the cushions to relax.

The first few centuries had been hard. He hadn't grown up, in the first place. By the time he was twenty, he had attained his full height—five feet nine. But he still looked like a seventeen-year-old.

And he had still looked that way nineteen hundred years later. It had been a long, hard drive to make enough money to live on during that time. Kids don't get well-paying jobs.

Actually, he'd lived a miserable hand-to-mouth existence for centuries. But the gradual collapse of the Christian ban on usury had opened the way for him to make some real money. Money makes more money, in a capitalistic system, if you have patience. Titus had time on his side.

It wasn't until the free-enterprise system had evolved that he started to get anywhere. But a deposit of several hundred pounds in the proper firm back in 1735 had netted a little extra money. The British East India Company had brought his financial standing up a great deal, and judicious investments ever since left him comfortably fixed. He derived considerable amusement from the extraordinary effects compound interest exerted on a bank account a century old.

To Be Continued

"Here you are, buddy," said the cab driver.

Gaius Titus climbed out and gave the driver a five note without asking for change. *Zeus,* he thought. *I might as well make a night of it.*

He hadn't been really drunk since the stock market collapse back in 1929.

Leslie MacGregor pushed open the door of the San Marino Bar in Greenwich Village and walked to the customary table in the back corner. Three people were already there, and the conversation was going well. Leslie waved a hand and the two men waved back. The girl grinned and beckoned.

"Come on over, Les," she yelled across the noisy room. "Mack has just sold a story!" Her deep voice was clear and firm.

Mack, the heavy-set man next to the wall, grinned self-consciously and picked up his beer.

Leslie strolled quietly over to the booth and sat down beside Corwyn, the odd man of the trio.

"Sold a story?" Leslie repeated archly.

Mack nodded. "*Chimerical Review,*" he said. "A little thing I called 'Pluck Up the Torch.' Not much, but its a sale, you know."

"If one wants to prostitute one's art," said Corwyn.

Leslie frowned at him. "Don't be snide. After all, Mack has to pay the rent." Then he turned toward the girl. "Lorraine, could I talk to you a moment?"

She brushed the blonde hair back from the shoulders of her black turtleneck sweater and widened the grin on her face.

"Sure, Les," she said in her oddly deep, almost masculine voice. "What's all the big secret?"

No secret, thought Gaius Titus. What I want is simple enough.

For a long time, he had thought that near-immortality carried with it the curse of sterility. Now he knew it was simply a matter of time and growing up. As he stood up to walk to the bar with Lorraine, he caught a glimpse of himself in the dusty mirror behind the bar. He didn't look much over twenty-five. But things had been changing in the past fifty years. He had never had a heavy beard before; he had not developed the husky baritone voice until a year before the outbreak of the First World War.

It had been difficult, at first, to hide his immortality. Changing names, changing residences, changing, changing, changing. Until he had found that he didn't have to change—not deep inside.

People don't recognize faces. Faces are essentially all alike. Two eyes, two ears, a nose, a mouth. What more is there to a face? Only the personality behind it.

A personality is something that is projected—something put on display for others to see. And Gaius Titus Menenius had found that two thousand years of experience had given him enough internal psychological reality to be able to project any personality he wanted to. All he needed was a change of dress and a change of personality to be

Robert Silverberg

a different person. His face changed subtly to fit the person who was wearing it; no one had ever caught on.

Lorraine sat down on the bar stool. "Beer," she said to the bartender. "What's the matter, Les? What's eating you?"

He studied her firm, strong features, her deep, mocking eyes. "Lorraine," he said softly, "will you marry me?"

She blinked. "Marry you? You? Marry?" She grinned again. "Who'd ever think it? A bourgeois conformist, like all the rest." Then she shook her head. "No, Les. Even if you're kidding, you ought to know better than that. What's the gag?"

"No gag," said Leslie, and Gaius Titus fought his surprise and shock at his third failure. "I see your point," Leslie said. "Forget it. Give my best to everyone." He got up without drinking his beer and walked out the door.

Leslie stepped out into the street and started heading for the subway. Then Gaius Titus, withdrawing the mask, checked himself and hailed a cab.

He got into the cab and gave the driver his home address. He didn't see any reason for further pursuing his adventures that evening.

He was mystified. How could *three* personality-facets fail so completely? He had been handling these three girls well ever since he had met them, but tonight, going from one to the next, as soon as he made any serious ventures toward any of them the whole thing folded. Why?

"It's a lousy world," he told the driver, assuming for the moment the mask of Phil Carlson, cynical newsman. "Damn lousy." His voice was a biting rasp.

"What's wrong, buddy?"

"Had a fight with all three of my girls. It's a lousy world."

"I'll buy that," the driver said. The cab swung up into Park. "But look at it this way, pal: who needs them?"

For a moment the mask blurred and fell aside, and it was Gaius Titus, not Phil Carlson, who said, "That's exactly right! Who needs them?" He gave the driver a bill and got out of the cab.

Who needs them? It was a good question. There were plenty of girls. Why should he saddle himself with Sharon, or Ginger, or Lorraine? They all had their good qualities—Sharon's social grace, Ginger's vigor and drive, Lorraine's rugged intellectualism. They were all three good-looking girls, tall, attractive, well put together. But yet each one, he realized, lacked something that the others had. None of them was really *worthy* by herself, he thought, apologizing to himself for what another man might call conceit, or sour grapes.

None of them would really do. But if somehow, some way, he could manage to combine those three leggy girls, those three personalities into one body, *there* would be a girl—

He gasped.

To Be Continued

He whirled and caught sight of the cab he had just vacated.

"Hey, cabby!" Titus called. "Come back here! Take me back to the San Marino!"

. She wasn't there. As Leslie burst in, he caught sight of Corwyn, sitting alone and grinning twistedly over a beer.

"Where'd they go? Where's Lorraine?"

The little man lifted his shoulders and eyebrows in an elaborate shrug. "They left about a minute ago. No, it was closer to ten, wasn't it? They went in separate directions. They left me here."

"Thanks," Leslie said.

Scratch Number One. Titus thought. He ran to the phone booth in the back, dialed Information, and demanded the number of the East Side Bar. After some fumbling, the operator found it.

He dialed. The bartender's tired face appeared in the screen.

"Hello, Sam," the barkeep said. "What's doing?"

"Do me a favor, Jerry," Sam said. "Look around your place for Ginger."

"She ain't here, Sam," the bartender said. "Haven't seen her since you two blew out of here a while back." Jerry's eyes narrowed. "I ain't never seen you dressed up like that before, Sam, you know?"

Gaius Titus crouched down suddenly to get out of range of the screen. "I'm celebrating tonight, Sam," he said, and broke the connection.

Ginger wasn't to be found either, eh? That left only Sharon. He couldn't call Kavanaugh's—they wouldn't give a caller any information about their patrons. Grabbing another taxi, he shot across town to Kavanaugh's.

Sharon wasn't there when Schuyler arrived. She hadn't been in since the afternoon, a waiter informed him, Schuyler had a drink and left. Gaius Titus returned to his apartment, tingling with an excitement he hadn't known for centuries.

He returned to Kavanaugh's the next night, and the next. Still no sign of her.

The following evening, though, when he entered the bar, she was sitting there, nursing an Old Fashioned. He slid onto the seat next to her. She looked up in surprise.

"Bill! Good to see you again."

"The same here," Gaius Titus said. "It's good to see you again—Ginger. Or is it Lorraine?"

She paled and put her hand to her mouth. Then, covering, she said, "What do you mean, Bill? Have you had too many drinks tonight?"

"Possibly," Titus said. "I stopped off in the San Marino before I came up. You weren't there, Lorraine. That deep voice is quite a trick, I have to admit. I had a drink with Mack and Corwyn. Then I went over to the East End, Ginger. You weren't there, either. So," he said, "there was only one place left to find you, Sharon."

She stared at him for a long moment. Finally she said, simply, "Who are you?"

Robert Silverberg

"Leslie MacGregor," Titus said. "Also Sam Spielman. and W. M. Schuyler. Plus two or three other people. The name is Gaius Titus Menenius, at your service."

"I still don't understand—"

"Yes, you do," Titus said. "You are clever—but not clever enough. Your little game had me going for almost a month, you know? And it's not easy to fool a man my age."

"When did you find out?" the girl asked weakly.

"Monday night, when I saw all three of you within a couple of hours."

"You're—"

"Yes. I'm like you," he said. "But I'll give you credit: I didn't see through it until I was on my way home. You were using my own camouflage technique against me, and I didn't spot it for what it was. What's your real name?"

"Mary Bradford," she said. "I was English, originally. Of fine Plantagenet stock. I'm really a Puritan at heart, you see." She was grinning slyly.

"Oh? Mayflower descendant?" Titus asked teasingly.

"No," Mary replied. "Not a descendant. A passenger. And I'll tell you—I was awfully happy to get out of England and over here to Plymouth Colony."

He toyed with her empty glass. "You didn't like England? Probably my fault. I was a minor functionary in King James's court in the early seventeenth century."

They giggled together over it. Titus stared at her, his pulse pounding harder and harder. She stared back. Her eyes were smiling.

"I didn't think there was another one," she said after a while. "It was so strange, never growing old. I was afraid they'd burn me as a witch. I had to keep changing, moving all the time. It wasn't a pleasant life. It's better lately—I enjoy these little poses. But I'm glad you caught on to me," she said. She reached out and took his hand. "I guess I would never have been smart enough to connect you and Leslie and Sam the way you did Sharon and Ginger and Lorraine. You play the game too well for me."

"In two thousand years," Titus said, not caring if the waiter overheard him, "I never found another one like me. Believe me, Mary, I looked. I looked hard, and I've had plenty of time to search. And now to find you, hiding behind the faces of three girls I knew!"

He squeezed her hand. The next statement followed logically for him. "Now that we've found each other," he said softly, "we can have a child. A third immortal."

Her face showed radiant enthusiasm. "Wonderful!" she said. "When can we get married?"

"How about tomor—" he started to say. Then a thought struck him.

"Mary?"

"What . . . Titus?"

"How old did you say you were? When were you born?" he asked.

She thought for a moment. "1597," she said. "I'm nearly four hundred."

To Be Continued   **49**

He nodded, dumb with growing frustration. Only four hundred? That meant—that meant she was now the equivalent of a three-year-old child!

"When can we get married?" she repeated.

"There's no hurry," Titus said dully, letting her hand drop. "We have eleven hundred years." ∎

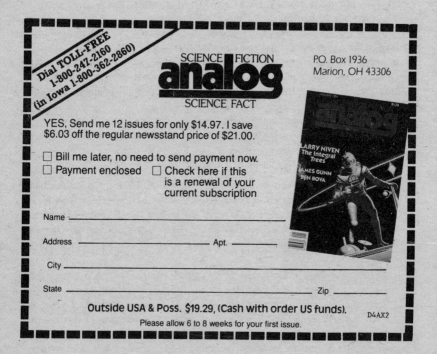

The End of Summer

Algis Budrys

"The End of Summer" was my first cover story for anyone, and I have the Kelly Freas original painting. I just looked up at it, and my heart still turns over.

I was twenty-three when I wrote that story. I'd felt it down in my mind for weeks, and finally I got the feeling it was time to sit and type. I still had no clear idea of what was going to come up out of there.

Since making my first sale—in March, 1952, with a short story to Astounding—I'd begun appearing in almost all the SF magazines, with short stories. I'd done one or two longer pieces, but ASF hadn't taken them. From the age of twelve I'd wanted to be known as a writer for John W. Campbell, Jr., and Astounding Science Fiction. Plenty of people who published short stories in ASF never became known as Campbell writers.

It was about eleven in the morning. I typed the heading and began the first sentence, whose exact phrases were only then forming. At ten o'clock that night, the piece was finished, exactly as you'll find it here.

It became my first novelette for Astounding. John didn't cry out any hurrahs when he took it, but I felt pretty good about the sale; it was a step up toward the day when I might have the lead story in an issue, and thus probably the cover. In my mind's eye was an unbroken row of ASF covers going back to October, 1943, the first issue I had bought, alone out in the southern New Jersey desolate chicken farm country. At the time, I could have told you the names of every one of the writers honored by those paintings. They were names of people who had raised me; names no person of intelligence and sensibility could forget.

In course of time, I discovered that my friend, Kelly Freas, had been given the story to illustrate. Kelly showed me the finished black-and-whites, which I thought were perfect. This was shortly after Edna and I had asked Kelly to be our best man. (John and Peg Campbell came to the wedding.) I don't know wht causes and effects are intermingled here, but one day right about this time—it was in fact the middle of summer, 1954; the story had been written in the spring and the wedding was in late July—Kelly told me that after seeing the interiors, John had decided to make it the cover story.

And so we were married; Edna and ASF and John and Kelly and the lad with the good grades in English Composition who had fretfully haunted the newsstands.

Now as to where the story came from. . . . Well, the title comes from visiting friends who lived year 'round on the shore. The memory vaults come from thinking on the problem posed by John R. Pierce in his story "Invariant" (ASF, April, '44). And that was as much rationality as I put into it. The rest of it was, simply, as close as the better part of my mind could come to the best story anyone could write around that idea; that is, an ASF story. It came out by itself; names, places, pacing, dialogue, all. What had put it there? Astounding Science Fiction *Magazine put it there.*

1

AMERICAPORT HADN'T changed since he'd last seen it, two hundred years before. It was set as far away from any other civilized area as possible, so that no plane, no matter how badly strayed, could possibly miss its landing and crash into a dwelling. Except for the straight-edge swath of the highway leading south, it was completely isolated if you forgot the almost deserted tube station. Its edge was dotted by hangars and a few offices, but the terminal building itself was small, and severely functional. Massive with bar concrete, aseptic with steel and aluminum, it was a gray, bleak place in the wilderness.

Kester Fay was so glad to see it that he jumped impatiently from the big jet's passenger lift. He knew he was getting curious looks from the ground crew clustered around the stainless-steel ship, but he would have been stared at in any case, and he had seen the sports car parked and waiting for him beside the Administration Building. He hurried across the field at a pace that attracted still more attention, eager to get his clearance and be off.

He swung his memory vault impatiently by the chain from his wristlet while the Landing Clearance officer checked his passport, but the man was obviously too glad to see someone outside the small circle of airlines personnel. He stalled interminably, and while Fay had no doubt that his life out here bored him to tears, it was becoming harder and harder to submit patiently.

"Christopher Jordan Fay," the man read off, searching for a fresh conversational opening. "Well, Mr. Fay, we haven't seen you here since '753. Enjoy your stay?"

"Yes," he answered as shortly as possible. Enjoyed it? Well, yes, he supposed he had, but it was hard to feel that way since he'd played his old American memories at augmented volume all through the flight across the Atlantic. Lord, but he was tired of Europe at this moment; weary of winding grassy lanes that meandered with classic patience among brooks and along creeks, under old stately trees! "It's good to be back where a man can stretch his legs, though."

The official chuckled politely, stamping forms. "I'll bet it is at that. Planning to stay long?"

Forever, if I can help it, Fay thought first. But then he smiled ruefully. His life had already been an overdone demonstration that forever was a long time. "For a while, at any rate," he answered, his impatience growing as he thought of the car again. He shuffled his feet on the case-hardened flooring.

"Shall I arrange for transportation to New York?"

Fay shook his head. "Not for me. But the man who drove my car up might be a customer."

The official's eyebrows rose, and Fay suddenly remembered that America, with its more liberal social attitudes, might tolerate him more than Europe had, but that there were still plenty of conservatives sheltered under the same banner.

As a matter of fact, he should have realized that the official was a Homebody; a

Civil Service man, no doubt. Even with a dozen safe places to put it down within easy reach, he still kept his memory vault chained to his wrist. Fay's own eyebrows lifted, and amusement glittered in his eyes.

"Driving down?" The official looked at Fay with a mixture of respect, envy, and disapproval.

"It's only fifteen hundred miles," Fay said with careful nonchalance. Actually, he felt quite sure that he was going to throttle the man if he wasn't let out of here and behind the wheel soon. But it would never do to be anything but bored in front of a Homebody. "I expect to make it in about three days," he added, almost yawning.

"Yes, sir," the man said, instantly wrapping himself in a mantle of aloof politeness, but muttering "Dilly!" almost audibly.

Fay'd hit home with that one, all right! Probably, the man had never set foot in an automobile. Certainly, he considered it a barefaced lie that anyone would undertake to average fifty mph during a driving day. Safe, cushiony pneumocars were his speed—and he an airlines employee!

Fay caught himself hastily. Everybody had a right to live any way he wanted to, he reminded himself.

But he could not restrain an effervescent grin at the man's sudden injured shift to aloofness.

"All right, sir," the official said crisply, returning Fay's passport. "Here you are. No baggage, of course?"

"Of course," Fay said agreeably, and if that had been intended as a slur at people who traveled light and fast, it had fallen exceedingly flat. He waved his hand cheerfully as he turned away, while the official stared at him sourly. "I'll be seeing you again, I imagine."

"I'm afraid not, sir," the man answered with a trace of malevolence. "United States Lines is shutting down passenger service the first of next year."

Momentarily nonplussed, Fay hesitated. "Oh? Too bad. No point to continuing, though, is there?"

"No, sir. I believe you were our first in a hectoyear and a half." Quite obviously, he considered that as much of a mark of Cain as necessary.

"Well . . . must be dull out here, eh?"

He cocked a satiric eye at the man and was gone, chuckling at that telling blow while the massive exit door swung ponderously shut behind him.

The car's driver was obviously a Worker who'd taken on the job because he needed money for some obscure, Workerish purpose. Fay settled the business in the shortest possible time, counting out hundred-dollar bills with a rapid shuffle. He threw in another for good measure, and waved the man aside, punching the starter vibrantly. He was back, he was home! He inhaled deeply, breathing the untrammeled air.

Curled around mountains and trailed gently through valleys, the road down through New York State was a joy. Fay drove it with a light, appreciative smile, guiding his car exuberantly, his muscles locked into communion with the automobile's grace and power as his body responded to each banked turn, each surge of acceleration below the downward crest of a hill. There was nothing like this in Europe—nothing. Over there, they left no room for his kind among their stately people.

He had almost forgotten what it was like to sit low behind the windscreen of a two-seater and listen to the dancing explosions of the unmuffled engine. It was good to be back, here on this open, magnificent road, with nothing before or behind but satin-smooth ferroconcrete and heaped green mountains to either side.

He was alone on the road, but thought nothing of it. There were very few who lived his kind of life. Now that his first impatience had passed, he was sorry he hadn't been able to talk to the jet's pilot. But that, of course, had been out of the question. Even with all the safety interlocks, there was the chance that one moment's attention lost would allow an accident to happen.

So, Fay had spent the trip playing his memory on the plane's excellent equipment, alone in the comfortable but small compartment forward of the ship's big cargo cabin.

He shrugged as he nudged the car around a curve in the valley. It couldn't be helped. It was a lonely life, and that was all there was to it. He wished there were more people who understood that it was the *only* life—the only solution to the problem which had fragmented them into so many social patterns. But there were not. And, he supposed, they were all equally lonely. The Homebodies, the Workers, the Students, and the Teachers. Even, he conceded, the Hoppers. He'd Hopped once himself, as an experiment. It had been a hollow, hysteric experience.

The road straightened, and, some distance ahead, he saw the white surface change to the dark macadam of an urban district. He slowed in response, considering the advisability of switching his safeties in, and decided it was unnecessary as yet. He disliked being no more than a pea in a safetied car's basket, powerless to do anything but sit with his hands and feet off the controls. No; for another moment, he wanted to be free to turn the car nearer the shoulder and drive through the shade of the thick shrubbery and overhanging trees. He breathed deeply of the faint fragrance in the air and once more told himself that *this* was the only way to live, the only way to find some measure of vitality. A Dilly? Only in the jealous vocabularies of the Homebodies, so long tied to their hutches and routines that the scope of mind and emotion had narrowed to fit their microcosm.

Then, without warning, still well on the white surface of open road, the brown shadow darted out of the bushes and flung itself at his wheels, barking shrilly.

He tried to snap the car out of the way, his face suddenly white, but the dog moved unpredictably, its abrupt yell of pain louder than the scream of Fay's brakes. He felt the soft bump, and then his foot jerked away from the clutch and the car stalled convulsively. Even with his engine dead and the car still, he heard no further sound from the dog.

Then he saw the Homebody boy running toward him up the road, and the expression of his face changed from shocked unpleasantness to remorseful regret. He sighed and climbed out of the car clumsily, trying to think of something to say.

The boy came running up and stopped beside the car, looking up the road with his face drawn into tearful anger.

"You *ran* over Brownie!"

Fay stared helplessly down at the boy. "I'm sorry, son," he said as gently as he could. He could think of nothing really meaningful to tell him. It was a hopeless situation. "I . . . I shouldn't have been driving so fast."

The boy ran to the huddled bundle at the shoulder of the road and picked it up in his arms, sobbing. Fay followed him, thinking that ten thousand years of experience were not enough—that a hundred centuries of learning and acquiring superficial maturity were still insufficient to shield the emotions trapped in a young boy's body, at the mercy of his glandular system, under a shock like this.

"Couldn't you see him?" the boy pleaded.

Fay shook his head numbly. "He came out of the shrubs—"

"You shouldn't have been driving so fast. You should have—"

"I know." He looked uselessly back up the road, the trees bright green in the sunshine, the sky blue.

"I'm sorry," he told the boy again. He searched desperately for something, some way, to make recompense. "I wish it hadn't happened." He thought of something, finally. "I . . . I know it wouldn't be the same thing, but I've got a dog of my own—a basset hound. He's coming over from Europe on a cargo ship. When he gets here, would you like to have him?"

"Your *own* dog?" For a moment, the boy's eyes cleared, but then he shook his head hopelessly. "It wouldn't work out," he said simply, and then, as though conscious of guilt at even considering that any other dog could replace his, tightened his arms on the lifeless bundle.

No, it hadn't been such a good idea, Fay realized. If he weren't so snarled up in remorse and confusion, he'd have seen that. Ugly had been his dog and couldn't be separated from him, or he from Ugly. He realized even more strongly just precisely what he had done to the boy.

"Something wrong? Oh—" The Homebody man who had come up the road stopped beside them, his face turning grave. Fay looked at him in relief.

"I had my automatics off," he explained to the man. "I wouldn't have, if I'd known there was a house around here, but I didn't see anything. I'm terribly sorry about the . . . about Brownie."

The man looked again at the dog in the boy's arms, and winced. Then he sighed and shrugged helplessly. "Guess it was bound to happen sometime. Should have been on a leash. There's still a law of averages."

Fay's fist clenched behind his back, out of sight. The well-worn words bit deep at the very foundation of his vitality, and his mind bridled, but in another moment the spasm of reflexive fear was gone, and he was glad he'd had this harmless outlet for his emotions. Besides, the man was right, and at this moment Fay was forced to be honest enough with himself to admit it. There was still a law of averages, whether Fay and his Dilly kind liked it or not.

"Go on back to the house, son," the man said with another sigh. "There's nothing we can do for Brownie. We'll bury him later. Right now you ought to wash up. I'll be along in a minute."

It was the way he said it—the fatalistic acceptance that no matter what the honest folk did, some blundering, heedless dilettante was going to thwart them—that scored Fay's emotions.

The boy nodded wordlessly, still crying, and began to walk away without looking at Fay again.

But Fay couldn't let him go. Like a man who picks at a splinter, he could not let this pass so simply. "Wait!" he said urgently.

The boy stopped and looked at him woodenly.

"I . . . I know there's nothing—I mean," Fay stumbled, "Brownie was your dog, and there can't be another one like him. But I do a lot of traveling—" He stopped again, flushing at the Homebody man's knowing look, then pushed on regardless. "I see a lot of people," he went on. "I'll try to find you a dog that hasn't ever belonged to anybody. When I do, I'll bring him to you. I promise."

The boy's lip twitched, suddenly revealing what ten thousand years had taught him. "Thanks, mister," he said half-scornfully, and walked away, cradling his dog.

He hadn't believed him, of course. Fay suddenly realized that no one ever believed a Dilly, whether he was telling the truth or not. He realized, too, that he had done the best he could, and nevertheless failed. He looked regretfully after the boy.

"You didn't have to do that," the man said softly, and Fay noted that some of his reserve and half-contemptuous politeness were gone. "I don't know whether to believe you or not, but you didn't have to do that. Anyway, I'll edit the dog out of his memories tonight. My wife and I'll clean the place up, and he won't notice anything." He paused, reflecting, his eyes dark. "Guess Madge and I'll cut it out of our own minitapes, too."

Fay clenched his teeth in sudden annoyance. Nobody ever believed a Dilly. "No," he said. "I wish you wouldn't do that. I meant what I said." He shook his head again. "I don't like editing. There's always a slip somewhere, and then you know you've got a hole in your memory, but you can never remember what it was."

The man looked at him curiously. "Funny thing for one of you people to say. I always heard you went for editing in a big way."

Fay kept his face from showing his thoughts. There it was again—that basic lack of understanding and a complete unwillingness to check secondhand tales. The very essence of his kind of life was that no memory, no experience, not be lived and preserved. Besides, he'd always heard that it was the Homebodies who had to edit whole hectoyears to keep from going mad with boredom.

"No," he contented himself with saying. "You're confusing us with the Hoppers. *They'll* try anything."

The End of Summer

The man curled his lip at the mention, and Fay reflected that the introduction of a common outsider seemed helpful in circumstances like this.

"Well . . . maybe you're right," the man said, still not completely trustful, but willing to take the chance. He gave Fay his name, Arnold Riker, and his address. Fay put the slip of paper carefully in his memory vault.

"Anytime I lose that, I'll have lost my memory, too," he commented.

The man grinned wryly. "More likely, you'll remember to forget it tonight," he said, some of his distrust returning at the sight of the spooled tapes.

Fay took that without protest. He supposed Riker had a right to feel that way. "Can I drive you down to your house?"

The man flicked an expressive glance along the car's length and shook his head. "Thanks. I'll walk. There's still a law of averages."

And you can take that phrase and carve it on Humanity's headstone, Fay thought bitterly, but did not reply.

He climbed into the car, flicked on the automatics, and froze, completely immobile from sharply ingrained habit that was the only way to avoid the careless move that just might open the safety switch. He did not even turn his head to look at the man he left behind as the car started itself slowly away, nor did he catch more than a passing glimpse of the house where the boy and his dog had lived together for ten kiloyears.

We guard our immortality so carefully. But there's still a law of averages.

2

Perversely, he drove more rapidly than normal for the rest of the trip. Perhaps he was trying to reaffirm his vitality. Perhaps he was running away. Perhaps he was trying to cut down the elapsed time between towns, where his automatics threaded him through the light pedestrian traffic and sent him farther down the road, with each new danger spot safely behind him. At any rate, he arrived at his Manhattan apartment while it was still daylight, stepping off the continuous-impulse elevator with some satisfaction. But his were eyes discontented.

The apartment, of course, was just as he had left it two hectoyears ago. The semirobots had kept it sealed and germicidal until the arrival of his return message yesterday.

He could imagine the activity that had followed, as books and music tapes were broken out of their helium-flooded vaults, rugs and furnishings were stripped of their cocoons, aerated, and put in place. From somewhere, new plants had come and been set in the old containers, and fresh liquor put in the cabinet. There would be food in the kitchen, clothes in the wardrobes—the latest styles, of course, purchased with credits against the left-behind apparel of two hectoyears before—and there were the same, old familiar paintings on the walls. Really old, not just By-Product stuff.

He smiled warmly as he looked around him, enjoying the swell of emotion at the

Algis Budrys

apartment's comfortable familiarity. He smiled once more, briefly, at the thought that he must some day devise a means of staying in a sealed apartment—wearing something like a fishing lung, perhaps—and watch the semirobots at their refurbishing process. It must be a fascinating spectacle.

But his glance had fallen on the memory vault which he had unchained and put on a coffee table. It faced him with the ageless, silent injunction painted on each of its faces: PLAY ME, and underneath this the block of smaller lettering that he, like everyone else, knew by heart:

> If your surroundings seem unfamiliar, or you have any other reason to suspect that your environment and situation are not usual, request immediate assistance from any other individual. He is obligated by strict law to direct you to the nearest free public playback booth, where you will find further instructions. Do not be alarmed, and follow these directions without anxiety, even if they seem strange to you. In extreme situations, stand still and do not move. Hold this box in front of you with both hands. This is a universally recognized signal of distress. Do not let anyone take this box away from you, no matter what the excuse offered.

He wondered momentarily what had made him notice it; he knew it so well that the pattern of type had long ago become no more than a half-seen design with a recognition value so high that it had lost all verbal significance.

Was it some sort of subconscious warning? He checked his memory hastily, but relaxed when he found none of the telltale vagueness of detail that meant it was time to let everthing else wait and get to a playback as fast as possible. He had refreshed his memory early this morning, before starting the last leg of his trip, and it seemed to be good for several more hours, at least.

What was it, then?

He frowned and went to the liquor cabinet, wondering if some train of thought had been triggered off by the accident and was trying to call attention to himself. And when he dropped into an easy chair a few minutes later, a drink in his hand and his eyes still brooding over the vault's legend, he realized that his second guess had been the right one. As usual, one level of his mind had been busy digesting while the surface churned in seeming confusion.

He smiled ruefully. Maybe he wasn't quite as much of a Dilly as he looked and would have liked to believe. Still, a man couldn't live ten thousand years and not put a few things together in his head. He took a sip of his drink and stared out over the city in the gathering twilight. Somewhere in the graceful furniture behind him a photoelectric relay clicked, and his high-fidelity set began to play the Karinius *Missa*. The apartment had not forgotten his moods.

No, he thought, the machines never forgot. Only men forgot, and depended on machines to help them remember. He stared at the vault, and a familiar sophistry occurred to him. "Well," he asked the box labeled PLAY ME, "which *is* my brain—you or the gray lump in my head?"

The answer depended on his moods, and on his various audiences. Tonight, alone, in an uncertain mood, he had no answer.

He took another drink and sat back, frowning.

At best, he'd offered the boy a shoddy substitute. Even presuming that the passage of ten kiloyears had somehow still left room for a dog without a master, the animal would have to be refamiliarized with the boy at least once or twice a day.

Why? Why did dogs who had always had the same master remember him without any difficulty, even though they seemed to have to reinvestigate their surroundings periodically? Why would Ugly, for instance, remember him joyfully when his ship came? And why would Ugly have to be refamiliarized with this apartment, in which he'd lived with Fay, off and on, for all this time?

The Kinnard dog, whose master insisted on building each new house in a carbon copy of the previous, didn't have anywhere near as much trouble. Why?

He'd heard rumors that some people were recording canine memories on minitape, but that sort of story was generally classified along with the jokes about the old virgin who switched vaults with her nubile young niece.

Still and all, there might be something in that. He'd have to ask Monkreeve. Monkreeve was the Grand Old Man of the crowd. He had memories the rest of them hadn't even thought of yet.

Fay emptied his glass and got up to mix another drink. He was thinking harder than he had for a long time—and he could not help feeling that he was making a fool of himself. Nobody else had ever asked questions like this. Not where others could hear them, at any rate.

He sat back down in his chair, fingers laced around the glass while the *Missa* ended and the *Lieutenant Kije* suite caught up the tempo of the city as it quickened beneath showers of neon.

PLAY ME. Like a music tape, the memory vault held his life tightly knit in the nested spindles of bright, imperishable minitape.

What, he suddenly asked himself, would happen if he didn't play it tonight?

"If your surroundings seem unfamiliar, or you have any other reason to suspect your environment and situation are not usual . . .

"Obligated by strict law to direct you . . .

"Do not be alarmed . . . "

What? What was behind the whispered stories, the jokes:

"What did the girl in the playback booth say to the young man who walked in by mistake?

"Man, this has been the *busiest* twenty-seventh of July!" [Laughter]

The thought struck him that there might be all sorts of information concealed in his fund of party conversation.

"If you wish to get to heaven,

Algis Budrys

Stay away from twenty-seven."

And there it was again. Twenty-seven. July twenty-seventh, this time conglomerated with a hangover reference to religion. And that was interesting, too. Man had religions, of course—schismatic trace sects that offered no universally appealing reward to make them really popular. But they must have been really big once, judging by the stamp they'd left on oaths and idiomatic expressions. Why? What did they have? Why had two billion people integrated words like "Heaven," "Lord God," and "Christ" into the language so thoroughly that they had endured ten kiloyears?

July twenty-seventh when? Year?

What would happen to him if he ignored PLAY ME just this once?

He had the feeling that he knew all this; that he had learned it at the same time that he had learned to comb his hair and cut his fingernails, take showers and brush his teeth. But he did all that more or less automatically now.

Maybe it was time he thought about it.

But nobody else did. Not even Monkreeve.

So what? Who was Monkreeve, really? Didn't the very fact that he had thought of it make it all right? That *was* the basis on which they judged everything else, wasn't it?

That boy and his dog had really started something.

He realized several things simultaneously, and set his glass down with a quick *thump*. He couldn't remember the dog's name. And he was definitely letting the simple problem of following his conscience—and his wounded pride—lead him into far deeper intellectual waters than any boy and his dog had a right.

His cheeks went cold as he tried to remember the name of this morning's hotel, and he shivered violently. He looked at his box labeled PLAY ME.

"Yes," he told it. "Yes, definitely."

3

Fay awoke to a bright, sunny morning. The date on his calendar clock was April 16, 11958, and he grinned at it while he removed the vault's contacts from the bare places on his scalp. He noted that all the memories he had brought back from Europe had been rerecorded for the apartment's spare vault, and that the current minitape had advanced the shining notch necessary to record yesterday.

He looked at that notch and frowned. It looked like an editing scratch, and was. It was always there, every morning, but he knew it covered nothing more than the normal traumatic pause between recording and playback. He'd been told that it was the one memory nobody wanted to keep, and certainly he'd never missed editing it—or, of course, remembered doing it. It was a normal part of the hypnotic action pattern set by the recorder to guide him when he switched over from record to playback, his mind practically blank by that time.

He'd never seen a tape, no matter whose, that did not bear that one scratch to mark each day. He took pride in the fact that a good many tapes were so hashed out and romanticized as to be almost pure fiction. He hadn't been lying to the boy's father—and he noted the presence of that memory with the utmost satisfaction—he had a driving basic need to see everything, hear everything, sense each day and its events to their fullest, and to remember them with sharp perfect clarity.

He laughed at the vault as he kicked it shut on his way to the bathroom. "Not until tonight," he said to PLAY ME, and then teetered for a breathless moment as he struggled to regain his balance. He set his foot down with a laugh, his eyes sparkling.

"Who needs a car to live dangerously?" he asked himself. But that brought back the memory of the boy, and his lips straightened. Nevertheless, it was a beautiful day, and the basic depression of yesterday was gone. He thought of all the people he knew in the city, one of whom, at least, would be sure to have a contact somewhere or the other that would solve his problem for him.

He ate his breakfast heartily, soaking for an hour in the sensual grip of his bathtub's safety slinging while he spooned the vitalizing porridge, then shrugged into a violet bathrobe and began calling people on the telephone.

He hadn't realized how long he'd been gone, he reflected, after Vera, his welcome to her apartment finished, had left him with a drink while she changed. It was, of course, only natural that some of the old crowd had changed their habits or themselves gone traveling in his absence. Nevertheless, he still felt a little taken aback at the old phone numbers that were no longer valid, or the really astonishing amount of people who seemed to have edited him out of their memories. Kinnard, of all people! And Lorraine.

Somehow he'd never thought Lorraine would go editor.

"Ready, Kes?"

Vera was wearing a really amazing dress. Apparently, America had gone back toward conservatism, as he might have guessed from his own wardrobe.

Vera, too, had changed somehow—too subtly for him to detect, here in surroundings where he had never seen her before. Hadn't she always been resistant to the fad of completely doing apartments over every seventy years? He seemed to remember it that way, but even with minitapes, the evidence of the eye always took precedence over the nudge of memory. Still, she at least knew where Monkreeve was, which was something he hadn't been able to find out for himself.

"Uh-huh. Where're we going?"

She smiled and kissed the tip of his nose. "Relax, Kes. Let it happen."

"Um."

"Grasshoppers as distinct from ants, people given to dancing and similar gay pursuits, or devotees to stimulants," Monkreeve babbled, gesturing extravagantly. "Take your pick of derivations." He washed down a pill of some sort and braced himself theatrically. "I've given up on the etymology. What'd you say your name was?"

Fay grimaced. He disliked Hoppers and Hopper parties—particularly in this instance. He wished heartily that Vera had told him what had happened to Monkreeve before she brought him here.

He caught a glimpse of her in the center of an hysterical knot of people, dancing with her seven petticoats held high.

"Who*ee!*" Monkreeve burst out, detecting the effects of the pill among the other explosions in his system. Fay gave him a searching look, and decided, from the size of his pupils, that he could probably convince himself into an identical state on bread pills, and more than likely was.

"Got a problem, hey, lad?" Monkreeve asked wildly. "Got a dog problem." He put his finger in his mouth and burlesqued Thought. "Got a dog, got a problem, got a problem, got a dog," he chanted. "Hell!" he exploded, "go see old Williamson. Old Williamson knows everything. Ask him anything. Sure," he snickered, "ask him anything."

"Thanks, Monk," Fay said. "Glad to've met you," he added in the accepted polite form with editors, and moved toward Vera.

"Sure, sure, Kid. Ditto and check. Whatcha say your name was?"

Fay pretented to be out of earshot, brushed by a couple who were dancing in a tight circle to no music at all, and delved into the crowd around Vera.

"Hi, Kes!" Vera exclaimed, looking up and laughing. "Did Monk give you any leads?"

"Monk has a monkey on his back, he thinks," Fay said shortly, a queasy feeling in his throat.

"Well, why not try that on the kid? He might like a change." Vera broke into fresh laughter. Suddenly an inspiration came to her, and she began to sing.

"Oh where, oh where, has my little dog gone? Oh where, oh where can he be?"

The rest of the crowd picked it up. Vera must have told them about his search, for they sang it with uproarious gusto.

Fay turned on his heel and walked out.

The halls of the University library were dim gray, padded with plastic sponge, curving gently with no sharp corners. Doorways slid into walls, the sponge muffled sound, and he wore issued clothes into which he had been allowed to transfer only those personal items which could not possibly cut or pry. Even his vault had been encased in a ball of cellular sponge plastic, and his guide stayed carefully away from him, in case he should fall or stumble. The guide carried a first aid kit, and like all the library staff, was a certified Doctor of Theoretical Medicine.

"This is Dr. Williamson's interview chamber," the guide told him softly, and pressed a button concealed under the sponge. The door slid back, and Fay stepped into the padded interior of the chamber, divided down the middle by a sheet of clear, thick plastic. There was no furniture to bump into, of course. The guide made sure he was safely in, out of the door's track, and closed it carefully after he had stepped out.

Fay sat down on the soft floor and waited. He started wondering what had happened to the old crowd, but he had barely found time to begin when the door on the other side of the partition opened and Dr. Williamson came in. Oddly enough, his physiological age was less than Fay's, but he carried himself like an old man, and his entire manner radiated the same feeling.

He looked at Fay distastefully. "Hopper, isn't it? What're you doing here?"

Fay got to his feet. "No, sir. Dilly, if you will, but not a Hopper." Coming so soon after the party, Williamson's remark bit deep.

"Six of one, half a dozen of the other, in time," Williamson said curtly. "Sit down." He lowered himself slowly, testing each new adjustment of his muscles and bones before he made the next. He winced faintly when Fay dropped to the floor with defiant overcarelessness. "Well—go on. You wouldn't be here if the front desk didn't think your research was at least interesting."

Fay surveyed him carefully before he answered. Then he sighed, shrugged mentally, and began. "I want to find a dog for a little boy," he said, feeling more than foolish.

Williamson snorted: "What leads you to believe this is the ASPCA'?"

"ASPCA, sir?"

Williamson threw his hands carefully up to heaven and snorted again. Apparently, everything Fay said served to confirm some judgment of mankind on his part.

He did not explain, and Fay finally decided he was waiting. There was a minute's pause, and then Fay said awkwardly: "I assume that's some kind of animal shelter. But that wouldn't serve my purpose. I need a dog that . . . that *remembers*."

Williamson put the tips of his fingers together and pursed his lips. "So. A dog that remembers, eh?" He looked at Fay with considerably more interest, the look in his eyes sharpening.

"You look like any other brainless jackanapes," he mused, "but apparently there's some gray matter left in your artfully coiffed skull after all." Williamson was partially bald.

"What would you say," Williamson continued, "if I offered to let you enroll here as an Apprentice Liberor?"

"Would I find out how to get that kind of dog?"

A flicker of impatience crossed Willaimson's face. "In time, in time. But that's beside the point."

"I . . . I haven't got much time, sir," Fay said haltingly. Obviously, Williamson had the answer to his question. But would he part with it, and if he was going to, why this rigmarole?

Willaimson gestured with careful impatience. "Time is unimportant. And especially here, where we avoid the law of averages almost entirely. But there are various uses for time, and I have better ones than this. Will you enroll? Quick, man!''

Algis Budrys

"I—Dr. Williamson, I'm grateful for your offer, but right now all I'd like to know is how to get a dog." Fay was conscious of a mounting impatience of his own.

Williamson got carefully to his feet and looked at Fay with barely suppressed anger.

"Young man, you're living proof that our basic policy is right. I wouldn't trust an ignoramus like you with the information required to cut his throat.

"Do you realize where you are?" He gestured at the walls. "In this building is the world's greatest repository of knowledge. For ten thousand years we have been accumulating opinion and further theoretical data on every known scientific and artistic theory extant in 1973. We have data that will enable Man to go to the stars, travel ocean bottoms, and explore Jupiter. We have here the raw material of symphonies and sonatas that make your current addictions sound like a tincup beggar's fiddle. We have the seed of paintings that would make you spatter whitewash over the daubs you treasure, and verse that would drive you mad. And you want me to find you a dog!"

Fay had gotten to his own feet. Williamson's anger washed over him in battering waves, but one thing remained clear, and he kept to it stubbornly.

"Then you won't tell me."

"No, I will *not* tell you! I thought for a moment that you had actually managed to perceive something of your environment, but you have demonstrated my error. You are dismissed." Williamson turned and stamped carefully out of his half of the interview chamber, and the door slid open behind Fay.

Still and all, he had learned something. He had learned that there was something important about dogs not remembering, and he had a date: 1973.

He sat in his apartment, his eyes once more fixed on PLAY ME, and tried a thought on for size: July 27, 1973.

It made more sense that way than it did when the two parts were separated—which could mean nothing, of course. Dates were like the jigsaw puzzles that were manufactured for physiological four-year-olds: they fit together no matter how the pieces were matched.

When had the human race stopped having children?

The thought smashed him bolt upright in his chair, spilling his drink.

He had never thought of that. Never once had he questioned the fact that everyone was frozen at some apparently arbitrary physiological age. He had learned that such-and-such combined anatomical and psychological configuration was indicative of one physiological age, that a different configuration indicated another. Or had he? Couldn't he tell instinctively—or, rather, couldn't he tell as though the word "age" were applicable to humans as well as inanimate objects?

A lesser thought followed close on the heels of the first: exactly the same thing could be said of dogs, or canaries or parakeets, as well as the occasional cat that hadn't gone wild.

"Gone" wild? Hadn't most cats always been wild?

Just exactly what memories were buried in his mind, in hiding—or rather, since he was basically honest with himself, what memories had he taught himself to ignore? And why?

His skin crawled. Suddenly his careful, flower-to-flower world was tinged with frost around him, and brown, bare, and sharply ragged stumps were left standing. The boy and his dog had been deep water indeed—for his tentative toe had baited a monster of continuous and expanding questions to fang him with rows of dangerous answers.

He shook himself and took another drink. He looked at PLAY ME, and knew where the worst answers must be.

4

He awoke, and there were things stuck to his temples. He pulled them loose and sat up, staring at the furnishings and the machine that sat beside his bed, trailing wires.

The lights were on, but the illumination was so thoroughly diffused that he could not find its source. The furniture was just short of the radical in design, and he had certainly never worn pajamas to bed. He looked down at them and grunted.

He looked at the machine again, and felt his temples where the contacts had rested. His fingers came away sticky, and he frowned. Was it some sort of encephalograph? Why?

He looked around again. There was a faint possibility that he was recovering from psychiatric treatment, but this was certainly no sanatorium room.

There was a white placard across the room, with some sort of printing on it. Since it offered the only possible source of information, he got off the bed cautiously and, when he encountered no dizziness or weakness, crossed over to it. He stood looking at it, lips pursed and brow furrowed, while he picked his way through the rather simplified orthography.

> Christopher Jordan Fay:
> If your surroundings seem unfamiliar, or you have any other reason to suspect that your environment and situation are unusual, do not be alarmed, and follow these directions without anxiety, even if they seem strange to you. If you find yourself unable to do so, for any reason whatsoever, please return to the bed and read the instructions printed on the machine beside it. In this case, the nearest ''free public playback booth'' is the supplementary cabinet you see built into the head of the bed. Open the doors and read the supplementary instructions printed inside. In any case, do not be alarmed, and if you are unable or unwilling to perform any of the actions requested above, simply dial ''0'' on the telephone you see across the room.

Fay looked around once more, identified the various objects, and read on.

　　　　　　　　　　　　　　　　　　　　　　　　　　　　　Algis Budrys

The operator, like all citizens, is required by strict law to furnish you with assistance.

If, on the other hand, you feel sufficiently calm or are commensurately curious, please follow these directions:

Return to the bed and restore the contacts to the places where they were attached. Switch the dial marked "Record-Playback-Auxiliary Record" to the "Auxiliary Record" position. You will then have three minutes to place your right forearm on the grooved portion atop the machine. Make certain your arm fits snugly—the groove is custom-molded to accept your arm perfectly in one position only.

Finally, lie back and relax. All other actions are automatic.

For your information, you have suffered from loss of memory, and this device will restore it to you.

Should you be willing to follow the above directions, please accept our thanks.

Fay's tongue bulged his left cheek, and he restrained a grin. Apparently, his generator had been an unqualified success. He looked at the printing again, just to be certain, and confirmed the suspicion that it had been done by his own hand. Then, as a conclusive check, he prowled the apartment in search of a calendar. He finally located the calendar-clock, inexpertly concealed in a bureau drawer, and looked at the date.

That was his only true surprise. He whistled shrilly at the date, but finally shrugged and put the clock back. He sat down in a convenient chair, and pondered.

The generator was working just as he'd expected, the signal bouncing off the heaviside layer without perceptible loss of strength, covering the Earth. As to what could happen when it exhausted its radioactive fuel in another five thousand years, he had no idea, but he suspected that he would simply refuel it. Apparently, he still had plenty of money, or whatever medium of exchange existed now. Well, he'd provided for it.

Interesting, how his mind kept insisting it was July 27, 1973. This tendency to think of the actual date as "the future" could be confusing if he didn't allow for it.

Actually, he was some ten-thousand and thirty-eight years old, rather than the thirty-seven his mind insisted on. But his memories carried him only to 1973, while, he strongly suspected, the Kester Fay who had written that naïve message had memories that *began* shortly thereafter.

The generator broadcast a signal which enabled body cells to repair themselves with one hundred percent perfection, rather than the usual less-than-perfect of living organisms. The result was that none of the higher organisms aged, in any respect. Just the higher ones, fortunately, or there wouldn't even be yeast derivatives to eat.

But, of course, that included brain cells, too. Memory was a process of damaging brain cells much as a phonograph recording head damaged a blank record disk. In order to relive the memory, the organism had only to play it back, as a record is played. Except that, so long as the generator continued to put out the signal, brain cells, too, repaired themselves completely. Not immediately, of course, for the body took a little time to act. But no one could possibly sleep through a night and remember anything about the day before. Amnesia was the price of immortality.

He stood up, went to the liquor cabinet he'd located in his search, and mixed himself a drink, noticing again how little, actually, the world had progressed in ten thousand years. Cultural paralysis, more than likely, under the impact of two and a half billion individuals each trying to make his compromise with the essential boredom of eternal life.

The drink was very good, the whiskey better than any he was used to. He envied himself.

They'd finally beaten amnesia, as he suspected the human race would. Probably by writing notes to themselves at first, while panic and hysteria cloaked the world and July 27th marched down through the seasons and astronomers went mad.

The stimulated cells, of course, did not repair the damage done to them before the generator went into operation. They took what they already had as a model, and clung to it fiercely.

He grimaced. Their improved encephalograph probably rammed in so much information so fast that their artificial memories blanketed the comparatively small amount of information which they had acquired up to the 27th. Or, somewhat more likely, the period of panic had been so bad that they refused to probe beyond it. If that was a tape-recording encephalograph, editing should be easily possible.

"I suspect," he said aloud, "that what I am remembering now is part of a large supressed area in my own memory." He chuckled at the thought that his entire life had been a blank to himself, and finished the drink.

And what he was experiencing now was an attempt on his own part to get that blank period on tape, circumventing the censors that kept him from doing it when he had his entire memory.

And that took courage. He mixed another drink and toasted himself. "Here's to you, Kester Fay—I'm glad to learn I've got guts."

The whiskey was extremely good.

And the fact that Kester Fay had survived the traumatic hiatus between the twenty-seventh and the time when he had his artificial memory was proof that They hadn't gotten to him before the smash-up.

Paranoid, was he?

He'd stopped the accelerating race toward Tee-Total War, hadn't he?

They hadn't been able to stop him, that was certain. He'd preserved the race of Man, hadn't he?

Psychotic? He finished the drink and chuckled. Intellectually, he had to admit that anyone who imposed immortality on all his fellow beings without asking their permission was begging for the label.

Algis Budrys

But, of course, he knew he wasn't psychotic. If he were, he wouldn't be so insistent on the English "Kester" for a nickname rather than the American "Chris."

He put the glass down regretfully. Ah, well—time to give himself *all* his memories back. Why was his right arm so strong?

He lay down on the bed, replaced the contacts, and felt the needle slip out of its recess in the forearm trough and slide into a vein.

Scopolamine derivative of some sort, he decided. Machinery hummed and clicked in the cabinets at the head of the bed, and a blank tape spindle popped into position in the vault, which rested on a specially built stand beside the bed.

Complicated, he thought dimly as he felt the drug pumping into his system. I could probably streamline it down considerably.

He found time to think once more of his basic courage. Kester Fay must still be a rampant individual, even in his stagnant, conservative, ten thousand-year-weighty civilization.

Apparently, nothing could change his fundamental character.

He sank into a coma with a faint smile.

The vault's volume control in the playback cycle was set to "Emergency Overload." Memories hammered at him ruthlessly, ravaging brain tissue, carving new channels through the packed silt of repair, foaming, bubbling, hissing with voracious energy and shattering impetus.

His face ran through agonized changes in his sleep. He pawed uncertainly and feebly at the contacts on his scalp, but the vital conditioning held. He never reached them, though he tried, and, failing, tried, and tried through the long night, while sweat pured down his face and soaked into his pillow, and he moaned, while the minitapes clicked and spun, one after the other, and gave him back the past.

It was July 27, 1973, and he shivered with cold, uncomprehendingly staring at the frost on the windows, with the note dated 7/27/73 in his hand.

It was July 27, 1973, and he was faint with hunger as he tried to get the lights to work. Apparently, the power was off. He struck a match and stared down at the series of notes, some of them smudged with much unremembered handling, all dated July 27, 1973.

It was July 27, 1973, and the men who tried to tell him it was really Fall in 1989, clustered around his bed in the crowded hospital ward, were lying. But they told him his basic patents on controlled artificial radioactivity had made it possible to power the complicated machinery they were teaching him to use. And though, for some reason, money as an interest-gathering medium was no longer valid, they told him that in his special case, in gratitude, they'd arranged things so there'd be a series of royalties and licensing fees, which would be paid into his accounts automatically. He wouldn't even have to check on them, or know specifically where they came from. But the important part came when they assured him that the machinery—the "vault," and the "minitapes," whatever they were, would cure his trouble.

He was grateful for that, because he'd been afraid for a long time that he was going insane. Now he could forget his troubles.

Kester Fay pulled the vault contacts off his forehead and sat up to see if there was an editing scratch on the tape.

But, of course, there wasn't. He knew it before he'd raised his head an inch, and he almost collapsed, sitting on the edge of the bed with his head in his hands.

He was his own monster. He had no idea of what most of the words he'd used in those memories had meant, but even as he sat there, he could feel his mind hesitatingly making the linkages and assigning tags to the jumbled concepts and frightening rationalizations he'd already remembered.

He got up gingerly, and wandered about the apartment, straightening out the drawers he'd upset during his amnesiac period. He came to the empty glass, frowned at it, shrugged, and mixed a drink.

He felt better afterwards, the glow of 100 Proof working itself into his system. The effects wouldn't last, of course—intoxication was a result of damage to the brain cells—but the first kick was real enough. Moreover, it was all he'd gotten accustomed to, during the past ten kiloyears, just as the Hoppers could drug themselves eternally.

Ten thousand years of having a new personality seemed to have cured the psychosis he'd had with his old one. He felt absolutely no desire to change the world single-handed.

Had it, now? Had it? Wasn't being a dilettante the result of an inner conviction that you were too good for routine living?

And didn't he want to turn the generator off, now that he knew what it did and where it was?

He finished the drink and bounced the glass in his palm. There was nothing that said he had to reach a decision right this minute. He'd had ten kiloyears. It could wait a little longer.

He bathed to the accompaniment of thoughts he'd always ignored before—thoughts about things that weren't his problem, then. Like incubators full of babies ten kiloyears old, and pregnant women, and paralytics.

He balanced that against hydrogen bombs, and still the scales did not tip.

Then he added something he had never known before, but that he had now, and understood why no one ever ventured to cross twenty-seven, or to remember it if he had. For one instant, he, too, stopped still at his bath and considered ripping the memory out of his minitapes.

He added Death.

But he knew he was lost, now. For better or worse, the water had closed over his head, and if he edited the memory now, he would seek it out again some day. For a moment, he wondered if that was precisely what he had done, countless times before.

He gave it up. It could wait—if he stayed sane. At any rate, he knew how to get the little boy his dog, now.

Algis Budrys

He built a signal generator to cancel out the effect of the big one, purring implacably in its mountain shaft, sending out its eternal, unshieldable signal. He blanketed one room of his apartment with the canceling wave, and added six months to his age by staying in it for hours during the eighteen months it took to mate Ugly and raise the best pup, for the stimulating wave was the answer to sterility, too. Fetuses could not develop.

He cut himself from the Dilly crowd, what was left of it, and raised the pup. And it was more than six months he added to his age, for all that time he debated and weighed, and remembered.

And by the time he was ready, he still did not know what he was going to do about the greater problem. Still and all, he had a new dog for the boy.

He packed the canceling generator and the dog in his car, and drove back up the road he had come.

Finally, he knocked on Riker's door, the dog under one arm, the generator under the other.

Riker answered his knock and looked at him curiously.

"I'm . . . I'm Kester Fay, Mr. Riker," he said hesitating. "I've brought your boy that dog I promised."

Riker looked at the dog and the bulky generator under his arm, and Fay shifted his load awkwardly, the dangling vault interfering with his movements. Light as it was, the vault was a bulky thing. "Don't you remember me?"

Riker blinked thoughtfully, his forehead knotting. Then he shook his head. "No . . . no, I guess not, Mr. Fay." He looked suspiciously at Fay's clothes, which hadn't been changed in three days. Then he nodded.

"Uh . . . I'm sorry, mister, but I guess I must have edited it." He smiled in embarrassment. "Come to think of it, I've wondered if we didn't have a dog sometime. I hope it wasn't too important to you."

Fay looked at him. He found it impossible to think of anything to say. Finally, he shrugged.

"Well," he said, "your boy doesn't have a dog now, does he?"

Riker shook his head. "Nope. You know—it's a funny thing, what with the editing and everything, but he knows a kid with a dog, and sometimes he pesters the life out of me to get him one." Riker shrugged. "You know how kids are."

"Will you take this one?" He held out the squirming animal.

"Sure. Mighty grateful. But I guess we both know this won't work out too well." He reached out and took the dog.

"This one sure will," Fay said. He gave Riker the generator. "Just turn this on for a while in the same room with your son and the dog. It won't hurt anything, but the dog'll remember."

Riker looked at him skeptically.

"Try it," Fay said, but Riker's eyes were narrowing, and he gave Fay both the dog and the generator back.

"No, thanks," he said, "I'm not trying anything like that from a guy that comes out of nowhere in the middle of the night."

"Please, Mr. Riker. I promise—"

"Buddy, you're trespassing. I won't draw more than half a hectoyear if I slug you."

Fay's shoulders slumped. "All right," he sighed, and turned around. He heard Riker slam the heavy door behind him.

But as he trudged down the walk, his shoulders lifted, and his lips set in a line.

There has to be an end somewhere, he thought. Each thing has to end, or there will never be any room for beginnings. He turned around to be sure no one in the house was watching, and released the dog. He'd be found in the morning, and things might be different by then.

He climbed into the car and drove quickly away, leaving the dog behind. Somewhere outside of town, he threw the canceling generator outside, onto the concrete highway, and heart it smash. He unchained his memory vault, and threw it out, too.

There had to be an end. Even an end to starlit nights and the sound of a powerful motor. An end to the memory of sunset in the Piazza San Marco, and the sight of snow on Chamonix. An end to good whiskey. For him, there had to be an end—so that others could come after. He pointed the car toward the generator's location, and reflected that he had twenty or thirty years left, anyway.

He flexed his curiously light arm. ■

Won't You Walk—
Theodore Sturgeon

An odd thing has happened to me throughout my writing life: a hint, or an impulse, or some such which sidles into what I am writing, ignoring my lack of any formal training or, indeed, any real information. Next thing I know—or years later—this "something" will show up in the marketplace, or in a new mental therapy, or in the form (as happened recently) of a long quotation in the Proceedings of the Institute of Electrical and Electronic Engineers *from one of my yarns, describing a futuristic device which is suddenly on the cutting edge of a modern technology. And sometimes a notion like that hasn't been used yet, but will be because it must be. A perfect example is buried in this story: it's a theraputic use of the glaring, flashing red light in the correction of certain negative self-evaluations. I know of no therapist who uses it in all the years since it appeared (in 1956) but I know someone will. There are, by the way, much better ways of doing this than by punching little holes in an audio tape; these had not been devised when I wrote the story. You'll understand all this when you read it.*

A word must be said about the title. Many readers have told me that if they think of it at all, they are satisfied that it has to do with learning to crawl before learning to walk. It has nothing to do with that. I chose it because it is the opening line of a poem, or song, or bit of doggerel which I seem to have known since I was a child, and therefore concluded that everyone must know it. As far as I have been able to find since, however, nobody *has ever heard of this source, and if anyone can identify it for me, I will be pleased. The line is:*

"Won't you walk into my parlor?"
Said the spider to the fly. . . .

JOE FRITCH WALKED UNDER THE MOON, and behind the bridge of his nose something rose and stung him. When he was a little boy, which was better than thirty years ago, this exact sensation was the prelude to tears. There had been no tears for a long time, but the sting came to him, on its occasions, quite unchanged. There was another goad to plague him too, as demanding and insistent as the sting, but at the moment it was absent. They were mutually exclusive.

His mind was a jumble of half-curses, half-wishes, not weak or pale ones by any means, but just unfinished. He need not finish any of them; his curses and his wishes were his personal cliché, and required only a code, a syllable for each. "He who hesitates—" people say, and that's enough. "Too many cooks—" they say wisely. "What's sauce for the goose—" Valid sagacities, every one, classic as the Parthenon and as widely known.

Such were the damnations and the prayers in the microcosm called Joe Fritch. "Oh, I wish—" he would say to himself, and "If only—" and "Some day, by God—" and for each of these there was a wish, detailed and dramatic, so thought-out, touched-up, policed and maintained that it had everything but reality to make it real. And in the other area, the curses, the code-words expressed wide meticulous matrices: "That Barnes—" dealt not only with his employer, a snide, selfish, sarcastic sadist with a presence like itching powder, but with every social circumstance which produced and permitted a way of life wherein a man like Joe Fritch could work for a man like Barnes. "Lutie—" was his wife's name, but as a code word it was dowdy breakfasts and I-can't-afford, that-old-dress and the finger in her ear, the hand beginning to waggle rapidly when she was annoyed; "Lutie—" said as the overture to this massive curse was that which was wanted and lost ("Joe?" "What, li'l Lutie?" "Nothing, Joe. Just . . . Joe—") and that which was unwanted and owned, like the mortgage which would be paid off in only eighteen more years, and the single setting of expensive flowery sterling which they would never, never be able to add to.

Something had happened after dinner—he could almost not remember it now; what bursts the balloon, the last puff of air, or the air it already contains? Is the final drop the only factor in the spilling-over of a brimming glass? Something about Marie Next Door (Lutie always spoke of her that way, a name like William Jennings Bryan) and a new TV console, and something about Lutie's chances, ten years ago, of marrying no end of TV consoles, with houses free-and-clear and a car and a coat, and all these chances forsworn for the likes of Joe Fritch. It had been an evening like other evenings, through 10:13 P.M. At 10:14 something silent and scalding had burst in the back of Joe's throat; he had risen without haste and had left the house. Another man might have roared an epithet, hurled an ashtray. Some might have slammed the door, and some, more skilled in maliciousness, might have left it open so the angry wife, sooner or later, must get up and close it. Joe had simply shambled out, shrinking away from her in the mindless way an amoeba avoids a hot pin. There were things he might have said. There were things he could have said to Barnes, too, time and time again, and to the elevator-starter who caught him by the elbow one morning and jammed him into a car, laughing at him through the gate before the doors slid shut. But he never said the things, not to anyone. Why not? Why not?

"They wouldn't listen," he said aloud, and again the sting came back of his nose.

He stopped and heeled water out of his left eye with the base of his thumb. This, and the sound of his own voice, brought him his lost sense of presence. He looked around like a child awakening in a strange bed.

It was a curved and sloping street, quite unlike the angled regimentation of his neighborhood. There was a huge elm arched over the street-lamp a block away, and to Joe's disoriented eye it looked like a photographic negative, a shadow-tree lit by darkness looming over a shadow of light. A tailored hedge grew on a neat stone wall beside him; across the street was a white picket fence enclosing a rolling acre and the dark mass of just the house he could never own, belonging, no doubt, to someone people listened to. Bitterly he looked at it and its two gates, its rolled white driveway, and, inevitably, the low, long coupé which stood in it. The shape of that car, the compact, obedient, directional eagerness of it, came to him like the welcome answer to some deep question within him, something he had thought too complex to have any solution. For a moment a pure, bright vision overwhelmed and exalted him; his heart, his very bones cried *well, of course!* and he crossed to the driveway, along its quiet grassy margin to the car.

He laid a hand on its cool ivory flank, and had his vision again. At the wheel of this fleetfooted dream-car, he would meet the morning somewhere far from here. There would be a high hill, and a white road winding up it, and over the brow of that hill, there would be the sea. Below, a beach, and rocks; and there would be people. Up the hill he would hurtle, through and over a stone wall at the top, and in the moment he was airborne, he would blow the horn. Louder, *bigger* than the horn would be his one bright burst of laughter. He had never laughed like that, but he would, he could, for all of him would be in it, rejoicing that they listened to him, they'd all be listening, up and down the beach and craning over the cliff. After that he'd fall, but that didn't matter. Nothing would matter, even the fact that his act was criminal and childish. All the "If only—" and "Some day, by God—" wishes, all the "That Barnes—" curses, for all their detail, lacked implementation. But this one, this one—

The window was open on the driver's side. Joe looked around; the street was deserted and the house was dark. He bent and slid his hand along the line of dimly-glowing phosphorescence that was a dashboard. Something tinkled, dangled—the keys, the keys!

He opened the door, got in. He could feel the shift in balance as the splendid machine accepted him like a lover, and they were one together. He pulled the door all but closed, checked it, then pressed it the rest of the way. It closed with a quiet, solid click, Joe grasped the steering wheel in both hands, settled himself, and quelled just the great trumpeting of laughter he had envisioned. *Later, later.* He reached for the key, turned it.

There was a soft purring deep under the hood. The window at his left slid up, nudging his elbow out of the way, seated itself in the molding above. The purring stopped. Then silence.

Joe grunted in surprise and turned the key again. Nothing. He fumbled along the dashboard, over the cowling, under its edge. He moved his feet around. Accelerator, brake. No clutch. A headlight dimmer switch. With less and less caution he pushed, turned and pulled at the controls on the instrument panel. No lights came on. The radio did not work. Neither did the cigarette lighter, which startled him when it came out in his hand. There wasn't a starter anywhere.

Joe Fritch, who couldn't weep, very nearly did then. If a man had a car burglar-proofed with some sort of concealed switch, wasn't that enough? Why did he have to amuse himself by leaving the keys in it? Even Barnes never thought of anything quite that sadistic.

For a split second he glanced forlornly at his glorious vision, then forever let it go. Once he sniffed; then he put his hand on the door control and half rose in his seat.

The handle spun easily, uselessly around. Joe stopped it, pulled it upward. It spun just as easily that way. He tried pulling it toward him, pushing it outward. Nothing.

He bit his lower lip and dove for the other door. It had exactly the same kind of handle, which behaved exactly the same way. Suddenly Joe was panting as if from running hard.

Now take it easy. Don't try to do anything. Think. Think, Joe.

The windows!

On his door there were two buttons; on the other, one. He tried them all. "I can't get out," he whispered. "I can't—" Suddenly he spun one of the door handles. He fluttered his hands helplessly and looked out into the welcome, open dark. *"Can't!"* he cried.

"That's right," said a voice. "You sure can't."

The sting at the base of Joe Fritch's nose—that was one of the unexpressed, inexpressible pains which had plagued him ever since he was a boy. Now came the other.

It was a ball of ice, big as a fist, in his solar plexus; and around this ball stretched a membrane; and the ball was fury, and the membrane was fear. The more terrified he became, the tighter the membrane shrank and the more it hurt. If ever he were frightened beyond bearing, the membrane would break and let the fury out, and that must not, must not happen, for the fury was so cold and so uncaring of consequence. This was no churning confusion—there was nothing confused about it. There was only compression and stretching and a breaking point so near it could be felt in advance. There was nothing that could be done about it except to sit quite still and wait until it went away, which it did when whatever caused it went away.

This voice, though, here in the car with him, it didn't go away. Conversationally it said, "Were you thinking of breaking the glass?"

Joe just sat. The voice said, "Look in the glove compartment." It waited five seconds, and said, "Go ahead. Look in the glove compartment."

Trembling, Joe reached over and fumbled the catch of the glove compartment. He felt around inside. It seemed empty, and then something moved under his fingers. It was a rectangle of wood, about six inches by three, extremely light and soft. Balsa. "I used to use a real piece of glass as a sample," said the voice, "but one of you fools got to bashing it around and broke two of his own fingers. Anyway, that piece of wood is exactly as thick as the windshield and windows." It was nearly three quarters of an inch thick. "Bulletproof is an understatement. Which reminds me," said the voice, stifling a yawn, "if you have a gun, for Pete's sake don't use it. The slug'll ricochet. Did you ever see the wound a ricocheted bullet makes?" The yawn again. " 'Scuse me. You woke me up."

Joe licked his lips, which made him shudder. The tongue and lip were so dry they scraped all but audibly. "Where are you?" he whispered.

"In the house. I always take that question as a compliment. You're hearing me on the car radio. Clean, hm-m-m? Flat to twenty-seven thousand cycles. Designed it myself."

Joe said, "Let me out."

"I'll let you out, but I won't let you go. You people are my bread and butter."

"Listen," said Joe, "I'm not a thief, or a . . . or a . . . or anything. I mean, this was just a sort of wild idea. Just let me go, huh? I won't *ever* . . . I mean, I promise." He scraped at his lip with his tongue again and added, "Please. I mean, please."

"Where were you going with my car, Mister I'm not-a-thief?"

Joe was silent.

A sudden blaze of light made him wince. His eyes adjusted, and he found it was only the light over the porte cochere which bridged the driveway where it passed the house. "Come on inside," said the voice warmly.

Joe looked across the rolling lawn at the light. The car was parked in the drive near the street; the house was nearly two hundred feet away. *Catch ten times as many with it parked way out here*, he thought wildly. And, *I thought Barnes was good at making people squirm*. And, *Two hundred feet, and him in the house. He can outthink me; could he outrun me?* "What do you want me inside for?"

"Would it make any difference how I answered that question?"

Joe saw that it wouldn't. The voice was calling the shots just now, and Joe was hardly in a position to make any demands. Resignedly he asked, "You're going to call the police?"

"Absolutely not."

A wave of relief was overtaken and drowned in a flood of terror. No one knew where he was. No one had seen him get into the car. Being arrested would be unpleasant, but at least it would be a known kind of unpleasantness. But what lay in store for him in this mysterious expensive house?

"You better just call the police," he said. "I mean, have me arrested. I'll wait where I am."

"No," said the voice. It carried a new tone, and only by the change did Joe realize how—how *kind* it had been before. Joe believed that single syllable completely. Again he eyed the two hundred feet. He tensed himself, and said, "All right. I'll come."

"Good boy," said the voice, kind again. 'Sleep sweet." Something went *pfffft!* on the dashboard and Joe's head was enveloped in a fine, very cold mist. He fell forward and hit his mouth on the big V emblem in the hub of the steering wheel. A profound astonishment enveloped him because he felt the impact but no pain.

He blacked out.

There was a comfortable forever during which he lay in a dim place, talking lazily, on and on. Something questioned him from time to time, and perhaps he knew he was not questioning himself; he certainly didn't care. He rested in a euphoric cloud, calmly relating things he thought he had forgotten, and while an objective corner of his mind continued to operate, to look around, to feel and judge and report, it was almost completely preoccupied with an astonished delight that he could talk about his job, his marriage, his sister Anna, even about Joey—whom he'd killed when he and Joey were ten years old—without either the self-pitying twinge of unshed tears or the painful fear which contained his rage.

Someone moved into his range of vision, someone with a stranger's face and a manner of someone familiar. He had something shiny in his hand. He advanced and bent over him, and Joe felt the nip of a needle in his upper arm. He lay quietly then, not talking because he had finished what he had to say, not moving because he was so comfortable, and began to feel warm from the inside out. That lasted for another immeasurable time. Then he detected movement again, and was drawn to it; the stranger crossed in front of him and sat down in an easy chair. Their faces were about at the same level, but Joe was not on an easy chair. Neither was it a couch. It was something in between. He glanced down and saw his knees, his feet. He was in one of those clumsy-looking, superbly comfortable devices known as a contour chair. He half-sat, half-reclined in it, looked at the other man and felt just wonderful. He smiled sleepily, and the man smiled back.

The man looked too old to be thirty, though he might be. He looked too young for fifty, though that was possible, too. His hair was dark, his eyebrows flecked with gray—a combination Joe thought he had never seen before. His eyes were light—in this dim room it was hard to see their color. The nose was ridiculous: it belonged to a happy fat man, and not someone with a face as long and lean as this one. The mouth was large and flexible; it was exactly what is meant by the term "generous," yet its lips were thin, the upper one almost nonexistent. He seemed of average height, say five ten or eleven, but he gave the impression of being somehow too wide and too flat. Joe looked at him and at his smile, and it flashed across his mind that the French call a smile *sourire*, which means literally "under a laugh"; and surely, in any absolute scale of merriment, this smile was just exactly that. "How are you feeling?"

"I feel fine," said Joe. He really meant it.

"I'm Zeitgeist," said the man.

Joe was unquestioningly aware that the man knew him, knew all about him, so he didn't offer his name in return. He accepted the introduction and after a moment let his eyes stray from the friendly face to the wall behind him, to some sort of framed document, around to the side where a massive bookcase stood. He suddenly realized that he was in a strange room. He snapped his gaze back to the man. "Where am I?"

"In my house," said Zeitgeist. He uncrossed his legs and leaned forward. "I'm the man whose car you were stealing. Remember?"

Joe did, with a rush. An echo of his painful panic struck him, made him leap to his feet, a reflex which utterly failed. Something caught him gently and firmly around the midriff and slammed him back into the contour chair. He looked down and saw a piece of webbing like that used in aircraft safety belts, but twice as wide. It was around his waist and had no buckle; or if it had, it was behind and under the back of the chair, well out of his reach.

"It's OK," Zeitgeist soothed him. "You didn't actually steal it, and I understand perfectly why you tried. Let's just forget that part of it."

"Who are you? What are you trying to do? Let me out of this thing!" The memory of this man approaching him with a glittering hypodermic returned to him. "What did you do, drug me?"

Zeitgeist crossed his legs again and leaned back. "Yes, several times, and the nicest part of it is that you can't stay that excited very long just now." He smiled again, warm.

Joe heaved again against the webbing, lay back, opened his mouth to protest, closed it helplessly. Then he met the man's eyes again, and he could feel the indignation and fright draining out of him. He suddenly felt foolish, and found a smile of his own, a timid, foolish one.

"First I anaesthetized you," said Zeitgeist informatively, apparently pursuing exactly the line of thought brought out by Joe's question, "because not for a second would I trust any of you to come across that lawn just because I asked you to. Then I filled you full of what we'd call truth serum if this was a TV play. And when you'd talked enough I gave you another shot to pull you out of it. Yes, I drugged you."

"What for? What do you want from me, anyway?"

"You'll find out when you get my bill."

"Bill?"

"Sure. I have to make a living just like anybody else."

"Bill for what?"

"I'm going to fix you up."

"There's nothing the matter with me!"

Zeitgeist twitched his mobile lips. "Nothing wrong with a man who wants to take an expensive automobile and kill himself with it?"

Joe dropped his eyes. A little less pugnaciously, he demanded, "What are you, a psychiatrist or something?"

"Or something," laughed Zeitgeist. "Now listen to me," he said easily. "There are classic explanations for people doing the things they do, and you have a textbook full. You were an undersized kid who lost his mother early. You were brutalized by a big sister who just wouldn't be a mother to you. When you were ten you threw one of your tantrums and crowded another kid, and he slipped on the ice and was hit by a truck and killed. Your sister lambasted you for it until you ran away from home nine years later. You got married and didn't know how to put your wife into the mother-image, so you treated her like your sister Anna instead; you obeyed, you didn't answer back, you did as little as possible to make her happy because no matter how happy she got you were subconsciously convinced it would do you no good. And by the way, the kid who was killed had the same name as you did." He smiled his kindly smile, wagged his head and *tsk-tsked*. "You should see what the textbooks say about *that* kind of thing. Identification: you are the Joey who was killed when you got mad and hit him. Ergo, don't ever let yourself get mad or you'll be dead. Joe Fritch, you know what you are? You're a mess."

"What am I supposed to say?" asked Joe in a low voice. Had he run off at the mouth that much? He was utterly disarmed. In the face of such penetrating revelation, anger would be ridiculous.

"Don't say anything. That is, don't try to explain—I already understand. How'd you like to get rid of all that garbage? I can do that for you. Will you let me?"

"Why should you?"

"I've already told you. It's my living."

"You say you're a psychiatrist?"

"I said nothing of the kind, and that's beside the point. Well?"

"Well, OK. I mean . . . OK."

Zeitgeist rose, smiling, and stepped behind Joe. There was a metallic click and the webbing loosened. Joe looked up at his host, thinking: *Suppose I won't? Suppose I just don't? What could he do?*

"There are lots of things I could do," said Zeitgeist with gentle cheerfulness. "Full of tricks, I am."

In spite of himself, Joe laughed. He got up. Zeitgeist steadied him, then released his elbow. Joe said, "Thanks . . . what are you, I mean, a mind reader?"

"I don't have to be."

Joe thought about it. "I guess you don't," he said.

"Come on." Zeitgeist turned away to the door. Joe reflected that anyone who would turn his back on a prisoner like that was more than just confident—he must

Theodore Sturgeon

have a secret weapon. *But at the moment confidence is enough.* He followed Zeitgeist into the next room.

It, too, was a low room, but much wider than the other, and its dimness was of quite another kind. Pools of brilliance from floating fluorescents mounted over three different laboratory benches made them like three islands in a dark sea. At about eye-level—as he stood—in the shadows over one of the benches, the bright green worm of a cathode-ray oscilloscope writhed in its twelve-inch circular prison. Ranked along the walls were instrument racks and consoles; he was sure he could not have named one in ten of them in broad daylight. The room was almost silent, but it was a living silence of almost indetectable clickings and hummings and the charged, noiseless *presence* of power. It was a waiting, busy sort of room.

"Boo," said Zeitgeist.

"I beg your . . . huh?"

Zeitgeist laughed. "You say it." He pointed. "Boooo."

Joe looked up at the oscilloscope. The worm had changed to a wiggling, scraggly child's scrawl, which, when Zeitgeist's long-drawn syllable was finished, changed into a green worm again. Zeitgeist touched a control knob on one of the benches and the worm became a straight line. "Go ahead."

"Boo," said Joe self-consciously. The line was a squiggle and then a line again. "Come on, a good loud long one," said Zeitgeist. This time Joe produced the same sort of "grass" the other man had. Or at least, it looked the same. "Good," said Zeitgeist. "What do you do for a living?"

"Advertising. You mean I didn't tell you?"

"You were more interested in talking about your boss than your work. What kind of advertising?"

"Well, I mean, it isn't advertising like in an agency. I mean, I work for the advertising section of the public relations division of a big corporation."

"You write ads? Sell them? Art, production, research—what?"

"All that. I mean, a little of all those. We're not very big. The company is, I mean, but not our office. We only advertise in trade magazines. The engineer'll come to me with something he wants to promote and I check with the . . . I mean, with Barnes, and if he OKs it I write copy on it and check back with the engineer and write it again and check back with Barnes and write it again; and after that I do the layout, I mean I draft the layout just on a piece of typewriter paper, that's all, I can't draw or anything like that, I mean; and then I see it through Art and go back and check with Barnes, and then I order space for it in the magazines and—"

"You ever take a vocational analysis?"

"Yes. I mean, sure I did. I'm in the right sort of job, according to the tests. I mean, it was the Kline-Western test."

"Good test," said Zeitgeist approvingly.

"You think I'm not in the right sort of job?" He paused, and then with sudden animation, "You think I should quit that lousy job, I mean, get into something else?"

"That's your business. All right, that's enough."

The man could be as impersonal as a sixpenny nail when he wanted to be. He worked absorbedly at his controls for a while. There was a soft whine from one piece of apparatus, a clicking from another, and before Joe knew what was happening he heard someone saying, "All that. I mean, a little of all those. We're not very big. The company is, I mean, but not our office. We only advertise—" on and on, in his exact words. His exact voice, too, he realized belatedly. He listened to it without enthusiasm. From time to time a light blazed, bright as a photo-flash but scalding red. Patiently, brilliantly, the oscilloscope traced each syllable, each pulse within each syllable. ". . . and check with Barnes, and then I order sp—" The voice ceased abruptly as Zeitgeist threw a switch.

"I didn't know you were recording," said Joe, "or I would have . . . I mean, said something different maybe."

"I know," said Zeitgeist. "That red light bother you?"

"It was pretty bright," said Joe, not wanting to complain.

"Look here." He opened the top of the recorder. Joe saw reels and more heads than he had ever seen on a recorder before, and a number of other unfamiliar components. "I don't know much about—"

"You don't have to," said Zeitgeist. "See there?" He pointed with one hand, and with the other reached for a button on the bench and pressed it. A little metal arm snapped up against the tape just where it passed over an idler. "That punched a little hole in the tape. Not enough to affect the recording." Zeitgeist turned the reel slowly by hand, moving the tape along an inch or so. Joe saw, on the moving tape, a tiny bright spot of light. When the almost invisible hole moved into it, the red light flared. "I pushed that button every time you said 'I mean.' Let's play it again."

He played it again, and Joe listened—an act of courage, because with all his heart he wanted to cover his ears, shut his eyes against that red blaze. He was consumed with embarrassment. He had never heard anything that sounded so completely idotic. When at last it was over, Zeitgeist grinned at him. "Learn something?"

"I did," said Joe devoutly.

"OK," said Zeitgeist, in a tone which disposed of the matter completely as far as he was concerned, at the same time acting as prelude to something new. The man's expressiveness was extraordinary; with a single word he had Joe's gratitude and his fullest attention. "Now listen to this." He made some adjustments, threw a switch. Joe's taped voice said, " . . . go back and check it with Ba-a-a-a-a-ah—" with the "ah" going on and on like an all-clear signal. "That bother you?" called Zeitgeist over the noise.

"It's awful!" shouted Joe. This time he did cover his ears. It didn't help. Zeitgeist switched off the noise and laughed at him. "That's understandable. Your own voice,

Theodore Sturgeon

and it goes on and on like that. What's bothering you is, it doesn't breathe. I swear you could choke a man half to death, just by making him listen to that. Well, don't let it worry you. That thing over there"—he pointed to a massive cabinet against the wall—"is my analyzer. It breaks up your voice into all the tones and overtones it contains, finds out the energy level of each, and shoots the information to that tone-generator yonder. The generator reproduces each component exactly as received, through seventy-two band-pass filters two hundred cycles apart. All of which means that when I tell it to, it picks out a single vowel sound—in this case your 'a' in 'Barnes'—and hangs it up there on the 'scope like a photograph for as long as I want to look at it."

"All that, to do what I do when I say 'ah'?"

"All that," beamed Zeitgeist. Joe could see he was unashamedly proud of his equipment. He leaned forward and flicked Joe across the Adam's apple. "That's a hell of a compact little machine, that pharynx of yours. Just look at that wave-form."

Joe looked at the screen. "Some mess."

"A little tomato sauce and you could serve it in an Italian resturant," said Zeitgeist. "Now let's take it apart."

From another bench he carried the cable of a large control box, and plugged it into the analyzer with a many-pronged jack. The box had on it nearly a hundred keys. He fingered a control at the end of each row and the oscilloscope subsided to its single straight line. "Each one of these keys controls one of those narrow two-hundred-cycle bands I was talking about," he told Joe. "Your voice—everybody's voice—has high and low overtones, some loud, some soft. Here's one at the top, one in the middle, one at the bottom." He pressed three widely separated keys. The speaker uttered a faint breathy note, then a flat tone, the same in pitch but totally different in quality; it was a little like hearing the same note played first on a piccolo and then on a viola. The third key produced only a murmuring hiss, hardly louder than the noise of the amplifier itself. With each note, the 'scope showed a single wavy line. With the high it was a steep but even squiggle. In the middle it was a series of shallow waves like a child's drawing of an ocean. Down at the bottom it just shook itself and lay there.

"Just what I thought. I'm not saying you're a soprano, Joe, but there's five times more energy in your high register than there is at the bottom Ever hear the way a kid's voice climbs the scale when he's upset—whining, crying, demanding? 'Spose I told you that all the protest against life that you're afraid to express in anger, is showing up here?" He slid his fingers across the entire upper register, and the speaker bleated. "Listen to that, the poor little feller."

In abysmal self-hatred, Joe felt the sting of tears. "Cut it out," he blurted.

"Caht eet ow-oot," mimicked Zeitgeist. Joe thought he'd kill him, then and there, but couldn't because he found himself laughing. The imitation was very good. "You know, Joe, the one thing you kept droning on about in the other room was something about 'they won't listen to me. Nobody will listen.' How many times, say, in the office, have you had a really solid idea and kept it to yourself because 'nobody will listen'? How many times have you wanted to do something with your wife, go somewhere, ask her to get something from the cleaners—and then decided not to because she wouldn't listen?'' He glanced around at Joe, and charitably turned away from the contorted face. ''Don't answer that: you know, and it doesn't matter to me.

''Now get this, Joe. There's something in all animals just about as basic as hunger. It's the urge to attack something that's retreating, and its converse: to be wary of something that won't retreat. Next time a dog comes running up to you, growling, with his ears laid back, turn and run and see if he doesn't take a flank steak out of your southern hemisphere. After you get out of the hospital, go back and when he rushes you, laugh at him and keep going on about your business, and see him decide you're not on his calorie chart for the day. Well, the same thing works with people. No one's going to attack you unless he has you figured out—especially if he figures you'll retreat. Walk around with a big neon sign on your head that says HEY EVERY-BODY I WILL RETREAT, and you're just going to get cobbered wherever you go. You've got a sign like that and it lights up every time you open your mouth. Caht eet owoot.''

Joe's lower lip protruded childishly. ''I can't help what kind of voice I've got.''

''Probably you can't. I can, though.''

''But how—''

''Shut up.'' Zeitgeist returned all the keys to a neutral position and listened a moment to the blaring audio. Then he switched it off and began flicking keys, some up, some down. ''Mind you, this isn't a matter of changing a tenor into a baritone. New York City once had a mayor with a voice like a Punch and Judy show, and he hadn't an ounce of retreat in him. All I'm going to do is cure a symptom. Some people say that doesn't work, but ask the gimpy guy who finds himself three inches taller and walking like other people, the first time he tries his built-up shoes. Ask the guy who wears a well-made toupee.'' He stared for a while at the 'scope, and moved some more keys. ''You want people to listen to you. All right, they will, whether they want to or not. Of course, *what* they listen to is something else again. It better be something that backs up this voice I'm giving you. That's up to you.''

''I don't under—''

''You'll understand a lot quicker if we fix it so you listen and I talk. OK?'' Zeitgeist demanded truculently, and sent over such an engaging grin that the words did not smart. ''Now, like I said, I'm only curing a symptom. What you have to get through your thick head is that the disease doesn't exist. All that stuff about your sister Anna, and Joey, that doesn't exist because it happened and it's finished and it's years ago and doesn't matter any more. Lutie, Barnes . . . well, they bother you mostly because they won't listen to you. *They'll listen to you now.* So that botherment is over with, too; finished, done with, nonexistent. For all practical purposes yesterday is as far beyond recall as twenty years ago; just as finished, just as dead. So the little boy who

Theodore Sturgeon

got punished by his big sister until he thought he deserved being punished—*he* doesn't exist. The man with the guilty feeling killing a kid called Joey, he doesn't exist either any more, and by the way he wasn't guilty in the first place. The copy man who lets a pipsqueak sadist prick him with petty sarcasms—he's gone too, because now there's a man who won't swallow what he wants to say, what he knows is right. He'll say it, just because *people will listen.* A beer stein is pretty useless to anyone until you put beer in it. The gadget I'm going to give you you won't do you a bit of good unless you put yourself, your real self into it.'' He had finished with the keys while he spoke, had turned and was holding Joe absolutely paralyzed with his strange light eyes.

Inanely, Joe said, ''G-gadget?''

''Listen.'' Zeitgeist hit the master switch and Joe's voice again came from the speaker. ''We only advertise in trade magazines. The engineer'll come to me with something he wants to promote and—''

And the voice was his voice, but it was something else, too. Its pitch was the same, inflection, accent; but there was a forceful resonance in it somewhere, somehow. It was a compelling voice, a rich voice; above all it was assertive and sure. (And when the 'I means' came, and the scalding light flashed, it wasn't laughable or embarrassing; it was simply unnecessary.)

''That isn't me.''

''You're quite right. It isn't. But it's the way the world will hear you. It's behind the way the world will treat you. And the way the world treats a man is the way the man grows, if he wants to and he's got any growing left in him. Whatever is in that voice you can *be* because I will help and the world will help. But you've got to help, too.''

''I'll help,'' Joe whispered.

''Sometimes I make speeches,'' said Zeitgeist, and grinned shyly. The next second he was deeply immersed in work.

He drew out a piece of paper with mimeographed rulings on it, and here and there in the ruled squares he jotted down symbols, referring to the keyboard in front of him. He seemed then to be totaling columns; once he reset two or three keys, turned on the audio and listened intently, then erased figures and put down others. At last he nodded approvingly, rose, stretched till his spine cracked, picked up the paper and went over to the third bench.

From drawers and cubbyholes he withdrew components—springs, pads, plugs, rods. He moved with precision and swift familiarity. He rolled out what looked like a file drawer, but instead of papers it contained ranks and rows of black plastic elements, about the size and shape of miniature match boxes, each with two bright brass contacts at top and bottom.

''We're living in a wonderful age, Joe,'' said Zeitgeist as he worked. ''Before long I'll turn the old soldering iron out to stud and let it father waffles. Printed circuits, sub-mini tubes, transistors. These things here are electrets, which I won't attempt to explain to you." He bolted and clipped, bent and formed, and every once in a while, referring to his list, he selected another of the black boxes from the file and added it to his project. When there were four rows of components, each row about one and a half by six inches, he made some connections with test clips and thrust a jack into a receptacle in the bench. He glanced up at the 'scope, grunted, unclipped one of the black rectangles and substituted another from the files.

"These days, Joe, when they can pack a whole radar set—transmitter, receiver, timing and arming mechanisms and a power supply into the nose of a shell, a package no bigger than your fist—these days you can do anything with a machine. Anything, Joe. You just have to figure out how. Most of the parts exist, they make 'em in job lots. You just have to plug 'em together." He plugged in the jack, as if to demonstrate, and glanced up at the 'scope. "Good. The rest won't take long." Working with tin-snips, then with a small sheet-metal brake, he said, "Some day you're going to ask me what I'm doing, what all this is for, and I'll just grin at you. I'm going to tell you now and if you don't remember what I say, well, then forget it.

"They say our technology has surpassed, or bypassed, our souls, Joe. They say if we don't turn from science to the spirit, we're doomed. I agree that we're uncom-fortably close to damnation, but I don't think we'll appease any great powers by throwing our gears and gimmicks over the cliff as a sacrifice, a propitiation. Science didn't get us into this mess; we *used* science to get us in.

"So I'm just a guy who's convinced we can use science to get us out. In other words, I'm not hanging the gunsmith every time someone gets shot. Take off your shirt."

"What?" said Joe, back from a thousand miles. "Oh." Bemused, he took off his jacket and shirt and stood shyly clutching his thin ribs.

Zeitgeist picked up his project from the bench and put it over Joe's head. A flat band of spring steel passed over each shoulder, snugly. The four long flat casings, each filled with components, rested against his collarbones, pressing upward in the small hollow just below the bones, and against his shoulder blades. Zeitgeist bent and manipulated the bands until they were tight but comfortable. Then he hooked the back pieces to the front pieces with soft strong elastic bands passing under Joe's arms. "OK? OK. Now—say something."

"Say what?" said Joe stupidly, and immediately clapped his hand to his chest. "*Uh!*"

"What happened?"

"It . . . I mean, it buzzed!"

Zeitgeist laughed. "Let me tell you what you've got there. In front, two little speakers, an amplifier to drive them, and a contact microphone that picks up your chest tones. In back, on this side, a band-pass arrangement that suppresses all those dominating high-frequency whimperings of yours and feeds the rest, the stuff you're weak in, up front to be amplified. And over here, in back—that's where the power supply goes. Go over there where you were and record something. And remember what I told you—you have to help this thing. Talk a little slower and you won't have to say 'I mean' while you think of what comes next. You *know* what comes next, anyway. You don't have to be afraid to say it."

Dazed, Joe stepped back to where he had been when the first recording was made, glanced for help up at the green line of the oscilloscope, closed his eyes and said, falteringly at first, then stronger and steadier, " 'Four score and seven years ago, our fathers brought forth upon this contin—' "

"Cut!" cried Zeitgeist. "Joe, see that tone-generator over there? It's big as a spinet piano. I can do a lot but believe me, you haven't got one of those strapped on you. Your amplifier can only blow up what it gets. You don't have much, but for Pete's sake give it what you have. Try talking with your lungs full instead of empty. Push your voice a little, don't just let it fall out of you."

"Nothing happens, though. I sound the same to myself. Is it working? Maybe it doesn't work."

"Like I told you before," said Zeitgeist with exaggerated patience, "people who are talking aren't listening. It's working all right. Don't go looking for failures, Joe. Plenty'll come along that you didn't ask for. Now go ahead and do as I said."

Joe wet his lips, took a deep breath. Zeitgeist barked, "Now slowly!" and he began: " 'Four score and seven years—' " The sonorous words rolled out, his chest vibrated from the buzzing, synchronized to his syllables. And though he was almost totally immersed in his performance, a part of him leaped excitedly, realizing that never in his whole life before had he listened, really listened, to that majestic language. When he was finished he opened his eyes and found Zeitgeist standing very near him, his eyes alight.

"Good," the man breathed. "Ah, but . . . good."

"Was it? Was it really?"

In answer, Zeitgeist went to the controls, rewound the tape, and hit the playback button.

And afterwards, he said gently to Joe, "You *can* cry—see?"

"Damn foolishness," said Joe.

"No it isn't," Zeitgeist told him.

Outside, it was morning—what a morning, with all the gold and green, thrust and rustle of a new morning in a new summer. He hadn't been out all night; he had died and was born again! He stood tall, walked tall, he carried his shining new voice sheathed like Excalibur, but for all its concealment, he was armed!

He had tried to thank Zeitgeist, and that strange man had shaken his head soberly and said, "Don't, Joe. You're going to pay me for it."

"Well I will, of course I will! Anything you say . . . how much, anyhow?"

Zeitgeist had shaken his head slightly. "We'll talk about it later. Go on—get in the car. I'll drive you to work." And, silently, he had.

Won't You Walk—

Downtown, he reached across Joe and opened the door. For him, the door worked. "Come see me day after tomorrow. After dinner—nine."

"OK. Why? Got another . . . treatment?"

"Not for you," said Zeitgeist, and his smile made it a fine compliment for both of them. "But no power plant lasts forever. Luck." And before Joe could answer the door was closed and the big car had swung out into traffic. Joe watched it go, grinning and shaking his head.

The corner clock said five minutes to nine. Just time, if he hurried.

He didn't hurry. He went to Harry's and got shaved, while they pressed his suit and sponged his collar in the back room. He kept the bathrobe they gave him pulled snugly over his amplifier, and under a hot towel he reached almost the euphoric state he had been in last night. He thought of Barnes, and the anger stirred in him. With some new internal motion he peeled away its skin of fear and set it free. Nothing happened, except that it lived in him instead of just lying there. It didn't make him tremble. It made him smile.

Clean, pressed, and smelling sweet, he walked into his building at eight minutes before ten. He went down to the express elevator and stepped into the one open door. Then he said, "Wait," and stepped out again. The operator goggled at him.

Joe walked up to the starter, a bushy character in faded brown and raveled gold braid. "Hey . . . you."

The starter pursed a pair of liver-colored lips and glowered at him. "Whaddayeh want?"

Joe filled his lungs and said evenly, "Day before yesterday you took hold of me and shoved me into an elevator like I was a burlap sack."

The starter's eyes flickered. "Not me."

"You calling me a liar, too?"

Suddenly the man's defenses caved. There was a swift pucker which came and went on his chin, and he said, "Look, I got a job to do, mister, rush hours, if I don't get these cars out of here it's *my* neck, I didn't mean nothing by it, I—"

"Don't tell me your troubles," said Joe. He glared at the man for a second. "All right, do your job, but don't do it on me like that again."

He turned his back, knowing he was mimicking Zeitgeist with the gesture and enjoying the knowledge. He went back to the elevator and got in. Through the closing gate he saw the starter, right where he had left him, gaping. The kid running the elevator was gaping, too.

"Eleven," said Joe.

"Yes, *sir*," said the boy. He started the car. "You told *him*."

"Bout time," said Joe modestly.

"Past time," said the kid.

Joe got out on the eleventh floor, feeling wonderful. He walked down the hall,

Theodore Sturgeon

thumped a door open, and ambled in. Eleanor Bulmer, the receptionist, looked up. He saw her eyes flick to the clock and back to his face. "Well!"

"Morning," he said expansively, from his inflated lungs. She blinked as if he had fired a cap pistol, then looked confusedly down at her typewriter.

He took a step toward his corner desk when there was a flurry, a botherment up from the left, then an apparition of thinning hair and exophthalmic blue eyes. Barnes, moving at a half-trot as usual, jacket off, suspenders, arm-bands pulling immaculate cuffs high and away from rust-fuzzed scrawny wrists. "Eleanor, get me Apex on the phone. Get me Apex on the—" And then he saw Joe. He stopped. He smiled. He had gleaming pale-yellow incisors like a rodent. He, too, flicked a glance at the clock.

Joe knew exactly what he was going to say, exactly how he was going to say it. He took a deep breath, and if old ghosts were about to rise in him, the friendly pressure of the amplifier just under his collar-bones turned them to mist. *Why, Miss Terr Fritch*, Barnes would say with exaggerated and dramatic politeness, *how ki-i-ind of you to drop in today.* Then the smile would snap off and the long series of not-to-be-answered questions would begin. Didn't he know this was a place of business? Was he aware of the customary starting time? Did it not seem that among fourteen punctual people, he alone—and so on. During it, seven typewriters would stop, a grinning stock boy would stick his head over a filing cabinet to listen, and Miss Bulmer, over whose nape the monologue would stream, would sit with her head bowed waiting for it to pass. Already the typewriters had stopped. And yes, sure enough: behind Barnes he could see the stock boy's head.

"Why, Miss Terr Fritch!" said Barnes happily.

Joe immediately filled his lungs, turned his back on Barnes, and said into the stunned silence, "Better get him Apex on the phone, Eleanor. He has the whole place at a standstill." He then walked around Barnes as if the man were a pillar and went to his desk and sat down.

Barnes stood with his bony head lowered and his shoulders humped as if he had been bitten on the neck by a fire-ant. Slowly he turned and glared up the office. There was an immediate explosion of typewriter noise, shuffling feet, shuffling papers. "I'll take it in my office," Barnes said to the girl.

He had to pass Joe to get there, and to Joe's great delight he could see how reluctant Barnes was to do it. "I'll see you later," Barnes hissed as he went by, and Joe called cheerfully after him, "You just betcha." Out in the office, somebody whistled appreciatively; somebody snickered. Joe knew Barnes had heard it. He smiled, and picked up the phone. "Outside, Eleanor. Personal."

Eleanor Bulmer knew Barnes didn't allow personal calls except in emergencies, and then preferred to give his permission first. Joe could hear her breathing, hesitating. Then, "Yes, Mr. Fritch." And the dial tone crooned in his ear. *Mr. Fritch*, he thought. *That's the first time she ever called me Mr. Fritch. What do you know. Why . . . why, she never called me anything before! Just "Mr. Barnes wants to see you," or "Cohen of Electrical Marketing on the line."*

Won't You Walk—

Mr. Fritch dialed his home. "Hello—Lutie?"

"Joe! Where were you all night?" The voice was waspish, harrying; he could see her gathering her forces, he could see her mountain of complaints about to be shoveled into the telephone as if it were a hopper.

"I called up to tell you I'm all right because I thought it was a good idea. Maybe it was a bad idea."

"What?" There was a pause, and then in quite a different tone she said, "Joe? Is this . . . Joe, is that you?"

"Sure," he said heartily. "I'm at work and I'm all right and I'll be home for dinner. Hungry," he added.

"You expect me to cook you a dinner after—" she began, but without quite her accustomed vigor.

"All right, then I won't be home for dinner," he said reasonably.

She didn't say anything for a long time, but he knew she was still there. He sat and waited. At last she said faintly, "Will veal cutlets be all right?"

On the second night after this fledging, Mr. Joseph Fritch strode into the porte-cochere and bounded up the steps. He ground the bell-push with his thumb until it hurt, and then knocked. He stood very straight until the door opened.

"Joe, boy! Come on in." Zeitgeist left the door and opened another. Joe had the choice of following or of standing where he was and shouting. He followed. He found himself in a room new to him, low-ceilinged like the others, but with books from floor to ceiling. In a massive fieldstone fireplace flames leaped cheerfully, yet the room was quite cool. Air-conditioned. Well, he guessed Zeitgeist just *liked* a fire. "Look," he said abruptly.

"Sit down. Drink?"

"No. Listen, you've made a mistake."

"I know, I know. The bill. Got it with you?"

"I have."

Zeitgeist nodded approvingly. Joe caught himself wondering why. Zeitgeist glided across to him and pressed a tall glass into his hand. It was frosty, beaded, sparkling. "What's in it?" he snapped.

Zeitgeist burst out laughing, and in Joe fury passed, and shame passed, and he found himself laughing, too. He held out his glass and Zeitgeist clinked with him. "You're a . . . a—Luck."

"Luck," said Zeitgeist. They drank. It was whisky, the old gentle muscular whisky that lines the throat with velvet and instantly heats the ear lobes. "How did you make out?"

Joe drank again and smiled. "I walked into that office almost an hour late," he began, and told what had happened. Then, "And all day it was like that. I didn't know a job . . . people . . . I didn't know things could be like that. Look, I told you I'd pay you. I said I'd pay you anything you—"

Theodore Sturgeon

"Never mind that just now. What else happened? The suit and all?"

"That. Oh, I guess I was kind of—" Joe looked into the friendly amber in his glass, "well, intoxicated. Lunch time I just walked into King's and got the suit. Two suits. I haven't had a new suit for four years, and then it didn't come from King's. I just signed for 'em," he added, a reflective wonderment creeping into his voice. "They didn't mind. Shirts," he said, closing his eyes.

"It'll pay off."

"It did pay off," said Joe, bouncing on his soft chair to sit upright on the edge, shoulders back, head up. His voice drummed and his eyes were bright. He set his glass down on the carpet and swatted his hands gleefully together. "There was this liaison meeting, they call it, this morning. I don't know what got into me. Well, I do; but anyway, like every other copywriter I have a project tucked away; you know—I like it but maybe no one else will. I had it in my own roughs, up to yesterday. So I got this bee in my bonnet and went in to the Art Department and started in on them, and you know, they caught fire, they worked almost all *night?* And at the meeting this morning, the usual once-a-month kind of thing, the brass from the main office looking over us step-children and wondering why they don't fold us up and go to an outside agency. It was so easy!" he chortled.

"I just sat there, shy like always, and there was old Barnes as usual trying to head off product advertising and go into institutionals, because he likes to write that stuff himself. Thinks it makes the brass think he loves the company. So soon as he said 'institutionals' I jumped up and agreed with him and said let me show you one of Mr. Barnes's ideas. Yeah! I went and got it and you should *see* that presentation; you could eat it! So here's two VPs and a board secretary with their eyes bugging out and old Barnes not daring to deny anything, and everybody in the place knew I was lying and thought what a nice fellow I was to do it that way. And there sat that brass, looking at my haircut and my tie and my suit and me, and *buying* it piece by piece, and Barnes, old Barnes sweating it out."

"What did they offer you?"

"They haven't exactly. I'm supposed to go see the chairman Monday."

"What are you going to do?"

"Say no. Whatever it is, I'll say no. I have lots of ideas piled up—nobody would *listen* before! Word'll get around soon enough; I'll get my big raise the only smart way a man can get a really big one—just before he goes to work for a new company. Meanwhile I'll stay and work hard and be nice to Barnes, who'll die a thousand deaths."

Zeitgeist chuckled. "You're a stinker. What happened when you went home?"

Joe sank back into his chair and turned toward the flames; whatever his thoughts were, they suffused him with firelight and old amber, strength through curing, through waiting. His voice was just that mellow as he murmured, "That wasn't you at all. That was me."

"Oh, sorry. I wasn't prying."

Won't You Walk—

"Don't get me wrong!" said Joe. "I want to tell you." He laughed softly. "We had veal cutlets."

A log fell and Joe watched the sparks shooting upward while Zeitgeist waited. Suddenly Joe looked across at him with a most peculiar expression on his face. "The one thing I never thought of till the time came. I couldn't wear that thing all night, could I now? I don't want her to know. I'll be . . . you said I'd grow to . . . that if I put my back into it, maybe some day I wouldn't need it." He touched his collarbone.

"That's right," said Zeitgeist.

"So I couldn't wear it. And then I couldn't talk. Not a word." Again, the soft laugh. "She wouldn't sleep, not for the longest time. 'Joe?' she'd say, and I'd know she was going to ask where I'd been that night. I'd say, 'Shh.' and put my hand on her face. She'd hold on to it. Funny. Funny, how you know the difference," he said in a near whisper, looking at the fire again. "She said, 'Joe?' just like before, and I knew she was going to say she was sorry for being . . . well, all the trouble we've had. But I said 'Shh.' " He watched the fire silently, and Zeitgeist seemed to know that he was finished.

"I'm glad," said Zeitgeist.

"Yeah."

They shared some quiet. Then Zeitgeist said, waving his glass at the mantel, "Still think the bill's out of line?"

Joe looked at it, at the man. "It's not a question of how much it's worth," he said with some difficulty. "It's how much I can pay. When I left here I wanted to pay you whatever you asked—five dollars or five hundred, I didn't care what I had to sacrifice. But I never thought it would be five *thousand!*" He sat up. "I'll level with you; I don't have that kind of money. I never did have. Maybe I never will have."

"What do you think I fixed you up for?" Zeitgeist's voice cracked like a target-gun. "What do you think I'm in business for? I don't gamble."

Joe stood up slowly. "I guess I just don't understand you," he said coldly. "Well, at those prices I guess I can ask you to service this thing so I can get out of here."

"Sure." Zeitgeist rose and led the way out of the room and down the hall to the laboratory. His face was absolutely expressionless, but not fixed; only relaxed.

Joe shucked out of his jacket, unbuttoned his shirt and took it off. He unclipped the elastics and pulled the amplifier off over his head. Zeitgeist took it and tossed it on the bench. "All right," he said, "get dressed."

Joe went white. "What, you want to haggle? Three thousand then, when I get it," he said shrilly.

Zeitgeist sighed. "Get dressed."

Joe turned and snatched at his shirt. "Blackmail. Lousy blackmail."

Zeitgeist said, "You know better than that."

There is a quality of permanence about the phrase that precedes a silence. It bridges the gap between speech and speech, hanging in midair to be stared at. Joe pulled on his shirt, glaring defiantly at the other man. He buttoned it up, he tucked in the tails, he put on his tie and knotted it, and replaced his tie-clasp. He picked up his coat. And all the while the words hung there.

He said, miserably, "I want to know better than that."

Zeitgeist's breath hissed out; Joe wondered how long he had been holding it. "Come here, Joe," he said gently.

Joe went to the bench. Zeitgeist pulled the amplifier front and center. "Remember what I told you about this thing—a mike here to pick up the chest tones, bandpasses to cut down on what you have too much of, and the amplifier here to blow up those low resonances? And this?" he pointed.

"The power supply."

"The power supply," Zeitgeist nodded. "Well, look; there's nothing wrong with the theory. Some day someone will design a rig this compact that will do the job, and it'll work just as I said." His pale gaze flicked across Joe's perplexed face and he laughed. "You're sort of impressed with all this, aren't you?" He indicated the whole lab and its contents.

"Who wouldn't be?"

"That's the mythos of science, Joe. The layman is as willing to believe in the super-powers of science as he once did in witches. Now, I told you once that I believe in the ability of science to save our souls . . . our *selves*, if you like that any better. I believe that it's legitimate to use any and all parts of science for this purpose. And I believe the mythos of science is as much one of its parts as Avogadro's Law or the conservation of energy. Any layman who's seen the size of a modern hearing-aid, who knows what it can do, will accept with ease the idea of a band-passing amplifier with five watts output powered by a couple of penlite cells. Well, we just can't do it. We will, but we haven't yet."

"Then what's this thing? What's all this gobbledegook you've been feeding me? You give me something, you take it away. You make it work, you tell me it can't work. I mean, what are you trying to pull?"

"You're squeaking. And you're saying 'I mean,' " said Zeitgeist.

"Cut it out," Joe said desperately.

The pale eyes twinkled at him, but Zeitgeist made a large effort and went back to his subject. "All this is, this thing you've been wearing, is the mike here, which triggers these two diaphragm vibrators here, powered by these little dry cells. No amplifier, no speaker, no nothing but this junk and the mythos."

"But it worked; I heard it right here on your tape machine!"

"With the help of half a ton of components."

"But at the office, the liaison meeting, I . . . I—Oh—"

"For the first time in your life you walked around with your chest out. You faced people with your shoulders back and you looked 'em smack in the eye. You dredged up what resonance you had in that flattened-out chest of yours and flung it in people's

Won't You Walk—

faces. I didn't lie to you when I said they *had* to listen to you. They had to as long as you believed they had to."

"Did you have to drag out all this junk to make me believe that?"

"I most certainly did! Just picture it: you come to me here all covered with bruises and guilt, suicidal, cowed, and without any realizable ambition. I tell you all you need to do is stand up straight and spit in their eye. How much good would that have done you?"

Joe laughed shakily. "I feel like one of those characters in the old animated cartoons. They'd walk off the edge of a cliff and hang there in midair, and there they'd stay, grinning and twirling their canes, until they looked down. Then—boom!" He tried another laugh, and failed with it. "I just looked down," he said hoarsely.

"You've got it a little backwards," said Zeitgeist. "Remember how you looked forward to graduating—to the time when you could discard that monkey-puzzle and stand on your own feet? Well, son, you just made it. Come on; this calls for a drink!"

Joe jammed his arms into his jacket. "Thanks, but I just found out I can talk to my wife."

They started up the hall. "What do you do this for, Zeitgeist?"

"It's a living."

"Is that streamlined mousetrap out there the only bait you use?"

Zeitgeist smiled and shook his head.

For the second time in fifteen minutes Joe said, "I guess I just don't understand you," but there was a world of difference. Suddenly he broke away from the old man and went into the room with the fireplace. He came back, jamming the envelope into his pocket. "I can handle this," he said. He went out.

Zeitgeist leaned in the doorway, watching him go. He'd have offered him a ride, but he wanted to see him walk like that, with his head up. ∎

Theodore Sturgeon

Operation Syndrome
Frank Herbert

(Due to some of the things that happen with publishing deadlines, Frank Herbert was unable to send a personal introduction. We did, however, get its content over the phone:)

In 1953 Frank Herbert was submitting stories to Astounding Science Fiction, *never discussing them with Campbell (as contributors often did) before sending them in, receiving long, critical letters and an occasional phone call in response. That was encouraging, and a good basis to continue submitting, but it didn't mean as much as a particular comment made by Campbell. He said to a mutual friend that what Frank really needed was to "sit down and write and not worry about whether people are going to like it." It was quite a breakthrough: to think that someone might actually want to publish his work! "Operation Syndrome" was bought soon after, marking his first SF sale and first of many to ASF, including the premier appearance of* Dune. *Even so, he never ever got to meet Campbell as anything more than a voice on the telephone.*

At the time Frank wrote this story, he was studying privately under a pair of psychologists whose approach and methods were effective, if unorthodox. To them theory was subordinate to insight and psychotherapy was an art; the experience "turned him loose . . ." and "Operation Syndrome" reflects many of the questions then on his mind. Among the myriad of influences on our thinking and on our lives, he wondered, what are the "unknowns"? What are the hidden factors affecting our thought patterns, which we don't really focus on and never recognize? For Frank Herbert, exploring these questions became a sort of "science fiction head trip": within the Whole Wide Universe of SF there must *be a way for these factors to become known.*

HONOLULU IS QUIET, the dead buried, the rubble of buildings cleaned away. A salvage barge rocks in the Pacific swell off Diamond Head. Divers follow a bubble trail down into the green water to the wreck of the Stateside skytrain. The Scramble Syndrome did this. Ashore, in converted barracks, psychologists work fruitlessly in the aftermath of insanity. This is where the Scramble Syndrome started: one minute the city was peaceful; a clock tick later the city was mad.

In forty days—nine cities infected.

The twentieth century's Black Plague.

SEATTLE

First a ringing in the ears, fluting up to a whistle. The whistle became the warning blast of a nightmare train roaring clackety-clack, clackety-clack across his dream.

A psychoanalyst might have enjoyed the dream as a clinical study. This psychoanalyst was not studying the dream; he was having it. He clutched the sheet around his neck, twisted silently on the bed, drawing his knees under his chin.

The train whistle modulated into the contralto of an expensive chanteuse singing "Insane Crazy Blues." The dream carried vibrations of fear and wildness.

"A million dollars don't mean a thing—"

Hoarse voice riding over clarion brass, bumping of drums, clarinet squealing like an angry horse.

A dark-skinned singer with electric blue eyes and dressed in black stepped away from a red backdrop. She opened her arms to an unseen audience. The singer, the backdrop lurched into motion, revolving faster and faster and faster until it merged into a pinpoint of red light. The red light dilated to the bell mouth of a trumpet sustaining a minor note.

The music shrilled; it was a knife cutting his brain.

Dr. Eric Ladde awoke. He breathed rapidly; he oozed perspiration. Still he heard the singer, the music.

I'm dreaming that I'm awake, he thought.

He peeled off the top sheet, slipped his feet out, put them on the warm floor. Presently, he stood up, walked to the window, looked down on the moontrail shimmering across Lake Washington. He touched the sound switch beside the window and now he could hear the night—crickets, spring peepers at the lakeshore, the far hum of a skytrain.

The singing remained.

He swayed, gripped at the windowsill.

Scramble Syndrome—

He turned, examined the bedside newstape: no mention of Seattle. Perhaps he was safe—illness. But the music inside his head was no illness.

He made a desperate clutch for self-control, shook his head, banged his ear with

Frank Herbert

the palm of his hand. The singing persisted. He looked to the bedside clock—1:05 A.M., Friday, May 14, 1999.

Inside his head the music stopped. But now—Applause! A roar of clapping, cries, stamping of feet. Eric rubbed his head.

I'm not insane . . . I'm not insane—

He slipped into his dressing gown, went into the kitchen cubicle of his bachelor residence. He drank water, yawned, held his breath—anything to drive away the noise, now a chicken-haggle of talking, clinking, slithering of feet.

He made himself a highball, splashed the drink at the back of his throat. The sounds inside his head turned off. Eric looked at the empty glass in his hand, shook his head.

A new specific for insanity—alcohol! He smiled wryly. *And every day I tell my patients that drinking is no solution.* He tasted a bitter thought: *Maybe I should have joined that therapy team, not stayed here trying to create a machine to cure the insane. If only they hadn't laughed at me—*

He moved a fiberboard box to make room beside the sink, put down his glass. A notebook protruded from the box, sitting atop a mound of electronic parts. He picked up the notebook, stared at his own familiar block printing on the cover: *Amanti Teleprobe—Test Book IX.*

They laughed at the old doctor, too, he thought. *Laughed him right into an asylum. Maybe that's where I'm headed—along with everyone else in the world.*

He opened the notebook, traced his finger along the diagram of his latest experimental circuit. The teleprobe in his basement laboratory still carried the wiring, partially dismantled.

What was wrong with it?

He closed the notebook, tossed it back into the box. His thoughts hunted through the theories stored in his mind, the knowledge saved from a thousand failures. Fatigue and despondency pulled at him. Yet, he knew that the things Freud, Jung, Adler, and all the others had sought in dreams and mannerisms hovered just beyond his awareness in an electronic tracer circuit.

He wandered back into his study-bedroom, crawled into the bed. He practiced yoga breathing until sleep washed over him. The singer, the train, the whistle did not return.

Morning lighted the bedroom. He awoke, trailing fragments of his nightmare into consciousness, aware that his appointment book was blank until ten o'clock. The bedside newstape offered a long selection of stories, most headed "Scramble Syndrome." He punched code letters for eight items, flipped the machine to audio and listened to the news while dressing.

Memory of his nightmare nagged at him. He wondered, "How many people awake in the night, asking themselves, 'Is it my turn now?' "

He selected a mauve cape, drew it over his white coveralls. Retrieving the notebook from the box in the kitchen, he stepped out into the chill spring morning. He turned up the temperature adjustment of his coveralls. The unitube whisked him to the Elliott

Bay waterfront. He ate at a seafood restaurant, the teleprobe notebook open beside his plate. After breakfast, he found an empty bench outside facing the bay, sat down, opened the notebook. He found himself reluctant to study the diagrams, stared out at the bay.

Mists curled from the gray water, obscuring the opposite shore. Somewhere in the drift a purse seiner sounded its hooter. Echoes bounced off the buildings behind him. Early workers hurried past, voices stilled: thin look of faces, hunted glances—the uniform of fear. Coldness from the bench seeped through his clothing. He shivered, drew a deep breath of the salt air. The breeze off the bay carried essence of seaweed, harmonic on the dominant bitter musk of a city's effluvia. Seagulls haggled over a morsel in the tide rip. The papers on his lap fluttered. He held them down with one hand, watching the people.

I'm procrastinating, he thought. *It's a luxury my profession can ill afford nowadays.*

A woman in a red fur cape approached, her sandals tapping a swift rhythm on the concrete. Her cape billowed behind in a puff of breeze.

He looked up to her face framed in dark hair. Every muscle in his body locked. She was the woman of his nightmare down to the minutest detail! His eyes followed her. She saw him staring, looked away, walked past.

Eric fumbled his papers together, closed the notebook and ran after her. He caught up, matched his steps to hers, still staring, unthinking. She looked at him, flushed, looked away.

"Go away or I'll call a cop!"

"Please, I have to talk to you."

"I said go away." She increased her pace; he matched it.

"Please forgive me, but I dreamed about you last night. You see—"

She stared straight ahead.

"I've been told *that* one before! Go away!"

"But you don't understand."

She stopped, turned and faced him, shaking with anger. "But I *do* understand! You saw my show last night! You've dreamed about me!" She wagged her head. "Miss Lanai, I *must* get to know you!"

Eric shook his head. "But I've never even heard of you or seen you before."

"Well! I'm not accustomed to being insulted either!" She whirled, walked away briskly, the red cape flowing out behind her. Again he caught up with her.

"Please—"

"I'll scream!"

"I'm a psychoanalyst."

She hesitated, slowed, stopped. A puzzled expression flowed over her face. "Well, that's a new approach."

He took advantage of her interest. "I really did dream about you. It was most disturbing. I couldn't shut it off."

Something in his voice, his manner—She laughed, "A real dream was bound to show up some day."

"I'm Dr. Eric Ladde."

She glanced at the caduceus over his breast pocket. "I'm Colleen Lanai; I sing."

He winced. "I know."

"I thought you'd never heard of me."

"You sang in my dream."

"Oh." A pause. "Are you really a psychoanalyst?"

He slipped a card from his breast pocket; handed it to her. She looked at it.

"What does 'Teleprobe Diagnosis' mean?"

"That's an instrument I use."

She returned the card, linked an arm through his, set an easy, strolling pace. "All right, doctor. You tell me about your dream and I'll tell you about my headaches. Fair exchange?" She peered up at him from under thick eyelashes.

"Do you have headaches?"

"Terrible headaches." She shook her head.

Eric looked down at her. Some of the nightmare unreality returned. He thought, "What am I doing here? One doesn't dream about a strange face and then meet her in the flesh the next day. The next thing I know the whole world of my unconscious will come alive."

"Could it be this Syndrome thing?" she asked. "Ever since we were in Los Angeles I've—" She chewed at her lip.

He stared at her. "You were in Los Angeles?"

"We got out just a few hours before that . . . before—" She shuddered. "Doctor, what's it like to be crazy?"

He hesitated. "It's no different from being sane—for the person involved." He looked out at the mist lifting from the bay. "The Syndrome appears similar to other forms of insanity. It's as though something pushed people over their lunacy thresholds. It's strange; there's a rather well defined radius of about sixty miles which it saturated. Atlanta and Los Angeles, for instance, and Lawton, had quite sharp lines of demarcation: people on one side of a street got it; people on the other didn't. We suspect there's a contamination period during which—" He paused, looked down at her, smiled. "And all you asked was a simple question. This is my lecture personality. I wouldn't worry too much about those headaches; probably diet, change of climate, maybe your eyes. Why don't you get a complete physical?"

She shook her head. "I've had six physicals since we left Karachi: same thing—four new diets." She shrugged. "Still I have headaches."

Eric jerked to a stop, exhaled slowly. "You were in Karachi, too?"

"Why, yes; that was the third place we hit after Honolulu."

He leaned toward her. "And Honolulu?"

She frowned. "What is this, a cross-examination?" She waited. "Well—"

He swallowed, thought, *How can one person have been in these cities the Syndrome hit and be so casual about it?*

She tapped a foot. "Cat got your tongue?"

He thought, *She's so flippant about it.*

He ticked off the towns on his fingers. "You were in Los Angeles, Honolulu, Karachi; you've hit the high spots of Syndrome contamination and—"

An animal cry, sharp, exclamatory, burst from her. "It got all of those places?"

He thought, *How could anyone be alive and not know exactly where the Syndrome has been?*

He asked, "Didn't you know?"

She shook her head, a numb motion, eyes wide, staring. "But Pete said—" She stopped. "I've been so busy learning new numbers. We're reviving the old time hot jazz."

"How could you miss it? TV is full of it, the newstapes, the transgraphs."

She shrugged. "I've just been so busy. And I don't like to think about such things. Pete said—" She shook her head. "You know, this is the first time I've been out alone for a walk in over a month. Pete was asleep and—" Her expression softened. "That Pete; He must not have wanted me to worry."

"If you say so, but—" He stopped. "Who's Pete?"

"Haven't you heard of Pete Serantis and the musikron?"

"What's a musikron?"

She shook back a curl of dark hair. "Have your little joke, doctor."

"No, seriously. What's a musikron?"

She frowned. "You *really* don't know what the musikron is?"

He shook his head.

She chuckled, a throaty sound, controlled. "Doctor, you talk about *my* not knowing about Karachi and Honolulu. Where have you been hiding your head? Variety has us at the top of the heap."

He thought, "She's serious!"

A little stiffly, he said, "Well, I've been quite busy with a research problem of my own. It deals with the Syndrome."

"Oh." She turned, looked at the gray waters of the bay, turned back. She twisted her hands together. "Are you sure about Honolulu?"

"Is your family there?"

She shook her head. "I have no family. Just friends." She looked up at him, eyes shining. "Did it get . . . everybody?"

He nodded, thought: *She needs something to distract her attention.*

He said, "Miss Lanai, could I ask a favor?" He plunged ahead, not waiting for an answer. "You've been three places where the Syndrome hit. Maybe there's a clue in your patterns. Would you consent to undergoing a series of tests at my lab? They wouldn't take long."

"I couldn't possibly; I have a show to do tonight. I just sneaked out for a few minutes by myself. I'm at the Gweduc Room. Pete may wake up and—'' She focused on his pleading expression. ''I'm sorry, doctor. Maybe some other time. You wouldn't find anything important from me anyway.''

He shrugged, hesitated. ''But I haven't told you about my dream.''

''You tempt me, doctor. I've heard a lot of phony dream reports. I'd appreciate the McCoy for just once. Why don't you walk me back to the Gweduc Room? It's only a couple of blocks.''

''Okay.''

She took his arm.

''Half a loaf—''

He was a thin man with a twisted leg, a pinched, hating face. A cane rested against his knee. Around him wove a spiderweb maze of wires—musikron. On his head, a domeshaped hood. A spy, unsuspected, he looked out through a woman's eyes at a man who had identified himself as Dr. Eric Ladde. The thin man sneered, heard through the woman's ears: ''Half a loaf—''

On the bayside walk, Eric and Colleen matched steps.

''You never did tell me what a musikron is.''

Her laughter caused a passing couple to turn and stare. ''OK. But I still don't understand. We've been on TV for a month.''

He thought, *She thinks I'm a fuddy; probably am!*

He said, ''I don't subscribe to the entertainment circuits. I'm just on the science and news networks.''

She shrugged. ''Well, the musikron is something like a recording and playback machine; only the operator mixes in any new sounds he wants. He wears a little metal bowl on his head and just thinks about the sounds—the musikron plays them.'' She stole a quick glance at him, looked ahead. ''Everyone says it's a fake; it really isn't.''

Eric stopped, pulled her to a halt. ''That's fantastic. Why—'' He paused, chuckled. ''You know, you happen to be talking to one of the few experts in the world on this sort of thing. I have an encephalo-recorder in my basement lab that's the last word in teleprobes . . . that's what you're trying to describe.'' He smiled. ''The psychiatrists of this town may think I'm a young upstart, but they send me their tough diagnostic cases.'' He looked down at her. ''So let's just admit your Pete's machine is artistic showmanship, shall we?''

''But it isn't just showmanship. I've heard the records before they go into the machine and when they come out of it.''

Eric chuckled.

She frowned. ''Oh, you're so supercilious.''

Eric put a hand on her arm. ''Please don't be angry. It's just that I know this field. You don't want to admit that Pete has fooled you along with all the others.''

She spoke in a slow, controlled cadence: ''Look . . . doctor . . . Pete . . . was . . . one . . . of . . . the . . . inventors . . . of . . . the . . . Musikron . . . Pete . . . and . . . old . . . Dr. . . . Amanti.'' She squinted her eyes, looking up at him. "You may be a big wheel in this business, but I know what I've heard."

"You said Pete worked on this musikron with a doctor. What did you say that doctor's name was?"

"Oh, Dr. Carlos Amanti. His name's on a little plate inside the musikron."

Eric shook his head. "Impossible. Dr. Carlos Amanti is in an asylum."

She nodded. "That's right; Wailiku Hospital for the Insane. That's where they worked on it."

Eric's expression was cautious, hesitant. "And you say when Pete thinks about the sounds, the machine produces them?"

"Certainly."

"Strange I'd never heard about this musikron before."

"Doctor, there are a lot of things you've never heard about."

He wet his lips with his tongue. "Maybe you're right." He took her arm, set a rapid pace down the walkway. "I want to see this musikron."

In Lawton, Oklahoma, long rows of prefabricated barracks swelter on a sunbaked flat. In each barracks building, little cubicles; in each cubicle, a hospital bed; on each hospital bed, a human being. Barracks XRO-29: a psychiatrist walks down the hall, behind him an orderly pushing a cart. On the cart, hypodermic needles, syringes, antiseptics, sedatives, test tubes. The psychiatrist shakes his head.

"Baily, they certainly nailed this thing when they called it the Scramble Syndrome. Stick an egg-beater into every psychosis a person could have, mix 'em up, turn 'em all on."

The orderly grunts, stares at the psychiatrist.

The psychiatrist looks back. "And we're not making any progress on this thing. It's like bailing out the ocean with a sieve."

Down the hallway a man screams. Their footsteps quicken.

The Gweduc Room's elevator dome arose ahead of Eric and Colleen, a half-melon inverted on the walkway. At the top of the dome a blue and red script-ring circled slowly, spelling out, "Colleen Lanai with Pete Serantis and the Musikron."

On the walkway before the dome a thin man, using a cane to compensate for a limp, paced back and forth. He looked up as Eric and Colleen approached.

"Pete," she said.

The man limped toward them, his cane staccato on the paving.

"Pete, this is Dr. Ladde. He's heard about Dr. Amanti and he wants to—"

Pete ignored Eric, stared fiercely at Colleen. "Don't you know we have a show tonight? Where have you been?"

"But, it's only a little after nine; I don't—"

Eric interrupted. "I was a student of Dr. Amanti's. I'm interested in your musikron. You see, I've been carrying on Dr. Amanti's researches and—"

The thin man barked, "No time!" He took Colleen's arm, pulled her toward the dome.

"Pete, please! What's come over you?" She held back.

Pete stopped, put his face close to hers. "Do you like this business?"

She nodded mutely, eyes wide.

"Then let's get to work!"

She looked back at Eric, shrugged her shoulders. "I'm sorry."

Pete pulled her into the dome.

Eric stared after them. He thought, "He's a decided compulsive type . . . very unstable. May not be as immune to the Syndrome as she apparently is." He frowned, looked at his wrist watch, remembered his ten o'clock appointment. "Damn!" He turned, almost collided with a young man in busboy's coveralls.

The young man puffed nervously at a cigarette, jerked it out of his mouth, leered. "Better find yourself another gal, Doc. That one's taken."

Eric looked into the young-old eyes, stared them down. "You work in there?"

The young man replaced the cigarette between thin lips, spoke around a puff of blue smoke. "Yeah."

"When does it open?"

The young man pulled the cigarette from his mouth, flipped it over Eric's shoulder into the bay. "We're open now for breakfast. Floor show doesn't start until seven tonight."

"Is Miss Lanai in the floor show?"

The busboy looked up at the script-ring over the dome, smiled knowingly. "Doc, she *is* the floor show!"

Again Eric looked at his wrist watch, thought, *I'm coming back here tonight.* He turned toward the nearest unitube. "Thanks," he said.

"You better get reservations if you're coming back tonight," said the busboy.

Eric stopped, looked back. He reached into his pocket, found a twenty-buck piece, flipped it to the busboy. The thin young man caught the coin out of the air, looked at it, said, "Thank *you*. What name, Doc?"

"Dr. Eric Ladde."

The busboy pocketed the coin. "Righto, Doc. Floorside. I come on again at six. I'll attend to you personally."

Eric turned back to the unitube entrance again and left immediately.

Under the smog-filtered Los Angeles sun, a brown-dry city.

Mobile Laboratory 31 ground to a stop before Our Lady of Mercy Hospital, churning up a swirl of dried palm fronds in the gutter. The overworked turbo-motor sighed to a stop, grating. The Japanese psychologist emerged on one side, the Swedish doctor on the other. Their shoulders sagged.

The psychologist asked, "Ole, how long since you've had a good night's sleep?"

The doctor shook his head. "I can't remember, Yoshi; not since I left Frisco, I guess."

From the caged rear of the truck, wild, high-pitched laughter, a sigh, laughter.

The doctor stumbled on the steps to the hospital sidewalk. He stopped, turned. "Yoshi—"

"Sure, Ole. I'll get some fresh orderlies to take care of this one." To himself he added, "If there are any fresh orderlies."

Inside the hospital, cool air pressed down the hallway. The Swedish doctor stopped a man with a clipboard. "What's the latest count?"

The man scratched his forehead with a corner of the clipboard. "Two and a half million last I heard, doctor. They haven't found a sane one yet."

The Gweduc Room pointed a plastine finger under Elliott Bay. Unseen by the patrons, a cage compressed a high density of sea life over the transparent ceiling. Illumabeams traversed the water, treating the watchers to visions of a yellow salmon, a mauve perch, a pink octopus, a blue jellyfish. At one end of the room, synthetic mother-of-pearl had been formed into a giant open gweduc shell—the stage. Colored spotlights splashed the backdrop with ribbons of flame, blue shadows.

Eric went down the elevator, emerged in an atmosphere disturbingly reminiscent of his nightmare. All it lacked was the singer. A waiter led him, threading a way through the dim haze of perfumed cigarette smoke, between tables ringed by men in formal black, women in gold lamé, luminous synthetics. An aquamarine glow shimmered from the small round table tops—the only lights in the Gweduc Room other than spotlights on the stage and illumabeams in the dark water overhead. A susurration of many voices hung on the air. Aromas of alcohol, tobacco, perfumes, exotic seafoods layered the room, mingled with a perspirant undertone.

The table nestled in the second row, crowded on all sides. The waiter extricated a chair; Eric sat down.

"Something to drink, sir?"

"Bombay Ale."

The waiter turned, merged into the gloom.

Eric tried to move his chair into a comfortable position, found it was wedged immovably between two chairs behind him. A figure materialized out of the gloom across from him; he recognized the busboy.

"Best I could get you, Doc."

"Would you tell Miss Lanai I'm here?"

"I'll try, Doc; but that Pete character has been watching her like a piece of prize property all afternoon. Not that I wouldn't do the same thing myself, you understand."

White teeth flashed in the smoke-layered shadows. The busboy turned, weaved his way back through the tables. The murmuring undercurrent of voices in the room damped out. Eric turned toward the stage. A portly man in ebony and chalk-striped coveralls bent over the microphone.

"Here's what you've been waiting for," he said. He gestured with his left hand. Spotlights erased a shadow, revealing Colleen Lanai, her hands clasped in front of her. An old-fashioned gown of electric blue to match her eyes sheathed the full curves.

"Colleen Lanai!"

Applause washed over the room, subsided. The portly man gestured with his right hand. Other spotlights flared, revealing Pete Serantis in black coveralls, leaning on his cane.

"Pete Serantis and—"

He waited for a lesser frenzy of clapping to subside.

" . . . The Musikron!"

A terminal spotlight illuminated a large metallic box behind Pete. The thin man limped around the box, ducked, and disappeared inside. Colleen took the microphone from the announcer, who bowed and stepped off the stage.

Eric became aware of a pressing mood of urgency in the room. He thought, "For a brief instant we forget our fears, forget the Syndrome, everything except the music and this instant."

Colleen held the microphone intimately close to her mouth.

"We have some more real oldies for you tonight," she said. An electric pressure of personality pulsed out from her. "Two of these songs we've never presented before. First, a trio—'Terrible Blues' with the musikron giving you a basic recording by Clarence Williams and the Red Onion Jazz Babies, Pete Serantis adding an entirely new effect; next, 'Wild Man Blues' and the trumpet is pure Louis Armstrong; last, 'Them's Graveyard Words,' an old Bessie Smith special." She bowed almost imperceptibly.

Music appeared in the room, not definable as to direction. It filled the senses. Colleen began to sing, seemingly without effort. She played her voice like a horn, soaring with the music, ebbing with it, caressing the air with it.

Eric stared, frozen, with all the rest of the audience.

She finished the first song. The noise of applause deafened him. He felt pain in his hands, looked down to find himself beating his palms together. He stopped, shook his head, took four deep breaths. Colleen picked up the thread of a new melody. Eric narrowed his eyes, staring at the stage. Impulsively, he put his hands to his ears and felt panic swell as the music remained undiminished. He closed his eyes, caught his breath as he continued to see Colleen, blurred at first, shifting, then in a steady image from a place nearer and to the left.

A wavering threnody of emotions accompanied the vision. Eric put his hands before his eyes. The image remained. He opened his eyes. The image again blurred, shifted to normal. He searched to one side of Colleen for the position from which he had been seeing her. He decided it could only be from inside the musikron and at the instant of decision discerned the outline of a mirror panel in the face of the metallic box.

"Through a one-way glass," he thought. "Through Pete's eyes."

He sat, thinking, while Colleen finished her third number. Pete emerged from the musikron to share the applause. Colleen blew a kiss to the audience.

"We'll be back in a little while."

She stepped down from the stage, followed by Pete; darkness absorbed them. Waiters moved along the tables. A drink was placed on Eric's table. He put money in the tray. A blue shadow appeared across from him, slipped into the chair.

"Tommy told me you were here . . . the busboy." She leaned across the table. "You mustn't let Pete see you. He's in a rage, a real pet. I've never seen anybody that angry."

Eric leaned toward her, caught a delicate exhalation of sandalwood perfume. It dizzied him. "I want to talk to you," he said. "Can you meet me after the show?"

"I guess I can trust you," she said. She hesitated, smiling faintly. "You're the professional type." Another pause. "And I think I need professional advice." She slipped out of the chair, stood up. "I have to get back before he suspects I didn't go to the powder room. I'll meet you near the freight elevator upstairs."

She was gone.

A cold breeze off the bay tugged at Eric's cape, puffing it out behind him. He leaned against the concrete railing, drawing on a cigarette. The glowing coal flowed an orange wash across the face, flaring, dimming. The tide rip sniggled and babbled; waves lap-lap-lapped at the concrete beneath him. A multi-colored glow in the water to his left winked out as the illumabeams above the Gweduc Room were extinguished. He shivered. Footsteps approached from his left, passed behind him—a man, alone. A muffled whirring sound grew, stopped. Light footsteps ran toward him, stopped at the rail. He smelled her perfume.

"Thanks," he said.

"I can't be long. He's suspicious. Tommy brought me up the freight elevator. He's waiting."

"I'll be brief. I've been thinking. I'm going to talk about travel. I'm going to tell you where you've been since you hooked up with Pete in Honolulu." He turned, leaned sideways against the railing. "You tried your show first in Santa Rosa, California, the sticks; then you went to Piquetberg, Karachi, Peykyavik, Portland, Hollandia, Lawton—finally, Los Angeles. Then you came here."

"So you looked up our itinerary."

He shook his head. "No." He hesitated. "Pete's kept you pretty busy rehearsing, hasn't he?"

"This isn't easy work."

"I'm not saying it is." He turned back to the rail, flipped his cigarette into the darkness, heard it hiss in the water. "How long have you known Pete?"

"A couple of months more or less. Why?"

He turned away. "What kind of a fellow is he?"

She shrugged. "He's a nice guy. He's asked me to marry him."

Eric swallowed. "Are you going to?"

She looked out to the dark bay. "That's why I want your advice. I don't know . . . I just don't know. He put me where I am, right on top of the entertainment heap." She turned back to Eric. "And he really is an awfully nice guy . . . when you get under that bitterness."

Eric breathed deeply, pressed against the concrete railing. "May I tell you a story?"

"What about?"

"This morning you mentioned Dr. Carlos Amanti, the inventor of the teleprobe. Did you know him?"

"No."

"I was one of his students. When he had the breakdown it hit all of us pretty hard, but I was the only one who took up the teleprobe project. I've been working at it eight years."

She stirred beside him. "What is this teleprobe?"

"The science writers have poked fun at it; they call it the 'mind reader.' It's not. It's just a means of interpreting some of the unconscious impulses of the human brain. I suppose some day it may approach mind reading. Right now it's a rather primitive instrument, sometimes unpredictable. Amanti's intention was to communicate with the unconscious mind, using interpretation of encephalographic waves. The idea was to amplify them, maintain a discrete separation between types, and translate the type variations according to thought images."

She chewed her lower lip. "And you think the musikron would help make a better teleprobe, that it would help fight the Syndrome?"

"I think more than that." He looked down at the paving.

"You're trying to tell me something without saying it," she said. "Is it about Pete?"

"Not exactly."

"Why'd you give that long recitation of where we'd been? That wasn't just idle talk. What are you driving at?"

He looked at her speculatively, weighing her mood. "Hasn't Pete told you about those places?"

She put a hand to her mouth, eyes wide, staring. She moaned. "Not the Syndrome . . . not all of those places, too?"

"Yes." It was a flat, final sound.

She shook her head. "What are you trying to tell me?"

"That it could be the musikron causing all of this."

"Oh, no!"

"I could be wrong. But look at how it appears. Amanti was a genius working near the fringe of insanity. He had a psychotic break. Then he helped Pete build a machine. It's possible that machine picks up the operator's brain wave patterns, transmits them as a scrambling impulse. The musikron *does* convert thought into a discernible energy—sound. Why isn't it just as possible that it funnels a disturbing impulse directly into the unconscious.'' He wet his lips with his tongue. "Did you know that I hear those sounds even with my hands over my ears, see you with my eyes covered. Remember my nightmare? My nervous system is responding to a subjective impulse."

"Does it do the same thing to everybody?"

"Probably not. Unless a person was conditioned as I have been by spending years in the aura of a similar machine, these impulses would be censored at the threshold of consciousness. They would be repressed as unbelievable."

Her lips firmed. She shook her head. "I don't see how all this scientific gobbledy-gook proves the musikron caused the Syndrome."

"Maybe it doesn't. But it's the best possibility I've seen. That's why I'm going to ask a favor. Could you get me the circuit diagrams for the musikron? If I could see them I'd be able to tell just what this thing does. Do you know if Pete has plans for it?"

"There's some kind of a thick notebook inside the musikron. I think that's what you mean."

"Could you get it?"

"Maybe, but not tonight . . . and I wouldn't dare tell Pete."

"Why not tonight?"

"Pete sleeps with the key to the musikron. He keeps it locked when it's not in use; so no one will get inside and get a shock. It has to be left on all the time because it takes so long to warm it up. Something about crystals or energy potential or some words like that."

"Where's Pete staying?"

"There are quarters down there, special apartments."

He turned away, breathed the damp salt air, turned back.

Colleen shivered. "I know it's not the musikron. I . . . they—" She was crying.

He moved closer, put an arm around her shoulders, waiting. He felt her shiver. She leaned against him; the shivering subsided.

"I'll get those plans." She moved her head restlessly. "That'll prove it isn't the musikron."

"Colleen . . . " He tightened his arm on her shoulders, feeling a warm urgency within him.

She moved closer. "Yes."

He bent his head. Her lips were warm and soft. She clung to him, pulled away, nestled in his arms.

"This isn't right," she said.

Again he bent his head. She tipped her head up to meet him. It was a gentle kiss.

She pulled away slowly, turned her head toward the bay. "It can't be like this," she whispered. "So quick—without warning."

He put his face in her hair, inhaled. "Like what?"

"Like you'd found your way home."

He swallowed. "My dear."

Frank Herbert

Again their lips met. She pulled away, put a hand to his cheek. "I have to go."

"When will I see you?"

"Tomorrow. I'll tell Pete I have to do some shopping."

"Where?"

"Do you have a laboratory?"

"At my home in Chalmers Place on the other side of the lake. It's in the directory."

"I'll come as soon as I can get the diagrams."

Again they kissed.

"I really have to go."

He held her tightly.

"Really." She pulled away. "Good night"—she hesitated—"Eric." Shadows flowed in around her.

He heard the whirring of the elevator, leaned back against the concrete, drawing deep breaths to calm himself.

Deliberate footsteps approached from his left. A handlight flashed in his face, the dull gleam of a night patrolman's brassard behind the light. The light moved to the caduceus at his breast.

"You're out late, doctor."

The light returned to his face, winked off. Eric knew he had been photographed—as a matter of routine.

"Your lipstick's smudged," the patrolman said. He walked away past the elevator dome.

Inside the silent musikron: a thin man, pinched face, hating. Bitter thought: *Now wasn't that a sweet love scene!* Pause. *The doctor wants something to read?* Wry smile. *I'll provide it. He'll have something to occupy his mind after we've gone.*

Before going to bed, Eric filed a transgraph to Mrs. Bertz, his secretary, telling her to cancel his appointments for the next day. He snuggled up to the pillow, hugging it. Sleep avoided him. He practiced Yoga breathing. His senses remained alert. He slipped out of bed, put on a robe and sandals. He looked at the bedside clock—2:05 A.M., Saturday, May 15, 1999. He thought, *Just twenty-five hours ago—nightmare. Now . . . I don't know.* He smiled. *Yes I do; I'm in love. I feel like a college kid.*

He took a deep breath. *I'm in love.* He closed his eyes and looked at a memory picture of Colleen. *Eric, if you only solve this Syndrome, the world is yours.* The thoughts skipped a beat. *I'm an incipient manic—*

Eric ruminated. *If Pete takes that musikron out of Seattle—What then?*

He snapped a finger, went to the vidiphone, called an all-night travel agency. A girl clerk finally agreed to look up the booking dates he wanted—for a special fee. He gave her his billing code, broke the connection and went to the microfilm rack across from the foot of his bed. He ran a finger down the title index, stopped at "Implications of Encephalographic Wave Forms, A Study of the Nine Brain Pulses, by Dr. Carlos Amanti.'' He pushed the selector opposite the tape, activated the screen above the rack and returned to his bed, carrying the remote-control unit.

The first page flashed on the screen; room lights dimmed automatically. He read:

''There is a scale of vibratory impulses spanning and exceeding the human auditory range which consistently produce emotional responses of fear in varying degrees. Certain of these vibratory impulses—loosely grouped under the term *sounds*—test the extremes of human emotional experience. One may say, within reason, that all emotion is response to stimulation by harmonic movement, by oscillation.

''Many workers have linked emotions with characteristic encephalographic wave responses: Carter's work on Zeta waves and love; Reymann on Pi waves and abstract thinking; Poulson on the Theta Wave Index to degrees of sorrow, to name a few.

''It is the purpose of my work to trace these characteristic responses and point out what I believe to be an entirely new direction for interpretation of—''

Because of the late hour, Eric had expected drowsiness to overtake his reading, but his senses grew more alert as he read. The words had the familiarity of much re-reading, but they still held stimulation. He recalled a passage toward the end of the book, put the film on motor feed and scanned forward to the section he wanted. He slowed the tape, returned the controls to single-page advance; there it was:

''While working with severely disturbed patients in the teleprobe, I have found a charged emotional feeling in the atmosphere. Others, unfamiliar with my work, have reported this same experience. This suggests that the characteristic emanations of a disturbed mentality may produce sympathetic reactions upon those within the un-shielded field of the teleprobe. Strangely, this disturbed sensation sometimes follows by minutes or even hours the period when the patient was under examination.

''I am hesitant to suggest a theory based upon this latter phenomenon. There is too much we do not know about the teleprobe—its latency period, for instance. However, it is possible that the combination of teleprobe and disturbed personality broadcasts a field with a depressant effect upon the unconscious functions of persons within that field. Be that as it may, this entire field of teleprobe and encephalographic wave research carries implications which—''

With a decisive gesture, Eric snapped off the projector, slipped out of bed and dressed. The bedside clock showed 3:28 A.M., Saturday, May 15, 1999. Never in his life had he felt more alert. He took the steps two at a time down to his basement lab, flipped on all the lights, wheeled out his teleprobe.

I'm on to something, he thought. *This Syndrome problem is too urgent for me to waste time sleeping.*

He stared at his teleprobe, an open framework of shelves, banks of tubes, maze of wiring, relaxing chair in the center with the metal hemisphere of the pickup directly above the chair. He thought, *The musikron is rigged for sound projection; that means a secondary resonance circuit of some kind.*

He pulled an unused tape recorder from a rack at the end of his bench, stripped the playback circuit from it. He took the recorder service manual, sketched in the changes

Frank Herbert

he would need, pausing occasionally to figure circuit loads and balances on a slide rule. Presently, not too satisfied with his work, but anxious to get started, he brought out the parts he would need and began cutting and soldering. In two hours he had what he wanted.

Eric took cutter pliers, went to the teleprobe, snipped away the recorder circuit, pulled it out as a unit. He wheeled the teleprobe cage to the bench and, delicately feeling his way, checking the circuit diagrams as he went, he wired in the playback circuit. From the monitor and audio sides, he took the main leads, fed them back into the first bank of the encephalographic pickup. He put a test power source on the completed circuit and began adding resistance units by eye to balance the impedance. It took more than an hour of testing and cutting, required several units of shielding.

He stepped back, stared at the machine. He thought, *It's going to oscillate all over the place. How does he balance this monster?*

Eric pulled at his chin, thinking. *Well, let's see what this hybrid does.*

The wall clock above his bench showed 6:45 A.M. He took a deep breath, hooked an overload fuse into a relay power switch, closed the switch. A wire in the pickup circuit blazed to incandescence; the fuse kicked out. Eric opened the switch, picked up a test meter, and returned to the machine. The fault eluded him. He went back to the circuit diagrams.

"Perhaps too much power—" He recalled that his heavy duty rheostat was at a shop being repaired, considered bringing out the auxiliary generator he had used on one experiment. The generator was beneath a pile of boxes in a corner. He put the idea temporarily aside, turned back to the teleprobe.

"If I could just get a look at that musikron."

He stared at the machine. "A resonance circuit—What else?" He tried to imagine the interrelationship of the components, fitting himself into the machine.

"I'm missing it some place! There's some other thing and I have the feeling I already know it, that I've heard it. I've got to see the diagrams on that musikron."

He turned away, went out of the lab and climbed the stairs to his kitchen. He took a coffee capsule from a package in the cupboard, put it beside the sink. The vidiphone chimed. It was the clerk from the travel bureau. Eric took down her report, thanked her, broke the connection. He did a series of subtractions.

"Twenty-eight hour time lag," he thought. "Every one of them. That's too much of a coincidence."

He experienced a moment of vertigo, followed by weariness. "I'd better get some rest. I'll come back to this thing when I'm more alert."

He padded into the bedroom, sat down on the bed, kicked off his sandals and lay back, too tired to undress. Sleep eluded him. He opened his eyes, looked at the clock: 7:00 A.M. He sighed, closed his eyes, sank into a somnolent state. A niggling worry gnawed at his consciousness. Again he opened his eyes, looked at the clock: 9:50 A.M. *But I didn't feel the time pass,* he thought. *I must have slept.* He closed his eyes.

His senses drifted into dizziness, the current in a stream, a ship on the current, wandering, hunting, whirling.

He thought, *I hope he didn't see me leave.*

His eyelids snapped open and, for a moment, he saw a unitube entrance on the ceiling above his head. He shook his head.

"That was a crazy thought. Where'd that come from?" he asked himself. "I've been working too hard."

He turned on his side, returned to the somnolent state, his eyes drooping closed. Instantly, he had the sensation of being in a maze of wires; an emotion of hate surged over him so strongly it brought panic because he couldn't explain it or direct it at anything. He gritted his teeth, shook his head, opened his eyes. The emotion disappeared, leaving him weak. He closed his eyes. Into his senses crept an almost overpowering aroma of gardenias, a vision of dawnlight through a shuttered window. His eyelids snapped open; he sat up in the bed, put his head in his hands.

Rhinencephalic stimulation, he thought. *Visual stimulation . . . auditory stimulation . . . nearly total sensorium response. It means something. But what does it mean?* He shook his head, looked at the clock: 10:10 A.M.

Outside Karachi, Pakistan, a Hindu holy man squatted in the dust beside an ancient road. Past him paraded a caravan of International Red Cross trucks, moving selected cases of Syndrome madness to the skytrain field on the Indus delta. Tomorrow the sick would be studied at a new clinic in Vienna. The truck motors whined and roared; the ground trembled. The holy man drew an ancient symbol with a finger in the dust. The wind of a passing truck stirred the pattern of Brahmaputra, twisting it. The holy man shook his head sadly.

Eric's front door announcer chimed as someone stepped onto the entrance mat. He clicked the scanner switch at his bedside, looked to the bedroom master screen; Colleen's face appeared on the screen. He punched for the door release, missed, punched again, caught it. He ran his hands through his hair, snapped the top clip of his coveralls, went to the entrance hall.

Colleen appeared tiny and hesitant standing in the hall. As he saw her, something weblike, decisive, meshed inside him—a completeness.

He thought, *Boy, in just one day you are completely on the hook.*

"Eric," she said.

Her body's warm softness clung to him. Fragrance wafted from her hair.

"I missed you," he said.

She pulled away, looked up. "Did you dream about me?"

He kissed her. "Just a normal dream."

"Doctor!"

A smile took the sting out of the exclamation. She pulled away, slipped off her fur-lined cape. From an inner pocket of the cape she extracted a flat blue booklet. "Here's the diagram. Pete didn't suspect a thing."

Abruptly, she reeled toward him, clutched at his arm, gasping.

He steadied her, frightened. "What's the matter, darling?"

She shook her head, drawing deep, shuddering breaths.

"It's nothing; just a . . . little headache."

"Little headache nothing." He put the back of his wrist against her forehead. The skin held a feverish warmth. "Do you feel ill?"

She shook her head. "No. It's going away."

"I don't like this as a symptom. Have you eaten?"

She looked up, calmer. "No, but I seldom eat breakfast . . . the waistline."

"Nonsense! You come in here and eat some fruit."

She smiled at him. "Yes, doctor . . . darling."

The reflection on the musikron's inner control surfaces gave an underlighted, demoniacal cast to Pete's face. His hand rested on a relay switch. Hesitant thought: *Colleen, I wish I could control your thoughts. I wish I could tell you what to do. Each time I try, you get a headache. I wish I knew how this machine really works.*

Eric's lab still bore the cluttered look of his night's activities. He helped Colleen up to a seat on the edge of the bench, opened the musikron booklet beside her. She looked down at the open pages.

"What are all those funny looking squiggles?"

He smiled. "Circuit diagram." He took a test clip and, glancing at the diagram, began pulling leads from the resonance circuit. He stopped, a puzzled frown drawing down his features. He stared at the diagram. "That can't be right." He found a scratch pad, stylus, began checking the booklet.

"What's wrong?"

"This doesn't make sense."

"How do you mean?"

"It isn't designed for what it's supposed to do."

"Are you certain?"

"I know Dr. Amanti's work. This isn't the way he works." He began leafing through the booklet. A page flopped loose. He examined the binding. The booklet's pages had been razored out and new pages substituted. It was a good job. If the page hadn't fallen out, he might not have noticed. "You said it was easy to get this. Where was it?"

"Right out on top of the musikron."

He stared at her speculatively.

"What's wrong?" Her eyes held open candor.

"I wish I knew." He pointed to the booklet. "That thing's as phony as a Martian canal."

"How do you know?"

"If I put it together that way"—a gesture at the booklet—"it'd go up in smoke the instant power hit it. There's only one explanation: Pete's on to us."

"But how?"

"That's what I'd like to know . . . how he anticipated you'd try to get the diagram for me. Maybe that busboy—"

"Tommy? But he's such a nice young fellow."

"Yeah. He'd sell his mother if the price was right. He could have eavesdropped last night."

"I can't believe it." She shook her head.

In the webwork of the musikron, Pete gritted his teeth. *Hate him! Hate him!* He pressed the thought at her, saw it fail. With a violent motion, he jerked the metal hemisphere off his head, stumbled out of the musikron. *You're not going to have her! If it's a dirty fight you want, I'll really show you a dirty fight!*

Colleen asked, "Isn't there some other explanation?"

"Can you think of one?"

She started to slide down from the bench, hesitated, lurched against him, pressing her head against his chest. "My head . . . my head—" She went limp in his arms, shuddered, recovered slowly, drew gasping breaths. She stood up. "Thank you."

In a corner of the lab was a canvas deck chair. He led her over to it, eased her down. "You're going to a hospital right now for a complete check-up—tracers, the works. I don't like this."

"It's just a headache."

"Peculiar kind of a headache."

"I'm not going to a hospital."

"Don't argue. I'm calling for reservations as soon as I can get over to the phone."

"Eric, I won't do it!" She pushed herself upright in the chair. "I've seen all the doctors I want to see." She hesitated, looked up at him. "Except you. I've had all those tests. There's nothing wrong with me . . . except something in my head." She smiled. "I guess I'm talking to the right kind of a doctor for that."

She lay back, resting, closed her eyes. Eric pulled up a stool, sat down beside her, holding her hand. Colleen appeared to sink into a light sleep, breathing evenly. Minutes passed.

If the teleprobe wasn't practically dismantled, I could test her, he thought.

She stirred, opened her eyes.

"It's that musikron," he said. He took her arm. "Did you ever have headaches like this before you began working with that thing?"

"I had headaches, but . . . well, they weren't this bad." She shuddered. "I kept having horrible dreams last night about all those poor people going insane. I kept waking up. I wanted to go in and have it out with Pete." She put her hands over her face. "How can you be certain it's the musikron. You can't be sure. I won't believe it! I can't."

Eric stood up, went to the bench and rummaged under loose parts for a notebook. He returned, tossed the book into her lap. "There's your proof."

She looked at the book without opening it. "What is this?"

Frank Herbert

"It's some figures on your itinerary. I had a travel bureau check your departure times. From the time Pete would have been shutting down the musikron to the moment all hell broke loose there's an even twenty-eight-hour time lapse. That same time lag is present in each case."

She pushed the notebook from her lap. "I don't believe it. You're making this up."

He shook his head. "Colleen, what does it mean to you that you have been each place where the Syndrome hit . . . that there was a twenty-eight-hour time lapse in each case. Isn't that stretching coincidence too far?"

"I know it's not true." Her lips thinned. "I don't know what I've been thinking of to even consider you were right." She looked up, eyes withdrawn. "It can't be true. If it was, it would mean Pete planned the whole thing. He's just not that kind of a guy. He's nice, thoughtful."

He started to put his hand on her arm. "But, Colleen, I thought—"

"Don't touch me. I don't care what you thought, or what I thought. I think you've been using your psychological ability to try to turn me away from Pete."

He shook his head, again tried to take her arm.

She pulled away. "No! I want to think and I can't think when . . . when you touch me." She stared at him. "I believe you're just jealous of Pete."

"That's not—"

A motion at the lab door caught his eye, stopped him. Pete stood there. leaning on his cane.

Eric thought, *How did he get there? I didn't hear a thing. How long has he been there?* He stood up.

Pete stepped forward. "You forgot to latch your door, doctor." He looked at Colleen. "Common enough thing. I did, too." He limped into the room, cane tapping methodically. "You were saying something about jealousy." A pause. "I understand about jealousy."

"Pete!" Colleen stared at him, turned back to Eric. "Eric, I—" She began, and then shrugged.

Pete rested both hands on his cane, looked up at Eric. "You weren't going to leave me anything, were you, doctor—the woman I love, the musikron. You were even going to hang me for this Syndrome thing."

Eric stopped, retrieved his notebook from the floor. He handed it to Pete, who turned it over, looked at the back.

"The proof's in there. There's a twenty-eight-hour time lag between the moment you leave a community and the moment madness breaks out. You already know it's followed you around the world. There's no deviation. I've checked it out."

Pete's face paled. "Coincidence. Figures can lie; I'm no monster."

Colleen turned toward Eric, back to Pete. "That's what I told him, Pete."

"Nobody's accusing you of being a monster, Pete . . . yet," Eric said. "You *could* be a savior. The knowledge that's locked up in that musikron could practically wipe out insanity. It's a positive link with the unconscious . . . can be tapped any time. Why, properly shielded—''

"Nuts! You're trying to get the musikron so you can throw your weight around." He looked at Colleen "And you sugar-talked her into helping you." He sneered. "It's not the first time I've been double-crossed by a woman; I guess I should've been a psychiatrist."

Colleen shook her head. "Pete, don't talk that way."

"Yeah . . . How else do you expect me to talk? You were a nobody; a canary in a hula chorus and I picked you up and set you down right on the top. So what do you do—" He turned away, leaning heavily on the cane. "You can have her, Doc; she's just your type!"

Eric put out a hand, withdrew it. "Pete! Stop allowing your deformity to deform your reason! It doesn't matter how we feel about Colleen. We've got to think about what the musikron is doing to people! Think of all the unhappiness this is causing people . . . the death . . . the pain—"

"People!" Pete spat out the word.

Eric took a step closer to him. "Stop that! You know I'm right. You can have full credit for anything that is developed. You can have full control of it. You can—"

"Don't try to kid me, Doc. It's been tried by experts. You and your big words! You're just trying to make a big impression on baby here. I already told you you can have her. I don't want her."

"Pete! You—"

"Look out, Doc; you're losing your temper!"

"Who wouldn't in the face of your pig-headedness?"

"So it's pig-headed to fight a thief, eh, Doc?" Pete spat on the floor, turned toward the door, tripped on his cane and fell.

Colleen was at his side. "Pete, are you hurt?"

He pushed her away. "I can take care of myself!" He struggled to his feet, pulling himself up on the cane.

"Pete, please—"

Eric saw moisture in Pete's eyes. "Pete, let's solve this thing."

"It's already solved, Doc." He limped through the doorway.

Colleen hesitated. "I have to go with him. I can't let him go away like this. There's no telling what he'll do."

"But don't you see what he's doing?"

Anger flamed in her eyes; she stared at Eric. "I saw what you did and it was as cruel a thing as I've ever seen." She turned and ran after Pete.

Her footsteps drummed up the stairs; the outer door slammed.

An empty fibreboard box lay on the floor beside the teleprobe. Eric kicked it across the lab.

"Unreasonable . . . neurotic . . . flighty . . . irresponsible—"

He stopped; emptiness grew in his chest. He looked at the teleprobe. "Sometimes, there's no predicting about women." He went to the bench, picked up a transistor, put it down, pushed a tumble of resistors to the back of the bench. "Should've known better."

He turned, started toward the door, froze with a thought which forced out all other awareness:

What if they leave Seattle?

He ran up the stairs three at a time, out the door, stared up and down the street. A jet car sped past with a single occupant. A woman and two children approached from his left. Otherwise, the street was empty. The unitube entrance, less than half a block away, disgorged three teen-age girls. He started toward them, thought better of it. With the tubes running fifteen seconds apart, his chance to catch them had been lost while he'd nursed his hurt.

He re-entered the apartment.

I have to do something, he thought. *If they leave, Seattle will go the way of all the others.* He sat down by the vidiphone, put his finger in the dial, withdrew it.

If I call the police, they'll want proof. What can I show them besides some time-tables? He looked out the window at his left. *The musikron! They'll see*—Again he reached for the dial, again withdrew. *What would they see? Pete would just claim I was trying to steal it.*

He stood up, paced to the window, stared out at the lake.

I could call the society, he thought.

He ticked off in his mind the current top officers of the King County Society of Psychiatric Consultants. All of them considered Dr. Eric Ladde a little too successful for one so young; and besides there was the matter of his research on the teleprobe; mostly a laughable matter.

But I have to do something . . . the Syndrome—He shook his head. *I'll have to do it alone, whatever I do.* He slipped into a black cape, went outside and headed for the Gweduc Room.

A cold wind kicked up whitecaps in the bay, plumed spray onto the waterfront sidewalk. Eric ducked into the elevator, emerged into a lunchroom atmosphere. The girl at the checktable looked up.

"Are you alone, doctor?"

"I'm looking for Miss Lanai."

"I'm sorry. You must have passed them outside. She and Mr. Serantis just left."

"Do you know where they were going?"

"I'm sorry; perhaps if you come back this evening—"

Eric returned to the elevator, rode up to the street vaguely disquieted. As he emerged from the elevator dome, he saw a van pull away from the service dome. Eric played a hunch, ran toward the service elevator which already was whirring down.

"Hey!"

The whirring stopped, resumed; the elevator returned to the street level, in it Tommy, the busboy.

"Better luck next time, Doc."

"Where are they?"

"Well—"

Eric jammed a hand into his coin pocket, fished out a fifty-buck piece, held it in his hand.

Tommy looked at the coin, back at Eric's eyes. "I heard Pete call the Bellingham skytrain field for reservations to London."

A hard knot crept into Eric's stomach; his breathing became shallow, quick; he looked around him.

"Only twenty-eight hours—"

"That's all I know, Doc."

Eric looked at the busboy's eyes, studying him.

Tommy shook his head. "Don't you start looking at me that way!" He shuddered. "That Pete give me the creeps; always staring at a guy; sitting around in that machine all day and no noises coming out of it." Again he shuddered. "I'm glad he's gone."

Eric handed him the coin. "You won't be."

"Yeah," Tommy stepped back into the elevator. "Sorry you didn't make it with the babe, Doc."

"Wait."

"Yeah?"

"Wasn't there a message from Miss Lanai?"

Tommy made an almost imperceptible motion toward the inner pocket of his coveralls. Eric's trained eyes caught the gesture. He stepped forward, gripped Tommy's arm.

"Give it to me!"

"Now look here, Doc."

"Give it to me!"

"Doc, I don't know what you're talking about."

Eric pushed his face close to the busboy's. "Did you see what happened to Los Angeles, Lawton, Portland, all the places where the Syndrome hit?"

The boy's eyes went wide. "Doc, I—"

"Give it to me!"

Tommy darted his free hand under his coveralls, extracted a thick envelope, thrust it into Eric's hand.

Eric released the boy's arm. Scrawled on the envelope was: "This will prove you were wrong about Pete." It was signed, "Colleen."

"You were going to keep this?" Eric asked.

Tommy's lips twisted. "Any fool can see it's the plans for the musikron, Doc. That thing's valuable."

Frank Herbert

"You haven't any idea," Eric said. He looked up. "They're headed for Bellingham?"

"Yeah."

The nonstop unitube put Eric at the Bellingham field in twenty-one minutes. He jumped out, ran to the station, jostling people aside. A skytrain lashed into the air at the far end of the field. Eric missed a step, stumbled, caught his balance.

In the depot, people streamed past him away from the ticket window. Eric ran up to the window, leaned on the counter. "Next train to London?"

The girl at the window consulted a screen beside her. "There'll be one at 12:50 tomorrow afternoon, sir. You just missed one."

"But that's twenty-four hours!"

"You'd arrive in London at 4:50 p.m., sir." She smiled. "Just a little late for tea." She glanced at his caduceus.

Eric clutched at the edge of the counter, leaned toward her. "That's twenty-nine hours—one hour too late."

He pushed himself away from the window, turned.

"It's *just* a four-hour trip, doctor."

He turned back. "Can I charter a private ship?"

"Sorry, doctor. There's an electrical storm coming; the traveler beam will have to shut down. I'm sure you couldn't get a pilot to go out without the beam. You do understand?"

"Is there a way to call someone on the skytrain?"

"Is this a personal matter, doctor?"

"It's an emergency."

"May I ask the nature of the emergency?"

He thought a moment, looking at the girl. He thought, *Same problem here . . . nobody would believe me.*

He said, "Never mind. Where's the nearest vidiphone? I'll leave a message for her at Plymouth Depot."

"Down that hallway to your right, doctor." The girl went back to her tickets. She looked up at Eric's departing back. "Was it a medical emergency, doctor?"

He paused, turned. The envelope in his pocket rustled. He felt for the papers, pulled out the envelope. For the second time since Tommy had given them to him, Eric glanced inside at the folded pages of electronic diagrams, some initialed "C.A."

The girl waited, staring at him.

Eric put the envelope back in his pocket, a thought crystalizing. He glanced up at the girl. "Yes, it was a medical emergency. But you're out of range."

He turned, strode outside, back to the unitube. He thought about Colleen. *Never trust a neurotic woman. I should have known better than to let my glands hypnotize me.*

He went down the unitube entrance, worked his way out to the speed strip, caught the first car along, glad to find it empty. He took out the envelope, examined its contents during the ride. There was no doubt about it; the envelope contained the papers Pete had razored from the musikron service book. Eric recognized Dr. Amanti's characteristic scrawl.

The wall clock in his lab registered 2:10 p.m. as Eric turned on the lights. He took a blank sheet of paper from his notebook, wrote on it with grease pencil:

"DEADLINE, 4:00 p.m., Sunday, May 16th."

He tacked the sheet above his bench, spread out the circuit diagrams from the envelope. He examined the first page.

Series modulation, he thought. *Quarter wave.* He ran a stylus down the page, checked the next page. *Multiple phase-reversing.* He turned to the next page. The stylus paused. He traced a circuit, went back to the first page. *Degenerative feedback.* He shook his head. *That's impossible! There'd just be a maze of wild harmonics.* He continued on through the diagrams, stopped and read through the last two pages slowly. He went through the circuits a second time, a third time, a fourth time, He shook his head. *What is it?*

He could trace the projection of much of the diagram, amazed at the clear simplicity of the ideas. The last ten pages though—they described a series of faintly familiar circuits, reminding him of a dual frequency crystal calibrator of extremely high oscillation. "10,000 KD" was marked in the margin. But there were subtle differences he couldn't explain. For instance, there was a sign for a lower limit.

A series of them, he thought. *The harmonics hunt and change. But it can't be random. Something has to control it, balance it.*

At the foot of the last page was a notation: "Important—use only C6 midget variable, C7, C8 dual, 4ufd."

They haven't made tubes in that series for fifty years, he thought. *How can I substitute?*

He studied the diagram.

I don't stand a chance of making this thing in time. And if I do; what then? He wiped his forehead. *Why does it remind me of a crystal oscillator?* He looked at the clock—two hours had passed. *Where did the time go?* he asked himself. *I'm taking too much time just learning what this is.* He chewed his lips, staring at the moving second hand of the clock, suddenly froze. *The parts houses will be closing and tomorrow's Sunday!*

He went to the lab vidiphone, dialed a parts house. No luck. He dialed another, checking the call sheet beside the phone. No luck. His fifth call netted a suggestion of a substitute circuit using transistors which might work. Eric checked off the parts list the clerk suggested, gave the man his package tube code.

"I'll have them out to you first thing Monday," the man said.

"But I have to have them today! Tonight!"

"I'm sorry, sir. The parts are in our warehouse; it's all locked up tight on Saturday afternoon."

Frank Herbert

"I'll pay a hundred bucks above list price for those parts."

"I'm sorry, sir; I don't have authorization."

"Two hundred."

"But—"

"Three hundred."

The clerk hesitated. Eric could see the man figuring. The three hundred probably was a week's wages.

"I'll have to get them myself after I go off duty here," the clerk said. "What else do you need?"

Eric leafed through the circuit diagrams, read off the parts lists from the margins. "There's another hundred bucks in it if you get them to me before seven."

"I get off at 5:30, doctor. I'll do my best."

Eric broke the circuit, returned to his bench, began roughing-in from the diagram with what materials he had. The teleprobe formed the basic element with surprisingly few changes.

At 5:40, the dropbell of his transgraph jangled upstairs. Eric put down his soldering iron, went upstairs, pulled out the tape. His hands trembled when he saw the transmission station. London. He read:

"Don't ever try to see me again. Your suspicions are entirely unfounded as you probably know by now. Pete and I to be married Monday. Colleen."

He sat down at the transmitter, punched out a message to American Express, coding it urgent for delivery to Colleen Lanai.

"Colleen: If you can't think of me, please think of what this means to a city full of people. Bring Pete and that machine back before it's too late. You can't be this inhuman."

He hesitated before signing it, punched out, "I love you." He signed it, "Eric."

He thought, *You damn' fool, Eric. After the way she ran out on you.*

He went into the kitchen, took a capsule to stave off weariness, ate a dinner of pills, drank a cup of coffee. He leaned back against the kitchen drainboard, waiting for the capsule to take hold. His head cleared; he washed his face in cold water, dried it, returned to the lab.

The front door announcer chimed at 6:42 P.M. The screen showed the clerk from the parts house, his arms gripping a bulky package. Eric punched the door release, spoke into the tube: "First door on your left, downstairs."

The back wall of his bench suddenly wavered, the lines of masonry rippling; a moment of disorientation surged through him. He bit his lip, holding to the reality of the pain.

It's too soon, he thought. *Probably my own nerves; I'm too tense.*

An idea on the nature of the Syndrome flashed into his mind. He pulled a scratch pad to him, scribbled, "Loss of unconscious autonomy; overstimulation subliminal receptors; gross perception—petit perception. Check C. G. Jung's collective unconscious."

Footsteps tapped down the stairway.

"This the place?"

The clerk was a taller man than he had expected. An air of near adolescent eagerness played across the man's features as he took in the lab. "What a layout!"

Eric cleared a space on the bench. "Put that stuff right here." Eric's eyes focused on the clerk's delicately sensitive hands. The man slid the box onto the bench, picked up a fixed crystal oscillator from beside the box, examined it.

"Do you know anything about electronic hookups?" Eric asked.

The clerk looked up, grinned. "W7CGO. I've had my own ham station over ten years."

Eric offered his hand. "I'm Dr. Eric Ladde."

"Baldwin Platte . . . Baldy." He ran one of his sensitive hands through thinning hair.

"Glad to know you, Baldy. How'd you like to make a thousand bucks over what I've already promised you?"

"Are you kidding, Doc?"

Eric turned his head, looked at the framework of the teleprobe. "If that thing isn't finished and ready to go by four o'clock tomorrow afternoon, Seattle will go the way of Los Angeles."

Baldy's eyes widened; he looked at the framework. "The Syndrome? How can—"

"I've discovered what caused the Syndrome . . . a machine like this. I have to build a copy of that machine and get it working. Otherwise—"

The clerk's eyes were clear, sober. "I saw your nameplate upstairs, Doc, and remembered I'd read about you."

"Well?"

"If you say positive you've found out what caused the Syndrome, I'll take your word for it. Just don't try to explain it to me." He looked toward the parts on the bench, back to the teleprobe. "Tell me what I'm supposed to do." A pause. "And I hope you know what you're talking about."

"I've found something that just can't be coincidence," Eric said. "Added to what I know about teleprobes, well—" He hesitated. "Yes, I know what I'm talking about."

Eric took a small bottle from the rear of his bench, looked at the label, shook out a capsule. "Here, take this; it'll keep you awake."

Baldy swallowed the capsule.

Eric sorted through the papers on his bench, found the first sheet. "Now, here's what we're dealing with. There's a tricky quarter-wave hookup coupled to an amplification factor that'll throw you back on your heels."

Baldy looked over Eric's shoulder. "Doesn't look too hard to follow. Let me work on that while you take over some of the tougher parts." He reached for the diagram, moved it to a cleared corner of the bench. "What's this thing supposed to do, Doc?"

Frank Herbert

"It creates a field of impulses which feed directly into the human unconscious. The field distorts—"

Baldy interrupted him. "OK, Doc. I forgot I asked you not to explain it to me." He looked up, smiled. "I flunked Sociology." His expression sobered. "I'll just work on the assumption you know what this is all about. Electronics I understand; psychology . . . no."

They worked in silence, broken only by sparse questions, muttering. The second hand on the wall clock moved around, around, around; the minute hand followed, and the hour hand.

At 8:00 A.M., they sent out for breakfast. The layout of the crystal oscillators still puzzled them. Much of the diagram was scrawled in a radio shorthand.

Baldy made the first break in the puzzle.

"Doc, are these things supposed to make a noise?"

Eric looked at the diagram. "What?" His eyes widened. "Of course they're supposed to make a noise."

Baldy wet his lips with his tongue. "There's a special sonar crystal set for depth sounding in submarine detection. This looks faintly like the circuit, but there are some weird changes."

Eric tugged at his lip; his eyes glistened. "That's it! That's why there's no control circuit! That's why it looks as though these things would hunt all over the place! The operator is the control—his mind keeps it in balance!"

"How's that?"

Eric ignored the question. "But this means we have the wrong kind of crystals. We've misread the parts list." Frustration sagged his shoulders. "And we're not even halfway finished."

Baldy tapped the diagram with a finger. "Doc, I've got some old surplus sonar equipment at home. I'll call my wife and have her bring it over. I think there are six or seven sonopulsators—they just might work."

Eric looked at the wall clock: 8:28 A.M. Seven and a half hours to go. "Tell her to hurry."

Mrs. "Baldy" was a female version of her husband. She carried a heavy wooden box down the steps, balancing it with an easy nonchalance.

"Hi, Hon. Where'll I put this stuff?"

"On the floor . . . anywhere. Doc, this is Betty."

"How do you do."

"Hiya, Doc. There's some more stuff in the car. I'll get it."

Baldy took her arm. "You better let me do it. You shouldn't be carrying heavy loads, especially down stairs."

She pulled away. "Go on. Get back to your work. This is good for me—I need the exercise."

Operation Syndrome

"But—"

"But me no buts." She pushed him.

He returned to the bench reluctantly, looking back at his wife. She turned at the doorway and looked at Baldy. "You look pretty good for being up all night, Hon. What's all the rush?"

"I'll explain later. You better get that stuff."

Baldy turned to the box she had brought, began sorting through it. "Here they are." He lifted out two small plastic cases, handed them to Eric, pulled out another, another. There were eight of them. They lined the cases up on the bench. Baldy snapped open the cover of the first one.

"They're mostly printed circuits, crystal diode transistors and a few tubes. Wonderful engineering. Don't know what the dickens I ever planned to do with them. Couldn't resist the bargain. They were two bucks apiece." He folded back the side plate. "Here's the crys—Doc!"

Eric bent over the case.

Baldy reached into the case. "What were those tubes you wanted?"

Eric grabbed the circuit diagram, ran his finger down the parts list. "C6 midget variable, C7, C8 dual, 4ufd."

Baldy pulled out a tube. "There's your C6." He pulled out another. "There's your C8." Another. "Your C7." He peered into the works. "There's a third stage in here I don't think'll do us any good. We can rig a substitute for the 4ufd component."

Baldy whistled tonelessly through his teeth. "No wonder that diagram looked familiar. It was based on this wartime circuit."

Eric felt a moment of exultation, sobered when he looked at the wall clock: 9:04 A.M.

He thought, "We have to work faster or we'll never make it in time. Less than seven hours to go."

He said, "Let's get busy. We haven't much time."

Betty came down the stairs with another box. "You guys eaten?"

Baldy didn't look up from dismantling the second plastic box. "Yeah, but you might make us some sandwiches for later."

Eric looked up from another of the plastic boxes. "Cupboard upstairs is full of food."

Betty turned, clattered up the stairs.

Baldy glanced at Eric out of the corners of his eyes. "Doc, don't say anything to Betty about the reason for all this." He turned his attention back to the box, working methodically. "We're expecting our first son in about five months." He took a deep breath. "You've got me convinced." A drop of perspiration ran down his nose, fell onto his hand. He wiped his hand on his shirt. "This has gotta work."

Betty's voice echoed down the stairs: "Hey, Doc, where's your can opener?"

Eric had his head and shoulders inside the teleprobe. He pulled back, shouted, "Motor-punch to the left of the sink."

　　　　　　　　　　　　　　　　　　　　　　　　　　Frank Herbert

Muttering, grumbling, clinking noises echoed down from the kitchen. Presently, Betty appeared with a plate of sandwiches, a red-tinted bandage on her left thumb. "Broke your paring knife," she said. "Those mechanical gadgets scare me." She looked fondly at her husband's back. "He's just as gadget happy as you are, Doc. If I didn't watch him like a spy-beam my nice old kitchen would be an electronic nightmare." She upended an empty box, put the plate of sandwiches on it. "Eat when you get hungry. Anything I can do?"

Baldy stepped back from the bench, turned. "Why don't you go over to Mom's for the day?"

"The whole day?"

Baldy glanced at Eric, back at his wife. "The Doc's paying me fourteen hundred bucks for the day's work. That's our baby money; now run along."

She made as though to speak, closed her mouth, walked over to her husband, kissed his cheek. "OK, Hon. Bye." She left.

Eric and Baldy went on with their work, the pressure mounting with each clock tick. They plodded ahead, methodically checking each step.

At 3:20 PM, Baldy released test clips from half of the new resonance circuit, glanced at the wall clock. He stopped, looked back at the teleprobe, weighing the work yet to be done. Eric lay on his back under the machine, soldering a string of new connections.

"Doc, we aren't going to make it." He put the test meter on the bench, leaned against the bench. "There just isn't enough time."

An electronic soldering iron skidded out from under the teleprobe. Eric squirmed out behind it, looked up at the clock, back at the unconnected wires of the crystal circuits. He stood up, fished a credit book from his pocket, wrote out a fourteen hundred buck credit check to Baldwin Platte. He tore out the check, handed it to Baldy.

"You've earned every cent of this, Baldy. Now beat it; go join your wife."

"But—"

"We haven't time to argue. Lock the door after you go so you can't get back in if—"

Baldy raised his right hand, dropped it. "Doc, I can't—"

"It's all right, Baldy." Eric took a deep breath. "I kind of know how I'll go if I'm too late." He stared at Baldy. "I don't know about you. You might, well—" He shrugged.

Baldy nodded, swallowed. "I guess you're right, Doc." His lips worked. Abruptly, he turned, ran up the stairs. The outside door slammed.

Eric turned back to the teleprobe, picked up an open lead to the crystal circuits, matched it to its receptor, ran a drop of solder across the connection. He moved to the next crystal unit, the next—

At one minute to four he looked at the clock. More than an hour's work remained on the teleprobe and then—He didn't know. He leaned back against the bench, eyes filmed by fatigue. He pulled a cigarette from his pocket, pressed the igniter, took a deep drag. He remembered Colleen's question: "What's it like to be insane?" He stared at the ember on his cigarette.

Will I tear the teleprobe apart? Will I take a gun, go hunting for Colleen and Pete? Will I run out—The clock behind him clicked. He tensed. *What will it be like?* He felt dizzy, nauseated. A wave of melancholia smothered his emotions. Tears of self-pity started in his eyes. He gritted his teeth. *I'm not insane . . . I'm not insane*—He dug his fingernails into his palms, drew in deep, shuddering breaths. Uncertain thoughts wandered through his mind.

I shall faint . . . the incoherence of morosis . . . demoniacal possession . . . dithyrambic dizziness . . . an anima figure concretionized out of the libido . . . corybantic calenture . . . mad as a March hare—

His head sagged forward.

. . . Non compos mentis . . . aliéné . . . avoir le diable au corps—What has happened to Seattle? What has happened to Seattle? What has—His breathing steadied; he blinked his eyes. Everything appeared unchanged . . . unchanged . . . unchanged—*I'm wandering. I must get hold of myself!*

The fingers of his right hand burned. He shook away the short amber of his cigarette. *Was I wrong? What's happening outside?"* He started for the stairs, made it halfway to the door when the lights went out. A tight band ringed his chest. Eric felt his way to the door, grasped the stair rail, climbed up to the dim, filtered light of the hall. He stared at the stained glass bricks beside the door, tensed at a burst of gunshots from outside. He sleepwalked to the kitchen, raised on tiptoes to look through the ventilator window over the sink.

People! The street swarmed with people—some running, some walking purposefully, some wandering without aim, some clothed, some partly clothed, some nude. The bodies of a man and child sprawled in blood at the opposite curbing.

He shook his head, turned, went into the living room. The lights suddenly flashed on, off, on, stayed. He punched video for a news program, got only wavy lines. He put the set on manual, dialed a Tacoma station. Again wavy lines.

Olympia was on the air, a newscaster reading a weather report: "Partly cloudy with showers by tomorrow afternoon. Temperatures—"

A hand carrying a sheet of paper reached into the speaker's field of vision. The newsman stopped, scanned the paper. His hand shook. "Attention! Our mobile unit at the Clyde Field jet races reports that the Scramble Syndrome has struck the twin cities of Seattle-Tacoma. More than three million people are reported infected. Emergency measures already are being taken. Road blocks are being set up. There are known to have been fatalities, but—"

A new sheet of paper was handed to the announcer. His jaw muscles twitched as he read. "A jet racer has crashed into the crowd at Clyde Field. The death toll is estimated at three hundred. There are no available medical facilities. All doctors

Frank Herbert

listening to this broadcast—all doctors—report at once to State disaster headquarters. Emergency medical—'' The lights again blinked out, the screen faded.

Eric hesitated. *I'm a doctor. Shall I go outside and do what I can, medically, or shall I go down and finish the teleprobe—now that I've been proved right? Would it do any good if I did get it working?* He found himself breathing in a deep rhythm. *Or am I crazed like all the others? Am I really doing what I think I'm doing? Am I mad and dreaming a reality?* He thought of pinching himself, knew that would be no proof. *I have to go ahead as though I'm sane. Anything else* really *is madness.*

He chose the teleprobe, located a handlight in his bedroom, returned to the basement lab. He found the long unused emergency generator under the crates in the corner. He wheeled it to the center of the lab, examined it. The powerful alcohol turbine appeared in working order. The pressure cap on the fuel reservoir popped as he released it. The reservoir was more than half full. He found two carboys of alcohol fuel in the corner where the generator had been stored. He filled the fuel tank, replaced the cap, pumped pressure into the tank.

The generator's power lead he plugged into the lab fuse box. The hand igniter caught on the first spin. The turbine whirred to life, keened up through the sonic range. Lab lights sprang to life, dimmed, steadied as the relays adjusted.

It was 7:22 P.M. by the wall clock when he soldered the final connection. Eric estimated a half hour delay before the little generator had taken over, put the time actually at near eight o'clock. He found himself hesitant, strangely unwilling to test the completed machine. His one-time encephalorecorder was a weird maze of crossed wiring, emergency shielding, crowded tubes, crystals. The only familiar thing remaining in the tubular framework was the half-dome of the head-contact hanging above the test chair.

Eric plugged in a power line, linked it to a portable switchbox which he placed in the machine beside the chair. He eased aside a sheaf of wires, wormed his way through, sat down in the chair. He hesitated, hand on the switch.

Am I really sitting here? he wondered. *Or is this some trick of the unconscious mind? Perhaps I'm in a corner somewhere with a thumb in my mouth. Maybe I've torn the teleprobe apart. Maybe I've put the teleprobe together so it will kill me the instant I close the switch.*

He looked down at the switch, withdrew his hand. He thought, *I can't just sit here; that's madness, too.*

He reached up to the helmetlike dome, brought it down over his head. He felt the pinpricks of the contacts as they probed through his hair to his scalp. The narco-needles took hold, deadening skin sensation.

This feels like reality, he thought. *But maybe I'm building this out of memory. It's hardly likely I'm the only sane person in the city.* He lowered his hand to the switch. *But I have to act as though I am.*

Almost of its own volition, his thumb moved, depressed the switch. Instantly, a soft ululation hung in the laboratory air. It shifted to dissonance, to harmony, wailing, half-forgotten music, wavered up the scale, down the scale.

In Eric's mind, mottled pictures of insanity threatened to overwhelm his consciousness. He sank into a maelstrom. A brilliant spectrograph coruscated before his eyes. In a tiny corner of his awareness, a discrete pattern of sensation remained, a reality to hold onto, to save him—the feeling of the teleprobe's chair beneath him and against his back.

He sank farther into the maelstrom, saw it change to gray, become suddenly a tiny picture seen through the wrong end of a telescope. He saw a small boy holding the hand of a woman in a black dress. The two went into a hall-like room. Abruptly Eric no longer saw them from a distance but was again himself at age nine walking toward a casket. He sensed again the horrified fascination, heard his mother's sobs, the murmurous, meaningless voice sounds of a tall, thin undertaker. Then, there was the casket and in it a pale, waxed creature who looked somewhat like his father. As Eric watched, the face melted and became the face of his uncle Mark; and then another mask, his high-school geometry teacher. Eric thought, *We missed that one in my psychoanalysis.* He watched the mobile face in the coffin as it again shifted and became the professor who had taught him abnormal psychology, and then his own analyst, Dr. Lincoln Ordway, and then—he fought against this one—Dr. Carlos Amanti.

So that's the father image I've held all these years, he thought. *That means—That means I've never really given up searching for my father. A fine thing for an analyst to discover about himself!* He hesitated. *Why did I have to recognize that? I wonder if Pete went through this in his musikron?* Another part of his mind said. *Of course not. A person has to want to see inside himself or he never will, even if he has the opportunity.*

The other part of his mind abruptly seemed to reach up, seize control of his consciousness. His awareness of self lurched aside, became transformed into a mote whipping through his memories so rapidly he could barely distinguish between events.

Am I dying? he wondered. *Is it my life passing in review?*

The kaleidoscopic progression jerked to a stop before a vision of Colleen—the way he had seen her in his dream. The memory screen lurched to Pete. He saw the two people in a relationship to himself that he had never quite understood. They represented a catalyst, not good or evil, merely a reagent which set events in motion.

Suddenly, Eric sensed his awareness growing, permeating his body. He knew the condition and action of each gland, each muscle fiber, each nerve ending. He focused his inner eye on the grayness through which he had passed. Into the gray came a tendril of red—shifting, twisting, weaving past him. He followed the red line. A picture formed in his mind, growing there like the awakening from anaesthetic. He looked down a long street—dim in the spring dusk—at the lights of a jet car thundering toward him. The car grew larger, larger, the lights two hypnotic eyes. With the vision came a thought: *My, that's pretty!*

Frank Herbert

Involuntary reactions took over. He sensed muscles tensing, jumping aside, the hot blast of the jet car as it passed. A plaintive thought twisted into his mind: *Where am I? Where's Mama? Where's Bea?*

Tightness gripped Eric's stomach as he realized he sat in another's consciousness, saw through another's eyes, sensed through another's nerves. He jumped away from the experience, pulling out of the other mind as though he had touched a hot stove.

So that's how Pete knew so much, he thought. *Pete sat in his musikron and looked through our eyes.* Another thought: *What am I doing here?* He sensed the teleprobe chair beneath him, heard the new self within him say, "I'm going to need more trained, expert help."

He followed another red tendril, searching, discarded it; sought another. The orientation was peculiar—no precise up or down or compass points until he looked out of the other eyes. He came to rest finally behind two eyes that looked down from an open window in the fortieth story of an office building, sensed the suicidal thoughts building up pressure within this person. Gently, Eric touched the center of consciousness, seeking the name—Dr. Lincoln Ordway, psychoanalyst.

Eric thought, *Even now I turn back to my own analyst.*

Tensely, Eric retreated to a lower level of the other's consciousness, knowing that the slightest misstep would precipitate this man's death wish, a jump through that window. The lower levels suddenly erupted a pinwheel or coruscating purple light. The pinwheel slowed, became a mandala figure—at the four points of the figure an open window, a coffin, a transitus-tree and a human face which Eric suddenly recognized as a distorted picture of himself. The face was boyish, slightly vacant.

Eric thought, *The analyst, too, is tied to what he believes is his patient.* With the thought, he willed himself to move gently, unobtrusively into the image of himself, began to expand his area of dominion over the other's unconscious. He pushed a tentative thought against the almost palpable wall which represented Dr. Ordway's focus of consciousness: *Linc* (a whisper), *don't jump. Do you hear me, Linc? Don't jump. The city needs your help.*

With part of his mind, Eric realized that if the analyst sensed his mental privacy being invaded that realization could tip the balance, send the man plunging out the window. Another part of Eric's mind took that moment to render up a solution to why he needed this man and others like him: The patterns of insanity broadcast by Pete Serantis could only be counterbalanced by a rebroadcast of calmness and sanity.

Eric tensed, withdrew slightly as he felt the analyst move closer to the window. In the other's mind, he whispered, "Come away from the window. Come away—" Resistance! A white light expanded in Eric's thoughts, rejected him. He felt himself swimming out into the gray maelstrom, receding. A red tendril approached and with it a question, not of his own origin, lifted into his mind:

Eric? What is this thing?

Eric allowed the pattern of teleprobe development to siphon through his mind. He ended the pattern with an explanation of what was needed.

Thought: *Eric, how did the Syndrome miss you?*

Conditioning by long exposure to my own teleprobe; high resistance to unconscious distortion built up by that work.

Funny thing; I was about to dive out the window when I sensed your interference. It was something—the red tendril moved closer—*like this.*

They meshed completely.

"What now?" asked Dr. Ordway.

"We'll need as much trained help as we can find in the city. Others would censor out this experience below the threshold of consciousness."

"The influence of your teleprobe may quiet everybody."

"Yes, but if the machine is ever turned off, or if people go beyond its area of influence, they'd be back in the soup."

"We'll have to go in the back door of every unconscious in the city and put things in order!"

"Not just *this* city; every city where the musikron has been and every city where Serantis takes it until we can stop him."

"How did the musikron do this thing?"

Eric projected a mixed pattern of concepts and pictures: "The musikron pushed us deep down into the collective unconscious, dangled us there as long as we remained within its area of influence. (Picture of rope hanging down into swirls of fog.) Then the musikron was turned off. (Picture of knife cutting the rope, the end falling, falling into a swirling gray maelstrom.) Do you see it?"

"If we have to go down into that maelstrom after all these people, hadn't we better get started?"

He was a short man digging with his fingers in the soft loam of his flowerbed, staring vacantly at shredded leaves—name, Dr. Harold Marsh, psychologist. Unobtrusively, softly, they absorbed him into the network of the teleprobe.

She was a woman, dressed in a thin housecoat, preparing to leap from the end of a pier—name, Lois Voorhies, lay analyst. Swiftly, they drew her back to sanity.

Eric paused to follow a thin red tendril to the mind of a neighbor, saw through the other's eyes sanity returning around him.

Like ripples spreading in a pond, a semblance of sanity washed out across the city. Electric power returned; emergency services were restored.

The eyes of a clinical psychologist east of the city transmitted a view of a jet plane arrowing toward Clyde Field. Through the psychologist's mind the network picked up the radiating thought patterns of a woman—guilt, remorse, despair.

Colleen!

Hesitantly, the network extended a pseudopod of thought, reached into Colleen's consciousness and found terror. *What is happening to me!*

Eric took over. *Colleen, don't be afraid. This is Eric. We are getting things back*

Frank Herbert

in order thanks to you and the musikron plans. He projected the pattern of their accomplishments.

I don't understand. You're—

You don't have to understand now. Hesitantly: *I'm glad you came.*

Eric, I came as soon as I heard—when I realized you were right about Pete and the musikron. She paused. *We're coming down to land.*

Colleen's chartered plane settled onto the runway, rolled up to a hangar and was surrounded by National Guardsmen.

She sent out a thought: *We have to do something about London. Pete threatened to smash the musikron, to commit suicide. He tried to keep me there by force.*

When?

Six hours ago.

Has it been that long since the Syndrome hit?

The network moved in: *What is the nature of this man Serantis?*

Colleen and Eric merged thoughts to project Pete's personality.

The network: *He'll not commit suicide, or smash his machine. Too self-centered. He'll go into hiding. We'll find him soon enough when we need him—unless he's lynched first.*

Colleen interrupted: *This National Guard major won't let me leave the airport.*

Tell him you're a nurse assigned to Maynard Hospital.

Individual thought from the network: *I'll confirm from this end.*

Eric: *Hurry . . . darling. We need all of the help we can get from people resistant to the teleprobe.*

Thoughts from the network: *That's as good a rationalization as any. Every man to his own type of insanity. That's enought nonsense—let's get to work!* ■

The Bright Illusion

C. L. Moore

I especially like this story because, shortly after I started it, it took over and practically wrote itself. Also, it's one of my early stories which I frequently referred to in writing my later ones because it covers so many different areas of fantasy.

THROUGH THE BLINDING shimmer of sun upon sand, Dixon squinted painfully at the curious mirage ahead. He was reeling with thirst and heat and weariness, and about him the desert heaved in long, blurred waves, but through the haze upon the desert, he peered anxiously at the thing and could not make it out.

Nothing he had ever seen or heard of could cause such a mirage as this. It was a great oval of yellow light, bulging up convexly from the earth like some translucent golden egg half buried in the sand. And over its surface there seemed to be an immense busyness, as if it was covered with tiny, shimmering things that moved constantly. He had never seen anything remotely resembling it before.

As he toiled through the sand toward the bright illusion, he became aware of darker specks around it haphazardly, specks that as he approached took on the aspect of men grotesquely sprawled in attitudes of death. He could not make it out. Of course it was a mirage, yet it did not recede as he advanced, and the details of those sprawled bodies became clearer and clearer, and the great translucent oval loomed up against the sky mystifyingly.

He thought he must be dreaming, or perhaps a little unbalanced by the heat and thirst. He had been struggling through this burning sand under this burning sun for a long while now, and there were times when the rush of illusion swallowed him up, and he could hear water splashing and fountains tinkling in the empty desert about him. This must be a hallucination, then, for it could scarcely be a mirage. He was almost upon it, and it had so real a look—those bodies, sprawling—

He stumbled over the first, for somehow his muscles did not co-ordinate very well now. It was the sun-withered body of an old man in the Legion uniform, his kepi fallen forward over his face. The next was that of an Arab in a tangle of dirty white garments, and beyond him was the almost-fresh corpse of a boy in khaki shorts and sun helmet.

Dixon wondered dully what had happened to them and why the bodies were in such varying stages of decomposition. He lifted a dragging head and peered at the great egg-shaped thing bulging up from the sand. It reminded him of a huge bubble of golden water, save that bubbles were round, and—

Belatedly, caution returned to him. These dead men must have met their deaths somehow through the presence of the great egg. He had better advance more cautiously or— And then the pull seized him. He had come too near. Something inexorable and slow was dragging him forward—or was it that the great bubble was advancing toward him?

Sky and sand reeled. And the distance between him and the great egg-shaped thing lessened and lessened and—and somehow he found himself flat against a great golden translucency that shivered against him with the strangest motion, as if it was alive and hungry for—

He felt that he should be afraid, yet somehow he was not aware of fear at all. The golden light was closing over him and around him with a queer, engulfing motion. He shut his eyes and relaxed utterly in the impassive grip of the thing.

Dixon was lying motionless in the midst of a golden radiance that seemed crystal clear, yet so obstructed his vision that he could see only a few yards away, and the desert landscape outside was as unreal as a dream. The most delicious sensation of rest and well-being was surging through him in slow waves that succeeded one another like ripples on a shore, each leaving an increasing residue of serenity and luxurious comfort. Thirst and hunger and weariness had vanished in a breath. He knew no fear or anxiety. In a trancelike calm he lay there, feeling the waves flow through him unbroken, staring up into the lucid golden light without wonder or surprise.

How long he lay there he never knew. In the perfect peace of the glow enfolding him, he was very dimly aware that the all-penetrating waves were washing through him in a way which queerly suggested searching. They permeated every atom of him, flooding his brain with light and calmness.

In his tranced quiet he knew, without actually realizing, that memory in lightning flashes was reeling through his mind. Abstract memories of things he had learned in college and in afterlife. Snatches of literature, fragments of sciences. Mathematical problems solved in breathtaking speed and supplanted by chemical formulas that melted into the bits of psychology remembered from schooldays. Impassively he lay there, scarcely realizing the flashing reviews that passed through his light-flooded brain.

And then the tempo of the ripples that went over him began to change. His mind awoke by degrees from its pleasant coma, though his body still lay relaxed. And now the wavelets in the queerest way were beating upon his brain tantalizingly. Little fragments of thoughts not his own blew through his mind and faded.

He struggled to grasp them. He clutched at the vanishing tags, striving to weld them together, feeling obscurely that if he could retain each small flutter as it wavered through his mind, if he could put them together and fuse them in a unit, he might understand.

Very slowly he succeeded. Very slowly the waves as they flowed through him began to surrender their meanings to his clutching mind: meanings that solidified and amplified with each succeeding wave, building themselves up slowly as ripple after ripple washed serenely through the straining brain that was learning so painfully to comprehend their significance.

By degrees Dixon realized that some intelligence was striving to communicate with him. The knowledge did not come in words or even word forms introduced into his brain. But it came, slowly and inexorably, building up and up as wave after measured wave flowed through him and vanished, leaving a residue of knowledge to be increased by the next.

And the vast, the almost divine, impersonality of it staggered him. This being —intelligence, presence—was so utterly abstract a thing that even in the knowledge it imparted to him there was no hint of personality or consciousness of individual being. There could have been no "I" in its supervocabulary of thought ripples.

C. L. Moore

Divinely serene, divinely abstract, it allowed knowledge to flow through the brain of the man suspended in its heart. And by measured degrees that knowledge built itself up in his mind.

He had been chosen. For a long while this being had been waiting here, trapping the men who came near enough, sending its light waves in floods through their minds to illuminate their thoughts and their capacity for knowledge, probing their intelligences. All those others lying outside had been found wanting. The being had discarded them and waited, in its serene passivity, until the right man came by.

This much flowed through his brain. Then there was a hiatus, to permit him to absorb the knowledge, to understand. After a while the wavelets began to beat through him again in their measured slowness. He became aware of vast, dim voids, blank stretches empty of space or time or any of the myriad dimensions. He knew that through these, while long periods elapsed which yet had no relation to the time he understood, the great light-bubble had traveled from some origin unthinkably far away, on a quest. He realized that it had at last emerged from those gray, formless voids into the interstellar space of his own universe; that it had made its way here, driven by a vast purpose he could not grasp, and had come to rest upon the desert sands, to lie in wait.

Again there was a gap in the thought waves, and again Dixon lay still, assimilating that stunning knowledge. And yet, somehow, he was not greatly surprised or in the remotest way skeptical. He waited.

Presently the flow began again. There was, in another part of space, a world which this being desired—or no, not desired; there was nothing so human or personal a thing as desire about it. A world which it meant to have; a very alien world, he gathered, from the sort he knew. Peopled by alien creatures and built in other dimensions than those which formed his own universe.

These people worshiped a powerful god. And it was this worship—this godhood—which the being that enfolded him meant to possess. It tried to give him a glimpse of why, but the thought waves which flowed through his brain were incomprehensible and remote—not knowledge, but a jumble of unrelated impressions, without coherence. After a few vain attempts to instill the reason for its purpose into his mind, the being apparently dismissed the point as unnecessary and went on.

This god which it meant to dispossess was very powerful; so powerful that of itself the being could do nothing to overthrow it, could not even pass the barriers set up to guard the strange world. It had need of an intelligent, animate creature from a world different enough in structure so that the god's peculiar powers would have no effect upon him.

Gradually the measured beats made it clear to Dixon that he was the chosen envoy. He was to be transported there, armed in potent ways, sent out into the new world to overthrow the god's domain and make way for his sponsor to take possession.

There was a long hiatus after that. Dixon lay quiet, rather stunned by the magnitude of the thing. The being which engulfed him must have sensed the growing rebellion in his mind, for after a while the beats began again. And Dixon knew that the proposition was not a compulsory one. But—the knowledge followed casually through him—though he was free to be released and set back upon his journey if he refused the plan, he would inevitably die soon, die very unpleasantly.

There was no water within any possible reach, and a band of veiled Tuaregs was scouring the desert nearby in search of that Arab who lay in a huddle of dirty white robes outside the egg-shaped bubble. If he did not die of thirst before they caught him, he would die in a manner infinitely more undesirable at their hands. But, of course, if he so desired, he was free to go.

Dixon digested this information thoughtfully, hesitatingly, though he knew he had no choice. His blind stumbling through the desert could have no other end than slow death, as he had been aware even before he came upon the great bubble. And if there were Tuaregs near— Even in the bodily trance that cradled him he shuddered. He had seen victims of Tuareg tortures, miraculously alive after days and days of— He turned his mind from that. No; he had no choice.

And gradually a little spark of excitement began to burn in him. What an adventure! And though death might lie at the end of it, there was at least a hope for life, and he knew he had not even that if he refused. Consent was forming in his mind, but, even before it crystallized, the being must have known, for about him the lucid radiance suddenly began to cloud and change. Milkiness flooded through it and through his body and his brain. Oblivion swallowed him up.

When realization returned to Dixon it came slowly. Layer by layer the oblivion melted from his mind. He had a vague impression of vast spaces traversed and barriers surmounted, and somehow he sensed an indefinable difference in the space that surrounded the bubble, though it was indefinite how he knew it. A little beat quivered through him, and another, clearing away the fogs of his consciousness. Then knowledge began to pulse again through him in measured flow.

They had crossed gulfs greater than he could comprehend. They were suspended now above the world of their destination. He was to look briefly upon it, for even through the protecting walls of the light-bubble the thing that he would see was so alien to him that in his present form he could not bear to gaze upon it long.

Then the light about Dixon cleared to translucence, and somehow he was looking out and down upon a scene that stunned his eyes with its violence. He had an instant's impression of a land that shrieked and raved with maniacal color beyond any conception of color as he knew it. He turned his eyes wincingly away and stared down at the scene immediately below. And though in point of actual space it must have been very far away, he could see everything quite clearly and with a wider radius of vision than he was accustomed to. It was as if in one glance he encompassed the whole circle of the horizon.

The world below was one vast city that reeled away in terrace below crazy terrace out to a skyline that shimmered with white dazzle. And the colors that blazed and howled and agonized over the insane angles of the place turned him sick and dizzy. They were incredible angles and impossible colors, the tints and the tilts of madness—wild, staggering lines and arcs and jagged peaks, crazy inclines broken by ridges of eruptive color, zigzag bridges, buildings that leaned out in gravity-defying angles.

All these incredible terraces mounted up and up in diminishing arcs to the topmost tier of all. This was small and smooth, though over its pavement the insane colors sprawled blotchily. And in the very center a mighty column rose, blacker than any darkness he had ever seen before. On its height burned a pale flame.

But the inhabitants! Dixon could see them quite clearly despite the distance. They were sinuous and serpentine, and their motions were blurs of swiftness, poems of infinite grace. They were not men—they had never been men in any stage of their evolution. And if the colors of the buildings were agony to his eyes, the living, unstable hues that writhed and crawled over the beings below were so frightful that his gaze rebelled. For this reason he never knew just how they were shaped.

There was one standing just below the great black pillar whereon burned the flame, and of this he had the clearest view. It was boneless and writhing, livid with creeping color. Its single great eye, lucid and expressionless, stared from an unfeatured, mouthless face, half scarlet and half purple, between which two shades a wedge of nameless green broadened as he looked away.

He had seen this much before the pellucid crystal began to cloud about him once more and the slow knowledge began its beat through his brain. He must look no longer, or something disastrous might happen to his benumbed senses. He understood by now that it was not in his own form that he was to go out into the crazy land. He was sure, even without that seeping knowledge, that his own body could never endure the colors of the place, nor could his own material feet read the dizzy angles. Many of the streets and bridges were too steep for human feet to walk.

And he was understanding, as the slow waves flowed on, how different these people were from his own kind. Not only in appearance; their very substance was different from flesh and blood, the atoms arranged in different patterns. They obtained nourishment in an incomprehensible way from some source he could not understand. Their emotions and habits and purposes were alien to all his experience, and among them even the sexes were not those he knew. They were more numerous than mankind's two, and their functions were entirely different. Reproduction here was based on an utterly alien principle.

When the pause came in the waves of knowledge, Dixon was a little dizzy with the complete strangeness of this place and with wonder how he would be enabled to enter it. He lay still, wondering, until the flow began again.

Then the knowledge of the way he was to be introduced into the strange god's domain began to surge in deliberate beats through his brain. It seemed simple, yet the magnitude of it was staggering. A sort of veil of illusion was to be dropped between him and these alien beings. To them, his form would seem one of their own. Through the veil his speech would be filtered and changed into their indescribable mode of communication. And to him they would have the appearance of humanity, their speech would be understandable, their curious emotions translated into familiarity.

Even their multiple sexes would be resolved arbitrarily into two. For though this being could not approach any nearer the strange god whose flame burned upon the pillar, it seemed to have immense power even from this distance in the crazy world below.

The slow-beating waves made him aware that during his sojourn in the strange place he would be guided and in a measure protected, and that his knowledge would still flow through his brain. All this was possible, he understood, because of his own complete difference from anything in this world—such a difference from anything in this world—such a difference that he would not cause even a ripple upon the surface of the god's consciousness until the time came for his overthrow.

Then again the cloudiness began to clear, until Dixon was looking out through crystal walls upon that reeling city below. For an instant it shuddered with mad colors before his aching eyes. And then over the whole crazy panorama the queerest blurring came. He looked down upon a changing world wherein the wild colors faded and ran together and the staggering angles of that mighty vista below were obscured in structural changes whose purpose he began to understand.

Before his eyes a splendid and stately city was taking shape. Out of the ruin of eye-wrenching color rose tier beyond tier of white pillars and translucent domes. Roofs of alabaster formed themselves under a sky whose pallor was deepening into blue.

When he tore his eyes away from that magnificent vista, terrace dropping away below terrace, crowned with domes and spires and columns wreathed in green, far out to the distant horizon, he saw that over the crowded streets with their swarms of multicolored horrors a stranger change was falling. Out of the mingling indistinctnesses of those colors without name, the semblance of humanity grew. People of noble stature and stately bearing, robed in garments of shining steel, took form before its eyes.

In less time than it takes to tell, a metropolis of familiar aspect stretched invitingly under his gaze. That nightmare of colors was gone as a nightmare goes, leaving no faintest trace behind. Yet he knew as he looked down that in reality nothing was changed. The writhing people still flashed with infinite speed and grace through tiptilted streets of gravity-defying angles. He blinked and looked again, but the illusion held steady—a stupendous city, smiling under a blue, familiar sky.

Slowly through his consciousness beat the realization that, once down there in the metamorphosed world, he must search out the temple of the god, find its vulnerable spot, provide as it were a window, so that through his eyes the being which had brought him here could see its enemy's weakness and instruct Dixon further. And it was impressed upon him, too, that all possible speed must be made, for though there was little danger that the god would realize the inimical presence, yet his very safeguard was his greatest danger. Dixon was so alien to the ultimate particles of his being that, though this protected him from the god, it made his maintenance in the strange world very difficult. It was a strain even upon the vast powers of the light-bubble being to keep that veil of illusion stretched protectingly between him and this world, the very sight and touch of which would send him mad if he was exposed to it long unguarded.

There was a little pause after this, and Dixon lay still, awed by the unthinkable difference between his own structure of mind and body and that of the strange place and people below. Then with breathtaking abruptness, darkness dropped over him. One instant he lay serenely cradled in golden radiance, the next he was dropping through blackness with a queer, high scream in his ears as if he fell through some resisting atmosphere which was not air. Physically he was protected, but he could hear the thin sound of it in varying intensities.

And then without warning the darkness broke, and he found his feet upon solid ground without any hint of jar. He was simply standing upon a marble pavement under a clear blue sky and looking out over a breath-stopping vista of world-city, dropping away in terrace below shining terrace to a distant skyline, out and away in broadening tiers. Light shimmered dazzlingly upon faraway steel figures moving through the streets below, away and away until they were no more than tiny pinpricks of shimmer on the horizon's edge. From each broad circular terrace a marble ramp led down to the next beneath, and over these the steel-bright people were swarming in busy hordes.

And Dixon knew, even as he stared with caught breath at the magnificence of it, that in reality he stood at the apex of a city of madness that reeled away below him in tier after crazy tier, a nightmare of meaningless angles and raving color, through whose streets things writhing and dreadful and acrawl with living hues were flashing with movements of blurring speed. All this splendor was a veil across his eyes. What unknowable activities were really taking place below? On what nameless errands were these busy crowds bound? Then a little sound at his side turned him from the dizzy thoughts tormenting his brain, and he flashed an abrupt glance sidewise, alert for danger. Then he caught his breath and stared.

She was slim as a sword blade in her steel robe, standing under the mighty tower of the black pillar, and she was lovelier than a dream. Her hair swung in black page-boy curls to her shoulders, and from under the darkness of it eyes as blue as steel met his unwaveringly. She was all bright metal to his first glance, steel-molded curves of her under the armored robe, steel lights upon her burnished hair, steel-bright eyes shining. All steel and brightness—but Dixon saw that her mouth was soft and colored like hot embers. And for an instant he wanted to burst into crazy song. It was an inexplicable feeling that he had never known before, a heady delight in being alive. But even through the exultation, he knew that he looked upon an illusion. He knew that she was a faceless, crawling thing, without sex, without any remotest kinship to anything he knew. And yet this illusion was very lovely and—

She was looking up at him with startled eyes, and now she spoke, a little breathlessly, in a sweet, tinkling voice. "You—you have come? Oh, whence have you come?" And he thought that she was striving hard not to believe something which she wanted with all her soul to think true.

There was no answer he could give. He glanced around helplessly at the blue, empty sky, at the great pillar rising behind her, at the pale flame burning so steadily upon its summit. The blaze held him for an instant, and in the instant he stood with eyes uplifted the girl must have thought she had her answer, for she caught her breath in a gasp that was half a sob, and in one swift motion she fell to her knees before him, a miracle of sliding grace in that close gown of steel, so that the light rippled all down her sweet, slim body and lay bluely on the wings of her hair that swung forward as she bent her head.

"I knew it! I knew!" she breathed. "I knew my god would send you! Oh, praise great IL, who has sent me such an envoy!"

Dixon looked down upon the bent black head, his eyes troubled. If she believed him a messenger from the god, it would simplify his task enormously. And yet . . . He had entertained no scruples about displacing the god of a maniacal world peopled with writhing monstrosities, but this was different, somehow. This girl . . .

"I am the high priestess of our god," she murmured, as if in answer to his half-formed query. "I have served IL with all my heart for many cycles now, but only he knows who I have prayed for the coming of an envoy among us. Such honor is enough to—to—" The sweet voice choked suddenly on a sob, as if the answer to her prayer was too much for her to endure unmoved.

Dixon bent and took her chin in his hand, lifting her face to his. The steel-bright eyes were dazzling with diffused tears. The red mouth trembled. She was looking up at him with awe and worship upon her face, and suddenly he knew that he wanted no worship from her. He resented that look of respect and awe. He wanted—well, he wanted her to see a man, not a divine messenger. He wanted to—

Then the queerest madness came over him, deliciously—and he acted. He stooped swiftly and set his lips over the trembling red lips of the girl, and for an instant the whole strange world reeled and swam in a heady pleasure like nothing he had ever known before.

When he straightened and stood looking down upon her, she met his eyes with purest bewilderment in hers, one hand hovering at her lips and incomprehension radiant in every line of her. Her blue gaze was traveling over him from head to foot in swift, puzzled glances.

And the realization swept back upon him tremendously. To her he wore the writhing shape that was hers in reality. That troubled blue gaze was the gaze of a single pale eye which traveled over the crawling limbs of a monster. He was not even sure that, to her, kneeling denoted homage and wondered in what alien way she was actually expressing her awe.

It was an uncanny feeling which was to haunt him through all his hours here—the knowledge that what he looked upon was unreal, the wonder as to what was actually taking place behind the mask of humanity which only he could see. That kiss—how had it seemed to her? What nameless gesture had he seemed to perform before her eyes—her eye? For he had kissed a monstrosity that had no mouth. Remembering the

C. L. Moore

glimpse he had caught of a one-eyed, featureless face crawling with alive colors, he shuddered and turned back to the kneeling girl as if for reassurance.

Dixon was aware of a curious emptiness within him because of this beauty which was only an illusion—had never been, would never be. He was looking straight into her steel-blue eyes now, and she was smiling very tremulously and with that puzzled look still upon her face. He could see the little shimmering tumult her heart made under the dazzle of her robe. And she was not even female. He narrowed his eyes and strove to pierce the mirage for a moment; to convince himself that here knelt a colored horror of sinuosity and sexlessness. And everything within him cried out protestingly. She was human—she was lovely—she was everything desirable and sweet. And she did not even exist save as a crawling horror upon whom in her normal guise he could never dare to look.

Then, as if to refute that, she flashed up at him a small, uncertain smile which made her so unmistakably human and sweet that he disbelieved everything but her own reality, and she said, "What—what was the meaning of that, O divine envoy?"

He frowned. "You are to call me Dixon," he said. "And that was—well, just a form of greeting."

"The way they greet one another in great IL's domain—in Paradise? Then . . ." She rose in one swift motion. Before he realized what was happening she had risen upon her sandaled toes and her warm mouth was brushing his. "Then I return your greeting, O Dixon."

Involuntarily his arms closed around her. Her body was firm and soft and warm in his clasp—the body of a living human girl, a mirage more real than reality. And again he wondered what nameless rites she was actually performing behind the illusory veil which masked her real, writhing self. And because she felt so pleasant in his arms he released her abruptly and stepped back, knowing the first quickening of uneasiness. Good heaven, could it be possible for a man to fall in love with a hallucination?

She looked up at him serenely, evidently feeling that she had mastered a difficult point of divine etiquette.

"How pleasant a thing is this new way of greeting!" she murmured, half to herself. "And now, O Dixon, you have but to command me in all things. What would you in IL's world-city?"

Dixon debated swiftly with himself. After all, lovely though she seemed, she was—and he must bear this in mind constantly, lest something dangerous befall—she was a sinuous, faceless thing, a creeping horror with the tints of an incredible spectrum. She was no more than this, and he must find his way, by her help, into the god IL's temple and let the light-being look through his eyes so that he might find IL's vulnerable spot. After that—well, he must do as he was commanded. IL would be overthrown, his own sponsor would usurp the godship, and that would be all. As for these beings which peopled the world, no doubt the change of gods would be a startling thing, but there was no help for it. He had but to perform his own part and then go.

"O Dixon!" the sweet, light voice of the girl broke in upon his thoughts. "O

Dixon, would you see how IL's temple is kept by his worshipers? Would you see how devoutly his world adores him?''

"Yes," said Dixon thankfully. "You may lead me to IL's temple."

She genuflected again, a poem of grace in that steel gown along which the light slid in long lines as she moved, and the dark hair swung forward about her face. Then she turned and crossed the terrace toward a ramp which led down into the city. They went down the slope of it—what eye-tormenting angles of spanning actually led downward he could not even guess—and emerged upon a broad street lined with pillared buildings. There were throngs of steel-robed people here who parted in devout rows as the priestess came down the ramp.

She paused at the head of the street and lifted her arms, and Dixon heard her voice ringing clearly over the crowd. "Great IL has answered our prayers at last," she cried. "He has sent an envoy from his own divinity. Here is the messenger from our god!"

A murmur went over the crowd—a murmur of awe and rejoicing. And then they knelt in long, sinuous rows as if a wind had blown across a field of sword blades. And with incredible swiftness the whisper ran back along the street, from mouth to mouth. He imagined it rippling out and out, down and down, from terrace to terrace, until it reached the ultimate limits of the whole tiered world.

They stepped down among the kneeling throngs, walking a lane of steel worshipers, and by the time they had reached the end of the street Dixon could see flecks of light far away below hurrying upward as the news spread. Up through the pillared streets and the green terraces they came swarming, men and women in robes of linked metal, with intent, awe-struck faces upturned. Dixon moved on with a long stride, a divine messenger from a god marching in triumph through a city without ends or boundaries, for as far as he could see the steel flecks that were people flashed up through the buildings below. And their multitudes were breathtaking. The whole vast city swarmed with living steel as wave after wave of armored people rolled upward toward the heights. His brain reeled with the numbers of them.

Over the bowed heads of the throngs as they advanced, Dixon glanced curiously at the buildings which lined the streets, casting about for some clue to the sort of life those people led. He found nothing. The marble pillars and walls rose as blankly as stage sets along the streets. A mask had been set for him over the realities of the place, but it was not a living mask. There were no shops, no markets, no residences, Rows of noncommittal pillars faced him blankly, betraying no secrets. Apparently the light-being had been unable to do more than mask the strangeness of this world. It could not infuse into it the spirit of a daily life so utterly alien as man's.

They went on through the dead-faced streets, down another ramp, and always the people dropped to their knees, perfectly the illusion of humanity. What, he wondered, were they actually doing? In what weird, incredible way were they really expressing their devotion? It was, of course, better not to know.

Dixon watched the girl before him walking proudly and lightly through the homage-stricken throngs, her dark head high, the steel robe rippling over the loveliness of her body as she moved. Presently she paused for him, smiling over her shoulder in a way that made his heart quicken, and turned in under the great arch of a doorway.

It was not a particularly imposing structure; no more than a marble-columned building with a huge dark portal. But, once inside, Dixon stopped in stunned astonishment in the vastness spread out before him.

It must have occupied the whole interior of all the terraces above—a mighty dome about which the building and streets overhead were the merest shell. In the dimness he could not descry the limits of it, but he saw that the whole vast temple was built in the shape of a great dome. For temple it must be. He knew that instinctively. There was the shadow of divinity in it, somehow—a vast calm. And for an instant, as he stared about the great place, he forgot even the presence of the girl at his side.

In the very center of the wide, dark floor lay a pool of pale radiance which somehow gave the impression that it seethed and boiled, though its surface lay untroubled under the lofty dome of the roof. And above the pool the ceiling was shaped like a burning lens to gather and concentrate the radiance arising from it. This centered at the apex of the roof in a dazzle of light at which he could not look directly. He realized that the center of this burning brilliance must be just under the pillar which crowned the topmost terrace—the pillar upon which burned the flame of IL.

Beyond the column of light rising from the pool, Dixon saw dimly in the gloom of the great temple the glimmer of steel robes. There was an arch in the far wall, so distant he could scarcely make it out, and in this doorway a small steel figure stood. As he watched, the sonorous boom of a gong rang through the dimness. The air trembled with sound, and through the shaking twilight the figure stepped out resolutely, crossing the floor with even, unhurried strides. He could not tell at the distance if it was man or woman, but it approached the radiant pool with, somehow, a sort of restrained eagerness that he was at a loss to understand. It reached the brink and did not pause. The haze of light rising from the pool swallowed it without a flicker. And the great dome was empty again save for themselves.

Dixon turned, awe-struck, to the girl, questions hovering on his mouth. Just in time he remembered his role and rephrased the query: "And how do you interpret this, priestess?"

She smiled up at him bewilderingly. It irritated him that his heart made that odd little leap whenever she smiled so, and he missed the first of her answer in watching the way her lips moved to frame the words she spoke.

". . . continually, at every beat of the signal," she was saying, "so that there is never an interval through all time when one of us has not completed his cycles and is ready to return into the flame." The gong sounded above her light voice. "See? Here comes another. And for countless ages it has been so, for our numbers are great enough so that the stream of voluntary sacrifices need never falter. So we nourish IL's flame and keep it burning."

Dixon said nothing. His eyes were upon her, but the bright illusion was swimming curiously in a mist that was closing down over him, and he was becoming aware of a strange pulsing of his own blood, as if—yes, as if familiar waves of knowledge were beginning their beat through his receptive brain. For a timeless interval he stood rigid, receiving that intelligence, feeling all he had seen and heard draining out of him into the vast reservoir of knowledge which was the light-being, feeling the voiceless commands of it flowing in. Ripple after ripple of the incoming tide rose in his brain. And gradually, in measured beats, he learned that this pool was the source of the pale flame burning upon the pillar, but that it was not essentially a part of it. The god IL drew his power from the dissolving lives of those people who sacrificed themselves—and this was the only way to destroy them, for they could not die otherwise—but IL was not present in the pool. IL was the flame on the column, no more, feeding upon the reflection from below. And if the rising light could be cut off temporarily IL's power would fail at its source. The invader could make an entrance and fight it out with him.

And now for an instant all the thought flow ceased; then in sharply clear ripples of intense emphasis came the syllables of a word. It was a word without meaning to Dixon, a word whose very sounds were unlike those of any language that man speaks. But he knew that he must speak it, and that the cadences of the sound would somehow open the way for the light-being to enter. With the impression of that word upon him the ripples ceased. A profound quiet reigned in his mind.

Out of that quiet the great domed temple slowly took form about him again. He heard the gong notes trembling through the air and saw another steel-robed figure pacing toward the pool. He turned his head and looked down into the high priestess's face at his shoulder. He had only to speak the word now and accomplish IL's overthrow—and then leave. Leave her—never see her again, except perhaps in dreams.

Her eyes met his with a little kindling under the blueness of them, and her mouth trembled into a smile as she met his gaze. She had the look of one eager and taut and waiting, and there was perfect faith in her eyes. And in that instant he knew he could not betray it.

"No," he murmured aloud. "No, my dear; I can't—I simply can't do it!"

Her brows drew together in exquisite bewilderment. "Do what?" she asked in a light whisper, to match his own lowered tone. "Do what?" But somehow the answer seemed not to interest her, for she did not pause for a reply. She had met his eyes and was staring up in a sort of dazed surprise, her blue gaze plunging into his with rigid intensity. And slowly she began to speak, in a tiny, breathless murmur. "I think . . . I think I see, O Dixon, the strangest things . . . in your eyes. Dreadful things and shapes without meaning . . . and something like a veil between us . . . Dixon . . . nothing is clear . . . and yet—and yet, Dixon, my own face is looking back at me out of your eyes."

He caught his breath suddenly in a painful gasp, and in one involuntary motion he had her in his arms. She clung to him blindly. He could feel the trembling that shivered through her steel-sheathed body, and her heart's pounding shook them both.

C. L. Moore

"I am afraid, Dixon—I am afraid!" she wailed softly. "What is it that frightens me so, Dixon?"

He did not answer. There was no answer. But he hugged her close and felt the sweet firmness of her body against his and knew helplessly that he loved the illusion that was herself and would always love it.

Dixon was frightened, too; frightened at the depth of the emotion that shook him, for he was remembering the clinging of her soft mouth to his, and how beautifully her body curved under the embrace of her metal robe, and that the loveliness which filled his arms and his heart was no more than an illusion to mask something so grotesque that he could never bear to look upon it unmasked. Lovely body, lovely face, sweet, warm mouth upon his—was this all? Could love rise from no more than a scrap of beautifully shaped flesh? Could any man love more than that with such intensity as shook him now?

He loosed her from one arm and set his finger under her chin, lifting her face to his. Her eyes met his own, blue and puzzled and afraid, and shining with something very splendid which all but blotted out her bewilderment and her terror.

"I love you," he murmured. "I don't care—I love you."

"Love?" she echoed in her light whisper. "Love?" And he saw in her eyes that the word had no meaning for her.

The room reeled about him for an instant. Somehow he had never thought of that. Knowing as he did of the immense gulf between them and the strangeness of the emotions which swayed these creatures of such alien race, yet it had not occurred to him that anywhere throughout the cosmos where living beings dwelt there could be a species to which love had no meaning. Was she, then, incapable of feeling it? Good heaven, was he doomed to love an empty body, soulless, the mirage masking a sexless being who could not return any emotion he knew?

He looked down and saw the diffused radiance behind her eyes, shining and very tender, and the bewilderment upon her face, and he thought, somehow, that he was hovering on the very brink of something vaster than anything he had ever known before—an idea too splendid to be grasped. Yet when he looked down into her eyes he thought he understood—almost—

Suddenly all about him the world trembled. It was as if the whole vast place were the reflection in a pool, and a ripple had passed blurringly over the surface. Then everything righted itself. But he understood. He had been here too long. The veil between him and this alien world was wearing thin.

"No—I *can't* go!" he groaned and gripped the girl closer in his arms.

He must have spoken aloud, for he felt her stir against him and heard her anxious voice. "Go? O Dixon, Dixon—take me with you! Don't leave me, Dixon!"

Some fantastic hope flowered suddenly within him. "Why not?" he demanded. "Why not? Tell me!" And he shook her a little in his urgency.

"I don't know," she faltered. "I only know that—that—O Dixon, that I shall be so lonely when you have gone. Take me—please take me!"

The Bright Illusion

"Why?" he demanded inexorably. For he thought now that he was hovering very near the understanding of the vast and splendid thing which had almost dawned upon him before the world shook.

"Because I . . . because . . . I don't understand it, Dixon, I can't tell you why—I haven't the words. But since you came I—is it that I have been waiting for you always? For I never knew until you came how lonely I had been. And I cannot let you go without me. O Dixon, is this what you call love?"

There was pain in her voice and in her veiled eyes. And the thought came to him that love was like an infectious germ, spreading pain wherever it rooted itself. Had he brought it to her—infected her, too, with the hopeless passion he knew? For it was wildly hopeless. In a moment or so he must leave this alien place forever, and no power existent could maintain very long the illusion veil through which they knew love.

Could his own new love for her endure the sight of her real self? And what would happen to this strange flowering of an emotion nameless and unknown to her—her love for him? Could it bear the look of his human shape, unmasked? And yet, he asked himself desperately, could a love as deep and sincere as the love he bore her be so transient a thing that he could not endure the sight of her in another guise? Could—

Again that queer flickering flashed over the world. Dixon felt the ground underfoot tilt dangerously, and for a moment insane colors stabbed at his eyes and the whole room reeled and staggered. Then it was still again. He had scarcely noticed. He swung her around to face him, gripping her shoulders and staring down compellingly into her eyes.

"Listen!" he said rapidly, for he knew his time was limited now, perhaps to seconds. "Listen! Have you any idea what you are asking?"

"Only to go with you," she said. "To be with you, wherever you are. And if you are indeed IL's messenger—perhaps a part of his godhead—then shall I enter the flame and give myself to IL? In that way can I join you and be one with you?"

He shook his head. "I am not from IL. I have been sent to destroy him. I'm a man from a world so different from yours that you could never bear to look upon me in my real form. You see me as an illusion, just as I see you. And I must go back to my own world now—alone."

Her eyes were dizzy with trying to understand.

"You are—not from IL? Not as you seem? Another world? Oh, but take me with you! I must go—I must!"

"But, my dearest, I can't. Don't you understand? You couldn't live an instant in my world—nor I much longer in yours."

"Then I will die," she said calmly. "I will enter the flame and wait for you in death. I will wait forever."

"My darling, not even that." He said it gently. "Not even in death can we be

C. L. Moore

together. For when you die you go back to IL, and I go—I go—back to another god, perhaps. I don't know. But not to IL."

She stood, blank-eyed, in his grasp, trying to force her mind into the incredible belief. When she spoke, the words came slowly, as if her thoughts were speaking aloud.

"I don't understand," she said. "But I know . . . you speak the truth. If I die by the flame—in the only way there is for me to die—we are parted forever. I can't! I won't! I will not let you go! Listen to me—" and her voice dropped to a soft whisper—"you say you came to destroy IL? Why?"

"As the envoy of another god, who would take his place."

"I have given my whole life to the worship of IL," she murmured to herself, very gently. And then, in a stronger voice: "But destroy him, Dixon! There may be a chance that way—there is none now. Oh, I may be a traitor—worse than a traitor. There is no word to describe one who betrays his god into destruction, no word terrible enough. But I would do it—yes, gladly, now. Destroy him, and let me seek another death somewhere, somehow—let me die as you die. Perhaps your god can release me into your sort of death, and I can wait for you there until you come. Oh, Dixon, please!"

The idea was a staggering one, but for a wild moment Dixon knew hope again. Might it not be that—that—

Quite suddenly he understood. He looked down on the loveliness of her with unseeing eyes. In these past few moments of insanity, learning that she loved him, too, enough that she begged death of him if in that way they might be united, in these few moments he came to realize that the flesh meant nothing. It was not her body he loved. And a great relief flooded him, to be sure that—sure that it was not merely infatuation, or desire for the loveliness which did not exist save as a mirage before his eyes. No, it was love, truly and completely, despite the shape she wore, despite the nameless sex that was hers. Love for herself—the essential self, however deeply buried beneath whatever terrible guise. And though her very substance was alien to him, and though no creature in all her ancestry had ever known love before, she loved him. Nothing else mattered.

And then without warning the great dome before him wavered and contorted into impossible angles, like the reflections in a flawed mirror. And Dixon felt the firm curved body in his arms melting fluidly into a different form and texture. It squirmed . . .

He stood at the entrance to a mighty room that staggered with frantic color, reeling with eye-stunning angles and incredible planes. And in his arms— He looked down. He clasped a creature at which he could not bear to look directly, a thing whose wild-looped limbs and sinuous body rippled and crawled with the moving tints of madness. It was slippery and horrible to the touch, and from the midst of a shifting, featureless face a great lucid eye stared up at him with desperate horror, as if it was looking upon something so frightful that the very sight was enough to unseat its reason.

Dixon closed his eyes after that one revolting glimpse, but he had seen in the eye upturned to him enough of dawning comprehension to be sure it was she whom he held. And he thought that despite the utter strangeness of that one staring eye there was somewhere in the clarity of it, and the steadfastness, a glimmer of the innermost spark which was the being he loved—that spark which had looked from the blue gaze he had seen in its human shape. With that inner spark of life she was the same.

He tightened his grip upon her—or it—though his flesh crept at the contact and he knew that the feel was as revolting to it as to himself, and looked out over that shallow, color-stained head upon the vast room before him. His eyes throbbed savagely from those fierce colors never meant for human eyes to see. And though the creature in his arms hung acquiescent, he knew the effort it must cost to preserve that calm.

A lump rose in his throat as he realized the significance of that—such utter faith in him, though he wore a shape terrible enough to bring the fear of madness into that great lucid eye when it rested upon him. But he knew he could not stand there long and retain his own sanity. Already the colors were raving almost audibly through his brain, and the ground heaved underfoot, and he was sure that neither of them could endure much more of this. So he gripped the dreadful thing which housed the being he loved, and almost of itself he felt that incredibly alien word rip itself from his lips.

It was not a word to be set down in any written characters. Its sound to his ears was vague and indeterminate, like a whisper heard over too great distances to have any form. But the moment it left his lips he felt a vast, imponderable shifting in the substance of the temple. And, like a shutter's closing, the room went black. Dixon gave one involuntary sob of relief as the maniacal colors ceased their assault upon his brain, and he felt the dreadful thing in his arms go rigid in the utter blackness. For a moment everything was still as death.

And then through the dark around them a tiny shiver ran, the least little stir of motion, the thinnest thread of sound. It pierced Dixon's very eardrums and shuddered thrillingly along his nerves. And with incredible swiftness that tiny stirring and that infinitesimal sound grew and swelled and ballooned into a maelstrom of rushing tumult, louder and louder, shriller and shriller. Around them in the blackness swooped and stormed the sounds of a mightier conflict than any living man could ever have heard before—a battle of gods, invisible to the blackness of utter void.

That stunning uproar mounted and intensified until he thought his head would burst with the infinite sound of it, and forces beyond comprehension stormed through the air. The floor seemed to dissolve under him, and space whirled in the dark so that he was conscious of neither up nor down. The air raved and shrieked. Blind and deafened and stunned by the magnitude of the conflict, Dixon hugged his dreadful burden and waited.

How long it went on he never knew. He was trying to think as the turmoil raged around his head, trying to guess what would come next; if the light-being in its victory could unite them in any way, in life or in death. He could think of that quite calmly now, death and union. For life without her, he knew unquestioningly, would be a sort of living death, alone and waiting. Living was where she was, and if she were dead, then life lay only in death for him. His head reeled with the wild wonderings and with the noise of battle raving about them both. For eternities, it seemed to him, the whole universe was a maelstrom, insanity shrieked in his ears, and all the powers of darkness swooped and screamed through the void about him. But, after an endless while, very gradually he began to realize that the tumult was abating. The roaring in his ears faded slowly; the wild forces storming through the dark diminished. By infinite degree the uproar died away. Presently again the stillness of death descended through the blackness upon the two who waited.

There was a long interval of silence, nerve-racking, ear-tormenting. And then, at long last, out of that darkness and silence spoke a voice, vast and bodiless and serene. And it was not the voice of the light-being. It spoke audibly in Dixon's brain, not in words, but in some nameless speech which used instead of syllables some series of thought forms that were intelligible to him.

"My chosen priestess," said the voice passionlessly, "so you would have had me destroyed?"

Dixon felt the convulsive start of the creature in his arms and realized dimly that the same worldless speech, then, was intelligible to them both. He realized that only vaguely, with one corner of his mind, for he was stunned and overwhelmed with the realization that it must be the god IL speaking—that his own sponsor had been overcome.

"And you, Dixon," the voice went on evenly, "sent by my enemy to open the way. You are a very alien creature, Dixon. Only by the power I wrested from that being which assaulted me can I perceive you at all, and your mind is a chaos to me. What spell have you cast over my chosen priestess, so that she no longer obeys me?"

"Have you never heard of love?" demanded Dixon aloud.

The query faded into the thick darkness without an echo, and a profound stillness followed in its wake. He stood in the blind dark and utter silence, clutching his love, waiting. Out of that quiet the god-voice came at last:

"Love"—in a musing murmur. "Love—no! there is no such thing in all my universe. What is it?"

Dixon stood helpless, mutely trying to frame an answer. For who can define love? He groped for the thought forms, and very stumblingly he tried to explain, knowing as he did so that it was as much for the benefit of her he held in his arms as for the god, because although she loved, she could not know the meaning of love, or what it meant to him. When he had ceased, the silence fell again heavily.

At last IL said, "So—the reigning principle of your own system and dimension. I understand that much. But there is no such thing here. Why should it concern you? Love is a thing between the two sexes of your own race. This priestess of mine is of another sex than those you understand. There can be no such thing as this love between you."

"Yet I saw her first in the form of a woman," said Dixon. "And I love her."

"You love the image."

"At first it may be that I did. But now—no; there's much more of it than that. We may be alien to the very atoms. Our minds may be alien, and all our thoughts, and even our souls. But, after all, alien though we are, that alienage is of superficial things. Stripped down to the barest elemental beginning, we have one kinship—we share life. We are individually alive, animate, freewilled. Somewhere at the very core of our beings is the one vital spark of life, which in the last analysis is *self*, and with that one spark we love each other."

The deepest silence fell again when he had ended—a silence of the innermost brain. Out of it at last IL said, "And you, my priestess? What do you say? Do you love him?"

Dixon felt the shape in his arms shudder uncontrollably. She—he could not think of her as "it"—stood in the very presence of her god, heard him address her in the black blindness of his presence, and the awe and terror of it was almost enough to shake her brain. But after a moment she answered in a small, faltering murmur, the very ghost of a reply, and in some curious mode of speech which was neither vocal nor entirely thought transfer. "I—I do not know that word, O mighty IL. I know only that there is no living for me outside his presence. I would have betrayed your godhead to free me, so that I might die in his way of death, and meet him again beyond—if there can be any beyond for us. I would do all this again without any hesitation if the choice was given me. If this is what you call love—yes; I love him."

"He is," said IL, "a creature of another race and world and dimension. You have seen his real form, and you know."

"I do not understand that," said the priestess in a surer voice. "I know nothing except that I cannot—will not live without him. It is not his body I . . . love, nor do I know what it is which commands me so. I know only that I do love him."

"And I you," said Dixon. It was a very strange sensation to be addressing her thus, from brain to brain. "The sight of you was dreadful to me, and I know how I must have looked to you. But the shock of that sight has taught me something. I know now. The shape you wear and the shape you seemed to wear before I saw you in reality are both illusions, both no more than garments which clothe that . . . that living, vital entity which is yourself—the real you. And your body does not matter to me now, for I know that it is no more than a mirage."

"Yes," she murmured. "Yes, I understand. You are right. The bodies do not matter now. It goes so much deeper than that."

"And what," broke in the voice of IL, "is your solution of this problem?"

It was Dixon who broke the silence that fell in mute answer to the query. "There can be no such thing as union for us anywhere in life. In death, perhaps—but I do not know. Do you?"

"No," said IL surprisingly.

"You—you do not? You, a god?"

"No. I have taken these beings who worship me back into the flame. The energy which was theirs in life supports me—but something escapes. I do not know what. Something too intangible even for me to guess at. No—I am a god, and I do not know what comes after death.''

Dixon pondered that for a long while. There was an implication in it somewhere which gave him hope, but his brain was so dazed he could not grasp it. At last the light broke, and he said joyfully, ''Then—why, then you cannot keep us apart! We can die and be free.''

''Yes. I have no hold over you. Even if I would wreak vengeance upon you for your part in my betrayal, I could not. For death will release you into—I do not know what. But it will be release.''

Dixon swallowed hard. Half-doubts and hesitations crowded his mind, but he heard his own voice saying steadily, ''Will you do that for us—release us?''

In the silence as he waited for an answer he was trying to realize that he stood on the threshold of death; trying to understand, his mind probing ahead eagerly for the answer which might lie beyond. And in the timeless moment he waited he was very sure, for whatever lay ahead could not be extinction and surely not separation. This was the beginning; surely it could not end so soon, unfulfilled, all the questions unanswered.

No; this love which linked them, two beings so alien, could not flicker out with their lives. It was too great—too splendid, far too strong. He was no longer uncertain, no longer afraid, and hope began to torment him exquisitely. What lay beyond? What vast existences? What starry adventures, together? Almost impatiently he poised on the brink of death.

Through this IL's voice spoke with a vast, passionless calm. ''Die, then,'' said IL.

For an instant the darkness lay unbroken about them. Then a little flicker ran indescribably through it. The air shook for a breathless moment.

And IL was alone. ∎

The Mechanic
Hal Clement

Science fiction is not prophesy. Its fun lies in finding new and surprising ways to look at ourselves and the world. Nevertheless, some of us like to feel that what we tell might possibly happen. Whenever we learn that the curtain seems to be rising on a brand new stage in the theater of human knowledge, we feel the temptation to write a few plays.

Astronomy was my first love, chemistry my second—both amply demonstrated by my obvious leaning toward space opera. However, when DNA and RNA were established as the carrier molecules of heredity a quarter-century or so ago, I couldn't resist the possibilities. I am what the crass mystics call a crass materialist, feeling quite certain that life phenomena will eventually prove explainable in detail in terms of physicical and chemical laws. I can see repair and reconstruction of the human body being reduced to semi-skilled routine as basic knowledge of genetic phenomena leads to engineering technique. The human mind, however, will resist that reduction much longer than the body; and it seems quite reasonable to me to expect that body-repair specialists will be regarded somewhat as drudges by the ''real'' doctors. The latter, then as now, will be working in the areas where the answers are less clearly known and the cure rate lower than one could wish.

It won't be a boring world, though. We'll just be taking a new set of ''of courses'' for granted. We'll be just as annoyed and impatient with what can't be done for us—either by doctors or delivery services. We'll be screaming for the good old days when all the body repair skill available to humanity could be had for fifty dollars—so that if you had a hundred, you could pay the undertaker too.

My teeth are so full of amalgam that I couldn't get through a radar screen in my birthday suit. Primitive. Crude. But I have the teeth. My father at my age didn't, and his father I never had a chance to meet.

DRIFTING IDLY, the *Shark* tended to look more like a manta ray than her name suggested; but at high cruise, as she was now, she bore more resemblance to a flying fish. She was entirely out of the water except for the four struts that carried her hydroplanes; the air propellers which drove her were high enough above the surface to raise very little spray. An orbiting monitor satellite could have seen the vessel herself from a hundred miles up, since her upper hull was painted in a vividly fluorescent pattern of red and yellow; but there was not enough wake to suggest to such a watcher that the wedge-shaped machine was traveling at nearly sixty-five knots.

Chester V. Winkle—everyone knew what the middle initial stood for, but no one mentioned it in his presence—sat behind the left bow port of his command with his fingers resting lightly on the pressure controls. He was looking ahead, but knew better than to trust his eyes alone. Most of his attention was devoted to the voice of the smaller man seated four feet to his right, behind the other ''eye'' of the manta. Yoshii Ishihara was not looking outside at all; his eyes were directed steadily at the sonar display screen which was all that stood between the *Shark* and disaster at her present speed among the ice floes and zeowhales at the Labrador Sea.

''Twenty-two targets in the sweep; about fourteen thousand meters to the middle of the group,'' he said softly.

''Heading?'' Winkle knew the question was superfluous; had a change been in order, the sonarman would have given it.

''As we go, for thirty-two hundred meters. Then twenty-two mils starboard. There's ice in the way.''

''Good. Any data on target condition yet?''

''No. It will be easier to read them when we stop, and will cost little time to wait. Four of the twenty-two are drifting, but the sea is rich here and they might be digesting. Stand by for change of heading.''

''Ready on your call.'' There was silence for about a minute.

''Starboard ten.''

''Starboard ten.'' The hydro-planes submerged near the ends of the *Shark*'s bow struts banked in response to the pressure of Winkle's fingers, though the hull remained nearly level. The compass needle on the panel between the view ports moved smoothly through ten divisions. As it reached the tenth, Ishihara, without looking up from his screen, called, ''Steady.''

''Steady she is,'' repied the commander.

''Stand by for twelve more to starboard—now.'' The *Shark* swung again and steadied on the new heading.

''That leaves us a clear path in,'' said the sonarman. ''Time to engine cut is four minutes.''

In spite of his assurance that the way was clear, Ishihara kept his eyes on his instrument—his standards of professional competence would permit nothing less while the *Shark* had way on her. Winkle, in spite of the sleepy appearance which combined with his name to produce a constant spate of bad jokes, was equally alert for visible obstructions ahead. Several ice floes could be seen; but none were directly in the vessel's path, and Winkle's fingers remained idle until his second officer gave the expected signal.

Then the whine of turbines began to drop in pitch, and the *Shark*'s broad form eased toward the swell below as the hydrofoils lost their lift. The hull extensions well out on her "wings" which gave the vessel catamaran-type stability when drifting kissed the surface gently, their added drag slowing the machine more abruptly; and twenty feet aft of the conning ports the four remaining members of the crew tensed for action.

"Slow enough for readings?" asked Winkle.

"Yes, sir. The homing signal is going out now. I'll have counts in the next thirty seconds." Ishihara paused. "One of the four drifters is underway and turning toward us. No visible response from the others."

"Which is the nearest of the dead ones?"

"Fifteen hundred meters, eight hundred forty mils port." Winkle's fingers moved again. The turbines that drove the big, counter-rotating air propellers remained idle, but water jets playing from ducts on the hydrofoil struts swung the ship in the indicated direction and set her traveling slowly toward the drifter. Winkle called an order over his shoulder.

"Winches and divers ready. The trap is unsafetied. Contact in five minutes."

"Winch ready," Dandridge's deep voice reported as he swept his chessboard to one side and closed a master switch. Mancini, who had been facing him across the board, slipped farther aft to the laboratory which occupied over half of the *Shark*'s habitable part. He said nothing, since no order had been directed at him, and made no move to uncage any of his apparatus while the vessel was still in motion.

"Divers standing by." Farrell spoke for himself and his assistant after a brief check of masks and valves—both were already dressed for Arctic water. They took their places at either side of the red-checkered deck area, just forward of the lab section, which marked the main hatch. Dandridge, glancing up to make sure that no one was standing on it, opened the trap from his control console. Its halves slid smoothly apart, revealing the chill green liquid slipping between the hulls. At the *Shark*'s present speed she was floating at displacement depth, so that the water averaged about four meters down from the hatch; but this distance was varied by a swell of a meter or so. Farrell stood looking down at it, waiting patiently for the vessel to stop; his younger assistant dropped prone by the edge of the opening and craned his neck through it in an effort to see forward.

Ishihara's voice was barely audible over the wind now that the hatch was open, but occasional words drifted back to the divers. "Six hundred . . . as you go . . . four . . . three . . ."

"I see it," Winkle cut in. "I'll take her." He called over his shoulder again, "Farrell . . . Stubbs . . . we're coming up on one. You'll spot it in a minute. I'll tell you when I lose it under the bow."

"Yes, sir," acknowledged Farrell. "See it yet, Rick?"

"Not yet," was the response. "Nothing but jellyfish."

"Fifty meters," called the captain. "Now thirty." He cut the water jets to a point where steerage way would have been lost if such a term had meant anything to the *Shark,* and continued to inch forward. "Twenty."

"I see it," called Stubbs.

"All right," answered the captain. "Ten meters. Five. It's right under me; I've lost it. Con me, diver."

"About five meters, sir. It's dead center . . . four . . . three . . . two . . . all right, it's right under the hatch. Magnets ready, Gil?"

The magnetic grapple was at the forward end of its rail, directly over the hatch, so Dandridge was ready; but Winkle was not.

"Hold up . . . don't latch on yet, Stubbs, watch the fish; are we drifting?"

"A little, sir. It's going forward and a little to port . . . now you're stopping it . . . there."

"Quite a bit of wind," remarked the captain as his fingers lifted from the hydrojet controls. "All right. Pick it up."

"Think the magnets will be all right, Marco?" asked Dandridge. "That whale looks funny to me." The mechanic joined the winchman and divers at the hatch and looked down at their floating problem.

At first glance the "whale" was ordinary enough. It was about two meters long, and perfectly cigar-shaped except where the intake ring broke the curve some forty centimeters back of the nose. The exhaust ports, about equally far from the tail end, were less visible since they were merely openings in the dark gray skin. Integument and openings alike were hard to see in detail, however; the entire organism was overgrown with a brownish, slimy-looking mass of filaments reminiscent both of mold and of sealskin.

"It's picked up something, all right," Mancini conceded. "I don't see why your magnets shouldn't work, though . . . unless you'd rather they didn't get dirty."

"All right. Get down the ladder and steer 'em, Rick." Dandridge caused a light alloy ladder to extend from the bow edge of the hatch as he spoke; then he fingered another switch which sent the grapples themselves slowly downward. Stubbs easily beat them to the foot of the ladder, hooked one leg through a rung, reached out with both arms and tried to steady the descending mass of metal. The *Shark* was pitching somewhat in the swell, and the eighty pounds of electromagnet and associated wiring were slightly rebellious. The youngest of the crew and the only nonspecialist among its members—he was still working off the two-year labor draft requirement which preceded higher education—Rick Stubbs got at least his share of the dirty work. He was not so young as to complain about it.

"Slower . . . slower . . . twenty c's to go . . . ten . . . hold it now . . . just a touch lower . . . all right, juice!" Dandridge followed the instructions, fed current to the magnets, and started to lift.

The Mechanic

"Wait!" the boy on the ladder called almost instantly. "It's not holding!"

The mechanic reacted almost as fast.

"Bring it up anyway!" he called. "The infection is sticking to the magnets. Let me get a sample!" Stubbs shrank back against the ladder as the slimy mass rose past him in response to Mancini's command. Dandridge grimaced with distaste as it came above deck level and into his view.

"You can have it!" he remarked, not very originally.

Mancini gave no answer, and showed no sign of any emotion but interest. He had slipped back into his lab as the material was ascending, and now returned with a two-liter flask and the biggest funnel he possessed.

"Run it aft a little," he said briefly. "That's enough . . . I'll miss some, and it might as well fall into the water as onto the deck." The grapple, which had crawled a few inches toward him on its overhead rail, stopped just short of the after edge of the hatch. Mancini, standing unconcernedly at the edge of the opening with the wind ruffling his clothes, held funnel and flask under the magnets.

"All right, Gil, drop it," he ordered. Dandridge obeyed.

Most of the mess fell obediently away from the grapple. Some landed in the funnel and proceeded to ooze down into the flask; some hit Mancini's extended arm without appearing to bother him; a little dropped onto the deck, to the winchman's visible disgust. Most fell past Stubbs back into the sea.

The mechanic took up some of the material from his arm and rubbed it between thumb and forefinger. "Gritty," he remarked. "And the magnets held this stuff, but not the whale's skeleton. That means that most of the skeleton must be gone, and I bet this grit is magnetite. I'll risk a dollar that this infection comes from that old 775-FeDE6 culture that got loose a few years ago from Passamaquoddy. I'll give it the works to make sure, though. You divers will have to use slings to get the fish aboard, I'm afraid.

"Rick, I'll send the magnets down first and you can rinse 'em off a bit in the water. Then I'll run out the sling and you can get it around the whale."

"All right, sir. Standing by." As the grapple went down again Dandridge called to the mechanic, who had turned back toward the lab.

"I suppose the whale is ruined, if you're right about the infection. Can we collect damages?" Mancini shook his head negatively.

"No one could collect from DE; they went broke years ago—from paying damages. Besides, the courts decided years ago that injury or destruction of a piece of pseudolife was recoverable property damage only if an original model was involved. This fish is a descendant of a model ten years old; it was born at sea. We didn't make it, and can't recover for it." He turned to his bench, but flung a last thought over his shoulder. "My guess that this pest is a DE escapee could be wrong, too. They worked out a virus for that strain a few months after it escaped, and I haven't heard of an iron infection in four years. This may be a mutation of it—that's still my best guess—but it could also be something entirely new." He settled himself onto a stool and began dividing the material from the flask into the dozens of tiny containers which fed the analyzers.

In the water below, Stubbs had plunged from the ladder and was removing slime from the grapple magnets. The stuff was not too sticky, and the grit which might be magnetite slightly offset the feeling of revulsion which the boy normally had for slimy materials, so he was able to finish the job quickly enough to keep Dandridge happy. At Rick's call, the grapple was retracted; a few moments later the hoist cable came down again with an ordinary sling at its extremity. Stubbs was still in the water, and Farrell had come part way down the ladder. The chief diver guided the cable down to his young assistant, who began working the straps around the torpedolike form which still bobbed between the *Shark*'s hulls.

It was quite a job. The zeowhale was still slippery, since the magnets had not come even close to removing all the foreign growth. When the boy tried to reach around it to fasten the straps it slithered away from him. He called for more slack and tried to pin it against one of the hulls as he worked, but still it escaped him. He was too stubborn to ask for help, and by this time Farrell was laughing too hard to have provided much anyway.

"Ride him, Buster!" the chief diver called as Stubbs finally managed to scissor the slippery cylinder with his legs. "That's it . . . you've got him dogged now!"

The boy hadn't quite finished, actually, but one strap did seem secure around the forward part of the hull. "Take up slack!" he called up to the hatch, without answering Farrell's remark.

Dandridge had been looking through the trap and could see what was needed; he reached to his control console and the hoist cable tightened.

"That's enough!" called Stubbs as the nose of the zeowhale began to lift from the water. "Hold it until I get another strap on, or this one will slip free!"

Winches obediently ceased purring. With its motion restrained somewhat, the little machine offered less opposition to the attachment of a second band near its stern. The young swimmer called, somewhat breathlessly, "Take it up!" and paddled himself slowly back to the ladder. Farrell gave him a hand up, and they reached the deck almost as quickly as the specimen.

Dandridge closed the hatch without waiting for orders, though he left the ladder down—there would be other pickups in the next few minutes, but the wind was cold and loud. Stubbs paid no attention; he barely heard the soft "eight hundred meters, seventy-five mils to starboard," as he made his way around the closing hatch to Mancini's work station. The mechanic's job was much more fascinating than the pilot's.

He knew better than to interrupt a busy professional with questions, but the mechanic didn't need any. Like several other men, not only on the *Shark* but among the crew of her mother ship, Mancini had come to like the youngster and respect his general competence; and like most professionals, his attitude toward an intelligent labor draftee was a desire to recruit him before someone else did. The man, therefore, began to talk as soon as he noticed the boy's presence.

"You know much about either chemical or field analysis, Rick?"

"A little. I can recognize most of your gear—ultracentrifuge, chromatographic and electrophoretic stuff, NMR equipment, and so on. Is that," he pointed to a cylindrical machine on another bench, "a diffraction camera?"

"Good guess. It's a hybrid that a friend of mine dreamed up which can be used either for electron microphotography or diffraction work. All that comes a bit later, though. One thing about analysis hasn't changed since the beginning; you try to get your initial sample into as many different homogeneous parts as possible before you get down to the molecular scale."

"So each of these little tubes you're filling goes through centrifuge, or solvation, or electrophoresis—"

"More usually, through all of them, in different orders."

"I should think that just looking at the original, undamaged specimen would tell you *something*. Don't you ever do that?"

"Sure. The good old light microscope will never disappear; as you imply, it's helpful to see a machine in its assembled state, too. I'll have some slides in a few more seconds; the mike is in that cabinet. Slide it out, will you?"

Stubbs obeyed, literally since the instrument was mounted on a track. The designers of the *Shark*'s laboratory had made it as immune to rough weather as they could. Mancini took the first of his slides, clipped it under the objective, and took one look.

"Thought so," he grunted. "Here, see for yourself."

Stubbs applied an eye to the instrument, played briefly with the fine focus—he had the normal basic training in fundamental apparatus—and looked for several seconds.

"Just a mess of living cells that don't mean much to me, and a lot of little octahedra. Are they what you mean?"

"Yep. Magnetite crystals, or I'm a draft-dodger." (His remark had no military significance; the term now referred to individuals who declined the unskilled-labor draft, voluntarily giving up their rights to higher education and, in effect, committing themselves to living on basic relief.) "We'll make sure, though." The mechanic slid another piece of equipment into position on the microscope stage, and peered once more into the field of view. Stubbs recognized a micromanipulator, and was not surprised when Mancini, after two minutes or so of silent work, straightened up and removed a small strip of metal from it. Presumably one of the tiny crystals was now mounted on the strip.

The mechanic turned to the diffraction camera, mounted the bit of metal in a clamp attached to it, and touched a button which started specimen and strip on a journey into the camera's interior. Moments later a pump started to whine.

"Five minutes to vacuum, five more for scanning," he remarked. "We might as well have a look at the fish itself while we wait; even naked-eye examination has its uses.'' He got up from his seat, stretched, and turned to the bench on which the ruined zeowhale lay. ''How much do you know about these things, Rick? Can you recognize this type?''

''I think so. I'd say it was a copper-feeder of about '35 model. This one would be about two years old.''

''Good. I'd say you were about right. You've been doing some reading, I take it.''

''Some. And the *Guppy*'s shop is a pretty good museum.''

''True enough. Do you know where the access regions are on this model?''

''I've seen some of them opened up, but I wouldn't feel sure enough to do it myself.''

''It probably wouldn't matter if you did it wrong in this case; this one is safely dead. Still, I'll show you; better see it right than do it wrong.'' He had removed the straps of the sling once the ''fish'' had been lowered onto a rack on the bench, so nothing interfered with the demonstration. ''Here,'' he pointed, ''the reference is the centerline of scales along the back, just a little lighter in color than the rest. Start at the intake ring and count eight scales back; then down six on either side, like that. That puts you on this scale . . . so . . . which you can get under with a scalpel at the start of the main opening.'' He picked up an instrument about the size of a surgical scalpel, but with a blunt, rounded blade. This he inserted under the indicated scale. ''See, it comes apart here with very light pressure, and you can run the cut back to just in front of the exhaust vents—like that. If this were a living specimen, the cut would heal under sealant spray in about an hour after the fish was back in the water. This one . . . hm-m-m. No wonder it passed out. I wonder what this stuff is?''

The body cavity of the zeowhale was filled with a dead-black jelly, quite different in appearance from the growth which had covered the skin. The mechanic applied retractors to the incision, and began silently poking into the material with a variety of ''surgical'' tools. He seemed indifferent to the feelings which were tending to bring Stubbs's stomach almost as much into daylight as that of the whale.

Pieces of rubbery internal machinery began to litter the bench top. Another set of tiny test tubes took samples of the black jelly, and followed their predecessors into the automatic analyzers. These began to hum and sputter as they went to work on the new material—they had long since finished with the first load, and a pile of diagrams and numerical tables awaited Mancini's attention in their various delivery baskets. He had not even taken time to see whether his guess about magnetite had been good.

Some of the organs on the desk were recognizable to the boy—for any large animal, of course, a heart is fairly obviously a heart when it has been dissected sufficiently to show its valve structure. A four-kilogram copper nugget had come from the factory section; the organism had at least started to fulfill its intended purpose before disease had ended its pseudolife. It had also been developing normally in other respects, as a twenty-five centimeter embryo indicated. The zeowhales and their kindred devices reproduced asexually; the genetic variation magnification, which is the biological advantage of sex, was just what the users of the pseudo-organisms did not want, at least until some factor could be developed which would tend to select for the characteristics they wanted most.

Mancini spent more than an hour at his rather revolting task before he finally laid down his instruments. Stubbs had not been able to watch him the whole time, since the *Shark* had picked up the other two unresponsive whales while the job was going on. Both had been infected in the same way as the first. The boy was back in the lab, though, when the gross dissection of the original one was finished. So was Winkle, since nothing more could be planned until Mancini produced some sort of report.

"The skeleton was gone completely," was the mechanic's terse beginning. "Even the unborn one hadn't a trace of metallic iron in it. That was why the magnets didn't hold, of course. I haven't had time to look at any of the analysis reports, but I'm certain that the jelly in the body cavity and the moldy stuff outside are part of the same life form, and that organism dissolved the metallic skeleton and precipitated the iron as magnetite in its own tissues. Presumably it's a mutant from one of the regular ironfeeding strains. Judging by its general cellular conformation, its genetic tape is a purine-pyrimidine nucleotide quite similar to that of natural life—"

"Just another of the original artificial forms coming home to roost?" interjected Winkle.

"I suppose so. I've isolated some of the nuclear material, but it will have to go back to the big field analyzer on the *Guppy* to make sure."

"There seem to be no more damaged fish in the neighborhood. Is there any other material you need before we go back?"

"No. Might as well wind her up, as far as I'm concerned—unless it would be a good idea to call the ship first while we're out here to find out whether any other schools this way need checking."

"You can't carry any more specimens in your lab even if they do," Winkle pointed out, glancing around the littered bench tops.

"True enough. Maybe there's something which wouldn't need a major checkup, though. But you're the captain; play it as you think best. I'll be busy with this lot until we get back to the *Guppy* whether we get straight there or not."

"I'll call." The captain turned away to his own station.

"I wonder why they made the first pseudo-life machines with gene tapes so much like the real thing," Stubbs remarked when Winkle was back in his seat. "You'd think they'd foresee what mutations could do, and that organisms too similar to genuine life might even give rise to forms which could cause disease in us as well as in other artificial forms."

"They thought of it, all right," replied Mancini. "That possibility was a favorite theme of the opponents of the whole process—at least, of the ones who weren't driven by frankly religious motives. Unfortunately, there was no other way the business could have developed. The original research of course had to be carried out on what you call 'real' life. That led to the specific knowledge that the cytosine-thymineadenineguanine foursome of ordinary DNA could form a pattern which was both self-replicating and able to control polypeptide and polysaccharide synthesis—''

"But I thought it was more complex than that; there are phosphates and sugars in the chain, and the DNA imprints RNA, and—''

"You're quite right, but I wasn't giving a chemistry lecture; I was trying to make an historical point. I'm saying that at first, no one realized that anything except those four specific bases could do the genetic job. Then they found that quite a lot of natural life forms had variations of those bases in their nucleotides, and gradually the reasons *why* those structures, or rather their potential fields, had the polymermolding ability they do became clear. Then, and only then, was it obvious that 'natural' genes aren't the only possible ones; they're simply the ones which got a head start on this planet. There are as many ways of building a gene as there are of writing a poem—or of making an airplane if you prefer to stay on the physical plane. As you seem to know, using the channels of a synthetic zeolite as the backbone for a genetic tape happens to be a very convenient technique when we want to grow a machine like the one we've just taken apart here. It's bulkier than the phosphate-sugarbase tape, but a good deal more stable.

"It's still handy, though, to know how to work with the real thing—after all, you know as well as I do that the reason you have a life expectancy of about a hundred and fifty years is that your particular gene pattern is on file in half a cubic meter of zeolite mesh in Denver under a nice file number . . . ''

"026-18-6533'' muttered the boy under his breath.

". . . which will let any halfway competent molecular mechanic like me grow replacement parts and tissues if and when you happen to need them.''

"I know all that, but it still seems dangerous to poke around making little changes in ordinary life forms,'' replied Rick. "There must be fifty thousand people like you in the world, who could tailor a dangerous virus, or germ, or crop fungus in a couple of weeks of lab and computer work, and whose regular activities produce things like that iron-feeder which can mutate into dangerous by-products.''

"It's also dangerous to have seven billion people on the planet, practically every one of whom knows how to light a fire,'' replied Mancini. "Dangerous or not, it was no more possible to go from Watson and Crick and the DNA structure to this zeowhale without the intermediate development than it would have been to get from the Wright brothers and their powered kite to the two-hour transatlantic ramjet without building Ford tri-motors and DC-3s in between. We have the knowledge, it's an historical fact that no one can effectively destroy it, so we might as well use it. The fact that so many competent practitioners of the art exist is our best safeguard if it does get a little out of hand at times.''

The boy looked thoughtful.

"Maybe you have something there,'' he said slowly. "But with all that knowledge, why only a hundred and fifty years? Why can't you keep people going indefinitely?''

"Do you think we should?'' Mancini countered with a straight face. Rick grinned.

"Stop ducking. If you could, you would—for some people anyway. Why can't you?" Mancini shrugged.

"Several hundred million people undoubtedly know the rules of chess." He nodded toward the board on Dandridge's control table. "Why aren't they all good players? You know, don't you, why doctors were reluctant to use hormones as therapeutic agents even when they became available in quantity?"

"I think so. If you gave someone cortisone it might do what you wanted, but it might also set other glands going or slow them down, which would alter the levels of other hormones, which in turn . . . well, it was a sort of chain reaction which could end anywhere."

"Precisely. And gene-juggling is the same only more so. If you were to sit at the edge of the hatch there and let Gil close it on you, I could rig the factors in your gene pattern so as to let you grow new legs; but there would be a distinct risk of affecting other things in your system at the same time. In effect, I would be taking certain *restraints* which caused your legs to stop growing when they were completed *off* your cell-dividing control mechanisms—the sort of thing that used to happen as a natural, random effect in cancer. I'd probably get away with it—or rather, you would—since you're only about nineteen and still pretty deep in what we call the stability well. As you get older, though, with more and more factors interfering with that stability, the job gets harder—it's a literal juggling act, with more and more balls being tossed to the juggler every year you live.

"You were born with a deep enough stability reserve to keep yourself operating for a few decades without any applied biochemical knowledge; you might live twenty years or ninety. Using the knowledge we have, we can play the game longer; but sooner or later we drop the ball. It's not that we don't know the rules; to go back to the chess analogy, it's just that there are too many pieces on the board to keep track of all at once."

Stubbs shook his head. "I've never thought of it quite that way. To me, it's always been just a repair job, and I couldn't see why it should be so difficult."

Mancini grinned. "Maybe your cultural grounding didn't include a poem called the 'Wonderful One-Hoss Shay.' Well, we'll be a couple of hours getting back to the *Guppy*. There are a couple of sets of analysis runs sitting with us here. Maybe, if I start trying to turn those into language you can follow, you'll have some idea of why the game is so hard before we get there. Maybe, too"—his face sobered somewhat—"you'll start to see why, even though we always lose in the end, the game is so much fun. It isn't just that our own lives are at stake, you know; men have been playing that kind of game for two million years or so. Come on."

He turned to the bench top on which the various analyzers had been depositing their results; and since Stubbs had a good grounding in mathematical and chemical fundamentals, their language ceased to resemble Basic English. Neither paid any attention as the main driving turbines of the *Shark* came up to quarter speed and the vessel began to pick her way out of the patch of ice floes where the zeowhales had been collecting metal.

By the time Winkle had reached open water and Ishihara had given him the clearance for high cruise, the other four had lost all contact with the outside world. Dandridge's chess board was in use again, with Farrell now his opponent. The molecular mechanic and his possible apprentice were deeply buried in a task roughly equivalent to explaining to a forty-piece orchestra how to produce ''Aida'' from overture to finale—without the use of written music. Stubbs's basic math was, for this problem, equivalent to having learned just barely his ''do, re, mi.''

There was nothing to distract the players of either game. The wind had freshened somewhat, but the swells had increased little if at all. With the *Shark* riding on her hydrofoils there was only the faintest of tremors as her struts cut the waves. The sun was still high and the sky almost cloudless. Between visual pilotage and sonar, life seemed as uncomplicated as it ever gets for the operator of a high-speed vehicle.

The *Guppy* was nearly two hundred kilometers to the south, far beyond sonar range. Four of her other boats were out on business, and Winkle occasionally passed a word or two with their commanders; but no one had anything of real importance to say. The desultory conversations were a matter of habit, to make sure that everyone was still on the air. No pilot, whether of aircraft, space vessel, surface ship, or submarine, attaches any weight to the proverb that no news is good news.

Just who was to blame for the interruption of this idyll remains moot. Certainly Mancini had given the captain his preliminary ideas about the pest which had killed their first whale. Just as certainly he had failed to report the confirmation of that opinion after going through the lab results with Stubbs. Winkle himself made no request for such confirmation—there was no particular reason why he should, and if he had it is hard to believe that he would either have realized all the implications or been able to do anything about them. The fact remains that everyone from Winkle at the top of the ladder of command to Stubbs at the bottom was taken completely by surprise when the *Shark*'s starboard after hydrofoil strut snapped cleanly off just below the mean planing water line.

At sixty-five knots, no human reflexes could have coped with the result. The electronic ones of the *Shark* tried, but the vessel's mechanical I.Q. was not up to the task of allowing for the lost strut. As the gyros sensed the drop in the right rear quadrant of their field of perception, the Autopilot issued commands to increase the angle of attack of the control foils on that strut. Naturally there was no response. The dip increased. By the time it got beyond the point where the machine thought it could be handled by a single set of foils, so that orders went out to decrease lift on the port-bow leg, it was much too late. The after portion of the starboard flotation hull smacked a wave top at sixty-five knots and, of course, bounced. The bounce was just in time to reinforce the letdown command to the port-bow control foils. The bow curve of the port hull struck in its turn, with almost undiminished speed and with two principal results.

About a third of the *Shark*'s forward speed vanished in less than the same fraction of a second as she gave up kinetic energy to the water in front, raising a cloud of spray more than a hundred meters and subjecting hull and contents to about four gravities of acceleration in a most unusual direction. The rebound was high enough to cause the starboard "wing" to dip into the waves, and the *Shark* did a complete double cartwheel. For a moment she seemed to poise motionless with port wing and hull entirely submerged and the opposite wing tip pointing at the sky; then, grudgingly, she settled back to a nearly horizontal position on her flotation hulls and lay rocking on the swell.

Externally she showed little sign of damage. The missing strut was, of course, under water anyway, and her main structure had taken only a few dents. The propellers had been twisted off by gyroscopic action during the cartwheel. Aside from this, the sleek form looked ready for service.

Inside, things were different. Most of the apparatus, and even some of the men, had been more or less firmly fixed in place; but the few exceptions had raised a good deal of mayhem.

Winkle and Ishihara were unconscious, though still buckled in their seats. Both had been snapped forward against their respective panels, and were draped with sundry unappetizing fragments of the dissected zeowhale. Ishihara's head had shattered the screen of his sonar instrument, and no one could have told at first glance how many cuts were supplying the blood on his face.

The chess players had both left impressions on the control panel of the winch and handling system, and now lay crumpled beside it. Neither was bleeding visibly, but Farrell's arms were both twisted at angles impossible to intact bones. Dandridge was moaning and just starting to try to get to his feet; he and Mancini were the only ones conscious.

The mechanic had been seated at one of his benches facing the starboard side of the ship when the impact came. He had not been strapped in his seat, and the four-g jerk had started to hurl him toward the bow. His right leg had stopped him almost as suddenly by getting entangled in the underpinning of the seat. The limb was not quite detached from its owner; oddly enough, its skin was intact. This was about the only bit of tissue below the knee for which this statement could be made.

Stubbs had been standing at the mechanic's side. They were to argue later whether it had been good or bad luck that the side in question had been the left. It depended largely on personal viewpoint. There had been nothing for Rick to seize as he was snatched toward the bow or, if there was, he had not been quick enough or strong enough to get it. He never knew just what hit him in flight; the motions of the *Shark* were so wild that it might have been deck, overhead, or the back of one of the pilot seats. It was evident enough that his path had intersected that of the big flask in which

Mancini had first collected the iron-feeding tissue, but whether the flask was still whole at the time remains unclear. It is hard to see how he could have managed to absorb so many of its fragments had it already shattered, but it is equally hard to understand how he could have scattered them so widely over his anatomy if it had been whole.

It was Stubbs, or rather the sight of him, that got Mancini moving. Getting his own shattered leg disentangled from the chair was a distracting task, but not distracting enough to let him take his eyes from the boy a few meters away. Arterial bleeding is a sight that tends to focus attention.

He felt sick, over and above the pain of his leg; whether it was the sight of Rick or incipient shock he couldn't tell. He did his best to ignore the leg as he inched across the deck, though the limb itself seemed to have other ideas. Unfortunately these weren't very consistent; sometimes it wanted—demanded—his whole mind, at others it seemed to have gone off somewhere on its own and hidden. He did not look back to see whether it was still with him; what was in front was more important.

The boy still had blood when Mancini reached him, as well as a functioning heart to pump it. He was not losing the fluid as fast as had appeared from a distance, but something would obviously have to be done about what was left of his right hand—the thumb and about half of the palm. The mechanic had been raised during one of the periods when first-aiders were taught to abjure the tourniquet, but had reached an age where judgment stands a chance against rules. He had a belt and used it.

A close look at the boy's other injuries showed that nothing could be done about them on the spot; they were bleeding slowly, but any sort of first aid would be complicated by the slivers of glass protruding from most of them. Face, chest, and even legs were slashed freely, but the rate of bleeding was not—Mancini hoped—really serious. The smaller ones were clotting already.

Dandridge was on his feet by now, badly bruised but apparently in the best shape of the six.

"What can I do, Marco?" he asked. "Everyone else is out cold. Should I use—"

"Don't use anything on them until we're sure there are no broken necks or backs; they may be better off unconscious. I know I would be."

"Isn't there dope in the first-aid kit? I could give you a shot of painkiller."

"Not yet, anyway. Anything that would stop this leg from hurting would knock me out, and I've got to stay awake if at all possible until help comes. The lab equipment isn't really meant for repair work, but if anything needs to be improvised from it I'll have to be the one to do it. I could move around better, though, if this leg were splinted. Use the raft foam from the handling locker."

Five minutes later Mancini's leg, from mid-thigh down, was encased in a bulky, light, but reasonably rigid block of foamed resin whose original purpose was to provide on-the-spot flotation for objects which were inconvenient or impossible to bring aboard.

It still hurt, but he could move around without much fear of doing the limb further damage.

"Good. Now you'd better see what communication gear, if any, stood up under this bump. I'll do what I can for the others. Don't move Ishi or the captain; work around them until I've done all I can."

Dandridge went forward to the conning section and began to manipulate switches. He was not a trained radioman—the *Shark* didn't carry one—but like any competent crew member he could operate all the vessel's equipment under routine conditions. He found quickly that no receivers were working, but that the regular transmitter drew current when its switches were closed. An emergency low-frequency beacon, entirely separate from the other communication equipment, also seemed intact; so he set this operating and began to broadcast the plight of the *Shark* on the regular transmitter. He had no way of telling whether either signal was getting out, but was not particularly worried for himself. The *Shark* was theoretically unsinkable—enough of her volume was filled with resin foam to buoy her entire weight even in fresh water. The main question was whether help would arrive before some of the injured men were beyond it.

After ten minutes of steady broacasting—he hoped—Dandrige turned back to the mechanic, to find him lying motionless on the deck. For a moment the winchman thought he might have lost consciousness; then Mancini spoke.

"I've done all I can for the time being. I've splinted Joe's arms and pretty well stopped Rick's bleeding. Ishi has a skull fracture and the captain at least a concussion; don't move either one. If you've managed to get in touch with the *Guppy*, tell them about the injuries. We'll need gene records from Denver for Rick, probably for Ishi, and possibly for the captain. They should start making blood for Rick right away, the second enough gene data is through; he's lost quite a bit."

"I don't know whether I'm getting out or not, but I'll say it all anyway," replied Dandridge, turning back to the board. "Won't you need some pretty extensive repair work yourself, though?"

"Not unless these bone fragments do more nerve damage than I think they have," replied Mancini. "Just tell them that I have a multiple leg fracture. If I know Bert Jellinge, he'll have gene blocks on all six of us growing into the machines before we get back to the *Guppy* anyway."

Dandridge eyed him more closely. "Hadn't I better give you a shot now?" he asked. "You said you'd done all you could, and it might be better to pass out from a sleepy shot than from pain. How about it?"

"Get that message out first. I can hold on, and what I've done is the flimsiest of patchwork. With the deck tossing as it is any of those splints may be inadequate. We can't strap any of the fellows down, and if the wave motion rolls one of them over I'll have the patching to do all ever again. When you get that call off, look at Rick once more; I think his bleeding has stopped, but until he's on a repair table I won't be happy about him."

"So you'd rather stay awake."

"Not exactly, but if you were in the kid's place, wouldn't *you* prefer me to?" Dandridge had no answer to that one; he talked into the transmitter instead.

His words, as it happened, were getting out. The *Conger*, the nearest of the *Shark*'s sister fish-tenders, had already started toward them; she had about forty kilometers to come. On the *Guppy* the senior mechanic had fulfilled Mancini's prediction; he had already made contact with Denver, and Rick Stubbs's gene code was about to start through the multiple-redundant communication channels used for the purpose—channels which, fortunately, had just been freed of the saturation caused by a serious explosion in Pittsburgh, which had left over five hundred people in need of major repair. The full transmission would take over an hour at the highest safe scanning rate; but the first ten minutes would have enough information, when combined with the basic human data already in the *Guppy*'s computers, to permit the synthesis of replacement blood.

The big mother-ship was heading toward the site of the accident so as to shorten the *Conger*'s journey with the victims. The operations center at Cape Farewell had offered a "mastodon"—one of the gigantic helicopters capable of lifting the entire weight of a ship like the *Shark*. After a little slide-rule work, the *Guppy*'s commander had declined; no time would have been saved, and the elimination of one ship-to-ship transfer for the injured men was probably less important than economy of minutes.

Mancini would have agreed with this, had he been able to join in the discussion. By the time Dandridge had finished his second transmission, however, the mechanic had fainted from the pain of his leg.

Objectively, the winchman supposed that it was probably good for his friend to be unconscious. He was not too happy, though, at being the only one aboard who could take responsibility for anything. The half hour it took for the *Conger* to arrive was not a restful one for him, though it could not have been less eventful. Even sixty years later, when the story as his grandchildren heard it included complications like a North Atlantic winter gale, he was never able to paint an adequate word picture of his feelings during those thirty minutes—much less an exaggerated one.

The manta-like structure of the tenders made transshipping most practical from bow-to-bow contact, but it was practical at all only on a smooth sea. In the present case, the *Conger*'s commander could not bring her bow closer than ten meters to that of the crippled ship, and both were pitching too heavily even for lines to be used.

One of the *Conger*'s divers plunged into the water and swam to the helpless vessel. Dandridge saw him coming through the bow ports, went back to his console, and rather to his surprise found that the hatch and ladder responded to their control switches. Moments later the other man was on the deck beside him.

The diver took in the situation after ten seconds of explanation by Dandridge and two of direct examination, and spoke into the transmitter which was part of his equipment. A few seconds later a raft dropped from the *Conger*'s hatch and two more men clambered down into it. One of these proved on arrival to be Mancini's opposite number, who wasted no time.

"Use the foam," he directed. "Case them all up except for faces; that way we can get them to the bench without any more limb motion. You say Marco thought there might be skull or spine fractures?"

"He said Ishi had a fractured skull and Winkle might have. All he said about spines was that we'd have to be careful in case it had happened."

"Right. You relax; I'll take care of it." The newcomer took up the foam generator and went to work.

Twenty minutes later the *Conger* was on her hydroplanes once more, heading for rendezvous with the *Guppy*.

In spite of tradition, Rick Stubbs knew where he was when he opened his eyes. The catch was that he hadn't the faintest idea how he had gotten there. He could see that he was surrounded by blood-transfusion equipment, electronic circulatory and nervous system monitoring gear, and the needle-capillary-and-computer maze of a regeneration unit, though none of the stuff seemed to be in operation. He was willing to grant from all this that he had been hurt somehow; the fact that he was unable to move his head or his right arm supported this notion. He couldn't begin to guess, however, what sort of injury it might be or how it had happened.

He remembered talking and working with Mancini at the latter's lab bench. He could not recall for certain just what the last thing said or done might be, though; somehow the picture merged with the foggy struggle back to consciousness which had culminated in recognition of his surroundings.

He could see no one near him, but this might be because his head wouldn't turn. Could he talk? Only one way to find out.

"Is anyone here? What's happened to me?" It didn't sound very much like his own voice, and the effort of speech hurt his chest and abdomen; but apparently words got out.

"We're all here, Rick. I thought you'd be switching back on about now." Mancini's face appeared in Stubbs's narrow field of vision.

"We're *all* here? Did everyone get hurt somehow? What happened?"

"Slight correction—most of us are here, one's been and gone. I'll tell you as much as I can; don't bother to ask questions, I know it must hurt you to talk. Gil was here for a while, but he just had a few bruises and is back on the job. The rest of us were banged up more thoroughly. My right leg was a jigsaw puzzle; Bert had an interesting time with it. I thought he ought to take it off and start over, but he stuck with it, so I got off with five hours of manual repair and two in regeneration instead of a couple of months hooked up to a computer. I'm still splinted, but that will be for only a few more days.

"No one knows yet just what happened. Apparently the *Shark* hit something going at full clip, but no one knows yet what it was. They're towing her in; I trust there'll be enough evidence to tell us the whole story."

"How about the other fellows?"

"Ishi is plugged in. He may need a week with computer regeneration control, or ten times that. We won't be able to assess brain damage until we find how close to consciousness he can come. He had a bad skull fracture. The captain was knocked out, and some broken ribs I missed on the first-aid check did internal damage. Bert is still trying to get him off without regeneration, but I don't think he'll manage it."

"You didn't think he could manage it with you, either."

"True. Maybe it's just that I don't think I could do it myself, and hate to admit that Jellinge is better at my own job than I am."

"How about Joe?"

"Both arms broken and a lot of bruises. He'll be all right. That leaves you, young fellow. You're not exactly a critical case, but you are certainly going to call for professional competence. How fond are you of your fingerprints."

"What? I don't track."

"Most of your right hand was sliced off, apparently by flying glass from my big culture flask. Ben Tulley from the *Conger*, which picked us up, found the missing section and brought it back; it's in culture now."

"What has that to do with fingerprints? Why didn't you or Mr. Jellinge graft it back?"

"Because there's a good deal of doubt about its condition. It was well over an hour after the accident before it got into culture. You know the sort of brain damage a few minutes without oxygen can do. I know the bone, tendon, and connective tissue in a limb is much less sensitive to that sort of damage, but an hour is a long time, chemically speaking. Grafting calls for healing powers which are nearly as dependent on genetic integrity as is nerve activity; we're just not sure whether grafting is the right thing to do in your case. It's a toss-up whether we should fasten the hand back on and work to make it take, or discard it and grow you a new one. That's why I asked how much you loved your fingerprints."

"Wouldn't a new hand have the same prints?"

"The same print classification, which is determined genetically, but not the same details, which are random."

"Which would take longer?"

"If the hand is in shape to take properly, grafting would be quicker—say a week. If it isn't, we might be six or eight times as long repairing secondary damage. That's longer than complete regeneration would take."

"When are you going to make up your minds?"

"Soon. I wondered whether you'd have a preference."

"How could I know which is better when you don't? Why ask me at all?"

"I had a reason—several, in fact. I'll tell you what they were after you've had two years of professional training in molecular mechanics, if you decide to come into the field. You still haven't told me which you prefer."

The boy looked up silently for a full minute. Actually, he spent very little of that time trying to make his mind up; he was wondering what Mancini's reasons might be. He gave up, flipped a mental coin, and said, "I think I'd prefer the original hand, if there's a real chance of getting it back and it won't keep me plugged into these machines any longer than growing a new one would."

"All right, we'll try it that way. Of course, you'll be plugged in for quite a while anyway, so if we do have trouble with the hand it won't make so much difference with your time."

"What do you mean? What's wrong besides the hand?"

"You hadn't noticed that your head is clamped?"

"Well, yes; I knew I couldn't move it, but I can't feel anything wrong. What's happened there?"

"Your face stopped most of the rest of the flask, apparently."

"Then how can I be seeing at all, and how is it that I talk so easily?"

"If I knew that much about probability, I'd stop working for a living and take up professional gambling. When I first saw you after your face had been cleaned off and before the glass had been taken out I wondered for a moment whether there hadn't been something planned about the arrangement of the slivers. It was unbelievable, but that's the way it happened. They say anything can happen once, but I'd advise you not to catch any more articles of glassware with your face."

"Just what was it like, Marco? Give me the details."

"Frankly, I'd rather not. There are record photos, of course, but if I have anything to say about it you won't see them until the rebuilding is done. Then you can look in a mirror to reassure yourself when the photos get your stomach. No"—as Stubbs tried to interrupt—"I respect what you probably think of as your clinical detachment, but I doubt very strongly that you could maintain it in the face of the real thing. I'm pretty sure that I couldn't, if it were my face." Mancini's thoughts flashed back to the long moments when he had been dragging his ruined leg across the *Shark*'s deck toward the bleeding boy, and felt a momentary glow—maybe that disclaimer had been a little too modest. He stuck to his position, however.

Rick didn't argue too hard, for another thought had suddenly struck his mind. "You're using regeneration on my face, without asking me whether I want it the way you did with my hand. Right?"

"That's right," Mancini said.

"That means I'm so badly damaged that ordinary healing won't take care of it."

Mancini pursed his lips and thought carefully before answering. "You'd heal, all right," he admitted at last. "You might just possibly, considering your age, heal without too much scarring. I'd hesitate to bet on that, though, and the scars you could come up with would leave you quite a mess."

Stubbs lay silent for a time, staring at the featureless ceiling. The mechanic was sure his expression would have been thoughtful had enough of the young face been visible to make one. He could not, however, guess at what was bothering the boy. As far as Mancini could guess from their work together there was no question of personal cowardice—for that matter, the mechanic could not see what there might be to fear. His profession made him quite casual about growing tissue, natural or artificial, on human bodies or anywhere else. Stubbs was in no danger of permanent disfigurement, crippling damage, or even severe pain; but something was obviously bothering the kid.

"Marco," the question came finally, "just where does detailed genetic control end, in tissue growth, and statistical effects take over?"

"There's no way to answer that both exactly and generally. Genetic factors are basically probability ones, but they're characterized by regions of high probability which we call stability wells. I told you about fingerprints, but each different situation would call for a different specific answer."

"It was what you said about prints that made me think of it. You're going to rebuild my face, you say. You won't tell me just how much rebuilding has to be done, but you admitted I *could* heal normally. If you rebuild, how closely will you match my original face? Does that statistical factor of yours take over somewhere along the line?"

"Statistical factors are everywhere, and work throughout the whole process," replied Mancini without in the least meaning to be evasive. "I told you that. By rights, your new face should match the old as closely as the faces of identical twins match each other, and for the same reason. I grant that someone who knows the twins really well can usually tell them apart, but no one will have your old face around for close comparison. No one will have any doubt that it's you, I promise."

"Unless something goes wrong."

"If it goes wrong enough to bother you, we can always do it over."

"But it *might* go really wrong."

Mancini, who would have admitted that the sun might not rise the next day if enough possible events all happened at once, did not deny this, though he was beginning to feel irritated. "Does this mean that you don't want us to do the job? Just take your chances on the scars?" he asked.

"Why do scars form, anyway?" was the counter. "Why can't regular, normal genetic material reproduce the tissue it produced in the first place? It certainly does sometimes; why not always?"

"That's pretty hard to explain in words. It has to do with the factors which stopped your nose growing before it became an elephant's trunk—or more accurately, with the factors which stopped your overall growth where they did. I can describe them completely, and I believe quite accurately, but not in Basic English."

"Can you measure those factors in a particular case?"

"Hm-m-m, yes; fairly accurately, anyway." Stubbs pounced on this with an eagerness which should have told the mechanic something.

"Then can't you tell whether these injuries, in my particular case, will heal completely or leave scars?"

"I . . . well, I suppose so. Let's see; it would take . . . hm-m-m; I'll have to give it some thought. It's not regular technique. We usually just rebuild. What's your objection, anyway? All rebuilding really means is that we set things going and then watch the process, practically cell by cell, and correct what's happening if it isn't right—following the plans you used in the first place."

"I still don't see why my body can't follow them without your help."

"Well, no analogy is perfect; but roughly speaking, it's because the cells which will have to divide to produce the replacement tissue had the blueprints which they used for the original construction stamped 'production complete; file in reference storage' some years ago, and the stamp marks covered some of the lines on the plans." Mancini's temper was getting a little short, as his tone showed. Theoretically his leg should not have been hurting him, but he had been standing on it longer than any repairman would have advised at its present stage of healing. And why did the kid keep beating around the bush?

Stubbs either didn't notice the tone or didn't care.

"But the plans—the information—that's still there; even I know that much molecular biology. I haven't learned how to use your analysis gear yet, much less to reduce the readings; but I can't see why you'd figure it much harder to read the plans under the 'file' stamp than to work out the ability of that magnetite slime to digest iron from the base configuration of a single cell's genes."

"Your question was why your body couldn't do it; don't change the rules in the middle of the game. I didn't say that *I* couldn't; I could. What I said was that it isn't usual, and I can't see what will be gained by it; you'd at least double the work. I'm not exactly lazy, but the work at best is difficult, precise, and time-consuming. If someone were to paint your portrait and had asked you whether you wanted it on canvas or paper, would you dither along asking about the brand of paint and the sizes of brushes he was going to use?"

"I don't think that's a very good analogy. I just want to know what to expect—"

"You can't *know* what to expect. No one can. Ever. You have to play the odds. At the moment, the odds are so high in your favor that you'd almost be justified in saying that you know what's going to happen. All I'm asking is that you tell me straight whether or not you want Bert and me to ride control as your face heals, or let it go its own way."

"But if you can grow a vine that produces ham sandwiches instead of pumpkins, why—" Mancini made a gesture of impatience. He liked the youngster and still hoped to recruit him, but there are limits.

"Will you stop sounding like an anti-vivisectionist who's been asked for a statement on heart surgery and give me a straight answer to a straight question? The chances are all I can give you. They are much less than fifty-fifty that your face will come out of this without scars on its own. They are much better than a hundred to one that even your mother will never know there's been a controlled regeneration job done on you unless you tell her. You're through general education, legally qualified to make decisions involving your own life and health, and morally obligated to make them instead of lying there dithering. Let's have an answer.''

For fully two minutes, he did not get it. Rick lay still, his expression hidden in dressings, eyes refusing to meet those of the man who stood by the repair table. Finally, however, he gave in.

"All right, do your best. How long did you say it would take?''

"I don't remember saying, but probably about two weeks for your face. You'll be able to enjoy using a mirror long before we get that hand unplugged, unless we're remarkably lucky with the graft.''

"When will you start?''

"As soon as I've had some sleep. Your blood is back to normal, your general pattern is in the machine; there's nothing else to hold us up. What sort of books do you like?''

"Huh?''

"That head's going to be in a clamp for quite a while. You may or may not like reading, but the only direction you can look comfortably is straight up. Your left hand can work a remote control, and the tape reader can project on the ceiling. I can't think of anything else to occupy you. Do you want some refreshing light fiction, or shall I start you on Volume One of *Garwood's Elementary Matrix Algebra for Biochemists?*''

A regeneration controller is a bulky machine, even though most of it has the delicacy and structural intricacy possible only to pseudolife—and, of course, to "real" life. Its sensors are smaller in diameter than human red blood cells, and there are literally millions of them. Injectors and samplers are only enough larger to take entire cells into their tubes, and these also exist in numbers which would make the device a hopeless one to construct mechanically. Its computer-controller occupies more than two cubic meters of molecular-scale "machinery" based on a synthetic zeolite framework. Mating the individual gene record needed for a particular job to the basic computer itself takes nearly a day; it would take a lifetime if the job had to be done manually, instead of persuading the two to "grow" together.

Closing the gap between the optical microscope and the test tube, which was blanketed under the word "protoplasm" for so many decades, also blurred the boundary between such initially different fields as medicine and factory design. Marco Mancini and Bert Jellinge regarded themselves as mechanics; what they would have been called a few decades earlier is hard to say. Even at the time the two had been born, no ten Ph.D.s could have supplied the information which now formed the grounding of their professional practice.

When their preliminary work—the "prepping"—on Rick Stubbs was done, some five million sensing tendrils formed a beard on the boy's face, most of them entering the skin near the edges of the injured portions. Every five hundred or so of these formed a unit with a pair of larger tubes. The sensors kept the computer informed of the genetic patterns actually active from moment to moment in the healing tissue—or at least, a statistically significant number of them. Whenever that activity failed to match within narrow limits what the computer thought should be happening, one of the larger tubes ingested a single cell from the area in question and transferred it to a large incubator—"large" in the sense that it could be seen without a microscope—just outside Rick's skin. There the cell was cultured through five divisions, and some of the product cells analyzed more completely than they could be inside a human body. If all were well after all, which was quite possible because of the limitations of the small sensors, nothing more happened.

If things were really not going according to plan, however, others of the new cells were modified. Active parts of their genetic material which should have been inert were inerted, quiet parts which should have been active were activated. The repaired cells were cultivated for several more divisions; if they bred true, one or more of them was returned to the original site—or at least, to within a few microns of it. Cell division and tissue building went on according to the modified plan until some new discrepancy was detected.

Most of this was, of course, automatic; too many millions of operations were going on simultaneously for detailed manual control. Nevertheless, Mancini and Jellinge were busy. Neither life nor pseudolife is infallible; mutations occur even in triply-redundant records. Computation errors occur even—or especially—in digital machines which must by their nature work by successive-approximation methods. It is much better to have a human operator, who knows his business, actually see that connective tissue instead of epidermis is being grown in one spot, or nerve instead of muscle cells in another.

Hence, a random selection of cells, not only from areas which had aroused the computer's interest but from those where all was presumably going well, also traveled out through the tubes. These went farther than just to the incubators; they came out to a point where gross microscopic study of them by a human observer was possible. This went on twenty-four hours a day, the two mechanics chiefly concerned and four others of their profession taking two-hour shifts at the microscope. The number of manhours involved in treating major bodily injury had gone up several orders of magnitude since the time when a sick man could get away with a bill for ten dollars from his doctor, plus possibly another for fifty from his undertaker.

The tendrils and tubes farthest from the damaged tissue were constantly withdrawing, groping their way to the action front, and implanting themselves anew, guided by the same chemical clues which brought leukocytes to the same area. Early versions of the technique had involved complex methods of warding off or removing the crowd of white cells from the neighborhood; the present idea was to let them alone. They were good scavengers, and the controller could easily allow for the occasional one which was taken in by the samplers.

* * *

So, as days crawled by, skin and fat and muscle and blood vessels, nerves and bones and tendons, gradually extended into their proper places in Stubbs's face and hand. The face, as Mancini had predicted, was done first; the severed hand had deteriorated so that most of its cells needed replacement, though it served as a useful guide.

With his head out of the clamp, the boy fulfilled another of the mechanic's implied predictions. He asked for a mirror. The man had it waiting, and produced it with a grin; but the grin faded as he watched the boy turn his face this way and that, checking his appearance from every possible angle. He would have expected a girl to act that way; but why should this youngster?

"Are you still the same fellow?" Mancini asked finally. "At least, you've kept your fingerprints." Rick put the mirror down.

"Maybe I should have taken a new hand," he said. "With new prints I might have gotten away with a bank robbery, and cut short the time leading to my well-earned retired leisure."

"Don't you believe it," returned Mancini grimly. "Your new prints would be on file along with your gene record and retinal pattern back in Denver before I could legally have unplugged you from the machine. I had to submit a written summary of this operation before I could start, even as it was. Forget about losing your legal identity and taking up crime."

Stubbs shrugged. "I'm not really disappointed. How much longer before I can write a letter with this hand, though?"

"About ten days; but why bother with a letter? You can talk to anyone you want; haven't your parents been on the 'visor every day?"

"Yes. Say, did you ever find out what made the *Shark* pile up?"

Mancini grimaced. "We did indeed. She got infected by the same growth that killed the zeowhale we first picked up. Did you by any chance run that fish into any part of the hull while you were attaching the sling?"

Rick stared aghast. "My gosh! Yes, I did. I held it against one of the side hulls because it was so slippery . . . I'm sorry . . . I didn't know—"

"Relax. Of course you didn't. Neither did I, then; and I never thought of the possibility later. One of the struts was weakened enough to fall at high cruise, though, and Newton's Laws did the rest."

"But does that mean that the other ships are in danger? How about the *Guppy* here? Can anything be done?"

"Oh, sure. It was done long ago. A virus for that growth was designed within a few weeks of its original escape; its gene structure is on file. The mutation is enough like the original to be susceptible to the virus. We've made up a supply of it, and will be sowing it around the area for the next few weeks wherever one of the tenders goes. But why change the subject, young fellow? Your folks *have* been phoning, because

I couldn't help hearing their talk when I was on watch. Why all this burning need to write letters? I begin to smell the proverbial rat.''

He noticed with professional approval that the blush on Rick's face was quite uniform; evidently a good job had been done on the capillaries and their auxiliary nerves and muscles. ''Give, son!''

''It's . . . it's not important,'' muttered the boy.

''Not important . . . oh, I see. Not important enough to turn you into a dithering nincompoop at the possibility of having your handsome features changed slightly, or make you drop back to second-grade level when it came to the responsibility for making a simple decision. I see. Well, it doesn't matter; she'll probably do all the deciding for you.''

The blush burned deeper. ''All right, Marco, don't sound like an ascetic; I know you aren't. Just do your job and get this hand fixed so I can write—at least there's still one form of communication you won't be unable to avoid overhearing while you're on watch.''

''What a sentence! Are you sure you really finished school? But it's all right, Rick—the hand will be back in service soon, and it shouldn't take you many weeks to learn to write with it again—''

''What?''

''It is a new set of nerves, remember. They're connected with the old ones higher up in your hand and arm, but even with the old hand as a guide they probably won't go to exactly the same places to make contact with touch transducers and the like. Things will feel different, and you'll have to learn to use a pen all over again.'' The boy stared at him in dismay. ''But don't worry. I'll do my best, which is very good, and it will only be a few more weeks. One thing, though—don't call your letter-writing problem my business; I'm just a mechanic. If you're really in love, you'd better get in touch with a doctor.'' ■

A Small Kindness
Ben Bova

I don't write many short stories. Whether it's some inborn trait or the result of working habits I've acquired over the years, I can't say. But I find myself much more comfortable with the long, complex characterizations and story developments that are possible in a novel than with the brief, incisive, carefully constrained strokes necessary to a short story. Most of the short stories I have written were hardly more than bare ideas, hastily fleshed out. Some of them have been out-and-out jokes, written in the form of a piece of short fiction.

"A Small Kindness" is much more than that, however. It must have come from deep within my unconscious mind, that dark storehouse peopled by phantoms who long to take on solid flesh and become as real as any character of fiction. In a way, this short story holds up a constrasting mirror to many of the themes I have written about elsewhere: the story seems to be saying that when the rich nations begin to develop industries in space, it will harm the poor nations; it even seems to say that UFOs actually are spacecraft from other worlds.

I use the term "seems to say" because this story literally wrote itself; my conscious mind had very little to do with it. Once I had determined to set up a confrontation in front of the Parthenon between a burned-out assassin and his assigned victim, my typing fingers flicked away on their own while I watched, surprised as any new reader would be at what was unfolding before my eyes.

I enjoyed reading "A Small Kindness." Sometimes I wonder if it wasn't actually written by one of those gentle, wise, patient aliens rather than by me.

JEREMY KEATING HATED THE RAIN. Athens was a dismal enough assignment, but in the windswept rainy night it was cold and black and dangerous. Everyone pictures Athens in the sunshine, he thought. The Acropolis, the gleaming ancient temples. They don't see the filthy modern city with its endless streams of automobiles spewing out so much pollution that the marble statues are being eaten away and the ancient monuments are in danger of crumbling.

Huddled inside his trench coat, Keating stood in the shadows of a deep doorway across the street from the taverna where his target was eating a relaxed and leisurely dinner. His last, if things went the way Keating planned.

He stood as far back in the doorway as he could, pressed against the cold stones of the building, both to remain unseen in the shadows and to keep the cold rain off himself. Rain or no, the automobile traffic still clogged Filellinon Boulevard, cars inching by bumber to bumper, honking their horns, squealing on the slickened paving. The worst traffic in the world, night and day. A million and a half Greeks, all in cars, all the time. They drove the way they lived—argumentatively.

The man dining across the boulevard in the warm, brightly lit taverna was Kabete Rungawa, of the Tanzanian delegation to the World Government conference. "The Black Saint of the Third World," he was called. The most revered man since Gandhi. Keating smiled grimly to himself. According to his acquaintances in the Vatican, a man has to be dead before he can be proclaimed a saint.

Keating was a tall man, an inch over six feet. He had the lean graceful body of a trained athlete, and it had taken him years of constant painful work to acquire it. The earlier part of his adult life he had spent behind a desk or at embassy parties, like so many other Foreign Service career officers. But that had been a lifetime ago, when he was a minor cog in the Department of State's global machine. When he was a husband and father.

His wife had been killed in the rioting in Tunis, part of the carefully orchestrated Third World upheaval that had forced the new World Government down the throats of the white, industrialized nations. His son had died of typhus in the besieged embassy, when they were unable to get medical supplies because the U.S. government could not decide whether it should negotiate with the radicals or send in the Marines.

In the end, they negotiated. But by then it was too late. So now Keating served as a roving attaché to U.S. embassies or consulates, serving where his special talents were needed. He had found those talents in the depth of his agony, his despair, his hatred.

Outwardly he was still a minor diplomatic functionary, an interesting dinner companion, a quietly handsome man with brooding eyes who seemed both unattached and unavailable. That made him a magnetic lure for a certain type of woman, a challenge they could not resist. A few of them had gotten close enough to him to trace the hairline scar across his abdomen, all that remained of the surgery he had needed after his first assignment, in Indonesia. After that particular horror, he had never been surprised or injured again.

With an adamant shake of his head, Keating forced himself to concentrate on the job at hand. The damp cold was seeping into him. His feet were already soaked. The cars still crawled along the rainy boulevard, honking impatiently. The noise was making him irritable, jumpy.

"Terminate with extreme prejudice," his boss had told him, that sunny afternoon in Virginia. "Do you understand what that means?"

Sitting in the deep leather chair in front of the section chief's broad walnut desk, Keating had nodded. "I may be new to this part of the department, but I've been around. It means to do to Rungawa what the Indonesians tried to do to me."

No one ever used the words *kill* or *assassinate* in these cheerfully lit offices. The men behind the desks, in their pinstripe suits, dealt with computer printouts and satellite photographs and euphemisms. Messy, frightening things like blood were never mentioned here.

The section chief steepled his fingers and gave Keating a long, thoughtful stare. He was a distinguished-looking man with silver hair and smoothly tanned skin. He might be the board chairman you meet at the country club, or the type of well-bred gentry who spends the summer racing yachts.

"Any questions, Jeremy?"

Keating shifted slightly in his chair. "Why Rungawa?"

The section chief made a little smile. "Do you like having the World Government order us around, demand that we disband our armed forces, tax us until we're as poor as the Third World?"

Keating felt the emotions burst into flame inside his guts. All the pain of his wife's death, of his son's lingering agony, of his hatred for the gloating ignorant sadistic petty tyrants who had killed them—all erupted in a volcanic tide of lava within him. But he clamped down on his body responses, used every ounce of training and willpower at his command to force his voice to remain calm. One thing he had learned about this organization, and about this section chief in particular: never let anyone know where you are vulnerable.

"I've got no great admiration for the World Government," he said.

The section chief's basilisk smile vanished. There was no need to appear friendly to this man. He was an employee, a tool. Despite his attempt to hide his emotions, it was obvious that all Keating lived for was to avenge his wife and child. It would get him killed, eventually, but for now his thirst for vengeance was a valuable handle for manipulating the man.

"Rungawa is the key to everything," the section chief said, leaning back in his tall swivel chair and rocking slightly.

Keating knew that the World Government, still less than five years old, was meeting in Athens to plan a global economic program. Rungawa would head the Tanzanian delegation.

"The World Government is taking special pains to destroy the United States," the section chief said, as calmly as he might announce a tennis score. "Washington was forced to accept the World Government, and the people went along with the idea because they thought it would put an end to the threat of nuclear war. Well, it's done that—at the cost of taxing our economy for every unemployed black, brown, and yellow man, woman, and child in the entire world.''

"And Rungawa?'' Keating repeated.

The section chief leaned forward, palms pressed on his desktop, and lowered his voice. "We can't back out of the World Government, for any number of reasons. But we can—with the aid of certain other Western nations—we can take control of it, if we're able to break up the solid voting bloc of the Third World nations.''

"Would the Soviets . . .''

"We can make an accommodation with the Soviets,'' the section chief said impatiently, waving one hand in the air. "Nobody wants to go back to the old Cold War confrontations. It's the Third World that's got to be brought to terms.''

"By eliminating Rungawa.''

"Exactly! He's the glue that holds their bloc together. 'The Black Saint.' They practically worship him. Eliminate him and they'll fall back into their old tangle of bickering selfish politicians, just as OPEC broke up once the oil glut started.''

It had all seemed so simple back there in that comfortable sunny office. Terminate Rungawa and then set about taking the leadership of the World Government. Fix up the damage done by the Third World's jealous greed. Get the world's economy back on the right track again.

But here in the rainy black night of Athens, Keating knew it was not that simple at all. His left hand gripped the dart gun in his trench coat pocket. There was enough poison in each dart to kill a man instantly and leave no trace for a coroner to find. The darts themselves dissolved on contact with the air within three minutes. The perfect murder weapon.

Squinting through the rain, Keating saw through the taverna's big plate glass window that Rungawa was getting up from his table, preparing to leave the restaurant.

Terminate Rungawa. That was his mission. Kill him and make it look as if he's had a heart attack. It should be easy enough. One old man, walking alone down the boulevard to his hotel. "The Black Saint'' never used bodyguards. He was old enough for a heart attack to be beyond suspicion.

But it was not going to be that easy, Keating saw. Rungawa came out of the taverna accompanied by three younger men. And he did not turn toward his hotel. Instead, he started walking down the boulevard in the opposite direction, toward the narrow tangled streets of the most ancient part of the city, toward the Acropolis. In the rain. Walking.

Frowning with puzzlement and aggravation, Keating stepped out of the doorway and into the pelting rain. It was icy cold. He pulled up his collar and tugged his hat down lower. He hated the rain. Maybe the old bastard will catch pneumonia and die naturally, he thought angrily.

As he started across the boulevard a car splashed by, horn bleating, soaking his trousers. Keating jumped back just in time to avoid being hit. The driver's furious face, framed by the rain-streaked car window, glared at him as the auto swept past. Swearing methodically under his breath, Keating found another break in the traffic and sprinted across the boulevard, trying to avoid the puddles even though his feet were already wet through.

He stayed well behind Rungawa and his three companions, glad that they were walking instead of driving, miserable to be out in the chilling rain. As far as he could tell, all three of Rungawa's companions were black, young enough and big enough to be bodyguards. That complicated matters. Had someone warned Rungawa? Was there a leak in the department's operation?

With Keating trailing behind, the old man threaded the ancient winding streets that huddled around the jutting rock of the Acropolis. The four blacks walked around the ancient citadel, striding purposefully, as if they had to be at an exact place at a precise time. Keating had to stay well behind them because the traffic along Theonas Avenue was much thinner, and pedestrians, in this rain, were nowhere in sight except for his quarry. It was quieter here, along the shoulder of the great cliff. The usual nightly *son et lumière* show had been cancelled because of the rain; even the floodlights around the Parthenon and the other temples had been turned off.

For a few minutes Keating wondered if Rungawa was going to the Agora instead, but no, the old man and his friends turned in at the gate to the Acropolis. The Sacred Way of the ancient Athenians.

It was difficult to see through the rain, especially at this distance. Crouching low behind shrubbery, Keating fumbled in his trench coat pockets until he found the miniature "camera" he had brought with him. Among other things, it was an infrared snooperscope. Even in the darkness and rain, he could see the four men as they stopped at the main gate. Their figures looked ghostly gray and eerie against a flickering dark background.

They stopped for a few moments while one of them opened the gate that was usually locked and guarded. Keating was more impressed than surprised. They had access to everything they wanted. But why do they want to go up to the Parthenon on a rainy wintry night? And how can I make Rungawa's death look natural if I have to fight my way past three bodyguards?

The second question resolved itself almost as soon as Keating asked it. Rungawa left his companions at the gate and started up the steep, rain-slickened marble stairs by himself.

"A man that age, in this weather, could have a heart attack just from climbing those stairs," Keating whispered to himself. But he knew that he could not rely on chance.

He had never liked climbing. Although he felt completely safe and comfortable in a jet plane and had even made parachute jumps calmly, climbing up the slippery rock face of the cliff was something that Keating dreaded. But he did it, nevertheless. It was not as difficult as he had feared. Others had scaled the Acropolis, over the thirty-some centuries since the Greeks had first arrived at it. Keating clambered and scrambled over the rocks, crawling at first on all fours while the cold rain spattered in his face. Then he found a narrow trail. It was steep and slippery, but his soft-soled shoes, required for stealth, gripped the rock well enough.

He reached the top of the flat-surfaced cliff in a broad open area. To his right was the Propylaea and the little temple of Athene Nike. To his left, the Arechtheum, with its Caryatides patiently holding up the roof as they had for twenty-five hundred years; the marble Maidens stared blindly at Keating. He glanced at them, then looked across the width of the clifftop to the half-ruined Parthenon, the most beautiful building on Earth, a monument both to man's creative genius and his destructive folly.

The rain had slackened, but the night was still as dark as the deepest pit of hell. Keating brought the snooperscope to his eyes again and scanned from left to right.

And there stood Rungawa! Directly in front of the Parthenon, standing there with his arms upraised, as if praying.

Too far away for the dart gun, Keating knew. For some reason, his hands started to shake. Slowly, struggling for absolute self-control, Keating put the "camera" back into his trench coat and took out the pistol. He rose to his feet and began walking toward Rungawa with swift but unhurried, measured strides.

The old man's back was to him. All you have to do, Keating told himself, is get to within a few feet, pop the dart into his neck, and then wait a couple of minutes to make certain the dart dissolves. Then go down the way you came and back to the *pension* for a hot bath and a bracer of cognac.

As he came to within ten feet of Rungawa he raised the dart gun. It worked on air pressure, practically noiseless. No need to cock it. Five feet. He could see the nails on Rungawa's upraised hands, the pinkish palms contrasting with the black skin of the fingers and the backs of his hands. Three feet. Rungawa's suit was perfectly fitted to him, the sleeves creased carefully. Dry. He was wearing only a business suit, and it was untouched by the rain, as well-creased and unwrinkled as if it had just come out of the store.

"Not yet, Mr. Keating," said the old man, without turning to look at Jeremy. "We have a few things to talk about before you kill me."

Keating froze. He could not move his arm. It stood ramrod straight from his left shoulder, the tiny dart gun in his fist a mere two feet from Rungawa's bare neck. But he could not pull the trigger. His fingers would not obey the commands of his mind.

Rungawa turned toward him, smiling, and stroked his chin thoughtfully for a moment.

"You may put the gun down now, Mr. Keating."

Jeremy's arm dropped to his side. His mouth sagged open; his heart thundered in his ears. He wanted to run away, but his legs were like the marble of the statues that watched them.

"Forgive me," said Rungawa. "I should not leave you out in the rain like that."

The rain stopped pelting Jeremy. He felt a gentle warmth enveloping him, as if he were standing next to a welcoming fireplace. The two men stood under a cone of invisible protection. Not more than a foot away, Jeremy could see the raindrops spattering on the stony ground.

"A small trick. Please don't be alarmed." Rungawa's voice was a deep rumbling bass, like the voice a lion would have if it could speak in human tongue.

Jeremy stared into the black man's eyes and saw no danger in them, no hatred or violence; only a patient amusement at his own consternation. No, more: a tolerance of human failings, a hope for human achievement, an *understanding* born of centuries of toil and pain and striving.

"Who are you?" Jeremy asked in a frightened whisper.

Rungawa smiled, and it was like sunlight breaking through storm clouds, "Ah, Mr. Keating, you are as intelligent as we had hoped. You cut straight to the heart of the matter."

"You knew I was following you. You set up this . . . meeting."

"Yes. Yes, quite true. Melodramatic of me, I admit. But would you have joined me at dinner if I had sent one of my aides across the street to invite you? I think not."

It's all crazy, Jeremy thought, I must be dreaming this.

"No, Mr. Keating, it is not a dream."

An electric jolt flamed through Jeremy. Jesus Christ, he can read my mind!

"Of course I can," Rungawa said gently, smiling, the way a doctor tells a child that the needle will hurt only for an instant. "How else would I know that you were stalking me?"

Jeremy's mouth went utterly dry. His voice cracked and failed him. If he had been able to move his legs he would have fled like a chimpanzee confronted by a leopard.

"Please do not be afraid, Mr. Keating. Fear is an impediment to understanding. If we had wanted to kill you, it would have been most convenient to let you slip while you were climbing up here."

"What . . ." Jeremy had to swallow and lick his lips before he could say. "Just who are you?"

"I am a messenger, Mr. Keating. Like you, I am merely a tool of my superiors. When I was assigned to this task, I thought it appropriate to make my home base Tanzania." The old man's smile returned, and a hint of self-satisfaction glowed in his eyes. "After all, Tanzania is where the earliest human tribes once lived. What more appropriate place for me to—um, shall we say, *associate* myself with the human race?"

"Associate . . . with the human race." Jeremy felt breathless, weak. His voice was hollow.

"I am not a human being, Mr. Keating. I come from a far distant world, a world that is nothing like this one."

"No . . . that can't . . ."

Rungawa's smile slowly faded. "Some of your people call me a saint. Actually, compared to your species, I am a god."

Jeremy stared at him, stared into his deep black eyes, and saw eternity in them, whirlpools of galaxies spinning majestically in infinite depths of space, stars exploding and evolving, worlds created out of dust.

He heard his voice, weak and childlike, say, "But you look human."

"Of course! Completely human. Even to your x-ray machines."

An alien. Jeremy's mind reeled. An extraterrestrial. With a sense of humor.

"Why not? Is not humor a part of the human psyche? The intelligences who created me made me much more than human, but I have every human attribute—except one. I have no need for vengeance, Mr. Keating."

"Vengeance," Jeremy echoed.

"Yes. A destructive trait. It clouds the perceptions. It is an obstacle in the path of survival."

Jeremy took a deep breath, tried to pull himself together. "You expect me to believe all this?"

"I can see that you do, Mr. Keating. I can see that you now realize that not *all* of the UFO stories have been hoaxes. We have never harmed any of your people, but we did require specimens for careful analysis."

"Why?"

"To help you find the correct path to survival. Your species is on the edge of a precipice. It is our duty to help you avoid extinction, if we can."

"Your duty?"

"Of course. Do not your best people feel an obligation to save other species from extinction? Have not these human beings risked their fortunes and their very lives to protect creatures such as the whale and the seal from slaughter?"

Jeremy almost laughed. "You mean you're from some interstellar Greenpeace project?"

"It is much more complex than that," Rungawa said. "We are not merely trying to protect you from a predator, or from an ecological danger. You human beings are your own worst enemy. We must protect you from ourselves—without your knowing it."

Before Jeremy could reply, Rungawa went on, "It would be easy for us to create a million creatures like myself and to land on your planet in great, shining ships and give you all the answers you need for survival. Fusion energy? A toy. World peace? Easily accomplished. Quadruple your global food production? Double your intelligence? Make you immune to every disease? All this we can do."

"Then why . . ." Jeremy hesitated, thinking. "If you did all that for us, it would ruin us, wouldn't it?"

Rungawa beamed at him. "Ah, you truly understand the problem! Yes, it would destroy your species, just as your Europeans destroyed the cultures of the Americas and Polynesia. Your anthropologists are wrong. There are superior cultures and inferior ones. A superior culture always crushes an inferior, even if he has no intention of doing so."

In the back of his mind, Jeremy realized that he had control of his legs again. He flexed the fingers of his left hand slightly, even the index finger that still curled around the trigger of the dart gun. He could move them at will once more.

"What you're saying," he made conversation, "if that if you landed here and handed us everything we want, our culture would be destroyed."

"Yes," Rungawa agreed. "Just as surely as you whites destroyed the black and brown cultures of the world. We have no desire to do that to you."

"So you're trying to lead us to the point where we can solve our own problems."

"Precisely so, Mr. Keating."

"That's why you've started this World Government," Keating said, his hand tightening on the gun.

"You started the World Government yourselves," Rungawa corrected. "We merely encouraged you, here and there."

"Like the riots in Tunis and a hundred other places."

"We did not encourage that."

"But you didn't prevent them, either, did you?"

"No. We did not."

Shifting his weight slightly to the balls of his feet, Keating said. "Without you the World Government will collapse."

The old man shook his head. "No, that is not true. Despite what your superiors believe, the World Government will endure even the death of 'The Black Saint.' "

"Are you sure?" Keating raised the gun to the black man's eye level. "Are you absolutely certain?"

Rungawa did not blink. His voice became sad as he answered. "Would I have relaxed my control of your limbs if I were not certain?"

Keating hesitated, but held the gun rock-steady.

"You are the test, Mr. Keating. You are the key to your species' future. We know how your wife and son died. Even though we were not directly responsible, we regret their deaths. And the deaths of all the others. They were unavoidable losses."

"Statistics," Keating spat. "Numbers on a list."

"Never! Each of them was an individual whom we knew much better than you could, and we regretted each loss of life as much as you do yourself. Perhaps more, because we understand what each of those individuals could have accomplished, had they lived."

"But you let them die."

"It was unavoidable, I say. Now the question is, can you rise above your own personal tragedy for the good of your fellow humans? Or will you take vengeance upon me and see your species destroy itself?"

"You just said the World Government would survive your death."

"And it will. But it will change. It will become a world dictatorship, in time. It will smother your progress. Your species will die out in an agony of overpopulation, starvation, disease, and terrorism. You do not need nuclear bombs to kill yourselves. You can manage it quite well enough merely by producing too many babies."

"The alternative is to let your people direct us, to become sheep without even knowing it, to jump to your tune."

"No!" Rungawa's deep voice boomed. "The alternative is to become adults. You are adolescents now. We offer you the chance to grow up and stand on your own feet."

"How can I believe that?" Keating demanded.

The old man's smile showed weariness. "The adolescent always distrusts the parent. That is the painful truth, is it not?"

"You have an answer for everything, don't you?"

"Everything, perhaps, except you. You are the key to your species' future, Mr. Keating. If you can accept what I have told you, and allow us to work with you despite all your inner thirst for vengeance, then the human species will have a chance to survive."

Keating moved his hand a bare centimeter to the left and squeezed the gun's trigger. The dart shot out with a hardly audible puff of compressed air and whizzed just past Rungawa's ear. The old man did not flinch.

"You can kill me if you want to," he said to Keating. "That is your decision to make."

"I don't believe you," Jeremy said. "I can't believe you! It's too much, it's too incredible. You can't expect a man to accept everything you've just told me . . . not all at once!"

"We do expect it," Rungawa said softly. "We expect that and more. We want you working with us, not against us."

Jeremy felt as if his guts were being torn apart. "Work with you?" he screamed. "With the people who murdered my wife and son?"

"There are children in the world. Do not deny them their birthright. Do not foreclose their future."

"You bastard!" Jeremy seethed. "You don't miss a trick, do you?"

"It all depends on you. Mr. Keating. You are our test case. What you do now will decide the future of the human species."

A thousand emotions raged through Jeremy. He saw Joanna being torn apart by the mob and Jerry in his cot screaming with fever, flames and death everywhere, the filth and poverty of Jakarta, and the vicious smile of the interrogator as he sharpened his razor.

He's lying, Jeremy's mind shouted at him. He's got to be lying. All this is some clever set of tricks. It can't be true. It can't be!

In a sudden paroxysm of rage and terror and frustration Jeremy hurled the gun high into the rain-filled night, turned abruptly and walked away from Rungawa. He did not look back, but he knew the old man was smiling at him.

It's a trick, he kept telling himself. A goddamned trick. He knew damned well I couldn't kill him in cold blood, with him standing there looking at me with those damned sad eyes of his. Shoot an old man in the face. I just couldn't do it. All he had to do was keep me talking long enough to lose my nerve. Goddamned clever black man. Must be how he lived to get so old.

Keating stamped down the marble steps of the Sacred Way, pushed past the three raincoated guards who had accompanied Rungawa, and walked alone and miserable back toward his *pension*.

How the hell am I going to explain this back at headquarters? I'll have to resign, tell them that I'm not cut out to be an assassin. They'll never believe that. Maybe I could get a transfer, get back into the political section, join the Peace Corps, anything!

He was still furious with himself by the time he reached his *pension*. Still shaking his head, angry that he had let the old man talk him out of his assigned mission. He must have been a medicine man or a voodoo priest when he was younger.

He pushed through the glassed front door of the *pension*, muttering to himself, "You let him trick you. You let that old black man hoodwink you."

The room clerk roused himself from his slumber and got up to reach Jeremy's room key from the rack behind his desk. He was a short, sturdily-built Greek, the kind who would have faced the Persian army at Marathon.

"You must have run very fast," he said to Keating in heavily accented English.

"Huh? What? Why do you say that?"

The clerk smiled, revealing tobacco-stained teeth. "You did not get wet."

Keating looked at the sleeve of his trench coat. It was perfectly dry. The whole coat was as clean and dry as if it had just come from a pressing. His feet were dry; his shoes and trousers and hat were dry.

He turned and looked out the front window. The rain was coming down harder than ever, a torrent of water.

"You run so fast you go between raindrops, eh?" The clerk laughed at his own joke.

Jeremy's knees nearly buckled. He leaned against the desk. "Yeah. Something like that."

The clerk, still grinning, handed him his room key. Jeremy gathered his strength and headed for the stairs, his head spinning.

As he went up the first flight, he heard a voice, even though he was quite alone on the carpeted stairs.

"A small kindness, Mr. Keating," said Rungawa, inside his mind. "I thought it would have been a shame to make you get wet all over again. A small kindness. There will be more to come."

Keating could hear Rungawa chuckling as he walked alone up the stairs. By the time he reached his room, he was grinning himself. ∎

The Unreachable Stars

Stanley Schmidt

In 1970 I had sold maybe four stories to John W. Campbell and had not yet dared to begin thinking of myself as professional. However, I had long wanted to meet His Awesomeness, and so when I found myself making a trip to the Northeast (from Ohio) I did manage to work up enough chutzpah *to ask if I might stop by. John said he would be delighted, because "bull sessions are a good way to get story ideas started."*

And so I went, though not without trepidation. I had read Harry Harrison's description of a meeting with Campbell as "like being fed through a buzz saw or a man-sized meat grinder," and I more or less expected to feel intimidated. Especially since the only story idea I was taking to talk about was so far short of half-baked that I could easily imagine his throwing me out after a few minutes, annoyed that I had wasted his time.

What I actually got was three hours of his undivided attention, lunch, and a high-powered dose of the most stimulating and enjoyable conversation I have ever experienced—less like a buzz saw than the intellectual equivalent of a good gymnastic workout. During one of those hours we kicked my idea back and forth, and in that hour together we worked more bugs out of it than I could have in a week of hard labor by myself. I went home and wrote the story and John not only bought the first draft he saw, but gave it a Kelly Freas cover and rushed it into print in the shortest possible time.

I think he did that because he, like I, was afraid that what I was writing about was a clear and present danger. If it happened, we would be the villains. "The Unreachable Stars" was not a "fun" story to write; it was something I had to get out of my system. I would like to believe that it made some small contribution to making sure it won't *be prophetic.*

ANTHON HILLAR COULD NOT QUITE get over his awe at the luxuriousness of the Regional Planning Director's office—and at the security measures which the government seemed to consider necessary. The director, a man of abnormally healthy and well-fed appearance, sat behind a massive desk with a row of lights spelling out "Olaf Karper" and stared at Anthon with an expression of mild amusement. But he stared by means of a closed-circuit television system, as if afraid to expose himself to the actual presence of a common person. And Anthon suddenly realized from the expression on the bureaucrat's face that he was not being taken at all seriously. "Well, then," he asked, suddenly defensive, "may I presume to ask what *you* think the stars are?"

Karper flashed a sardonic grin, apparently meant for someone out of view in his inner office. "I don't waste a great deal of thought on them," he confessed with a shrug. "I suppose they're what the nursery rhymes say—globs of fire, or something, somewhere off in the sky. So what? Hardly matters to command much of the attention of a busy administrator here on Earth."

"But they *are!*" Anthon insisted, leaning earnestly forward in the uncomfortable straight chair provided for visitors. "If these books I've found are right, they may be very important indeed. If they really are like other suns, pouring light and heat on other planets like Earth—or like Earth used to be—and if we can find ways to send people there . . ." He saw how little impression he was making on the Regional Director and his voice sagged as he finished, "They could provide some relief. At the very least a fresh chance for a few people . . ."

He gave up. And when Karper spoke he didn't even mention the soaring idea Anthon had been trying to get across. He just said, "About those books of yours, young man. Where did you say you found them?"

Anthon sighed impatiently. "One of the new energy-and-food complexes in Kaliforn," he repeated. "I already told you, I was supervising a construction group tearing up a historical preserve to make room. We were in an old burial region and we hit an unusually large, elaborate tomb. Some rich Twenty-first Century eccentric or something; I don't know. But it contained a lot of relics of the age—including books and papers. Our machines broke into an outer chamber and we found the ones I told you about. There may be more. But the rest of the vault is stronger. We'll need special equipment to open it without damaging any other artifacts that may—"

"And you came straight to me to ask for the special help," Karper interrupted, "rather than going to your immediate supervisor?"

"Yes. The issue seemed too important—"

"Hm-m-m! Proper channels are provided to be properly gone through, young man. Your supervisor can hardly be expected to like your bypassing him. I don't like it either. And I don't know *how* you bluffed and bullied your way past my secretaries." He paused, shaking his head and meditatively chewing a fingernail. "You thought it was too important," he repeated finally. "Now how on Earth did you decide that?"

"As soon as I saw what the books were about—"

Karper's eyebrows shot up in mock astonishment. "And how did you do that? You read Ancient English?"

"I told you," Anthon snapped, increasingly tired of repeating himself in circles, "I showed them to a friend. A professor of Ancient English in a Government School—"

"Who?"

"Mylo Gotfry. I told you that, too." Anthon suddenly felt—for the first time—an unaccustomed qualm. Had it been wise, he wondered, to mention Gotfry's name?

"Odd," Karper mused, again chewing his fingernail, "that a construction worker should be so friendly with a scholar. Can you explain that to me?"

"I can," Anthon said, his exasperation rising dangerously. "but what difference does it make? You keep harping on these petty things about me and ignoring what I came about. There's a pile of lost knowledge preserved out there and I want to be sure we get it out safely. Don't you care at all about that? Wouldn't you even like to find out if the stars *might* offer some kind of a way out?"

"Frankly," Karper muttered with obvious irritation, "I think this whole notion of other suns and planets is hogwash—and that goes double for the idea of people going to such places. But—" Abruptly his manner became suave, ingratiating . . . patronizing. Making quite a show of it, he produced a writing pad on which Anthon saw but could not quite read a couple of scrawled words, and prepared to write some more. "If it will make you feel better, why don't you tell me exactly how to find this vault of yours, and I'll see that proper action is taken."

Anthon stared distastefully at the director's face for a long time, feeling a grow-ing—and frightening—realization that "proper action" was not what he wanted. "Forget it," he said curtly, and as he said the words he rose from the chair, not allowing himself time to reconsider, and strode hastily from the room.

"Well, can you beat that!" Karper blinked in astonishment as Anthon Hillar's back disappeared through the door on his phonescreen.

"Do you want me to have him stopped before he leaves the building?" his secretary asked, reaching for call buttons.

"No." Karper shook his head absently. "The man's a crackpot, obviously. Not worth any more of our time." But as the secretary left and Karper tried to get back to what he had been doing before the interruption, his thoughts kept returning to the strange young construction worker. There were things about his story . . .

Karper couldn't be sure, of course. Such things were not included in his training. But the wild ideas Hillar claimed to have unearthed sounded vaguely subversive. It obviously would not do to have rumors spreading that there was a way out—when, of course, there wasn't.

And if, by any farfetched chance, there actually *was* anything to the ideas . . . if, impossible as it seemed, there *was* a way out—

In either case, Hillar should be in custody, and his vault should be found and opened under strictest security. And that scholar—Gotfry—who had already seen some of the books . . .

Softly cursing his blunder in letting Hillar walk away so easily, Karper hurriedly punched buttons on his phonescreen and waited for a connection. When an image finally formed on the screen, he saluted it quickly and said, "Sir, something's come up and I need your advice. The man left my office just minutes ago and he can't have gone far . . . "

Karper was quite right that Anthon had not, at that moment, gone far—in terms of distance. But it took little time or effort for a man to lose himself effectively in the city's throngs.

And that was exactly what Anthon intended to do.

He had no plans yet. His decision had come suddenly and surprised him as much as Karper, and he had not yet considered what he would do next. It had just suddenly seemed clear that the ideas from the tomb were more likely to be reburied than revived by Karper and his fellow bureaucrats. And Anthon felt that they were much too important for that.

So he had left. Unceremoniously, but probably not in such a way as to prompt any immediate punitive action.

Still, there was no point in taking unnecessary risks. So as soon as he left the government building, he merged into the dense crowd jamming the street and threaded a zigzag course away from the building, moving fast but trying to avoid an appearance of suspicious haste. Blending in was easy—the crowd contained such a multitude of so many nondescript types that it was hard to follow any individual through it for long.

Not far away, the crowd thinned somewhat and the broad boulevard splintered into narrow streets penetrating the deep, dingy canyons of a residential district. Here Anthon felt slightly more conspicuous. Every few steps, beggars held their cups out and stared pointedly at him. He hurried on past them, past the thin hungry people who were everywhere, past the shabby rows of crowded apartments where they lived and died and watched blaring television sets. The day was hot, even at its end, and air-conditioners poured excess heat into the street all along both sides. Anthon felt uncomfortable here—crime was commonplace, and the drugged and sick and mendicant had all become more numerous even within his own memory. And why not? Every man, woman, and child received a "fair share" of food and energy—but every year the fair share was a little smaller. Naturally more people would try to supplement theirs—or give up.

And when Anthon thought of Olaf Karper's round ruddy face and plush office against this background, he smelled a rat in the rationing process.

He was shaking as he reached the East 367th Street transport exchange and hurried down the ramp to the tunnels. The crowd circulated here, too, jostling for space on the moving standee strips of the intracity group and the enclosed trains of the Express system. Small private vehicles whizzed by in the Open lanes, and beggars sat cross-legged in reserved places along the walls. Anthon fought his way to a Seaward Express platform and got onto the second train. There were no seats, so he stood, gripping an overhead rail, as the train lurched forward into the dark tube. Looking straight ahead, he thought dazedly, *All Earth is like this! And it wasn't always . . .*

The train hummed quietly for a few minutes, then lurched to a stop and waited as its passengers streamed to the exits. Anthon streamed with them, across the platform interchange and up to street level.

The smell of the sea was in the air here—though largely masked by the smells of the city—and things were a bit quieter. Anthon relaxed slightly. He was miles from Karper's office now, and almost certainly free of pursuers—unless Karper had taken his story much more to heart than Anthon believed likely. That meant he could now begin giving some real thought to his own actions.

He entered the continuous row of buildings that hid the beach from the street. There would be food dispensers and tables off a lobby, and it would be easier to think on a less empty stomach.

He found the machines with little effort. The room has half empty, and over the general chatter Anthon easily heard an enraged patrolman in the corner lecturing an embarrassed ten-year-old on how he must never, *ever* throw glass in the aluminum slot on the recycling terminal. But it barely registered on his mind—he had heard it before, and the offense was one he would never think of committing himself. He stuck his ration plate in a food dispenser, made his selection, and let his mind settle onto his own affairs.

He stood alone at an empty table to eat his meal and ponder his situation. What had got into him, anyway? Fired by the ideas Mylo had found in the old books and papers, he had gone to Karper with grandiose but vague ideas of acting on them. True, he *had* bypassed his supervisor—but it had seemed necessary at the time.

And then the interview with Karper had proved so fruitless that he had impulsively walked out in the middle of it. A nearly unthinkable breach of etiquette, he realized now, and as such probably a mistake—but not a crime.

And for that reason he almost certainly had no cause to expect trouble from that quarter.

But now he faced decisions. His idea, when he left, had been that he might do something on his own.

A vague idea—just like the ones that had taken him to Karper in the first place. The words from the tomb—fragile paper books imperfectly preserved in the sealed darkness, loose sheets coated with clear plastic—had tickled his imagination with the idea that there were other worlds and men might reach them. But they had told him nothing of *how*. And he knew so little.

Frustrated, but determned not to be unnerved by it, he finished his meal and went to the rear of a lower level. A service corridor led him outside on the sea side of the building, and he sat down on the narrow seawall with his feet dangling high above the breaking surf. It was one of the few places he knew where he could find a semblance of solitude.

It was getting dark. The rows upon rows of window lights in the building at his back danced in constantly shifting reflections on the dark water that stretched to the horizon.

And above them, in the sky, other points of light twinkled from fixed locations—the stars, whatever they were. Anthony could see nearly a dozen, and the old book said there were really thousands that could be seen where there was no city glow. Anthon tried to picture that, and failed.

But if there were . . .

And there was the moon, now a bright crescent low in the west. The closest of all other worlds, according to the books, and a desolate place not fit for living.

Yet, if the plastic sheets did not lie, the ancients had *walked* there!

Looking at the sky and remembering what Mylo had read to him, Anthon felt the same excitement that had sent him to Karper welling up again. Exotic names haunted him.

Where *was* Cape Kendy?

Then he remembered how little he knew and the excitement collapsed in a limp heap. *I don't know where to begin,* he thought bluntly. *Face it. I might as well go back to work in the morning and forget all this. But it was a nice dream.*

He stood up abruptly, jerking his eyes away from the sky, and turned back to the door to the building. *Maybe,* he thought savagely, defensively, *those papers were just a hoax anyway . . . .*

He started inside—and stopped in midstride as a voice spoke inside his head. "No," it said quietly but distinctly—and Anthon knew it was coming from somewhere else, "they're no hoax."

Ozrlag looked up as soon as he had thought it and saw Mithjar standing in the doorway, glaring sternly and flicking his forked tail slowly from side to side. Flustered, trying to move his four-fingered paw as inconspicuously as possible, he shut off the transmitter and looked sheepishly at Mithjar, waiting. "Hello," he said finally, weakly.

Mizhjar blinked his nicitating membranes indifferently. "Just what," he said grimly, "do you think you were doing just now?"

"I . . ." Ozrlag began uncertainly.

"Never mind," Mizhjar interrupted, snapping his tail impatiently. "I know what you were doing. The question is *why?*" He strode toward Ozrlag, powerful muscles rippling under his soft pink down, and stood looking ominously down at his seated apprentice. "Don't you realize that people are *trying* to observe a culture in its natural state down there?"

"Yes, sir," Ozrlag gulped—or at least did what would correspond to gulping among the jömür. "But . . ." He had already started to recover from the shock of discovery by his adviser, and already he was preparing to attempt a defense. "This Anthon is special. We'd been studying this culture for seven seasons before we noticed him, and how far did we get? All we knew was that it was anomalous—a subsistence economy with a high-level technology. Nuclear power in full swing—though apparently frozen at the breeder reactor stage—and a vast population on the brink of starvation. Weird. Paradoxical. But *how did it get that way?* We had big teams scanning local archives through native minds and finding no clues. There seemed to be a big gap in their records, as if they had no interest in history. What Anthon found seems likely to start filling the gap."

"And we already have a group concentrating on what Anthon found," Mizhjar pointed out, "through Mylo Gotfry. You still haven't said anything to explain your arrogance in making a direct contact."

"Anthon thinks there's more where that came from," Ozrlag said. "He tried to get special help to get at it—because he's interested in the space-travel concept, which he seems never to have met before. Just now he was about to give up—and that would cost us access to this new information. So I thought it would be to our advantage to prod him a little." Ozrlag paused, looking expectantly at Mizhjar, then added defensively, "Look, I didn't give us away. I just made one little comment, as an anonymous mental voice. He could interpret it as his own conscience, or divine inspiration, or whatever's fashionable this season."

The expression on Mizhjar's feline face softened slightly, to Ozrlag's considerable relief. "I'll grant," he said, just a bit grudgingly, "that we'd all like to know what's in the other documents—if there *are* any other documents. But I'm still not sure you chose the wisest way to try to get at them. And look here." He motioned vaguely at the monitor panel—a panel which, like most on board the orbiting ship, would have struck a human visitor as oddly blank. But that was simply because most of the instrument readouts were directly telepathic, and Mizhjar's apparently random gesture directed Ozrlag unerringly to the intended item. "This ruler type that Anthon went to—Karper—is *not* going to help him help us. But it looks like Anthon's request unsettled him quite a bit, and the government's going to go after whatever other documents there are on its own."

Ozrlag hadn't noticed that before, but it was obvious now. Less obvious were the reasons. He started to comment, but before he started, Mizhjar continued.

"Just what they intend isn't clear—anyway to me. I don't think they're sure themselves, yet. But there's a good possibility that they'll destroy that material, or at least impound it, rather than trying to read it. So it behooves us to get there first—with somebody who wants to read it."

"Anthon?" Ozrlag asked, startled.

Mizhjar nodded. "Yes. and he might be reluctant, in his present mood."

"So," Ozrlag said slowly, hardly believing Mizhjar had come around to this in these few minutes, "I can keep talking to him?"

"I'm afraid you'll have to," Mizhjar said with obvious reluctance. "But, please . . . try to be discreet."

Anthon's first reaction to the voice in his head was puzzlement—and a bit of concern for his own mental health, since he had never been subject to hallucinations. He paused, just outside the door, and listened intently. But all he heard was the sea pounding the wall behind him, and the soft hum of the building's service machinery.

He shrugged and entered the building, shoving the imagined voice into the back of his mind. Resigned to the futility of what he had hoped to do, he headed back toward the street and the transport exchange. He would go home and count this day lost; tomorrow he would return to his job, take whatever minor punishment was coming to him, and then live out his days as he had always expected to.

The train was purring through its black tunnel, its few passengers reflected brightly in the small windows, when Anthon heard the silent voice again. "Giving up?" it chided gently. "With so much at stake? A fresh chance, and you pass it up?"

It was too distinct to ignore. Anthon grudgingly acknowledged its reality and tried to think rationally about it. Either it was a trick his own mind was playing on him, or *somebody* was somehow communicating directly with him. Anthon had heard folk tales of such communication. He had never believed them, but he was not one to dismiss possibilities without even a cursory examination.

He glanced around to make sure no other passengers were close. Then he whispered. "Who are you?"

He listened—if that is the right word. But no answer came.

Several seconds passed with no sound but the hum of the train and faint laughter from the far end of the car.

Then the "voice" came again, cool and with no indication of having heard Anthon's question. "The stars, Anthon, the stars!" it said. "Are you going to let them slip through your fingers? Aren't you going to *try* to get the other documents from the tomb?"

"The stars," Anthony muttered, quoting Karper, "are hogwash."

"No, Anthon," the voice insisted. "The stars are real. And they have new worlds—"

"How do *you* know?" Anthon snapped.

No answer.

Anthon waited. Then, "Whoever you are—can you hear me?"

Silence. Just the hum of the train.

Anthon shrugged. *OK,* he thought, annoyed. *So maybe I don't know how to talk back so he can hear me. Or maybe it* is *just a hallucination.*

Either way, he didn't like it.

The train screeched into the exchange nearest his home and he got off. Without further delay, the train streaked noisily out of sight while Anthon crossed the platform interchange—cautiously, for transport exchanges attracted thugs at night—and caught a lift to his street.

The street, like most residentials, was a narrow canyon between highrow dwellings, still sweltering in the exhaust of a thousand air-conditioners even this late at night. A few bright stars hung in the narrow slice of sky between roof fronts and shimmered in the turbulent air.

And Anthon felt haunted. He no longer heard the voice—although occasionally he seemed to catch a wisp of something so faint he couldn't be sure it was real—but the questions it had raised were again churning in his mind. He had thought the issue was closed—and now, whether the voice was real or imagined, it was tormenting him again.

Suppose, he thought, *the stars* are *real. Then you* are *throwing something big away. Can you do that and live with yourself?*

What can I do? another part of his mind countered. *I don't know where to begin.*

You begin, came the reply—and Anthon wondered idly if this dialogue was all in his own mind or if that voice was actually helping—*with the tomb. All the documents*—

And suddenly Anthon's mind pulled together into a unit again as he realized the magnitude of what he had just thought. Of course that was the place to begin! His attempt to get at whatever was still in the tomb had failed—but they had barely scratched the surface of what Mylo already had. Possible *that* contained a key.

For a fleeting instant, Anthon wondered about the tomb itself. While he had heard of such elaborate burials before, with artifacts preserved along with the body, he knew they were not usual in any part of the Twenty-first Century. What sort of man had had himself buried so oddly, with a library he could never read again—and why?

Had he, Anthon wondered abruptly, been trying to tell those who followed him something?

Then the thought passed and Anthon filled with new determination. He paused at the door of his own apartment and turned his new plan over once in his mind, examining it. He would go back to Mylo and learn all he could from the documents already in hand. And then, armed with that knowledge, he could better seek whatever else he needed to restore the lost arts.

Maybe, he thought jauntily as he turned away from his unopened door and started back to the street, *I'll even go find Cape Kendy myself!*

Ozrlag saw Anthon's decision and swore—and among the jömür, profanity is a highly developed and highly regarded art form. Reluctantly, he summoned Mizhjar.

Mizhjar's first words, when he arrived, were, *"Now* what have you done?"

"Please!" Ozrlag winced. "Must you always assume I've botched something? It's just that . . . well, my attempts to goad Anthon into going back after whatever documents are still in that tomb aren't working quite according to plan. I've got him interested in space travel again—but now he fancies himself as some sort of savior of his people." Mizhjar's whiskers curled questioningly and Ozrlag explained, "That is, he sees space travel as a way out of their domestic problems, and since the government doesn't seem interested, he wants to learn about it himself. He's going back to Mylo Gotfry to get started."

"Ridiculous!" Mizhjar snarled.

"Of course," Ozrlag agreed. "But even more importantly, a wasteful duplication of effort. We already have historians and comparative scientists scanning that material through Gotfry. Anthon isn't going to do a thing for us there. And meanwhile he's doing nothing to keep Karper from grabbing whatever new stuff there is out from under our noses."

Mizhjar nodded slightly. "What are you leading up to, Ozrlag?"

"I tried to obey your instructions to be discreet," said Ozrlag, "and this is where it got me. I couldn't be explicit enough. All I could do was prod him to follow his own inclinations—and they led him in a direction just different enough from what we had in mind to be utterly useless to us. Considering the possible importance of new documents to our cultural studies, I wondered if you would consider it wise to let him in on a little secret. If he knew who we are and what we want, and saw the possibility of mutual benefit—"

"*No!*" Mizhjar's tufted ears snapped erect and he broke in without waiting for Ozrlag to finish. He was obviously not at all amused. "That sort of thing is *strictly* a last resort. I can imagine circumstances in which you'd have no choice—but things haven't got that bad yet. Keep applying the same kind of pressure you've been using, but slant it toward getting at the new information before it's lost. You can do that, can't you? Play on this obsession of his. Use it to our advantage. And don't disillusion him too soon. You understand?"

Ozrlag, approximately speaking, sighed. "Yes, sir. I'll do my best."

Mylo Gotfry now lived, as befitted one entrusted with the education of future government officials, in a well-appointed penthouse among the foothills two hundred miles from Anthon's home. It was midday when Anthon stepped off the last strip and looked quickly around, less to marvel at the tiered expanse of rooftops stretching down into the valley and up the neighboring hills than to detect any sign of possible personal danger. If felt rather silly, almost paranoid—but the fact was that he had now been away from work without authorization for several hours, and that sort of thing simply isn't done. He *would* be hunted, and though he was far from home, Karper knew of his association with Mylo. He did not dare feel safe here.

Feeling a completely unaccustomed apprehensiveness—he had never been a fugitive before—he entered the building. He scanned the door-lined corridor furtively from the end before entering it, and when a lift stopped for him he watched the door open from a hidden alcove across the hall to be sure the car was empty.

His tensest moment came when the lift discharged him into a glassed-in vestibule on the roof. There was virtually no cover here, Anthon realized uncomfortably—no place to hide if they happened to trace him here.

But they were not here now, and things improved slightly in the corridor that served all the rooftop apartments. It was all glassed in, like the vestibule where the lift came up, to give the tenants the illusion of being outside without the annoyance of being rained on. But the immediate neighborhoods of many of the apartments were decorated by artificial shrubbery to heighten the illusion—rather sparse, but better than nothing.

Breathing only a little easier, Anthon reached Mylo's door and stopped. He put his ear to the door, listening for voices other than Mylo's, but heard nothing.

He knocked.

As he waited, he mulled over his solidifying plans, feeling growing confidence. Sure, the other worlds were far away—that was obvious from their appearance as tiny spots in the sky. Of course they wouldn't be able to absorb enough people to relieve the crowding on Earth. But that crowding had grown so bad that increasing numbers found local conditions intolerable—and Anthon was sometimes plagued by doubts about how long such a civilization could survive at all. If it didn't—or even if it just remained as it was—it seemed increasingly desirable to give even a few people a chance to try again, to start fresh on an unspoiled world and avoid the mistakes of their ancestors.

Their ancestors had been on the way to achieving that possibility—and, apparently, had abandoned the attempt. Anthon had no idea why, but he had found a way to learn what they had known and try to build on it. His mistake had been going to Karper prematurely—before he had thought it out to the point where he could offer more than vague conjecture. But after he had studied the documents Mylo had here, he would be able to offer concrete suggestions. And Mylo was, in his way, a rather influential man. . . .

Meanwhile, Mylo was also a clever man. Clever enough to help Anthon stay out of sight while he studied the old books and papers.

Anthon realized with a start that he had been standing here letting his thoughts wander for a long time, and Mylo had not answered. He knocked again.

Again a long silence. This time Anthon's thoughts focused on a question: What was wrong in there?

He didn't knock again. He stepped behind the artificial shrubs and stood under the window, small and set high in the wall to insure privacy while letting sunlight in. Hooking his hands over the narrow sill, he hauled himself up and rested his weight on his forearms while he looked inside.

Mylo was there, right across the room, but Anthon had never seen him like this before. He sat at a table, the ancient volumes piled before him, his bald head tilted toward Anthon and glistening with sweat. He didn't look up—his eyes never left the tattered volume he held open in front of him. He was flipping through the pages, in order and quite methodically, but so fast that he couldn't possibly be actually reading them.

With growing alarm, Anthon rapped on the windowpane.

Mylo didn't even look up. He kept flipping through the pages as if he had not heard Anthon.

Anthon dropped to the roof. Something was very wrong—and very strange—with Mylo. And Anthon wasn't at all sure what he should try to do about it. Should he break in—or leave as fast as he could?

He was about to decide on breaking in when that "voice" returned, and this time there was a commanding sense of urgency in it. *"Anthon! Hide—right now!"*

The tone was so compelling that Anthon was stretched flat on the roof, between the wall and the shrubs, before he even thought of questioning it. And then when he started to think about what he had done, he heard footsteps coming up the corridor from the lift.

He froze, waiting, breathing as lightly as he could. The footsteps passed right by him, separated from him only by the thin plastic plants, and then he saw four male feet turn and stop at Mylo's door. Lying very still, he rolled his eyes upward. He could see their faces now, and if they happened to look this way they would see him, too.

One of them was Olaf Karper. The other Anthon didn't recognize, but he was tall and rugged, with a craggy face and brilliant red hair, and he wore a government suit.

Karper knocked on Mylo's door. He and the stranger waited silently for half a minute, then he knocked again.

This time a full minute passed. Then Karper looked up at the stranger and said, "He doesn't answer, sir. I have no idea why he should suspect anything—unless Hillar came here and warned him. Do I have your permission to break the door down?"

Anthon frowned—or would have, had he dared to allow himself that luxury. Karper made it sound as if they were looking for Mylo, instead of Anthon.

The stranger nodded. "Go ahead, Olaf."

Karper drew back a step from the door and took a small metal instrument from a deep pocket. He made an adjustment on it, then pointed it at the lock and seemed to brace himself.

At the anticlimactic sound of a latch turning inside, Karper lowered his instrument. Anthon heard the door open and Mylo appeared, looking pale, dazed, and disoriented. "What is it?" he asked, his voice weak and tired. Anthon felt slightly relieved, but there was still much that needed explaining.

The tall readhead flashed a card at Mylo. "Mylo Gotfry? Artu Landen, Senior Security. You know a chap named Anthon Hillar?"

Mylo frowned slightly. He looked as if he were gradually getting his bearings back. "I do," he said. "Why?"

"He brought you some books—old books, to translate. We want those."

"I don't understand. They're just—"

"Don't argue. They're suspected of conflict with the people's interest. Here's my warrant. Now, the books, please."

Mylo read the warrant carefully, slowly, then turned without a word and disappeared into the apartment, leaving the door open. He reappeared shortly, carrying the pile from the table.

Security Officer Landen looked at them. "Old, all right," he muttered. "Are these all?"

"Yes." Mylo added no title of respect.

Landen hesitated briefly, then nodded to Karper. "Better make sure he didn't forget any, Olaf." Karper squeezed through the door past Mylo. While he waited, Landen lifted a book off the top and thumbed curiously through it, shaking his head. Then he took several books off the pile and tucked them under his arm.

Karper came back out and reported, "That seems to be all of them, sir."

Landen smiled slightly and nodded at the books Mylo still held. "Good. Get the rest, will you, Olaf?" Then, to Mylo, "Gotfry, you know as well as I that this sort of work is to be done only under official supervision. I won't take any action against you this time, but I'd advise you to steer clear of unauthorized moonlighting in the future." He turned without waiting for an answer and started briskly back to the lift, closely followed by Karper and the rest of the books.

Mylo looked after them for no more than a second, then turned, looking vaguely puzzled, and went back inside and shut the door. Anthon lay still, waiting to be sure Landen and Karper were really gone, and tried to make sense out of what had just happened. They hadn't been interested in Mylo after all, it seemed. Apparently they weren't even very concerned about Anthon. Instead, they wanted the books—and Artu Landen was Senior Security! Why would anybody that high suddenly care about those books—while ignoring a construction supervisor absent without leave?

After what seemed a reasonable time, Anthon cautiously stuck his head out between the shrubs and looked down toward the lift. It looked safe. He stood up and started toward Mylo's door.

"No," said the voice in his head.

Anthon hesitated, frowing and thinking rapidly. Too much was going on that he didn't understand. In particular, he was getting tired of being kept in the dark by whoever was behind that "voice."

"Why not?" he thought, and when no answer came he took another step forward.

"Don't," said the voice.

Anthon stopped again, but not indecisively. He was pretty sure now that, if the voice was actually coming from outside, its owner *could* read his thoughts. Its remarks were always too well timed for coincidence. In fact, thinking back, he remembered one point in last night's exchange on the train when the voice had seemed to slip and answer him directly. So he should be able to bargain. "You don't seem to want me to know who you are," he thought pointedly, "but you also don't want me to talk to Mylo. I'd like some information from you. Will you answer some questions—or shall I knock?" He lifted his hand toward the door.

He felt an odd throbbing in his brain, a sort of sub-verbal command to wait. Then that faded and the voice said, with obvious reluctance, "What do you want to know?"

"So," Anthon smiled slightly, lowering his hand, "you *can* read me. I thought so. Let's begin with the obvious. Who are you?"

No words formed, but Anthon "felt" the owner of the voice frantically seeking a way to avoid answering. "You've been needling me with the idea that the stars and their planets are real," he prompted, "as if you're certain of it. You've *experienced* interstellar travel?"

Pause. Then, quietly, "Yes."

"You're *from* one of those other worlds?"

"Yes."

A slight, remote hope rose. "Are you human?"

"That's a hard word to define," the voice said wryly. "In some senses, we would say yes. But we aren't of your kind."

Anthon had suspected that. He thought of the odd state he had found Mylo in before Landen and Karper had come. The idea of a connection was hard to escape. He asked bluntly, "What were you doing to Mylo Gotfrey a few minutes ago?"

Another pause as the voice—Ozrlag, Anthon knew suddenly, without knowing how—tried to hedge and again found itself trapped. "We are interested in the origins of your present culture, but most of the information about them seems to have been suppressed. So we were especially interested in the contents of the documents you found. We were having your friend read them for us—using his ability to translate the archaic language. When you arrived, we were having him go through them very rapidly, because we anticipated trouble from the government and we wanted to get as much as possible before it came." Ozrlag seized the opportunity to change the subject, quickening the pace of his thoughts. "As you see, the trouble we anticipated has already come. And don't think it will stop here. We both wanted what was in those books, Anthon—you did and we did. Now neither of us may get it. But there may be more in the unopened compartments of that burial vault—the ones you tried to get Karper to help you open. You'd like to see it and we'd like to see it—and it's pretty obvious your government would also like to get their hands on it. Maybe we can stop them—but it will take speed and cooperation."

Anthon frowned. "Are you suggesting a deal?"

"Yes. Go back to the vault—tonight. Lead us to it, and . . . and we'll send someone from our expedition to meet you and help you open it."

"Where is your expedition?" Anthon asked suspiciously.

"Never mind that," Ozrlag thought curtly. "You be there—and so will we."

Anthon drew a deep breath. "I think," he replied coolly, "that you want it more than I do. I'll agree—but only if you agree to provide more in return than you've offered so far."

"Such as?"

"Such as this." Anthon paused to compose his thoughts before beginning the proposition which had suddenly occurred to him. "There's no certainty that I'll be able to learn all I need to know about space travel from the books in the tomb. But you have experience. You can give us advice. You can help us get started."

"That's a big order," Ozrlag said after a while. "I doubt that you realize how big."

"No matter." Anthon was firm. "That's what I expect in return. If you want my help—take it or leave it."

A long pause—and, it seemed to Anthon—although he couldn't say why—a troubled pause. And then Ozrlag answered with similar firmness, "We'll tell you what we can—but only *after* you've led us to the vault."

Anthon thought it over. He seemed to have no more bargaining points. And the recent actions of Karper and Landen suggested strongly that getting to the vault first was a matter of some urgency.

He nodded slightly. "Agreed."

Ozrlag shut off the transmitter and turned away from it with an emphatic, *Whew! Well, it's happened. Hope Mizhjar believes it.* The realization of the turn events had taken, and what he had got himself into in terms of promises, was a little awesome. *But,* as he reminded himself quite truthfully, *there's no point in worrying much over that . . . .*

He got on the interphone to Amzhraz, the head of the research group that had been working through Gotfry. "Evidently you know your books were confiscated," he said without preamble. "Did you get anything you can use?"

Amzhraz made a modified affirmative gesture—disappointed, but not completely frustrated. "Yes, by pushing him. We'll try to keep track of the books, but we can't make just anybody read them for us. The language problem, you know. But we got enough to piece together quite an interesting picture. Look at this." He held a compact summary up to the phone.

Ozrlag glanced at it and his whiskers writhed in puzzlement. "Interesting," he agreed, "to put it mildly. I'm afraid I don't have time to study it right now, but I certainly will." He broke the connection, braced himself, and called Mizhjar.

"You did *what?*" Mizhjar rasped, drawing his lips tight against his teeth, when Ozrlag had finished summarizing.

"I admitted we were from offplanet," Ozrlag repeated quietly, forcing himself to remain calm, "and interested in their culture. And I . . . er . . . said we would send one of us to help him open the rest of that tomb."

Mizhjar struggled silently with his temper. Then he said tightly, "Ozrlag, you'd be a lot easier to take if you weren't so impulsive. What made you do a fool thing like that?"

"You said yourself," Ozrlag reminded, "that you could imagine circumstances where I would have no choice. They seemed to have arrived. Anthon—and the others—had me in a corner.''

'''I also said that anything like this was strictly a last resort, and I think you were too hasty—as usual—in deciding a last resort was called for. A moment's thought . . .'' He broke off, radiating exasperation. "Exactly what pressure did Anthon put on you?''

Ozrlag cringed slightly. "He was suspicious and about to barge in on Mylo Gotfry when he had just been reading for us. I tried to stop him, but he threatened to go ahead unless I'd answer some questions. I was afraid if he talked to Gotfry right then he'd find out—''

"So you *told* him more than he would have learned from Gotfry! *Think* about what you did, Ozrlag! What did you accomplish? You just blundered in and . . .''

"He would have learned some of it anyway,'' Ozrlag interrupted hotly, "and then his curiosity would have driven him after the rest. I'm not convinced that I really made things worse than they would have been anyway. And meanwhile Karper had brought another ruler and they confiscated the books Gotfry had been reading. They'll be hunting for the others, too, since they know about the tomb. Anthon's probably our only chance to get at them first. He's actually serious about this thing, Mizhjar. And since he was going to know at least something about us anyway, sending somebody down cautiously at night didn't seem so—''

Mizhjar was twisting his tail in slow, ominous patterns. "You've got a glib tongue, Ozrlag,'' he said carefully. "But you still need some judgment to go with it. Your argument has a bit of merit—just a bit. And enough damage is already done that we might as well go through with it, just in case there really is something important still in that vault. But who should go? It'll be a touchy job. So far only Anthon knows about us—Gotfry has some inkling, but he doesn't understand—but whoever goes down to the surface risks discovery by others. He'll be after valuable information for our cultural studies—but at the risk of jeopardizing the continuation of those studies at any level. And at considerable personal risk.'' He looked straight at Ozrlag, his expression stony. "Since this was your bright idea, I think *you* should be the one to go.''

"*Me?*'' Ozrlag yelped.

"You,'' Mizhjar said with finality. "I think you may learn something from it. Since so much depends on your not making an ass of yourself, I suggest you get over to Amzhraz and start briefing yourself. And when you go down there—you'd better be careful''

"But . . . '' Ozrlag started to protest and then broke off. The phonescreen had already gone blank.

Very briefly, he felt almost panic-stricken. Then, as he watched the after image fade away, he smiled to himself.

He had thought of another project.

To avoid the risk of unintended further damage to the tomb in which the books had been found, Anthon had transferred his crew's operations to another area before visiting Karper. He had even had the foresight to avoid making any fuss over that site, or giving the men any indication that it was the reason for suddenly moving their work elsewhere. Thus now, as he picked his way across the mutilated ground with no light but that of the moon, stars, and skyglow, he did not really expect to meet anybody. But his nerves and senses were tuned to a high pitch because of things that *could* happen—and in anticipation of meeting a traveler from the stars. He wasn't even sure, after the conversation he had heard between Landen and Karper, if they were looking for him. But he was sure he didn't want to be apprehended now. He had bigger things to do.

The air was getting slightly chilly and Anthon was very conscious of the smell of recently turned damp earth. And then he "heard" Ozrlag: "Anthon . . . you're nearly there? Don't answer out loud."

"Yes," Anthon said silently.

"You're alone?"

"I think so." Ozrlag must have known that—unless his mind-reading abilities were limited and he needed to check them against perceptions of Anthon's which he could not see directly.

"Good. Stop where you are. I'll join you in a minute." Anthon stopped, anxiously scanning the darkness around him for his first glimpse of an extraterrestrial. He tried to imagine what Ozrlag would look like, and, of course, how he would be traveling . . .

He wasn't sure exactly when he first caught sight of him. He just knew, after a while, that an indistinct shape had detached itself from the darkness and was moving toward him across the ground, perhaps a dozen yards away, eyes glowing faint yellow. As Ozrlag came closer, Anthon saw that he was walking upright on two legs and waving a long tail behind him, looking uncannily like a large cat modified for an erect posture and standing about four feet tall. But his slit pupils were horizontal, his tail was forked, he had a fine fuzzy covering instead of long fur, and fingers instead of paws—and he was wearing simple clothes and carrying a hexagonal suitcase-like thing in one hand. Anthon felt an unaccustomed excitement as the alien strode up, stopped three feet in front of him, and looked up at his face. But he saw no evidence that Ozrlag felt any similar emotion at meeting him.

"And so we meet," said Ozrlag—but he said it silently, the same way he had said everything so far. Anthon felt vaguely disappointed not to hear his actual voice, but he could easily see good reasons. Ozrlag continued briskly, "Nobody else is to know of my visit. Nobody. You understand that?"

Anthon nodded. "I understand."

"How great is the danger of our being discovered? Take me to the tomb while you answer."

Anthon started walking. "I don't know. I've been away, and I'm not sure what Karper and Landen—and my boss—are after. My guess is that they want to confiscate and suppress whatever's in the tomb—although I don't know why. But, if they're really interested, they'll be able to find the vault easily enough. I never told my boss exactly where it is, but he knows roughly where I was working right before I went to Karper. So if they asked him, he could help them narrow their search quite a bit.''

Ozrlag was keeping pace with Anthon's long strides with no apparent effort. ''I was afraid of that,'' he thought. ''We'll just have to hope we get there and get what we want before they do.'' Anthon tried to interpret the emotional tone he seemed to sense with the words. He had an impression that Ozrlag was quite nervous about something, but he couldn't tell what—or even if that were actually the right interpretation.

They reached the vault. It sat, partly uncovered and surrounded by a thin moat of muddy water, at the bottom of a depression made by earthmovers. The region was full of such depressions, many of them containing ruins or monuments, but few of the other structures were quite as large or quite as substantial as this one. Still, the difference was not so obvious as to automatically attract the attention of any casual passerby.

Anthon and Ozrlag warily circled the rim of the depression, looking for signs of present, or recent activity around the tomb. Seeing none, Anthon nodded and started down the slope. Ozrlag scurried on ahead and began opening his suitcase.

And a light appeared from nowhere, swept over the depression, and locked on Anthon. ''Hold it right there!'' a voice barked. ''Security check!''

Anthon stopped where he was, with a sinking feeling. Ozrlag was already down, but his chances of escaping discovery were slight. And the blinding light remained fixed on Anthon's face as the person wielding it trotted closer. For an instant he toyed with the idea of trying to run, but then the watchman came close enough so Anthon could see that the lantern was attached to the barrel of a decidedly ugly handgun. Anthon stood very still.

As the watchman drew up in front of him, he stuck a walkie-talkie back into its holster and lowered the lantern just enough to make it a shade less unpleasant. ''It's you, all right!'' the watchman declared triumphantly, grinning and showing several gaps in his teeth. ''They thought you'd come back here. You just stand there, son. They'll be along in a jiffy.''

Anthon stood—being held at gunpoint provided undeniable incentive. The watchman kept glancing around nervously, as if looking for something, but he never took the light—and gun—off Anthon.

''They'' came within two minutes. A supervisor's cart whirred across the ground, bounced to a halt ten feet away, and Karper and Landen jumped out opposite sides of it. ''That's the one.'' Karper said with obvious satisfaction. ''And I'd guess this must be the place. Thought he might lead us to it.''

''There was someone else with him, sir,'' the watchman said. ''But I didn't get a good look and I don't know where he went. Do I still need to keep this one covered?''

''No,'' Landen answered. ''He's under control. Look for the other one.''

The watchman took the lantern off Anthon and swept the area with it, first around the rim and then down in the depression. Finding nothing, he started around the rim, keeping the light aimed down at the tomb. Suddenly he stopped. "Something moved down there," he whispered. He took a sudden quick step, there was a flurry of movement in the depression, and then Ozrlag was caught in the beam, his back against the tomb and staring up as if the light had him pinned there. It was the first light bright enough to show colors since he had met Anthon.

Landen swore softly. "What on Earth is *that?*"

Karper blinked and shook his head. "A giant pink pussycat?" he giggled nervously.

"Shall I shoot it?" the watchman asked. He sounded eager.

"No," Landen answered at once. "But stay ready." He turned to Anthon. "What do you know about that thing down there, Hillar?"

"That's Ozrlag," Anthon said, distorting the jömür sounds slightly to fit his mouth. He looked squarely at Karper. "He's from one of those other planets you called hogwash. He came down to help me open the rest of the vault and get out whatever other books are there. Because"—and here he sped up as if to hurry past things which were dangerous but had to be said—"I didn't want you to get hold of those like you got the first batch. I don't understand why you want to suppress the idea of space travel, but it isn't going to work. Because even if you get these books too, Ozrlag's people are here and they know all about space travel and they're going to tell us!"

Karper's shock at the tirade was obvious and not surprising, but it was Landen who answered. "Why do you assume we want to supress it, Anthon?" he asked quietly.

Now Anthon was taken by surprise. "Don't you?" he asked.

"It was a possibility," Landen admitted, "but only as a last resort. Look . . . we know the state the world's in, too. It's discouraging. People—a lot of people—would jump at the chance to go somewhere else. *If* the chance existed, there'd be fierce competition for the available spots. We might have to play it down to avoid new domestic troubles. We'd *certainly* have troubles if word spread that there was a way out when there really wasn't. So if this space travel idea turned out to be just a myth—yes, we'd suppress it. But if it actually held water, we'd want to learn to use it. So before anything else, we wanted to find out." He glanced down at Ozrlag. "Your friend here throws a whole new light on things. How can I talk to him?"

"Just talk," Anthon said. "Or even just think without talking. I don't know how it works, but he'll understand you."

Landen looked down at Ozrlag and tried to affect a friendly smile. "So," he said, "you folks can tell us about interstellar travel, eh? Well, we'll be *delighted* to hear what you have to say!"

Ozrlag seemed, somehow, to shrink from them, and his "voice" spoke to all of them. "No," it said very quietly, "you won't. I hate to disappoint all of you, but what you want to do . . . you can't."

Something in Anthon tensed. "Are you trying to say," he asked, completely confused, "that interstellar travel is impossible after all?"

"I'm saying," Ozrlag returned slowly, "that for *you*, it is impossible."

Landen and Karper glanced at each other. Anthon fought to keep his mind steady and absorb what Ozrlag was saying. "What do you mean?" he asked tightly.

"Your ancestors played you a dirty trick," said Ozrlag. "Anthon . . . you, at least, knew we were reading the first batch of documents you found here by using Mylo Gotfry as an intermediary. You knew he was going fast. Our researchers have absorbed far more from those documents than you have—enough so that we now have a pretty good idea of how your world got the way it is."

"Come to the point!" Landen snapped.

"As soon as I can," Ozrlag replied, refusing to hurry. "You won't understand it without the background. Not long before this tomb was built—during the lifetime of the man buried here—some of your ancestors took the first small steps into space—the first small steps away from confinement to the home world. They reached your moon; they sent a few instruments to other planets of this system. And then they stopped.

"Why did they stop? Because of public pressure to use the resources that were being used in space on domestic problems instead . . . things like pollution and over-population and poverty. Poverty turned out to be the one that got the most demand, and the governments gave it. They tried to end it with handouts. It didn't really work, of course, any more than it's ever worked for anybody else. But it gave a comforting illusion for a while—especially since population was at such a level that to implement the poverty program they were incidentally forced to solve some of the pollution and energy problems. They had to continue developing their technology far enough to get breeder reactors into routine use for power generation—but after that they let innovation die out. And the breederization and ecology readjustment programs increased their capacity for feeding people so drastically that they could quit worrying about over-population. They wouldn't strain their new capacities for a long time—and given the choice of a real effort to curb population growth, or a way of absorbing more children, they overwhelmingly opted to absorb more people.

"But, of course, eventually the population did catch up again—and things deteriorated to what you have now. A culture with nuclear power driving television sets and air-conditioners—anyway until the fuel runs out, as it surely will—and so many people they all have a full-time struggle to get enought to eat. And no way out."

Anthon felt himself starting to shake with emotion. His dream was crumbling. "No way out?" he echoed. "The stars—"

"You can't get there from here," Ozrlag said harshly. "You *could* have—if they'd continued their efforts from the start. But they chose to stop space travel and let population growth continue unchecked; they should have done just the opposite, on both counts. I said going to the Moon was a small first step. I meant it. It was a tremendously impressive undertaking at the time, but you can hardly conceive how much more difficult it is to reach the stars. It can be done—but only with many, many man-years of dedicated work once you've passed the Moon-rocket stage. But *you* won't even be able to get that far, now—because it would require a kind of education and research that your static culture hasn't had for centuries, and it would require great amounts of manpower and material. And a subsistence economy can't spare manpower and material for anything except keeping itself alive."

"But," Karper protested, "if you already know the techniques and can teach us—"

"It still won't work," Ozrlag interrupted bluntly. "Even if we provided all the teachers gratis—which is a bit much to expect—you simply can't spare the students. Try to realize, we're talking about *massive* education and construction projects, even for as small a problem as going to the Moon. *Even if we try to help you*, you're trapped. I'm sorry." He looked pensively at the tomb. "I think the man who was buried here was upset at the space programs being killed at that crucial time. I think he saw, at least dimly, why it was wrong, and preserved his books in the hope they would help somebody get started again later. He didn't realize that his message would arrive too late to help."

Anthon stared numbly into space at the wreckage of his idea. He distantly heard Landen saying. "But there are more direct kinds of aid. You people have starships already, and there must be something we could provide in exchange." He paused, then blurted out, "And if coersion is necessary, we have you as a hostage."

It sounded futile to Anthon, but then he noticed that Ozrlag unmistakably grinned at Landen's suggestion. "Well," the jömür said, "I doubt that I'm a very *valuable* hostage, at the moment, but I'll see what can be arranged."

And at those words Anthon felt a thin thread of hope stil alive within him.

EPILOGUE

Anthon paused in the door of the jömür ship to survey his new home before becoming the first man to set foot on it. Never before had he seen such a wealth of growing plants as those which carpeted the hills rolling of to the horizon, or a sky like the one he saw now, utterly clear and deep blue except for a bank of billowy white clouds in the west. Never had he heard such a chorus of smaller living things, or felt such refreshing breezes.

Full of exhilaration at his role as chosen leader of the new colony, he shouldered his ax and gun and strode down the gangway onto the soft grass. He waited and watched proudly as the other men, women, and children followed him onto their new world. In five minutes they were all there, waiting, as Ozrlag came down alone to say good-bye.

"Terrific!" Anthon laughed as Ozrlag approached. "A new beginning—thanks to you. How many people will you be transplanting altogether, and how long will it take?"

"Hm-m-m?" Ozrlag's surprise at the question was unmistakable. "Why, this is all, as far as I know."

"*All?*" Anthon's jaw dropped. He hadn't been in on arranging the details himself, of course, but he'd been led to believe . . . "I thought—" he began.

"I thought we'd been over all this," Ozrlag interrupted, hardly listening. "Earth couldn't possibly offer us anything to finance a lot of these superferry trips, now, could it? And even if we wanted, obviously we couldn't move enough to make a dent in the population. But when we found out you and some others were interested in trying to make a better go of it elsewhere . . . well, it was easy to arrange for one small group, and it fit right in with a project I'd thought of for my apprenticeship—''

"Apprenticeship?" Anthon echoed.

"Yes. I thought you knew. I'm an apprentice sociologist and I thought a good topic for an experimental study would be the efforts of intelligent beings transplanted from a place like Earth to get along on a fresh world—''

"Ozrlag!"

The call broke in sharply, its tone peremptory. Mizhjar had appeared at the top of the gangway and was insistently beckoning for Ozrlag to return.

Ozrlag turned back to him with what Anthon did recognize as a good-natured but impersonal smile. "Good-bye," he said to the whole group, "and good luck!"

Anthon stared silently after him, stunned, as he hurried up the gangway and he and Mizhjar disappeared into the ship. Then, as the gangway began to slither back into the ship, he turned back to his colony.

And saw it transfigured. The hills were vast expanses of loneliness now, the chorus from the woods warned of animal pests yet unknown, the chill breeze bore the stink of alien poisons, and the clouds that had billowed pleasantly now loomed menacingly. The idyllic landscape had suddenly become a hostile power against which Anthon was pitted with little help, unskilled and meagerly provisioned.

Guinea pigs, he thought bitterly. He heard the ship starting to lift off behind him, but he didn't look back. *Guinea pigs transplanted from one place where we could barely live to another that dares us to do even that.*

The ship was gone now, and Anthon finally fully realized that, for *his* people, the stars would remain unreachable long past his lifetime.

But maybe not forever, he thought fiercely, choking down his disappointment. *Our ancestors were at this point once. Maybe we* can *avoid some of their mistakes. And then someday . . .*

He picked up his ax and gun and gestured to the others to follow him. They had work to do. One last time, he quietly cursed his ancestors' shortsightedness. then he let his eyes wander to the sky and to a distant future he would never see, and somehow he managed to smile.

Someday . . . ■

Rescue Squad

Katherine MacLean

Most of us fill out the income tax forms and employment forms with barely suppressed rage. What happens to a healthy, friendly, hardworking type who won't fill out forms? He's going to starve, right?

His friends know that George has one extra trouble. Beyond a friendly sharing of other people's feelings when he is with them, he can also feel other people's fears, even at a distance. Like hearing a distant scream.

Can this help him? He's going to starve; right?

HUNGER IS NOT a bad thing. Some guys who knew Zen and jaine yogi had told me they could go without food thirty days. They showed me how. The only trouble is, when you skip meals, you shake. When I touched a building it felt like the world was trembling.

If I told the employment board that my student support money had run out, they'd give me an adult support pension and a ticket to leave New York and never come back. I wasn't planning on telling them.

Ahmed the Arab came along the sidewalk, going fast, his legs rangy and swinging. Ahmed used to be king of our block gang when we were smaller, and he used to ask me to help him sometimes. This year Ahmed had a job working for the Rescue Squad. Maybe he would let me help him; maybe he could swing a job for me.

I signaled him as he came close. "Ahmed."

He went on by, hurrying. "OK, George, come on."

I fell into stride beside him. "What's the rush?"

"Look at the clouds, man. Something's getting ready to happen. We've got to stop it."

I looked at the clouds. The way I felt was smeared all over the sky. Dangerous dark dirty clouds bulged down over the city, looking ready to burst and spill out fire and dirt. In high school Psychology-A they said that people usually see clouds and blots in shapes to match their mood. My mood was bad, I could see that, but I still did not know what the sky really looked like—dark, probably, but harmless.

"What is it?" I asked. "Is it smog?"

Ahmed stopped walking, and looked at my face. "No. It's fear."

He was right. Fear lay like a fog across the air. Fear was in the threatening clouds and in the darkness across the faces of the people. People went by under the heavy sky, hunched as if there were a cold rain falling. Buildings above us seemed to be swaying outward.

I shut my eyes, but the buildings seemed to sway out farther.

Last year when Ahmed had been training for the Rescue Squad he'd opened up a textbook and tried to explain something to me about the difference between inner reality and outer reality, and how mobs can panic when they all see the same idea. I opened my eyes and studied the people running at me, past me, and away from me as the crowds rushed by. Crowds always rush in New York. Did they all see the buildings as leaning and ready to fall? Were they afraid to mention it?

"Ahmed, you Rescue Squad fink," I said, "what would happen if we yelled Earthquake good and loud? Would they all panic?"

"Probably so." Ahmed was looking at me with interest, his lean face and black eyes intent. "How do you feel, George? You look sick."

"I feel lousy. Something wrong in my head. Dizzy." Talking made it worse. I braced my hand against a wall. The walls rocked, and I felt as if I were down flat while I was still standing up.

"What in creation is wrong with me?" I asked. "I can't get sick from skipping a meal or so, can I?'' Mentioning food made my stomach feel strange and hollow and dry. I was thinking about death suddenly. "I'm not even hungry," I told Ahmed. "Am I sick?"

Ahmed, who had been king of our block gang when we were kids, was the one who knew the answers.

"Man, you've got good pickup." Ahmed studied my face, "Someone near here is in trouble and you're tuned in to it." He glanced at the sky east and west. "Which way is it worst? We've got to find him fast."

I looked up Fifth Avenue. The giant glass office building loomed and glittered insecurely, showing clouds through in dark green, and reflecting clouds in gray as if dissolving into the sky. I looked along Forty-Second Street to the giant arches of the Transport Center. I looked down Fifth Avenue, past the stone lions of the library, and then west to the neon signs and excitement. The darkness came at me with teeth, like a giant mouth. Hard to describe.

"Man, it's bad." I was shaken. "It's bad in every direction. It's the whole city!"

"It can't be," Ahmed said. "It's loud, we must be near where the victim is."

He put his wrist radio up to his mouth and pushed the signal button. "Statistics, please." A voice answered. "Statistics." Ahmed articulated carefully. "Priority call. Rescue Badge 54B. Give me today's trends in hospital admissions; all rises above sigma reciprocal 30. Point the center of any area with a sharp rise in"—he looked at me analytically— "dizziness, fatigue, and acute depressions." He considered me further. "Run a check on general anxiety syndromes and hypochondria." He waited for the Statistics Department to collect data.

I wondered if I should be proud or ashamed of feeling sick.

He waited—lean, efficient, impatient, with black eyebrows and black intense eyes. He'd looked almost the same when he was ten and I was nine. His family were immigrants, speaking some unAmerican language, but they were the proud kind. Another person would burn with hate or love for girls, but Ahmed would burn about Ideas. His ideas about adventure made him king of our block gang. He'd lead us into strange adventures and grown-up no-trespassing places just to look at things, and when we were trapped he'd consult a little pack of cards, or some dice, and lead us out of trouble at high speed—like he had a map. He had an idea that the look and feel of a place told you its fate; a bad-luck place looked bad. When he consulted me, or asked me how a place looked to me, I'd feel proud.

He'd left us behind. We all dropped out of high school, but Ahmed the Arab got good marks, graduated and qualified for advanced training. All the members of our gang had taken their adult retirement pensions and left the city, except me and Ahmed the Arab—and I heard Ahmed was the best detector in the Rescue Squad.

The wrist radio whistled and he put it to his ear. The little voice crackled off figures and statistical terms. Ahmed looked around at the people passing, surprised, then looked at me more respectfully. "It's all over Manhattan. Women coming in with psychosomatic pregnancy. Pregnant women are coming in with nightmares. Men are coming in with imaginary ulcers and cancers. Lots of suicides and lots of hospital commitments for acute suicidal melancholy. You are right. The whole city is in trouble.''

He started along Forty-Second Street toward Sixth Avenue, walking fast. ''Need more help. Try different techniques.'' A hanging sign announced, *Gypsy Tea Room, Oriental Teas, Exotic Pastries, Readings of Your Personality and Future.* Ahmed pushed through a swinging door and went up a moving escalator two steps at a time, with me right after him. We came out into the middle of a wide, low-ceiling restaurant, with little tables and spindly chairs.

Four old ladies were clustered around one table nibbling at cupcakes and talking. A businessman sat at a table near the window reading the *Wall Street Journal.* Two teener students sat leaning against the glass wall window looking down into Forty-Second Street and its swirling crowds. A fat woman sat at a table in a corner, holding a magazine up before her face. She lowered it and looked at us over the top. The four old ladies stopped talking and the businessman folded his *Wall Street Journal* and put it aside as if Ahmed and I were messengers of bad news. They were all in a miserable, nervous mood like the one I was in—expecting the worst from a doomed world.

Ahmed threaded his way among the tables toward the corner table where the fat woman sat. She put her magazine aside on another table as we approached. Her face was round and pleasant, with smile creases all over it. She nodded and smiled at me and then did not smile at Ahmed at all, but instead stared straight back into his eyes as he sat down in front of her.

He leaned across the table. ''All right, Bessie, you feel it, too. Have you located who it is?''

She spoke in a low, intense voice, as if afraid to speak loudly: ''I felt it first thing I woke up this morning, Ahmed. I tried to trace it for the Rescue Squad, but she's feeling, not thinking. And it's echoing off too many other people because they keep thinking up reasons why they feel so—'' She paused and I knew what she was trying to describe. Trying to describe it made it worse.

She spoke in a lower voice and her round face was worried. ''The bad dream feeling is hanging on, Ahmed. I wonder if I'm—''

She didn't want to talk about it, and Ahmed had his mouth open for a question, so I was sorry for her and butted in.

''What do you mean about people make echoes? How come all this crowd—'' I waved my hand in a vague way, indicating the city and the people. The Rescue Squad was supposed to rescue lost people. The city was not lost.

Ahmed looked at me impatiently. ''Adults don't like to use telepathy. They pretend they can't. but say a man falls down an elevator shaft and breaks a leg. No one finds him, and he can't reach a phone so he'll get desperate and pray and start using mind power. He'll try to send his thoughts as loud as he can. He doesn't know how loud he can send. But the dope doesn't broadcast his name and where he is, he just broadcasts: 'Help, I've got a broken leg!' People around the area pick up the thought, and his friends pick up the thought, and even people far away who are a lot like him, same age, same business, they all start thinking. 'Help, I've got a broken leg!' They come limping into the emergency clinics and get x-rays of good legs. The doctors tell them to go home. But they are picking up the thought, 'Help! I'm going to die unless I get help!' so they hang around the clinics and bother the doctors. They are scared. The Rescue Squad uses them as tracers. Whenever there is an abnormal wave of people applying for help in one district, we try to find the center of the wave and locate someone in real trouble.''

The more he talked the better I felt. It untuned me from the bad mood of the day, and Rescue Squad work was beginning to sound like something I could do. I know how people feel just by standing close to them. Maybe the Rescue Squad would let me join if I showed that I could detect people.

"Great," I said. "What about preventing murders? How do you do that?"

Ahmed took out his silver badge and looked at it. "I'll give you an example. Imagine an intelligent, sensitive kid with a vivid imagination. He is being bullied by a stupid father. He doesn't say anything back; he just imagines what he will do to the big man when he grows up. Whenever the big man gets him mad the kid clenches his fists and smiles and puts everything he's got into a blast of mental energy, thinking of himself splitting the big man's skull with an ax. He thinks loud. A lot of people in the district have nothing much to do, nothing much to think about. They never plan or imagine much and they act on the few thoughts that come to them. Get it?"

"The dopes act out what he is thinking," I grinned.

Ahmed looked at my grin with a disgusted expression and turned back to the fat woman. "Bessie, we've got to locate this victim. What do the tea leaves say about where she is?"

"I haven't asked." Bessie reached over to the other table and picked up an empty cup. It had a few soggy tea leaves in the bottom. "I was hoping that you would find her." She heaved herself to her feet and waddled into the kitchen.

I was still standing. Ahmed looked at me with a disgusted expression. "Quit changing the subject. Do you want to help resuce someone or don't you?"

Bessie came back with a round pot of tea and a fresh cup on a tray. She put the tray on the table and filled the cup, then poured half of the steaming tea back into the pot. I remembered that a way to get information from the group-mind is by seeing how people interpret peculiar shapes like ink blots and tea leaves, and I stood quietly, trying not to bother her.

She lowered herself slowly in to her chair, swirled the tea in the cup, and looked in. We waited. She rocked the cup, looking; then shut her eyes and put the cup down. She sat still, eyes closed, the eyelids squeezed tight in wrinkles.

"What was it?" Ahmed asked in a low voice.

"Nothing, nothing, just a—" She stopped and choked. "Just a damned, lousy maggotty skull."

That had to be a worse sign than getting the ace of spades in a card cut. Death. I began to get that sick feeling again. Death for Bessie?

"I'm sorry," Ahmed said. "But push on, Bessie. Try another angle. We need the name and address."

"She was not thinking about her name and address," Bessie's eyes were still tightly shut.

Suddenly Ahmed spoke in a strange voice. I'd heard that voice years ago when he was head of our gang—when he hypnotized another kid. It was a deep smooth voice and it penetrated inside of you.

"You need help and no one has come to help you. What are you thinking?"

The question got inside my head. An answer opened up and I started to answer, but Bessie answered first. "When I don't think, just shut my eyes and hold still, I don't feel anything, everything goes far away. When the bad things begin to happen I can stay far away and refuse to come back." Bessie's voice was dreamy.

The same dark sleepy ideas had formed in my own head. She was saying them for me. Suddenly I was afraid that the darkness would swallow me. It was like a night cloud, or a pillow, floating deep down and inviting you to come and put your head on it, but it moved a little and turned and showed a flash of shark teeth, so you knew it was a shark waiting to eat anyone who came close.

Bessie's eyes snapped open and she straightened herself upright her eyes so wide open that white showed around the rims. She was scared of sleeping. I was glad she had snapped out of it. She had been drifting down into the inviting dark toward that black monster.

"If you went in too deep, you could wake up dead," I said and put a hand on Ahmed's shoulder to warn him to slow down.

"I don't care which one of you speaks for her," he said, without turning around. "But you have to learn to separate your thoughts from hers. You're not thinking of dying—the victim is. She's in danger of death, somewhere." He leaned across the table to Bessie again, "Where is she?"

I tightened my grip on Ahmed's shoulder, but Bessie obediently picked up the teacup in fat fingers and looked in again. Her face was round and innocent, but I judged she was braver than I was.

I went around to Bessie's side of the table to look into the teacup over her shoulder. A few tea leaves were at the bottom of the cup, drifting in an obscure pattern. She tapped the side of the cup delicately with a fat finger. The pattern shifted. The leaves made some sort of a picture, but I could not make out exactly what it was. It looked like it meant something, but I could not see it clearly.

Bessie spoke sympathetically. "You're thirsty, aren't you? There, there, Honey-bunch. We'll find you. We haven't forgotten you. Just think where you are and we will—" Her voice died down to a low, fading mumble, like a windup doll running down. She put the cup down and put her head down into her spread hands.

I heard a whisper. "Tired of trying, tired of smiling. Let die. Let death be born. Death will come out to destroy the world, the worthless dry, rotten—"

Ahmed reached across and grasped her shoulders and shook them. "Bessie, snap out of it. That's not you. It's the *other one.*"

Bessie lifted a changed face from her hands. The round smiling look was gone into sagging sorrowful folds like an old bloodhound. She mumbled, "It's true. Why wait for someone to help you and love you? We are born and die. No one can help that. No reason to hope. Hope hurts. Hope hurt *her.*" It bothered me to hear Bessie talk. It was like she were dead. It was a corpse talking.

Bessie seemed to try to pull herself together and focus on Ahmed to report, but one eye went off focus and she did not seem to see him.

She said, "Hope hurts. She hates hope. She tried to kill it. She felt my thinking and she thought my feelings of life and hope were hers. I was remembering how Harry always helped me, and she blasted in blackness and hate—" She put her face down in her hands again. "Ahmed, he's dead. She killed Harry's ghost in my heart. He won't ever come back anymore, even in dreams." Her face was dead, like a mask.

He reached over and shook her shoulder again. "Bessie, shame on you, snap out of it."

She straightened and glared. "It's true. All men are beasts. No one is going to help a woman. You want me to help you at your job and win you another medal for finding that girl, don't you? You don't care about her." Her face was darkening, changing to something worse, that reminded me of the black shapes of the clouds.

I had to pull her out of it, but I didn't know what to do.

Ahmed clattered the spoon against the teacup with a loud clash and spoke in a loud casual voice: "How's the restaurant business, Bessie? Are the new girls working out?"

She looked down at the teacup, surprised, and then looked vaguely around the restaurant. "Not many customers right now. It must be an off hour. The girls are in the kitchen." Her face began to pull back into its own shape, a pleasant restaurant-service mask, round and ready to smile. "Can I have the girls get you anything, Ahmed?"

She turned to me with a habit of kindness, and her words were less mechanical. "Would you like anything, young man? You look so energetic standing there! Most young people like our Turkish honey rolls." She still wasn't focused on me, didn't see me, really, but—I smiled back at her, glad to see her feeling better.

"No thank you, Ma'am," I said and glanced at Ahmed to see what he would want to do next.

"Bessie's honey rolls are famous," Ahmed said. "They are dripping with honey and have so much almond flavor they burn your mouth." He rose easily, looking lazy. "I guess I'll have a dozen to take along."

The fat woman sat blinking her eyes up at him. Her round face did not look sick and sagging anymore, just sort of rumpled and meaningless, like your own face looks in the mirror in the morning. "Turkish honey-and-almond rolls," she repeated. "One dozen." She rang a little bell in the middle of the table and rose.

"Wait for me downstairs," Ahmed told me. He turned back to Bessie.

"Remember the time a Shriners Convention came in and they all wanted lobster and palm reading at once? Where did you get all those hot lobsters?" They moved off together to the counter which displayed cookies and rolls. A pretty girl in a frilled apron trotted out of the kitchen and stood behind the counter.

Bessie laughed, starting with a nervous high-pitched giggle and ending up in a deep ho-ho sound like Santa Claus. "Do I remember? What a hassle! Imagine me on the phone trying to locate twenty palm readers in ten minutes! I certainly was grateful when you sent over those twenty young fellows and girls to read palms for my Shriners. I was really nervous until I saw they had their marks really listening, panting for the next word. I thought you must have gotten a circus tribe of gypsies from the cooler. *Ho-ho*. I didn't know you had sent over the whole police class in Suspect Personality Analysis."

I went out the door, down to the sidewalk. A few minutes later Ahmed came down the escalator two steps at a time and arrived at the sidewalk like a rocket. "Here, carry these." He thrust the paper bag of Turkish honey rolls at me. The warm, sweet smell was good. I took the bag and plunged my hand in.

"Just carry them. Don't eat any." Ahmed led the way down the subway stairs to the first underground walkway.

I pulled my hand out of the bag and followed. I was feeling so shaky I went down the stairs slowly, one at a time instead of two at a time. When I got there Ahmed was looking at the signs that pointed in different directions, announcing what set of tracks led to each part of the city. For the first time I saw that he was uncertain and worried. He didn't know which way to go. It was a strange thought for me, that Ahmed did not know which way to go. It meant he had been running, without knowing which way to run.

He was thinking aloud: "We know that the victim is female, adult, younger than Bessie, probably pregnant, and is trapped some place where there is no food or water for her. She expected help from the people she loves, and was disappointed, and now is angry with the thought of love and hates the thought of people giving help."

I remembered Bessie's suddenly sick and flabby face, after the victim had struck out at Bessie's thought of giving help. *Angry* seemed to be the understatment of the year. I remembered the wild threatening sky, and I watched the people hurrying by, pale and anxious. Two chicks passed in bad shape. One was holding her stomach and muttering about Alka Seltzer, and the other had redrimmed eyes as if she had just been weeping. Can one person in trouble do that to a whole city full of people?

"Who is she, Ahmed?" I asked. "I mean, *what* is she anyhow?"

"I don't understand it myself," Ahmed said. Suddenly he attacked me again with his question, using that deep hypnotic voice to push me backward into the black whirlpools of the fear of death. *"If you were thirsty, very thirsty, and there was only one place in the city you could go to buy a thirst quencher, where—"*

"I'm not thirsty." I tried to swallow, and my tongue felt swollen, my mouth seemed dry and filled with sand, and my throat was coated with dry gravel. The world tilted over sideways. I braced my feet to stand up. "I *am* thirsty. How did you do that? I want to go to the White Horse Tavern on Bleecker Street and drink a gallon of ginger ale and a bottle of brown beer."

"You're my compass. Let's go there. I'll buy for you."

Ahmed ran down the Eighth Avenue subway stairs to the chair tracks. I followed, clutching the bag of sweet smelling rolls as if it were a heavy suitcase full of rocks. The smell made me hungry and weak. I could still walk, but I was pretty sure that, if Ahmed pushed me deep into that black mood just once more, they'd have to send me back on a stretcher.

On the tracks we linked our chairs and Ahmed shifted the linked chairs from belt to belt until we were traveling at a good speed. the chairs moved along the tunnels, passing under bright store windows with beautiful mannequins dancing and displaying things to buy. I usually looked up when we got near the forest fire and waterfall three-dimensional pics, but today I did not look up. I sat with my elbows braced on my knees and my head hanging. Ahmed looked at me alertly, his black eyebrows furrowed and dark eyes scanning me up and down like I was a medical diagram.

"Man, I'd like to see the suicide statistics right now. One look at you and I know it's bad."

I had enough life left to be annoyed. "I have my own feelings, not just some chick's feelings. I've been sick all day. A virus or something."

"Damnit, will you never understand? We've got to rescue this girl because she's broadcasting. She's broadcasting feeling sick!"

I looked at the floor between my feet. "That's a lousy reason. Why can't you rescue her just because she's in trouble? Let her broadcast. High School Psych-A said that everybody broadcasts."

"Listen," Ahmed leaned forward ready to tell me an idea. His eyes began to glitter as the idea took him. "Maybe she broadcasts too loud. Statistics has been running data on trends and surges in popular action. They think that people who broadcast too loud might be causing some of the mass action."

"I don't get you, Ahmed."

"I mean like they get a big surge of people going to Coney Island on a cloudy day, and they don't have subway cars ready for it, and traffic ties up. They compare that day with other cloudy days, the same temperature and the same time of year other years, and try to figure out what caused it. Sometimes it's a factory vacation; but sometimes it's one man, given the day off who goes to the beach, and an extra crowd of a thousand or so people from all over the city, people that don't know him, suddenly make excuses, clear schedules, and go to the beach, sometimes arriving at almost the same time, jamming up the subways for an hour, and making it hard for the Traffic Flow Control people.''

"Is it a club?'' I was trying to make out what he meant, but I couldn't see what it had to do with anything.

"No,'' he said. "They didn't know each other. It's been checked. The Traffic Flow experts have to know what to expect. They started collecting names from the crowds. They found that most of the people in each surge are workers with an IQ below one hundred, but somehow doing all right with their lives. They seemed to be controlled by one man in the middle of the rush who had a reason to be going in that direction. The Statistics people call the man in the middle the *Archetype*. That's an old Greek word. The original that other people are copied from—one real man and a thousand echoes.''

The idea of some people being echoes made me uneasy. It seemed insulting to call anyone an echo. "They must be wrong,'' I said.

"Listen.'' Ahmed leaned forward, his eyes brightening. "They think they are right—one man and a thousand echoes. They checked into the lives of the ones that seemed to be in the middle. The Archetypes are energetic ordinary people living average lives. When things go as usual for the Archetype, he acts normal and everybody controlled by him acts normal, get it?''

I didn't get it, and I didn't like it. "An average healthy person is a good Joe. He wouldn't want to control anyone,'' I said, but I knew I was sugaring the picture. Humans can be bad. People love power over people. "Listen,'' I said, "some people like taking advice. Maybe it's like advice?''

Ahmed leaned back and pulled his chin. "It fits. Advice by ESP is what you mean. Maybe the Archetype doesn't know he is broadcasting. He does just what the average man wants to do. Solves the same problems—and does it better. He broadcasts loud, pleasant, simple thoughts and they are easy to listen to if you have the same kind of life and problems. Maybe more than half the population below an IQ of 100 have learned to use telepathic pickup and let the Archetypes do their thinking for them.''

Ahmed grew more excited, his eyes fixed on the picture he saw in his head. "Maybe the people who are letting Archetypes run their lives don't even know they are following anyone else's ideas. They just find those healthy, problem-solving thoughts going on in a corner of their mind. Notice how the average person believes that thinking means sitting quietly and looking far away, resting your chin in your hand like someone listening to distant music? Sometimes they say, 'When there's too much noise I *can't hear myself think.*' But when an intellectual, a real thinker is thinking—'' He had been talking louder with more excitement as the subject got hold of him. He was leaning forward, his eyes glittering.

I laughed, interrupting. "When an intellectual is thinking he goes into high gear, leans forward, bugs his eyes at you and practically climbs the wall with each word, like you, Ahmed. Are you an Archetype?''

He shook his head. "Only for my kind of person. If an average kind of person started picking up my kind of thinking, it wouldn't solve his problems—so he would ignore it.''

He quit talking because I was laughing so hard. Laughing drove away the ghosts of despair that were eating at my heart. ''Your kind of person! Ho ho. Show me one. Ha ha. Ignore it? Hell, if a man found your thoughts in his head he'd go to a psychiatrist. He'd think he was going off his rails.''

Ahead we saw the big ''14'' signs signaling Fourteenth Street. I shifted gears on the linked seats and we began to slide sideways from moving cables to slower cables, slowing and going uphill.

We stopped. On the slow strip coming along a girl was kneeling sideways in one of the seats. I thought she was tying a shoelace, but when I looked back I saw she was lying curled up, her knees under her chin, her thumb in her mouth. Regression. Retreat into infancy. Defeat.

Somehow it sent a shiver of fear through me. Defeat should not come so easily. Ahmed had leaped out of his chair and was halfway toward the stairs.

''Ahmed!'' I shouted.

He looked back and saw the girl. The seat carried her slowly by in the low-speed lane.

He waved for me to follow him and bounded up the moving stairs. ''Come on,'' he yelled back, ''before it gets worse.''

When I got up top I saw Ahmed disappearing into the White Horse Tavern. I ran down the block and went in after him, into the cool shadows and paneled wood—nothing seemed to move. My eyes adjusted slowly and I saw Ahmed with his elbows on the counter, sipping a beer, and discussing the weather with the bartender.

It was too much for me. The world was out of its mind in one way and Ahmed was out of his mind in a different way. I could not figure it out, and I was ready to knock Ahmed's block off.

I was thirsty, but there was no use trying to drink or eat anything around that nut. I put my elbows on the bar a long way from Ahmed and called over to the bartender. ''A quart of Bock to go.'' I tilted my head at Ahmed, ''He'll pay for it.''

I sounded normal enough, but the bartender jumped and moved fast. He plunked a bottle in a brown paper bag in front of me and rubbed the bar in front of me with wood polish.

''Nice weather,'' he said, and looked around his place with his shoulders hunched, looking over his shoulders. ''I wish I was outside walking in the fresh air. Have you been here before?''

''Once,'' I said, picking up the bag. ''I liked it.'' I remembered the people who had shown me the place. Jean Fitzpatrick—she had shown me some of her poetry at a party—and a nice guy, her husband. Mort Fitzpatrick had played a slide whistle in his own tunes when we were walking along over to the tavern, and some bearded friends of theirs walked with us and talked odd philosophy and strange shared trips.

The girl told me that she and her husband had a house in the neighborhood, and invited me to a party there, which I turned down, and she asked me to drop in anytime.

I knew she meant the "anytime" invitation. They were villagers, Bohemians, the kind who collect art, and strange books, and farout people. Villagers always have the door open for people with strange stories and they always have a pot of coffee ready to share with you.

"Do Jean Fitzpatrick and Mort Fitzpatrick still live around here?" I asked the bartender.

"I see them around. They haven't been in recently." He began to wipe and polish the bar away from me, moving toward Ahmed. "For all I know they might of moved."

Ahmed sipped his beer and glanced at us sidelong, like a stranger.

I walked out into the gray day with a paper bag under my arm with its hard weight of Bock beer inside. I could quit this crazy, sickmaking business of being a detector. I could go look up somebody in the Village like Jean Fitzpatrick and tell how sick the day had been, and how I couldn't take it and had chickened out, until the story began to seem funny and the world became someplace I could stand.

Ahmed caught up with me and put a hand on my arm. I stopped myself from spinning around to hit him and just stood—staring straight ahead.

"You angry?" he asked, walking around me to get a look at my face. "How do you feel?"

"Ahmed, my feelings are my own business. OK? There is a girl around here I want to look up. I want to make sure she is all right. OK? Don't let me hold you up on Rescue Squad business. Don't wait for me. OK?" I started walking again, but the pest was walking right behind me. I had spelled it out, clear and loud that I didn't want company. I did not want to flatten him, because at other times he had been my friend.

"May I come along?" he asked politely. "Maybe I can help."

I shrugged, walking along toward the river. What difference did it make? I was tired and there was too much going on in New York City. Ahmed would go away soon on his business. The picture of talking to the girl was warm, dark, relaxing. We'd share coffee and tell each other crazy little jokes and let the world go forgotten.

The house of the Fitzpatricks was one of those little tilted houses left over from a hundred years ago when the city was a town, lovingly restored by hand labor and brightened under many coats of paint by groups of volunteer decorators. It shone with white paint and red doors and red shutters and windowboxes under each window growing green vines and weeds and wild flowers. The entire house was overhung by the gigantic girders of the Hudson River Drive with its hissing flow of traffic making a faint rumble through the air and shaking the ground underfoot.

I knocked on the bright red door. No one answered. I found an unused doorbutton at the side and pushed it. Chimes sounded, but nothing stirred inside.

Village places usually are lived in by guests. Day or night someone is there: broke artists, travelers, hitchhikers, stunned inefficient looking refugees from the student or research worlds staving off a nervous breakdown by a vacation far away from pressure. It was considered legitimate to put your head inside and holler for attention if you couldn't raise anyone by knocking and ringing. I turned the knob to go in. It would not turn. It was locked.

I felt like they had locked the door when they saw me coming. The big dope, musclehead George is coming, lock the door. This was a bad day, but I couldn't go any farther. There was no place to go but here.

I stood shaking the knob dumbly, trying to turn it. It began to make a rattling noise like chains, and like an alarm clock in a hospital. The sound went through my blood and almost froze my hand. I thought something was behind the door, and I thought it was opening and a monster with a skull face was standing there waiting.

I turned my back to the door and carefully, silently went down the two steps to the sidewalk. I had gone so far off my rails that I thought I heard the door creaking open, and I thought I felt the cold wind of someone reaching out to grab me.

I did not look back, just strode away, walking along the same direction I had been going, pretending I had not meant to touch that door.

Ahmed trotted beside me, sidling to get a view of my face, scuttling sideways and ahead of me like a big crab.

"What's the matter? What is it?"

"She's not— Nobody was—" It was a lie. Somebody or something was in that house. Ignore it, walk away faster.

"Where are we going now?" Ahmed asked.

"Straight into the river," I said and laughed. It sounded strange and hurt my chest like coughing. "The water is a mirage in the desert and you walk out on the dry sand looking for water to drown in. The sand is covered with all the lost dried things that sank out of sight. You die on the dry sand, crawling, looking for water. Nobody sees you. People sail overhead and see the reflection of the sky in the fake waves. Divers come and find your dried mummy on the bottom and make notes, wondering because they think there is water in the river. But it is all a lie."

I stopped. The giant docks were ahead, and between them the ancient, small wharfs. There was no use going in that direction, or in any direction. The world was shriveled and old, with thousands of years of dust settling on it—a mummy case. As I stood there the world grew smaller, closing in on me like a lid shutting me into a box. I was dead, lying down, yet standing upright on the sidewalk. I could not move.

"Ahmed," I said, hearing my voice from a great distance, "get me out of this. What's a friend for?"

He danced around me like some evil goblin. "Why can't you help yourself?"

"I can't move," I answered, being remarkably reasonable.

He circled me, looking at my face and the way I stood. He was moving with stops and starts, like a bug looking for a place to bite. I imagined myself shooting a spray can of insecticide at him.

Katherine MacLean

Suddenly he used the *voice*, the clear deep hypnotic voice that penetrates into the dark private world where I live when I'm asleep and dreaming.

"Why can't you move?"

The gulf opened up beneath my feet. "Because I'd fall," I answered.

He used the voice again, and it penetrated to an interior world where the dreams lived and were real all the time. I was shriveled and weak, lying on dust and bits of old cloth. A foul and dusty smell was in my nostrils and I was looking down over an edge where the air came up from below. The air from below smelled better. I had been there a long time. Ahmed's voice reached me, it asked—

"How far would you fall?"

I measured the distance with my eye. I was tired and the effort to think was very hard. Drop ten or twelve feet to the landing, then tangle your feet in the ladder lying there and pitch down the next flight of steep stairs . . . Death waited at the bottom.

"A long way," I answered. "I'm too heavy. Stairs are steep."

"Your mouth is dry," he said.

I could feel the thirst like flames, drying up my throat, thickening my tongue as he asked the question, the jackpot question.

"Tell me, what is your name?"

I tried to answer with my right name, George Sanford. I heard a voice croak. "Jean Dalais."

"Where do you live?" he asked in the penetrating voice that rang inside my skull and rang into the evil other world where I, or someone was on the floor smelling dust for the duration of eternity.

"Downstairs," I heard myself answer.

"Where are you now?" he asked in the same penetrating voice.

"In hell," the voice answered from my head.

I struck out with careful aim to flatten him with the single blow. He was dangerous. I had to stop him, and leave him stopped. I struck carefully, with hatred. He fell backward and I started to run. I ran freely, one block, two blocks. My legs were my own, my body was my own, my mind was my own. I was George Sanford and I could move without fear of falling. No one was behind me. The sun shone through clouds, the fresh wind blew along the empty sidewalks. I was alone. I had left that capsule world of dead horror standing behind me like an abandoned phone booth.

This time I knew what to do to stay out of it. Don't think back. Don't remember what Ahmed was trying to do. Don't bother about rescuing anyone. Take a walk along the edge of the piers in the foggy sunshine and think cheerful thoughts, or no thoughts at all.

I looked back and Ahmed was sitting on the sidewalk far back. I remembered that I was exceptionally strong and the coach had warned me to hold myself back when I hit. Even Ahmed? But he had been thinking, listening, off guard.

What had I said? *Jean Dalais*. Jean Fitpatrick had showed me some of her poetry, and that had been the name signed to it. Was Jean Dalais really Jean Fitzpatrick? It was probably her name before she married Mort Fitzpatrick.

I had run by the white house with the red shutters. I looked back. It was only half a block back. I went back, striding before fear could grip me again and rattled the knob and pulled at the red door and looked at the lock.

Ahmed caught up with me.

"You know how to pick locks?" I asked him.

"It's too slow," he answered in a low voice. "Let's try the windows."

He was right. The first window we tried was only stuck by New York soot. With our hands black and grimy with soot we climbed into the kitchen. The kitchen was neat except for a dried-up salad in a bowl. The sink was dry, the air was stuffy.

It was good manners to yell announcement of our trespassing.

"Jean!" I called. I got back echoes and silence, and something small falling off a shelf upstairs. The ghosts rose in my mind again and stood behind me, their claws outstretched. I looked over my shoulder and saw only the empty kitchen. My skin prickled. I was afraid of making a noise. Afraid death would hear me. Had to yell; afraid to yell. Had to move; afraid to move. Dying from cowardice. Someone else's thoughts, with the odor of illness, the burning of thirst, the energy of anger. I was shriveling up inside.

I braced a hand on the kitchen table. "Upstairs in the attic," I said. I knew what was wrong with me now. Jean Dalais was an Archetype. She was delirious and dreaming that she was I. Or I was really Jean Dalais suffering through another dream of rescue, and I was dreaming that strange people were downstairs in my kitchen looking for me. I, Jean, hated these hallucinations. I struck at the dream images of men with the true feeling of weakness and illness, with the memory of the time that had passed with no one helping me and the hatred of a world that trapped you and made hope a lie, trying to blast the lies into vanishing.

The George Sanford hallucination slid down to a sitting position on the floor of the kitchen. The bottle of Bock in its paper bag hit the floor beside him with a heavy clunk, sounding almost real. "You go look, Ahmed," said the George Sanford mouth.

The other figure in the dream bent over and placed a phone on the floor. It hit the linoleum with another clunk and a musical chiming sound that seemed to be heard upstairs. "Hallucinations getting more real. Can hear 'em now," muttered the Sanford self—or was it Jean Dalais who was thinking?

"When I yell, dial O and ask for the Rescue Squad to come over." Ahmed picked up the paper bag of Bock. "OK, George?" He started looking through the kitchen drawers. "Great stuff, beer, nothing better for extreme dehydration. Has salt in it. Keeps the system from liquid shock."

He found the beer opener and slipped it into his hip pocket. "Liquid shock is from sudden changes in the water-versus-salt balance," he remarked, going up the stairs softly, two at a time. He went out of sight and I heard his footsteps, very soft and inquiring. Even Ahmed was afraid of stirring up ghosts.

What had Bessie said about the victim? "Hope hurts." She had tried to give the victim hope and the victim had struck her to the heart with a dagger of hatred and shared despair.

That was why I was sitting on the floor!

Danger George *don't think!* I shut my eyes and blanked my mind.

The dream of rescue and the man images were gone. I was Jean Dalais sinking down into the dark, a warm velvet darkness, no sensation, no thought, only distantly the pressure of the attic floor against my face.

A strange thump shook the floor and a scraping sound pulled at my curiosity. I began to wake again. It was a familiar sound, familiar from the other world and the other life, six days ago, an eternity ago, almost forgotten. The attic floor pushed against my face with a smell of dust. The thump and the scraping sound came again, metal against wood. I was curious. I opened dry, sand-filled eyes and raised my head, and the motion awakened my body to the hell of thirst and the ache of weakness.

I saw the two ends of the aluminum ladder sticking up through the attic trapdoor. The ladder was back now. It had fallen long ago, and now it was back, looking at me, expecting me to climb down it. I cursed the ladder with a mental bolt of hatred. What good is a ladder if you can't move? Long ago I had found that moving around brought on labor pains. Not good to have a baby here. Better to hold still.

I heard a voice. "She's here. George. Call the Rescue Squad." I hated the voice. Another imaginary voice in the long nightmare of imaginary rescues. Who was "George?" I was Jean Dalais.

George. Someone had called "George." Downstairs in the small imagined kitchen I imagined a small image of a man grope for a phone beside him on the floor. He dialed "O" clumsily. A female voice asked a question. The man image said "Rescue Squad," hesitantly.

The phone clicked and buzzed and then a deep voice said, "Rescue Squad."

In the attic I knew how a dream of the Rescue Squad should go. I had dreamed it before. I spoke through the small man-image. "My name is Jean Fitzpatrick. I am at 29 Washington Street. I am trapped in my attic without water. If you people weren't fools, you would have found me long ago. Hurry. I'm pregnant." She made the man-image drop the receiver. The dream of downstairs faded again as the man-image put his face in his hands.

My dry eyes were closed, the attic floor again pressed against my face. Near me was the creak of ladder rungs taking weight, and then the creaks of the attic floor something heavy moving on it gently, then the rustle of clothing as somebody moved; the click of a bottle opener against a cap; the clink of the cap hitting the floor; the bubbling and hissing of a fizzing cool liquid. A hand lifted my head carefully and a cold bottle lip pushed against my mouth. I opened my mouth and the cool touch of liquid pressed within it and down the dry throat. I began to swallow.

George Sanford, me, took his hands away from his eyes and looked down at the phone. I was not lying down; I was not drinking; I was not thirsty. Had I dialed the

Rescue Squad when Ahmed called me? A small mannequin of a man in Jean Fitzpatrick's mind had called and hung up, but the mannequin was me, George Sanford—six feet one and a half inches. I am no woman's puppet. The strength of telepathy is powered by emotion and need, and the woman upstairs had enough emotion and need, but no one could have done that to me if I did not want to help. No one.

A musical, two-toned note of a siren approaching, growing louder. It stopped before the door. Loud knocks came at the door. I was feeling all right but still dizzy and not ready to move.

"Come in," I croaked. They rattled the knob. I got up and let them in, then stood hanging on to the back of a chair.

Emergency squad orderlies in blue and white. "You sick?"

"Not me, a woman upstairs." I pointed and they rushed up the stairs, carrying their stretcher and medical kits.

There was no thirst or need driving her mind to intensity any more, but our minds were still connected somehow, for I felt the prick of a needle in one thigh, and then the last dizziness and fear dimmed and vanished, the world steadied out in a good upright position, the kitchen was not a dusty attic but only a clean empty kitchen and all the sunshine of the world was coming in the windows.

I took a deep breath and stretched, feeling the muscles strong and steady in my arms and legs. I went up to the second floor and steadied the ladder for the Rescue Squad men while they carried the unconscious body of a young woman down from the attic.

She was curly-haired with a dirt-and-tear streaked face and skinny arms and legs. She was bulging in the middle, as pregnant as a pumpkin.

I watched the blue and white Rescue truck drive away.

"Want to come along and watch me make out my report?" Ahmed asked.

On the way out of the kitchen I looked around for the Turkish honey rolls, but the bag was gone. I must have dropped it somewhere.

We walked south a few blocks to the nearest police station. Ahmed settled down at a desk they weren't using to fill out his report, and I found a stack of comic magazines in the waiting room and chose the one with the best action on the cover. My hands shook a little because I was hungry, but I felt happy and important.

Ahmed filled out the top, wrote a few lines, and then started working the calculator on the desk. He stopped, stared off into space, glanced at me, and started writing again, glancing at me every second. I wondered what he was writing about me. I wanted the Rescue Squad brass to read good things about me so they would hire me for a job.

"I hunch good, don't I, Ahmed?"

"Yes." He filled something into a space, read the directions for the next question and began biting the end of his pen and staring at the ceiling.

"Would I make a good detector?" I asked.

Katherine MacLean

"What kind of mark did you get in Analysis of Variance in high school?"

"I never took it. I flunked probability in algebra, in six B—"

"The Rescue Squad wants you to fill out reports that they can run into the statistics machines. Look" —I went over and he showed me a space where he had filled out some numbers and a funny symbol like a fallen down d— "can you read it, George?"

"What's it say?"

"It says probability .005. That means the odds were two hundred to one against you finding the White Horse Tavern just by accident, when it was the place the Fitzpatrick woman usually went to. I got the number by taking a rough count of the number of bars in the phone book. More than two hundred wrong bars, and there was only one bar you actually went to. Two hundred divided by one, or two hundred. If you had tried two bars before finding the right one your chance of being wrong would have been two hundred divided by two. That's one hundred. Your score for being right was your chance of being wrong, or the reciprocal of your chance of being right by luck. Your score is two hundred. Understand? Around here they think forty is a good score."

I stared at him, looking stupid. The school had tried relays of teachers and tutors on me for two terms before they gave up trying to teach me. It didn't seem to mean anything. It didn't seem to have anything to do with people. Without probability algebra and graphs I found out they weren't going to let me take Psychology B, History, Social Dynamics, Systems Analysis, Business Management, Programming or Social Work. They wouldn't even let me study to be a Traffic Flow cop. I could have taken Electronics Repair but I wanted to work with people, not TV sets, so I dropped out. I couldn't do school work; but the kind of thing the Rescue Squad wanted done, I could do.

"Ahmed, I'd be good in the Rescue Squad. I don't need statistics. Remember I told you were pushing Bessie in too deep. I was right, wasn't I? And you were wrong. That shows I don't need training."

Ahmed looked sorry for me. "George, you don't get any score for that. Every soft-hearted slob is afraid when he sees someone going into a traumatic area in the subjective world. He always tries to make them stop. You would have said I was pushing her too deep anyhow, even if you were wrong."

"But I was right."

Ahmed half rose out of his chair, then made himself calm down.

He settled back, his lips pale and tight against his teeth. "It doesn't matter if you were right, unless you are right against odds. You get credit for picking the White Horse Tavern out of all the taverns you could have picked, and you get credit for picking the girl's house out of all the addresses you could have picked. I'm going to multiply the two figures by each other. It will run your score over eighty thousand probably. That's plenty of credit."

"But I only went to the tavern because I was thirsty. You can't credit me with that.

You made me thirsty somehow. And I went to the girl's house because I wanted to see her. Maybe she was pulling at me."

"I don't care what your reasons were! You went to the right place, didn't you? You found her, didn't you?" Ahmed stood up and shouted. "You're talking like a square. What do you think this is, 1950, or sometime your grandmother was running a store? I don't care what your reasons are, nobody cares anymore what the reasons are. We only care about results, understand? We don't know why things happen, but if everyone makes out good reports about them, with clear statistics, we can run the reports into the machines, and the machines will tell us exactly what is happening, and we can work with that, because they're facts, and it's the real world. I know you can find people. Your reasons don't matter. Scientific theories about the causes don't matter!"

He was red in the face and shouting, like I'd said something against his religion or something. "I wish we could get theories for some of it. But, if the statistics say that if something funny happens here and something else funny always happens over there, next, we don't have to know how the two connect; all we have to do is expect the second thing every time we see the first thing happen. See?"

I didn't know what he was talking about. My tutors had said things like that to me, but Ahmed felt miserable enough about it to shout. Ahmed was a friend.

"Ahmed," I said, "would I make a good detector?"

"You'd make a great detector, you dope!" He looked down at his report. "But you can't get into the Rescue Squad. The rules say that you've got to have brains in your head instead of rocks. I'll help you figure out some place else you can get a job. Stick around. I'll loan you fifty bucks as soon as I finish this report. Go read something."

I felt lousy, but I stood there fighting it, because this was my last chance at a real job, and there was something right about what I was trying to do. The Rescue Squad needed me. Lost people were going to need me.

"Ahmed," I said, trying to make my meaning very clear to him. "I *should* be in your department. You gotta figure out a way to get me in."

It's hard watching a strong confident guy go through a change. Generally Ahmed always knows what he is doing, he never wonders. He stared down at his report, holding his breath, he was thinking so hard. Then he got away from the desk and began to pace up and down. "What the hell is wrong with me? I must be going chicken. Desk work is softening me up." He grabbed up his report off the desk. "Come on, let's go buck the rules. Let's fight City Hall."

"We can't hire your friend." The head of the Rescue Squad shook his head. "He couldn't pass the tests. You said so yourself."

"The *rules* say that George has to pass the pen and paper tests." Ahmed leaned forward on the desk and tapped his hand down on the desk top, emphasizing words. "The rules are *trash* rules made up by trash bureaucrats so that nobody can get a job but people with picky little old-maid minds like them! Rules are something we use to deal with people we don't know and don't care about. We know George and we know we want him! How do we fake the tests?''

The chief held out one hand, palm down. ''Slow down, Ahmed. I appreciate enthusiasm, but maybe we can get Goerge in legitimately. I know he cut short an epidemic of hysteria and psychosomatics at the hospitals and saved the hospitals a lot of time and expense. I want him in the department if he can keep that up. But let's not go breaking up the system to get him in. We can use the system.''

The chief opened the intercom switch and spoke into the humming box. ''Get me Accounting, will you?'' The box answered after a short while the chief spoke again. He was a big, square built man, going slightly flabby. His skin was loose and slightly gray. ''Jack, listen, we need the services of a certain expert. We can't hire him. He doesn't fit the height and weight regulations, or something like that. How do we pay him?''

The man at the other end spoke briefly in accounting technicalities: '' . . . Contingencies, services, fees. Consultant. File separate requisitions. file accounting slips each month for total specifying spearate services rendered, time and results, with statistics of probability rundown on departmental expenses saved by outside help and city expenses saved by the Rescue Squad action, et cetera, et cetera. Get it?''

''OK, thanks.'' He shut off the chatterbox and spoke to Ahmed. ''We're in. Your friend is hired.''

My feet were tired standing there. My hands were shaking slightly so I had stuffed them into my pockets, like a nonchalant pose. I was passing the time thinking of restaurants, all the good ones that served the biggest plates for the least money. ''When do I get paid?'' I asked.

''Next month,'' Ahmed said. ''You get paid at the end of every month for the work you did on each separate case. Don't look so disappointed. You are a consultant expert now. You are on my expense account. I'm supposed to buy your meals and pay your transportation to the scene of the crime whenever I consult you.''

''Consult me now,'' I said.

We had a great Italian meal at an old-fashioned Italian restaurant: lasagna, antipasto, French bread in thick, tough slices, lots of butter, four cups of hot black coffee and spumoni for dessert, rich and sweet. Everything tasted fresh and cooked just right, and they served big helpings. I stopped shaking after the second cup of coffee.

There was something funny about that restaurant. Somebody was planning a murder, but I wasn't going to mention it to Ahmed until after dessert.

He'd probably want me to rescue somebody instead of eating. ■

Gulf

Robert A. Heinlein

In one of the fall, 1948, issues of Astounding Science Fiction *(as* Analog *was known then) a fan letter appeared, listing a number of stories which would appear in a future issue. John Campbell and I got our heads together, and thus was born the "time travel" issue.*

One of the stories listed for that future issue was "Gulf" by Robert A. Heinlein. I determined that this should be a superman story, and after pondering, asked my wife what could cause a superman to be different from other humans. "Easy," she said, "he thinks better than other people." Thus was born "Gulf."

"Gulf" is the lead story in Assignment in Eternity, *which has been published in the USA, England, Italy, Spain, France, Holland, Israel, and Sweden. It is still in print in many of those countries.*

Kettle Belly Baldwin was such a juicy character that I used him again in Friday. *A number of letters have come in since the publication of that book asking whether it's the same character, since he's grown into an old man between the two stories.*

THE FIRST-QUARTER ROCKET from Moonbase put him down at Pied-a-Terre. The name he was traveling under began—by foresight—with the letter "A"; he was through port inspection and into the shuttle tube to the city ahead of the throng. Once in the tube car he went to the men's washroom and locked himself in.

Quickly he buckled on the safety belt he found there, snapped its hooks to the wall fixtures, and leaned over awkwardly to remove a razor from his bag. The surge caught him in that position; despite the safety belt he bumped his head—and swore. He straightened up and plugged in the razor. His moustache vanished; he shortened his sideburns, trimmed the corners of his eyebrows, and brushed them up.

He towelled his hair vigorously to remove the oil that had sleeked it down, combed it loosely into a wavy mane. The car was now riding in a smooth, unaccelerated 300 mph; he let himself out of the safety belt without unhooking it from the walls and, working very rapidly, peeled off his moonsuit, took from his bag and put on a tweedy casual outfit suited to outdoors on Earth and quite unsuited to Moon Colony's air-conditioned corridors.

His slippers he replaced with walking shoes from the bag; he stood up. Joel Abner, commercial traveler, had disappeared; in his place was Captain Joseph Gilead, explorer, lecturer, and writer. Of both names he was the sole user; neither was his birth name.

He slashed the moonsuit to ribbons and flushed it down the water closet, added "Joel Abner's" identification card; then peeled a plastic skin off his travel bag and let the bits follow the rest. The bag was now pearl grey and rough, instead of dark brown and smooth. The slippers bothered him; he was afraid they might stop up the car's plumbing. He contented himself with burying them in the waste receptacle.

The acceleration warning sounded as he was doing this; he barely had time to get back into the belt. But, as the car plunged into the solenoid field and surged to a stop, nothing remained of Joel Abner but some unmarked underclothing, very ordinary toilet articles, and nearly two dozen spools of microfilm equally appropriate—until examined—to a commercial traveler or a lecturer-writer. He planned not to let them be examined as long as he was alive.

He waited in the washroom until he was sure of being last man out of the car, then went forward into the next car, left by its exit, and headed for the lift to the ground level.

"New Age Hotel, sir," a voice pleaded near his ear. He felt a hand fumbling at the grip of his travel bag.

He repressed a reflex to defend the bag and looked the speaker over. At first glance he seemed an under-sized adolescent in a smart uniform and pillbox cap. Further inspection showed premature wrinkles and the features of a man at least forty. The eyes were glazed. A pituitary case, he thought to himself, and on the hop as well. "New Age Hotel," the runner repeated. "Best mechanos in town, chief. There's a discount if you're just down from the moon."

Captain Gilead, when in town as Captain Gilead, always stayed at the old Savoy.

But the notion of going to the New Age appealed to him; in that incredibly huge, busy, and ultramodern hostelry he might remain unnoticed until he had had time to do what had to be done.

He disliked mightily the idea of letting go his bag. Nevertheless it would be out of character not to let the runner carry the bag; it would call attention to himself—and the bag. He decided that this unhealthy runt could not outrun him even if he himself were on crutches; it would suffice to keep an eye on the bag.

"Lead on, comrade," he answered heartily, surrendering the bag. There had been no hesitation at all; he had let go the bag even as the hotel runner reached for it.

"Okay, chief." The runner was first man into an empty lift; he went to the back of the car and set the bag down beside him. Gilead placed himself so that his foot rested firmly against his bag and faced forward as other travelers crowded in. The car started.

The lift was jammed; Gilead was subjected to body pressures on every side—but he noticed an additional, unusual, and uncalled-for pressure behind him.

His right hand moved suddenly and clamped down on a skinny wrist and a hand clutching something. Gilead made no further movement, nor did the owner of the hand attempt to draw away or make any objection. They remained so until the car reached the surface. When the passengers had spilled out he reached behind him with his left hand, recovered his bag and dragged the wrist and its owner out of the car.

It was, of course, the runner; the object in his fist was Gilead's wallet. "You durn near lost that, chief," the runner announced with no show of embarrassment. "It was falling out of your pocket."

Gilead liberated the wallet and stuffed it into an inner pocket. "Fell right through the zipper," he answered cheerfully. "Well, let's find a cop."

The runt tried to pull away. "You got nothing on me!"

Gilead considered the defense. In truth, he had nothing. His wallet was already out of sight. As to witnesses, the other lift passengers were already gone—nor had they seen anything. The lift itself was automatic. He was simply a man in the odd position of detaining another citizen by the wrist. And Gilead himself did not want to talk to the police.

He let got that wrist. "On your way, comrade. We'll call it quits."

The runner did not move. "How about my tip?"

Gilead was beginning to like this rascal. Locating a loose half credit in his change pocket he flipped it at the runner, who grabbed it out of the air but still didn't leave. "I'll take your bag now. Gimme."

"No thanks, chum. I can find your delightful inn without further help. One side, please."

"Oh, yeah? How about my commission? I gotta carry your bag, else how they gonna know I brung you in? Gimme."

Gilead was delighted with the creature's unabashed insistence. He found a two-

Robert A. Heinlein

credit piece and passed it over. "There's your cumshaw. Now beat it, before I kick your tail up around your shoulders."

"You and who else?"

Gilead chuckled and moved away down the concourse toward the station entrance to the New Age Hotel. His subconscious sentries informed him immediately that the runner had not gone back toward the lift as expected, but was keeping abreast him in the crowd. He considered this. The runner might very well be what he appeared to be, common city riffraff who combined casual thievery with his overt occupation. On the other hand—

He decided to unload. He stepped suddenly off the sidewalk into the entrance of a drugstore and stopped just inside the door to buy a newspaper. While his copy was being printed, he scooped up, apparently as an afterthought, three standard pneumo mailing tubes. As he paid for them he palmed a pad of gummed address labels.

A glance at the mirrored wall showed him that his shadow had hesitated outside but was still watching him. Gilead went on back to the shop's soda fountain and slipped into an unoccupied booth. Although the floor show was going on—a remarkably shapely ecdysiast was working down toward her last string of beads—he drew the booth's curtain.

Shortly the call light over the booth flashed discreetly; he called, "Come in!" A pretty and very young waitress came inside the curtain. Her plastic costume covered without concealing.

She glanced around. "Lonely?"

"No, thanks, I'm tired."

"How about a redhead, then? Real cute—"

"I really am tired. Bring me two bottles of beer, unopened, and some pretzels."

"Suit yourself, sport." She left.

With speed he opened the travel bag, selected nine spools of microfilm, and loaded them into the three mailing tubes, the tubes being of the common three-spool size. Gilead then took the filched pad of address labels, addressed the top one to "Raymond Calhoun, P. O. Box 1060, Chicago" and commenced to draw with great care in the rectangle reserved for electric-eye sorter. The address he shaped in arbitrary symbols intended not to be read, but to be scanned automatically. The hand-written address was merely a precaution, in case a robot sorter should reject his hand-drawn symbols as being imperfect and thereby turn the tube over to a human postal clerk for re-addressing.

He worked fast, but with the care of an engraver. The waitress returned before he had finished. The call light warned him; he covered the label with his elbow and kept it covered.

She glanced at the mailing tubes as she put down the beer and a bowl of pretzels. "Want me to mail those?"

He had another instant of split-second indecision. When he had stepped out of the tube car he had been reasonably sure, first, that the *persona* of Joel Abner, commercial traveler, had not been penetrated, and, second, that the transition from Abner to Gilead had been accomplished without arousing suspicion. The pocket-picking episode had not alarmed him, but had caused him to reclassify those two propositions from calculated certainties to unproved variables. He had proceeded to test them at once; they were now calculated certainties again—of the opposite sort. Ever since he had spotted his erstwhile porter the New Age runner standing outside this same drugstore his subconscious had been clanging like a burglar alarm.

It was clear not only that he had been spotted but that they were organized with a completeness and shrewdness he had not believed possible.

But it was mathematically probable to the point of certainty that they were not operating through this girl. They had no way of knowing that he would choose to turn aside into this particular drugstore. That she could be used by them he was sure—and she had been out of sight since his first contact with her. But she was clearly not bright enough, despite her alleycat sophistication, to be approached, subverted, instructed and indoctrinated to the point where she could seize an unexpected opportunity, all in a space of time merely adequate to fetch two bottles of beer. No, this girl was simply after a tip. Therefore she was safe.

But her costume offered no possibility of concealing three mailing tubes, nor would she be safe crossing the concourse to the post office. He had no wish that she be found tomorrow morning dead in a ditch.

"No," he answered immediately. "I have to pass the post office anyway. But it was a kind thought. Here." He gave her a half credit.

"Thanks." She waited and stared meaningfully at the beer. He fumbled again in his change pocket, found only a few bits, reached for his wallet and took out a five-pluton note.

"Take it out of this."

She handed him back three singles and some change. He pushed the change toward her, then waited, frozen, while she picked it up and left. Only then did he hold the wallet closer to his eyes.

It was not his wallet.

He should have noticed it before, he told himself. Even though there had been only a second from the time he had taken it from the runner's clutched fingers until he had concealed it in a front pocket, he should have known it—known it and forced the runner to disgorge, even if he had had to skin him alive.

But why was he sure that it was not his wallet? It was the proper size and shape, the proper weight and feel—real ostrich skin in these days of synthetics. There was the weathered ink stain which had resulted from carrying a leaky stylus in the same pocket. There was a V-shaped scratch on the front which had happened so long ago he did not recall the circumstances.

Yet it was not his wallet.

He opened it again. There was the proper amount of money, there were what seemed to be his Explorers' Club card and his other identity cards, there was a dog-eared flat-

234   **Robert A. Heinlein**

photo of a mare he had once owned. Yet the more the evidence showed that it was his, the more certain he became that it was not his. These things were forgeries; they did not *feel* right.

There was one way to find out. He flipped a switch provided by a thoughtful management; the booth became dark. He took out his penknife and carefully slit a seam back of the billfold pocket. He dipped a finger into a secret pocket thus disclosed and felt around; the space was empty—nor in this case had the duplication of his own wallet been quite perfect; the space should have been lined, but his fingers encountered rough leather.

He switched the light back on, put the wallet away, and resumed his interrupted drawing. The loss of the card which should have been in the concealed pocket was annoying, certainly awkward, and conceivably disastrous, but he did not judge that the information on it was jeopardized by the loss of the wallet. The card was quite featureless unless examined by black light; if exposed to visible light—by someone taking the real wallet apart, for example—it had the disconcerting quality of bursting explosively into flame.

He continued to work, his mind busy with the wider problem of why they had taken so much trouble to try to keep him from knowing that his wallet was being stolen—and the still wider and more disconcerting question of why they had bothered with *his* wallet. Finished, he stuffed the remainder of the pad of address labels into a crack between cushions in the booth, palmed the label he had prepared, picked up the bag and the three mailing tubes. One tube he kept separate from the others by a finger.

No attack would take place, he judged, in the drug store. The crowded concourse between himself and the post office he would ordinarily have considered equally safe—but not today. A large crowd of people, he knew, were equal to so many trees as witnesses if the dice were loaded with any sort of a diversion.

He slanted across the bordering slidewalk and headed directly across the middle toward the post office, keeping as far from other people as he could manage. He had become aware of two men converging on him when the expected diversion took place.

It was a blinding light and a loud explosion, followed by screams and startled shouts. The source of the explosion he could imagine; the screams and shouts were doubtless furnished free by the public. Being braced, not for this, but for anything, he refrained even from turning his head.

The two men closed rapidly, as on cue.

Most creatures and almost all humans fight only when pushed. This can lose them decisive advantage. The two men made no aggressive move of any sort, other than to come close to Gilead—nor did they ever attack.

Gilead kicked the first of them in the knee cap, using the side of his foot, a much more certain stroke than with the toe. He swung with his travel bag against the other at the same time, not hurting him but bothering him, spoiling his timing. Gilead followed it with a heavy kick to the man's stomach.

The man whose knee cap he had ruined was on the pavement, but still active—reaching for something, a gun or a knife. Gilead kicked him in the head and stepped over him, continued toward the post office.

Slow march—slow march all the way! He must not give the appearance of running away; he must be the perfect respectable citizen, going about his lawful occasions.

The post office came close, and still no tap on the shoulder, no denouncing shout, no hurrying footsteps. He reached the post office, was inside. The opposition's diversion had worked, perfectly—but for Gilead, not for them.

There was a short queue at the addressing machine. Gilead joined it, took out his stylus and wrote addresses on the tubes while standing. A man joined the queue almost at once; Gilead made no effort to keep him from seeing what address he was writing; it was "Captain Joseph Gilead, the Explorers' Club, New York." When it came his turn to use the symbol printing machine he still made no effort to conceal what keys he was punching—and the symbol address matched the address he had written on each tube.

He worked somewhat awkwardly as the previously prepared gummed label was still concealed in his left palm.

He went from the addressing machine to the mailing receivers; the man who had been behind him in line followed him without pretending to address anything.

Thwonk! and the first tube was away with a muted implosion of compressed air. *Thwonk!* again and the second was gone—and at the same time Gilead grasped the last one in his left hand, sticking the gummed label down firmly over the address he had just printed on it. Without looking at it he made sure by touch that it was in place, all corners sealed, then *thwonk!* it joined its mates.

Gilead turned suddenly and trod heavily on the feet of the man crowded close behind him. "Wups! pardon *me*." he said happily and turned away. He was feeling very cheerful; not only had he turned his dangerous charge over into the care of a mindless, utterly reliable, automatic machine which could not be coerced, bribed, drugged, nor subverted by any other means and in whose complexities the tube would be perfectly hidden until it reached a destination known only to Gilead, but also he had just stepped on the corns of one of the opposition.

On the steps of the post office he paused beside a policeman who was picking his teeth and staring out at a cluster of people and an ambulance in the middle of the concourse. "What's up?" Gilead demanded.

The cop shifted his toothpick. "First some damn fool sets off fireworks," he answered, "then two guys get in a fight and blame near ruin each other."

"My goodness!" Gilead commented and set off diagonally toward the New Age Hotel.

He looked around for his pick-pocket friend in the lobby, did not see him. Gilead strongly doubted if the runt were on the hotel's staff. He signed in as Captain Gilead,

Robert A. Heinlein

ordered a suite appropriate to the *persona* he was wearing, and let himself be conducted to the lift.

Gilead encountered the runner coming down just as he and his bellman were about to go up. "Hi, Shorty!" he called out while deciding not to eat anything in this hotel. "How's business?"

The runt looked startled, then passed him without answering, his eyes blank. It was not likely, Gilead considered, that the runt would be used after being detected; therefore some sort of drop box, call station, or headquarters of the opposition was actually inside the hotel. Very well, that would save everybody a lot of useless commuting—and there would be fun for all!

In the meantime he wanted a bath.

In his suite he tipped the bellman who continued to linger.

"Want some company?"

"No, thanks, I'm a hermit."

"Try this then." The bellman inserted Gilead's room key in the stereo panel, fiddled with the controls, the entire wall lighted up and faded away. A svelte blonde creature, backed by a chorus line, seemed about to leap into Gilead's lap. "That's not a tape," the bellman went on, "That's a live transmission direct from the Tivoli. We got the best equipment in town."

"So you have," Gilead agreed, and pulled out his key. The picture blanked; the music stopped. "But I want a bath, so get out—now that you've spent four credits of my money."

The bellman shrugged and left. Gilead threw off his clothes and stepped into the "fresher." Twenty minutes later, shaved from ear to toe, scrubbed, soaked, sprayed, pummeled, rubbed, scented, powdered, and feeling ten years younger, he stepped out. His clothes were gone.

His bag was still there; he looked it over. It seemed okay, itself and contents. There were the proper number of microfilm spools—not that it mattered. Only three of the spools mattered and they were already in the mail. The rest were just shrubbery, copies of his own public lectures. Nevertheless he examined one of them, unspooling a few frames.

It was one of his own lectures all right—but not one he had had with him. It was one of his published transcriptions, available in any large book store. "Pixies everywhere," he remarked and put it back. Such attention to detail was admirable.

"Room service!"

The service panel lighted up. "Yes, sir?"

"My clothes are missing. Chase 'em up for me."

"The valet has them, sir."

"I didn't order valet service. Get 'em back."

The girl's voice and face were replaced, after a slight delay, by those of a man. "It is not necessary to order valet service here, sir. 'A New Age guest receives the best.' "

"Okay, get 'em back—chop, chop! I've got a date with the Queen of Sheba."

"Very good, sir." The image faded.

With wry humor he reviewed his situation. He had already made the possibly fatal error of underestimating his opponent through—he now knew—visualizing that opponent in the unimpressive person of "the runt." Thus he had allowed himself to be diverted; he should have gone anywhere rather than to the New Age, even to the old Savoy, although that hotel, being a known stamping ground of Captain Gilead, was probably as thoroughly booby-trapped by now as this palatial dive.

He must not assume that he had more than a few more minutes to live. Therefore he must use those few minutes to tell his boss the destination of the three important spools of microfilm. Thereafter, if he still were alive, he must replenish his cash to give him facilities for action—the amount of money in "his" wallet, even if it were returned, was useless for any major action. Thirdly, he must report in, close the present assignment, and be assigned to his present antagonists as a case in themselves, quite aside from the matter of the microfilm.

Not that he intended to drop Runt & Company even if not assigned to them. True artists were scarce—nailing him down by such a simple device as stealing his pants! He loved them for it and wanted to see more of them, as violently as possible.

Even as the image on the room service panel faded he was punching the scrambled keys on the room's communicator desk. It was possible—certain—that the scramble code he used would be repeated elsewhere in the hotel and the supposed privacy attained by scrambling thereby breached at once. This did not matter; he would have his boss disconnect and call back with a different scramble from the other end. To be sure, the call code of the station to which he was reporting would thereby be breached, but it was more than worthwhile to expend and discard one relay station to get this message through.

Scramble pattern set up, he coded—not New Washington, but the relay station he had selected. A girl's face showed on the screen. "New Age service, sir. Were you scrambling?"

"Yes."

"I am veree sorree, sir. The scrambling circuits are being repaired. I can scramble for you from the main board."

"No, thanks, I'll call in clear."

"I yam ve-ree sor-ree, sir."

There was one clear-code he could use—to be used only for crash priority. This was crash priority. Very well—

He punched the keys again without scrambling and waited. The same girl's face appeared presently. "I am verree sorree, sir; that code does not reply. May I help you?"

"You might send up a carrier pigeon." He cleared the board.

The cold breath on the back of his neck was stronger now; he decided to do what he could to make it awkward to kill him just yet. He reached back into his mind and coded in clear the *Star-Times*.

No answer.

He tried the *Clarion*—again no answer.

No point in beating his head against it; they did not intend to let him talk outside to anyone. He rang for a bellman, sat down in an easy chair, switched it to "shallow massage," and luxuriated happily in the chair's tender embrace. No doubt about it; the New Age *did* have the best mechanos in town—his bath had been wonderful; this chair was superb. Both the recent austerities of Moon Colony and the probability that this would be his last massage added to his pleasure.

The door dilated and a bellman came in—about his own size, Gilead noted. The man's eyebrows went up a fraction of an inch on seeing Gilead's oyster-naked condition. "You want company?"

Gilead stood up and moved toward him. "No, dearie," he said grinning, "I want *you*"—at which he sank three stiffened fingers in the man's solar plexus.

As the man grunted and went down Gilead chopped him in the side of the neck with the edge of his hand.

The shoulders of the jacket were too narrow and the shoes too large; nevertheless two minutes later "Captain Gilead" had followed "Joel Abner" to oblivion and Joe, temporary and free-lance bellman, let himself out of the room. He regretted not being able to leave a-tip with his predecessor.

He sauntered past the passenger lifts, firmly misdirected a guest who had stopped him, and found the service elevator. By it was a door to the "quick drop." He opened it, reached out and grasped a waiting pulley belt, and, without stopping to belt himself into it, contenting himself with hanging on, he stepped off the edge. In less time than it would have taken him to parachute the drop he was picking himself up off the cushions in the hotel basement and reflecting that lunar gravitation surely played hob with a man's leg muscles.

He left the drop room and started out in an arbitrary direction, but walking as if he were on business and belonged where he was—any exit would do and he would find one eventually.

He wandered in and out of the enormous pantry, then found the freight door through which the pantry was supplied.

When he was thirty feet from it, it closed and an alarm sounded. He turned back.

He encountered two policemen in one of the many corridors under the giant hotel and attempted to brush on past them. One of them stared at him, then caught his arm. "Captain Gilead—"

Gilead tried to squirm away, but without showing any skill in the attempt. "What's the idea?"

"You are Captain Gilead."

"And you're my Aunt Sadie. Let go of my arm, copper."

The policeman fumbled in his pocket with his other hand, pulled out a notebook.

Gilead noted that the other officer had moved a safe ten feet away and had a Markheim gun trained on him.

"You, Captain Gilead," the first officer droned, "are charged on a sworn complaint with uttering a counterfeit five-pluton note at or about thirteen hours this date at the Grand Concourse drugstore in this city. You are cautioned to come peacefully and are advised that you need not speak at this time. Come along."

The charge might or might not have something to it, thought Gilead; he had not examined closely the money in the substituted wallet. He did not mind being booked, now that the microfilm was out of his possession; to be in an ordinary police station with nothing more sinister to cope with than crooked cops and dumb desk sergeants would be easy street compared with Runt & Company searching for him.

On the other hand the situation was too pat, unless the police had arrived close on his heels and found the stripped bellman, gotten his story and started searching.

The second policeman kept his distance and did not lower the Markheim gun. That made other considerations academic. "Okay, I'll go," he protested. "You don't have to twist my arm that way."

They went up to the weather level and out to the street—and not once did the second cop drop his guard. Gilead relaxed and waited. A police car was balanced at the curb. Gilead stopped. "I'll walk," he said. "The nearest station is just around the corner. I want to be booked in my own precinct."

He felt a teeth-chattering chill as the blast from the Markheim hit him; he pitched forward on his face.

He was coming to, but still could not co-ordinate, as they lifted him out of the car. By the time he found himself being half-carried, half-marched down a long corridor he was almost himself again, but with a gap in his memory. He was shoved through a door which clanged behind him. He steadied himself and looked around.

"Greetings, friend," a resonant voice called out. "Drag up a chair by the fire."

Gilead blinked, deliberately slowed himself down, and breathed deeply. His healthy body was fighting off the effects of the Markheim bolt; he was almost himself.

The room was a cell, old-fashioned, almost primitive. The front of the cell and the door were steel bars; the walls were concrete. Its only furniture, a long wooden bench, was occupied by the man who had spoken. He was fiftyish, of ponderous frame, heavy features set in a shrewd, good-natured expression. He was lying back on the bench, head pillowed on his hands, in animal ease. Gilead had seen him before.

"Hello, Dr. Baldwin."

The man sat up with a flowing economy of motion that moved his bulk as little as possible. "I'm not Dr. Baldwin—I'm not Doctor anything, though my name is Baldwin." He stared at Gilead. "But I know you—seen some of your lectures."

Gilead cocked an eyebrow. "A man would seem naked around the Association of Theoretical Physicists without a doctor's degree—and you were at their last meeting."

Baldwin chuckled boomingly. "That accounts for it—that has to be my cousin on my father's side, Hartley M.—Stuffy citizen Hartley. I'll have to try to take the curse

Robert A. Heinlein

off the family name, now that I've met you, Captain.'' He stuck out a huge hand. ''Gregory Baldwin, 'Kettle Belly' to my friends. New and used helicopters is as close as I come to theoretical physics. *''Kettle Belly Baldwin, King of the Kopters'* —you must have seen my advertising.''

''Now that you mention it, I have.''

Baldwin pulled out a card. ''Here. If you ever need one, I'll give you a ten percent off for knowing old Hartley. Matter of fact, I can do right well by you in a year-old Curtiss, a family car without a mark on it.''

Gilead accepted the card and sat down. ''Not at the moment, thanks. You seem to have an odd sort of office, Mr. Baldwin.''

Baldwin chuckled again. ''In the course of a long life these things happen, Captain. I won't ask you why you are here or what you are doing in that monkey suit. Call me Kettle Belly.''

''Okay.'' Gilead got up and went to the door. Opposite the cell was a blank wall; there was no one in sight. He whistled and shouted—no answer.

''What's itching you, Captain?'' Baldwin asked gently.

Gilead turned. His cellmate had dealt a solitaire hand on the bench and was calmly playing.

''I've got to raise the turnkey and send for a lawyer.''

''Don't fret about it. Let's play some cards.'' He reached in a pocket. ''I've got a second deck; how about some Russian bank?''

''No, thanks. I've got to get out of here.'' He shouted again—still no answer.

''Don't waste your lung power, Captain,'' Baldwin advised him. ''They'll come when it suits them and not a second before. I *know*. Come play with me; it passes the time.'' Baldwin appeared to be shuffling the two decks; Gilead could see that he was actually stacking the cards. The deception amused him; he decided to play—since the truth of Baldwin's advice was so evident.

''If you don't like Russian bank,'' Kettle Belly went on, ''here is a game I learned as a kid.'' He paused and stared into Gilead's eyes. ''It's instructive as well as entertaining, yet it's simple, once you catch on to it.'' He started dealing out the cards. ''It makes a better game with two decks, because the black cards don't mean anything. Just the twenty-six red cards in each deck count—with the heart suit coming first. Each card scores according to its position in that sequence. The ace of hearts is one and the king of hearts counts thirteen; the ace of diamonds is next at fourteen and so on. Savvy?''

''Yes.''

''And the blacks don't count. They're blanks . . . spaces. Ready to play?''

''What are the rules?''

''We'll deal out one hand for free; you'll learn faster as you see it. Then, when you've caught on, I'll play you for a half interest in the atomics trust—or ten bits in cash.'' He resumed dealing, laying the cards out rapidly in columns, five to a row. He paused, finished. ''It's my deal, so it's your count. See what you get.''

It was evident that Baldwin's stacking had brought the red cards into groups, yet there was no evident advantage to it, nor was the count especially high—nor low. Gilead stared at it, trying to figure out the man's game. The cheating, as cheating seemed too bold to be probable.

Suddenly the cards jumped at him, arranged themselves in a meaningful array. He read:

> XTHXY
>
> CANXX
>
> XXXSE
>
> HEARX
>
> XUSXX

The fact that there were only two fives-of-hearts available had affected the spelling but the meaning was clear. Gilead reached for the cards. "I'll try one. I can beat that score." He dipped into the tips belonging to the suit's owner. "Ten bits it is."

Baldwin covered it. Gilead shuffled, making even less attempt to cover up than had Baldwin. He dealt:

> WHATS
>
> XXXXX
>
> XYOUR
>
> GAMEX
>
> XXXXX

Baldwin shoved the money toward him and anted again. "Okay, my turn for revenge." He laid out:

> XXIMX
>
> XONXX
>
> YOURX
>
> XXXXX
>
> XSIDE

"I win again," Gilead announced gleefully. "Ante up."

He grabbed the cards and manipulated them:

> YEAHX
>
> XXXXX
>
> PROVE
>
> XXITX
>
> XXXXX

Baldwin counted and said, "You're too smart for me. Gimme the cards." He produced another ten-bit piece and dealt again:

> XXILX
>
> HELPX
>
> XXYOU
>
> XGETX
>
> OUTXX

"I should have cut the cards," Gilead complained, pushing the money over. "Let's double the bets." Baldwin grunted and Gilead dealt again:

XNUTS

IMXXX

SAFER

XXINX

XGAOL

"I broke your luck," Baldwin gloated. "We'll double it again?"

XUXRX

XNUTS

THISX

NOXXX

XJAIL

The deal shifted:

KEEPX

XTALK

INGXX

XXXXX

XBUDX

Baldwin answered:

THISX

XXXXX

XXNEW

AGEXX

XHOTL

As he stacked the cards again Gilead considered these new factors. He was prepared to believe that he was hidden somewhere in the New Age Hotel; in fact the counter-proposition that his opponents had permitted two ordinary cops to take him away to a normal city jail was most unlikely—unless they had the jail as fully under control as they quite evidently had the hotel. Nevertheless the point was not proven. As for Baldwin, he might be on Gilead's side; more probably he was planted as an *agent provocateur*—or he might be working for himself.

The permutations added up to six situations, only one of which made it desirable to accept Baldwin's offer for help in a jail break—said situation being the least likely of the six.

Nevertheless, though he considered Baldwin a liar, net, he tentatively decided to accept. A static situation brought him no advantage; a dynamic situation—*any* dynamic situation—he might turn to his advantage. but more data were needed. "These cards are sticky as candy," he complained. "You letting your money ride?"

"Suits." Gilead dealt again:

XXXXX

WHYXX

AMXXX
XXXXI
XHERE

"You have the damnedest luck," Baldwin commented:

FILMS
ESCAP
BFORE
XUXXX
KRACK

Gilead swept up the cards, was about to "shuffle," when Baldwin said, "Oh oh, school's out." Footsteps could be heard in the passage. "Good luck, boy," Baldwin added.

Baldwin knew about the films, but had not used any of the dozen ways to identify himself as part of Gilead's own organization. Therefore he was planted by the opposition, or he was a third factor.

More important, the fact that Baldwin knew about the films proved his assertion that this was not a jail. It followed with bitter certainty that he, Gilead, stood no computable chance of getting out alive. The footsteps approaching the cell could be ticking off the last seconds of his life.

He knew now that he should have found means to report the destination of the film before going to the New Age. But Humpty Dumpty was off the wall, entropy always increases—but the films *must* be delivered.

The footsteps were quite close.

Baldwin might get out alive.

But who was Baldwin?

All the while he was "shuffling" the cards. The action was not final; he had only to give them one true shuffle to destroy the message being set up in them. A spider settled from the ceiling, landed on the other man's hand. Baldwin, instead of knocking it off and crushing it, most carefully reached his arm out toward the wall and encouraged it to lower itself to the floor. "Better stay out of the way, shorty." he said gently, "or one of the big boys is likely to step on you."

The incident, small as it was, determined Gilead's decision—and with it, the fate of a planet. He stood up and handed the stack deck to Baldwin. "I owe you exactly ten-sixty," he said carefully. "Be sure to remember it—I'll see who our visitors are."

The footsteps had stopped outside the cell door.

There were two of them, dressed neither as police nor as guards; the masquerade was over. One stood well back, covering the maneuver with a Markheim, the other unlocked the door. "Back against the wall, Fatso," he ordered. "Gilead, out you come. And take it easy, or, after we freeze you, I'll knock out your teeth just for fun."

Baldwin shuffled back against the wall; Gilead came out slowly. He watched for any opening but the leader backed away from him without once getting between him and the man with the Markheim. "Ahead of us and take it slow," he was ordered. He complied, helpless under the precautions, unable to run, unable to fight.

Baldwin went back to the bench when they had gone. He dealt out the cards as if playing solitaire, swept them up again, and continued to deal himself solitaire hands. Presently he "shuffled" the cards back to the exact order Gilead had left them in and pocketed them.

The message had read: XTELLXFBSXPOBPXDEBTXXXCHI.

His two guards marched Gilead into a room and locked the door behind him, leaving themselves outside. He found himself in a large window overlooking the city and a reach of the river; balancing it on the left hung a solid portraying a lunar landscape in convincing color and depth. In front of him was a rich but not ostentatious executive desk.

The lower part of his mind took in these details; his attention could be centered only on the person who sat at that desk. She was old but not senile, frail but not helpless. Her eyes were very much alive, her expression serene. Her translucent, well-groomed hands were busy with a frame of embroidery.

On the desk in front of her were two pneumo mailing tubes, a pair of slippers, and some tattered, soiled remnants of cloth and plastic.

She looked up. "How do you do, Captain Gilead?" she said in a thin, sweet soprano suitable for singing hymns.

Gilead bowed. "Well, thank you—and you, Mrs. Keithley?"

"You know me, I see."

"Madame would be famous if only for her charities."

"You are kind. Captain, I will not waste your time. I had hoped that we could release you without fuss, but—" She indicated the two tubes in front of her. "—you can see for yourself that we must deal with you further."

"So?"

"Come, now, Captain. You mailed *three* tubes. These two are only dummies, and the third did not reach its apparent destination. It is possible that it was badly addressed and has been rejected by the sorting machines. If so, we shall have it in due course. But it seems much more likely that you found some way to change its address—likely to the point of pragmatic certainty."

"Or possibly I corrupted your servant."

She shook her head slightly. "We examined him quite thoroughly before—"

"Before he died?"

"Please, Captain, let's not change the subject. I must know where you sent that other tube. You cannot be hypnotized by ordinary means; you have an acquired immunity to hypnotic drugs. Your tolerance for pain extends beyond the threshold of unconsciousness. All of these things have already been proved, else you would not be in the job you are in; I shall not put either of us to the inconvenience of proving them again. Yet I must have that tube. What is your price?"

"You assume that I have a price."

She smiled. "If the old saw has any exceptions, history does not record them. Be reasonable, Captain. Despite your admitted immunity to ordinary forms of examination, there are ways of breaking down—of *changing*—a man's character so that he becomes really quite pliant under examination . . . ways that we learned from the commissars. But those ways take time and a woman my age has no time to waste."

Gilead lied convincingly. "It's not your age, ma'am; it is the fact that you know that you must obtain that tube at once or you will never get it." He was hoping—more than that, he was *willing*—that Baldwin would have sense enough to examine the cards for one last message . . . and act on it. If Baldwin failed and he, Gilead, died, the tube would eventually come to rest in a dead-letter office and would in time be destroyed.

"You are probably right. Nevertheless, Captain, I will go ahead with the Mindszenty technique if you insist upon it. What do you say to ten million plutonium credits?"

Gilead believed her first statement. He reviewed in his mind the means by which a man bound hand and foot, or worse, could kill himself unassisted. "Ten million plutons and a knife in my back?" he answered. "Let's be practical."

"Convincing assurance would be given before you need talk."

"Even so, it is not my price. After all, you are worth at least five hundred million plutons."

She leaned forward. "I like you, Captain. You are a man of strength. I am an old woman, without heirs. Suppose you became my partner—and my successor?"

"Pie in the sky."

"No, no! I mean it. My age and sex do not permit me actively to serve myself; I must rely on others. Captain, I am very tired of inefficient tools, of men who can let things be spirited away right from under their noses. Imagine!" She made a little gesture of exasperation, clutching her hand into a claw, "You and I could go far, Captain. I need you."

"But I do not need you, madame. And I won't have you."

She made no answer, but touched a control on her desk. A door on the left dilated; two men and a girl came in. The girl Gilead recognized as the waitress from the Grand Concourse Drug Store. They had stripped her bare, which seemed to him an unnecessary indignity since her working uniform could not possible have concealed a weapon.

The girl, once inside, promptly blew her top, protesting, screaming, using language unusual to her age and sex—an hysterical, thalmic outburst of volcanic proportions.

"Quiet, child!"

The girl stopped in midstream, looked with surprise at Mrs. Keithley, and shut up. Nor did she start again, but stood there, looking even younger than she was and somewhat aware of and put off stride by her nakedness. She was covered now with goose flesh, one tear cut a white line down her dust-smeared face, stopped at her lip. She licked at it and sniffled.

Robert A. Heinlein

"You were out of observation once, Captain," Mrs. Keithley went on, "during which time this person saw you twice. Therefore we will examine her."

Gilead shook his head. "She knows no more than a goldfish. But go ahead—five minutes of hypno will convince you."

"Oh, no, Captain! Hypno is sometimes fallible; if she is a member of your bureau, it is certain to be fallible." She signalled to one of the men attending the girl; he went to a cupboard and opened it. "I am old-fashioned," the old woman went on. "I trust simple mechanical means much more than I do the cleverest of clinical procedures."

Gilead saw the implements that the man was removing from cupboard and started forward. "Stop that?" he commanded, "You can't do that—"

He bumped his nose quite hard.

The man paid him no attention. Mrs. Keithley said, "Forgive me, Captain. I should have told you that this room is not one room, but two. The partition is merely glass, but very special glass—I use the room for difficult interviews. There is no need to hurt yourself by trying to reach us."

"Just a moment!"

"Yes, Captain?"

"Your time is already running out. Let the girl and me go free *now*. You are aware that there are several hundred men searching this city for me even now—and that they will not stop until they have taken it apart panel by panel."

"I think not. A man answering your description to the last factor caught the South Africa rocket twenty minutes after you registered at the New Age hotel. He was carrying your very own identifications. He will not reach South Africa, but the manner of his disappearance will point to desertion rather than accident or suicide."

Gilead dropped the matter. "What do you plan to gain by abusing this child? You have all she knows; certainly you do not believe that we could afford to trust in such as she?"

Mrs. Keithley pursed her lips. "Frankly, I do not expect to learn anything from her. I may learn something from you."

"I see."

The leader of the two men looked questioningly at his mistress; she motioned him to go ahead. The girl stared blankly at him, plainly unaware of the uses of the equipment he had gotten out. He and his partner got busy.

Shortly the girl screamed, continued to scream for a few moments in a high adulation. Then it stopped as she fainted.

They roused her and stood her up again. She stood, swaying and staring stupidly at her poor hands, forever damaged even for the futile purposes to which she had been capable of putting them. Blood spread down her wrists and dripped on a plastic tarpaulin, placed there earlier by the second of the two men.

Gilead did nothing and said nothing. Knowing as he did that the tube he was protecting contained matters measured in millions of lives, the problem of the girl, as a problem, did not even arise. It disturbed a deep and very ancient part of his brain, but almost automatically he cut that part off and lived for the time in his forebrain.

Consciously he memorized the faces, skulls, and figures of the two men and filed the data under "personal." Thereafter he unobtrusively gave his attention to the scene out the window. He had been noting it all through the interview but he wanted to give it explicit thought. He recast what he saw in terms of what it would look like had he been able to look squarely out the window and decided that he was on the ninety-first floor of the New Age hotel and approximately one hundred and thirty meters from the north end. He filed this under "professional."

When the girl died, Mrs. Keithley left the room without speaking to him. The men gathered up what was left in the tarpaulin and followed her. Presently the two guards returned and, using the same foolproof methods, took him back to his cell.

As soon as the guards had gone and Kettle Belly was free to leave his position against the wall he came forward and pounded Gilead on the shoulders. "Hi, boy! I'm sure glad to see you—I was scared I would never lay eyes on you again. How was it? Pretty rough?"

"No, they didn't hurt me; they just asked some questions."

"You're lucky. Some of those crazy damn cops play mean when they get you alone in a back room. Did they let you call your lawyer?"

"No."

"Then they ain't through with you. You want to watch it, kid."

Gilead sat down on the bench. "The hell with them. Want to play some more cards?"

"Don't mind if I do. I feel lucky." Baldwin pulled out the double deck, riffled through it. Gilead took them and did the same. Good! they were in the order he had left them in. He ran his thumb across the edges again—yes, even the black nulls were unchanged in sequence; apparently Kettle Belly had simply stuck them in his pocket without examining them, without suspecting that a last message had been written in to them. He felt sure that Baldwin would not have left the message set up if he had read it. Since he found himself still alive, he was much relieved to think this.

He gave the cards one true shuffle, then started stacking them. His first lay-out read:

XXXXX
ESCAP
XXATX
XXXXX
XONCE

"Gotcha that time!" Baldwin crowded. "Ante up:"

DIDXX
XYOUX
XXXXX
XXXXX

CRACK

"Let it ride," announced Gilead and took the deal:

XXNOX
BUTXX
XXXXX
XLETS
XXGOX

"You're too derned lucky to live," complained Baldwin. "Look—we'll leave the bets doubled and double the lay-out. I want a fair chance to get my money back."

His next lay-out read:

XXXXX
XTHXN
XXXXX
THXYX
NEEDX
XXXUX
ALIVX
XXXXX
PLAYX
XXXUP

"Didn't do you much good, did it?" Gilead commented, took the cards and started arranging them.

"There's something mighty funny about a man that wins all the time," Baldwin grumbled. He watched Gilead narrowly. Suddenly his hand shot out, grabbed Gilead's wrist. "I thought so;" he yelled. "A goddam card sharp—"

Gilead shook his hand off. "Why, you obscene fat slug!"

"Caught you! *Caught you!*" Kettle Belly reclaimed his hold, grabbed the other wrist as well. They struggled and rolled to the floor.

Gilead discovered two things: this awkward, bulky man was an artist at every form of dirty fighting and he could simulate it convincingly without damaging his partner. His nerve holds were an inch off the nerve; his kneeings were to thigh muscle rather than to the crotch.

Baldwin tried for a chancery strangle; Gilead let him take it. The big man settled the flat of his forearm against the point of Gilead's chin rather than against his Adam's apple and proceeded to "strangle" him.

There were running footsteps in the corridor.

Gilead caught a glimpse of the guards as they reached the door. They stopped momentarily; the bell of the Markheim was too big to use through the steel grating, the charge would be screened and grounded. Apparently they did not have pacifier bombs with them, for they hesitated. Then the leader quickly unlocked the door, while the man with the Markheim dropped back to the cover position.

Baldwin ignored them, while continuing his stream of profanity and abuse at Gilead.

He let the first man almost reach them before he suddenly said in Gilead's ear, "Close your eyes!" At which he broke just as suddenly.

Gilead sensed an incredibly dazzling flash of light even through his eyelids. Almost on top of it he heard a muffled crack; he opened his eyes and saw that the first man was down, his head twisted at a grotesque angle.

The man with the Markheim was shaking his head; the muzzle of his weapon weaved around. Baldwin was charging him in a waddle, back and knees bent until he was hardly three feet tall. The blinded guard could hear him, let fly a charge in the direction of the noise; it passed over Baldwin.

Baldwin was on him; the two went down. There was another cracking noise of ruptured bone and another dead man. Baldwin stood up, grasping the Markheim, keeping it pointed down the corridor. "How are your eyes, kid?" he called out anxiously.

"They're all right."

"Then come take this chiller." Gilead moved up, took the Markheim. Baldwin ran to the dead end of the corridor where a window looked out over the city. The window did not open; there was no "copter step" beyond it. It was merely a straight drop. He came running back.

Gilead was shuffling possibilities in his mind. Events had moved by Baldwin's plan, not by his. As a result of his visit to Mrs. Keithley's "interview room" he was oriented in space. The corridor ahead and a turn to the left should bring him to the quick-drop shaft. Once in the basement and armed with a Markheim, he felt sure that he could fight his way out—with Baldwin in trail if the man would follow. If not—well, there was too much at stake.

Baldwin was into the cell and out again almost at once. "Come along!" Gilead snapped. A head showed at the bend in the corridor; he let fly at it and the owner of the head passed out on the floor.

"Out of my way, kid!" Baldwin answered. He was carrying the heavy bench on which they had "played" cards. He started up the corridor with it, toward the sealed window, gaining speed remarkably as he went.

His makeshift battering ram struck the window heavily. The plastic bulged, ruptured, and snapped like a soap bubble. The bench went on through, disappeared from sight, while Baldwin teetered on hands and knees, a thousand feet of nothingness under his chin.

"Kid!" he yelled. "Close in! Fall back!"

Gilead backed toward him, firing twice more as he did so. He still did not see how Baldwin planned to get out, but the big man had demonstrated that he had resourcefulness—and resources.

Baldwin was whistling through his fingers and waving. In violation of all city traffic rules a helicopter separated itself from the late afternoon throng, cut through a lane, and approached the window. It hovered just far enough away to keep from fouling it blades. The driver opened the door, a line snaked across and Kettle Belly caught

Robert A. Heinlein

it. With great speed he made it fast to the window's polarizer knob, then grabbed the Markheim. "You first," he snapped. "Hurry!"

Gilead dropped to his knees and grasped the line; the driver immediately increased his tip speed and tilted his rotor; the line tautened. Gilead let it take his weight, then swarmed across it. The driver gave him a hand up while controlling his craft like a highschool horse with his other hand.

The 'copter bucked; Gilead turned and saw Baldwin coming across, a fat spider on a web. As he himself helped the big man in, the driver reached down and cut the line. The ship bucked again and slid away.

There were already men standing in the broken window. "Get lost, Steve!" Baldwin ordered. The driver gave his tip jets another notch and tilted the rotor still more; the 'copter swooped away. He eased it into the traffic stream and inquired, "Where to?"

"Set her for home—and tell the other boys to go home, too. No—you've got your hands full; I'll tell them!" Baldwin crowded up into the other pilot's seat, slipped on phones and settled a quiet-mike over his mouth. The driver adjusted his car to the traffic, set up a combination on his pilot, then settled back and opened a picture magazine.

Shortly Baldwin took off the phones and came back to the passenger compartment. "Takes a lot of 'copters to be sure you have one cruising by when you need it," he said conversationally. "Fortunately, I've got a lot of 'em. Oh, by the way, this is Steve Halliday. Steve, meet Joe—Joe, what is your last name?"

"Greene," answered Gilead.

"Howdy," said the driver and let his eyes go back to his magazine.

Gilead considered the situation. He was not sure that it had been improved. Kettle Belly, whatever he was, was more than a used 'copter dealer—*and* he knew about the films. This boy Steve looked like a harmless young introvert but, then, Kettle Belly himself looked like a lunk. He considered trying to overpower both of them, remembered Kettle Belly's virtuosity in rough-and-tumble fighting, and decided against it. Perhaps Kettle Belly really was on his side, completely and utterly. He heard rumors that the Department used more than one echelon of operatives and he had no way of being sure that he himself was on the top level.

"Kettle Belly," he went on, "could you set me down at the airport first? I'm in one hell of a hurry."

Baldwin looked him over. "Sure, if you say so. But I thought you would want to swap those duds. You're as conspicuous as a preacher at a stag party. And how are you fixed for cash?"

With his fingers Gilead counted the change that had come with the suit. A man without cash had one arm in a sling. "How long would it take?"

"Ten minutes extra, maybe."

Gilead thought again about Kettle Belly's fighting ability and decided that there was no way for a fish in water to get any wetter. "Okay." He settled back and relaxed completely.

Presently he turned again to Baldwin. "By the way, how did you manage to sneak in that dazzle bomb?"

Kettle Belly chuckled. "I'm a large man, Joe; there's an awful lot of me to search." He laughed again. "You'd be amazed at where I had that hidden."

Gilead changed the subject. "How did you happen to be there in the first place?"

Baldwin sobered. "That's a long and complicated story. Come back some day when you're not in such a rush and I'll tell you all about it."

"I'll do that—soon."

"Good. Maybe I can sell you that used Curtiss at the same time."

The pilot alarm sounded; the driver put down his magazine and settled the craft on the roof of Baldwin's establishment.

Baldwin was as good as his word. He took Gilead to his office, sent for clothes—which showed up with great speed—and handed Gilead a wad of bills suitable to stuff a pillow. "You can mail it back," he said.

"I'll bring it back in person," promised Gilead.

"Good. Be careful out on the street. Some of our friends are sure to be around."

"I'll be careful." He left, as casually as if he had called there on business, but feeling less sure of himself than usual. Baldwin himself remained a mystery and, in his business, Gilead could not afford mysteries.

There was a public phone booth in the lobby of Baldwin's building. Gilead went in, scrambled, then coded a different relay station from the one he had attempted to use before. He gave his booth's code and instructed the operator to scramble back. In a matter of minutes he was talking to his chief in New Washington.

"Joe! Where the hell have you been?"

"Later, boss—get this." In departmental oral code as an added precaution, he told his chief that the films were in post office box 1060, Chicago, and insisted that they be picked up by a major force at once.

His chief turned away from the view plate, then returned, "Okay, it's done. Now what happened to you?"

"Later, boss, later. I think I've got some friends outside who are anxious to rassle with me. Keep me here and I may get a hole in my head."

"Okay—but head right back here. I want a full report; I'll wait here for you."

"Right." He switched off

He left the booth light-heartedly, with the feeling of satisfaction that comes from a hard job successfully finished. He rather hoped that some of his "friends" would show up; he felt like kicking somebody who needed kicking.

But they disappointed him. He boarded the transcontinental rocket without alarms and slept all the way to New Washington.

He reached the Federal Bureau of Security by one of many concealed routes and went to his boss's office. After scan and voice check he was let in. Bonn looked up and scowled.

Gilead ignored the expression; Bonn usually scowled. "Agent Joseph Briggs, three-four-oh-nine-seven-two, reporting back from assignment, sir," he said evenly.

Bonn switched a desk control to "recording" and another to "covert." "You are, eh? Why, thumb-fingered idiot! how do you dare to show your face around here?"

"Easy now, boss—what's the trouble?"

Bonn fumed incoherently for a time, then said, "Briggs, twelve star men covered that pick up—and the box was empty. Post office box ten-sixty, Chicago, indeed! Where are those films? Was it a cover up? Have you got them with you?"

Gilead-Briggs restrained his surprise. "No. I mailed them at the Grand Concourse post office to the address you just named." He added, "The machine may have kicked them out; I was forced to letter by hand the machine symbols."

Bonn looked suddenly hopeful. He touched another control and said, "Carruthers! On that Briggs matter: Check the rejection stations for that routing." He thought and then added, "Then try a rejection sequence on the assumption that the first symbol was acceptable to the machine but mistaken. Also for each of the other symbols; run them simultaneously—crash priority for all agents and staff. After that try combinations of symbols taken two at a time, then three at a time, and so on." He switched off.

"The total of that series you just set up is every postal address in the continent," Briggs suggested mildly. "It can't be done."

"It's got to be done! Man, have you any idea of the *importance* of those films you were guarding?"

"Yes. The director at Moon Base told me what I was carrying."

"You don't act as if you did. You've lost the most valuable thing this or any other government can possess—the absolute weapon. Yet you stand there blinking at me as if you had mislaid a pack of cigarettes."

"Weapon?" objected Briggs. "I wouldn't call the nova effect that, unless you class suicide as a weapon. And I don't concede that I've lost it. As an agent acting alone and charged primarily with keeping it out of the hands of others. I used the best means available in an emergency to protect it. That is well within the limits of my authority. I was spotted, by some means—"

"You shouldn't have been spotted!"

"Granted. But I was. I was unsupported and my estimate of the situation did not include a probability of staying alive. Therefore I had to protect my charge by some means which did not depend on my staying alive."

"But you *did* stay alive—you're here."

"Not my doing nor yours, I assure you. I should have been covered. It was your order, you will remember, that I act alone."

Bonn looked sullen. "That was necessary."

"So? In any case, I don't see what all the shooting is about. Either the films show up, or they are lost and will be destroyed as unclaimed mail. So I go back to the Moon and get another set of prints."

Bonn chewed his lip. "You can't do that."

"Why not?"

Bonn hesitated a long time. "There were just two sets. You had the originals, which were to be placed in a vault in the Archives—and the others were to be destroyed at once when the originals were known to be secure."

"Yes? What's the hitch?"

"You don't see the importance of the procedure. Every working paper, every file, every record was destroyed when these films were made. Every technician, every assistant, received hypno. The intention was not only to protect the results of the research but to wipe out the very fact that the research had taken place. There aren't a dozen people in the system who even know of the existence of the nova effect."

Briggs had his own opinions on this point, based on recent experience, but he kept still about them. Bonn went on, "The Secretary has been after me steadily to let him know when the originals were secured. He has been quite insistent, quite critical. When you called in, I told him that the films were safe and that he would have them in a few minutes."

"Well?"

"Don't you see, you fool—he gave the order at once to destroy the other copies."

Briggs whistled. "Jumped the gun, didn't he?"

"That's not the way he'll figure it—mind you, the President was pressuring *him*. He'll say that *I* jumped the gun."

"And so you did."

"No, *you* jumped the gun. You told me the films were in that box."

"Hardly. I said I had sent them there."

"No, you didn't"

"Get out the tape and play it back."

"There is no tape—by the President's own order no records are kept on this operation."

"So? Then why are you recording now?"

"Because," Bonn answered sharply, "someone is going to pay for this and it is not going to be me."

"Meaning," Briggs said slowly, "that it is going to be me."

"I didn't say that. It might be the Secretary."

"If his head rolls, so will yours. No, both of you are figuring on using me. Before you plan on that, hadn't you better hear my report? It might affect your plans. I've got news for you, boss."

Bonn drummed the desk. "Go ahead. It had better be good."

In a passionless monotone Briggs recited all events as recorded by sharp memory from receipt of the films on the Moon to the present moment. Bonn listened impatiently.

Finished, Briggs waited. Bonn got up and strode around the room. Finally he stopped and said, "Briggs, I never heard such a fantastic pack of lies in my life. A fat man who plays cards! A wallet that wasn't your wallet—your clothes stolen! And

Mrs. Keithley—Mrs. *Keithley!* Don't you know that she is one of the strongest supporters of the Administration?''

Briggs said nothing. Bonn went on, "Now I'll tell you what actually did happen. Up to the time you grounded at Pied-a-Terre your report is correct, but—''

"How do you know?''

"Because you were covered, naturally. You don't think I would trust this to one man, do you?''

"Why didn't you tell me? I could have hollered for help and saved all this.''

Bonn brushed it aside. "You engaged a runner, dismissed him, went in that drugstore, came out and went to the post office. There was no fight in the concourse for the simple reason that no one was following you. At the post office you mailed three tubes, one of which may or may not have contained the films. You went from there to the New Age Hotel, left it twenty minutes later and caught the transrocket for Cape Town. You—''

"Just a moment,'' objected Briggs. "How could I have done that and still be here now?''

"Eh?'' For a moment Bonn seemed stumped. "That's just a detail; you were positively identified. For that matter, it would have been a far, far better thing for you if you stayed on that rocket. In fact—'' The bureau chief got a far-away look in his eyes. "—you'll be better off for the time being if we assume officially that you did stay on that rocket. You are in a bad spot, Briggs, a very bad spot. You did not muff this assignment—you sold out!''

Briggs looked at him levelly. "You are preferring charges?''

"Not just now. That is why it is best to assume that you stayed on that rocket—until matters settle down, clarify.''

Briggs did not need a graph to show him what solution would come out when "matters clarified.'' He took from a pocket a memo pad, scribbled on it briefly, and handed it to Bonn.

It read: "I resign my appointment effective immediately.'' He had added signature, thumbprint, date, and hour.

"So long, boss,'' he added. He turned slightly, as if to go.

Bonn yelled, "Stop! Briggs, you are under arrest.'' He reached toward his desk.

Briggs cuffed him in the windpipe, added one to the pit of Bonn's stomach. He slowed down then and carefully made sure that Bonn would remain out for a satisfactory period. Examination of Bonn's desk produced a knockout kit; he added a two-hour hypodermic, placing it inconspicuously beside a mole near the man's backbone. He wiped the needle, restored everything to its proper place, removed the current record from the desk and wiped the tape of all mention of himself, including door check. He left the desk set to "covert'' and "do not disturb'' and left by another of the concealed routes to the Bureau.

He went to the rocket port, bought a ticket, unreserved, for the first ship to Chicago. There was twenty minutes to wait; he made a couple of minor purchases from clerks rather than from machines, letting his face be seen. When the Chicago ship was called he crowded forward with the rest.

At the inner gate, just short of the weighing-in platform, he became part of the crowd present to see passengers off, rather than a passenger himself. He waved at someone in the line leaving the weighing station beyond the gate, smiled, called out a good-by, and let the crowd carry him back from the gate as it closed. He peeled off from the crowd at the men's washroom. When he came out there were several hasty but effective changes in his appearance.

More important, his manner was different.

A short, illicit transaction in a saloon near a hiring hall provided the work card he needed; fifty-five minutes later he was headed across country as Jack Gillespie, loader and helper driver on a diesel freighter.

Could his addressing of the pneumo tube had been bad enough to cause the automatic postal machines to reject it? He let the picture of the label, as it had been when he had completed it, build in his mind until it was as sharp as the countryside flowing past him. No, his lettering of the symbols had been perfect and correct; the machines would accept it.

Could the machine have kicked out the tube for another cause, say a turned-up edge of the gummed label? Yes, but the written label was sufficient to enable a postal clerk to get it back in the groove. One such delay did not exceed ten minutes, even during the rush hour. Even with five such delays the tube would have reached Chicago more than one hour before he reported to Bonn by phone.

Suppose the gummed label had peeled off entirely; in such case the tube would have gone to the same destination as the two cover-up tubes.

In which case Mrs. Keithley would have gotten it, since she had been able to intercept or receive the other two.

Therefore the tube had reached the Chicago post office box.

Therefore Kettle Belly *had* read the message in the stacked cards, had given instructions to someone in Chicago, had done so while at the helicopter's radio. After an event, "possible" and "true" are equivalent ideas, whereas "probable" becomes a measure of one's ignorance. To call a conclusion "improbable" *after the event* was self-confusing amphigory.

Therefore Kettle Belly Baldwin had the films—a conclusion he had reached in Bonn's office.

Two hundred miles from New Washington he worked up an argument with the top driver and got himself fired. From a local booth in town where he dropped he scrambled through to Baldwin's business office. "Tell him I'm a man who owes him money."

Shortly the big man's face built up on the screen. "Hi, kid! How's tricks?"

"I'm fired."

"I thought you would be."

"Worse than that—I'm wanted."

"Naturally."

Robert A. Heinlein

"I'd like to talk with you."

"Swell. Where are you?"

Gilead told him.

"You're clean?"

"For a few hours, at least."

"Go to the local airport. Steve will pick you up."

Steve did so, nodded a greeting, jumped his craft into the air, set his pilot, and went back to his reading. When the ship settled down on course, Gilead noted it and asked, "Where are we going?"

"The boss's ranch. Didn't he tell you?"

"No." Gilead knew it was possible that he was being taken for a one-way ride. True, Baldwin had enabled him to escape an otherwise pragmatically certain death—it was certain that Mrs. Keithley had not intended to let him stay alive longer than suited her uses, else she would not have had the girl killed in his presence. Until he had arrived at Bonn's office, he had assumed that Baldwin had saved him because he knew something that Baldwin most urgently wanted to know—whereas now it looked as if Baldwin had saved him for altruistic reasons.

Gilead conceded the existence in this world of altruistic reasons, but was inclined not to treat them as "least hypothesis" until all other possible hypotheses had been eliminated; Baldwin might have had his own reasons for wishing him to live long enough to report to New Washinton and nevertheless be leased to wipe him out now that he was a wanted man whose demise would cause no comment.

Baldwin might even be a partner in these dark matters of Mrs. Keithley. In some ways that was the simplest explanation though it left other factors unexplained. In any case Baldwin was a key actor—and he had the films. The risk was necessary.

Gilead did not worry about it. The factors known to him were chalked up on the blackboard of his mind, there to remain until enough variables become constants to permit a solution by logic. The ride was very pleasant.

Steve put him down on the lawn of a large rambling ranch house, introduced him to a motherly old party named Mrs. Garver, and took off. "Make yourself at home, Joe," she told him. "Your room is the last one in the east wing—shower across from it. Supper in ten minutes."

He thanked her and took the suggestion, getting back to the living room with a minute or two to spare. Several others, a dozen or more of both sexes, were there. The place seemed to be a sort of a dude ranch—not entirely dude, as he had seen Herefords on the spread as Steve and he were landing.

The other guests seemed to take his arrival as a matter of course. No one asked why he was there. One of the women introduced herself as Thalia Wagner and then took him around the group. Ma Garver came in swinging a dinner bell as this was going on and they all filed into a long, low dining room. Gilead could not remember when he had had so good a meal in such amusing company.

After eleven hours of sleep, his first real rest in several days, he came fully, suddenly awake at a group of sounds his subconscious could not immediately classify and refused to discount. He opened his eyes, swept the room with them, and was at once out of bed, crouching on the side away from the door.

There were hurrying footsteps moving past his bedroom door. There were two voices, one male, one female, outside the door; the female was Thalia Wagner, the man he could not place.

Male: "tsɯmaeq?"

Female: "nøʁ!"

Male: "zulntsɨ."

Female: "ɨpbit New Jersey."

These are not precisely the sounds that Gilead heard, first because of the limitation of phonetic symbols, and second because his ears were not used to the sounds. Hearing is a function of the brain, not of the ear; his brain, sophisticated as it was, nevertheless insisted on forcing the sounds that reached his ears into familiar pockets rather than stop to create new ones.

Thalia Wagner identified, he relaxed and stood up. Thalia was part of the unknown situation he accepted in coming here; a stranger known to her he must accept also. The new unknowns, including the odd language, he filed under "pending" and put aside.

The clothes he had had were gone, but his money—Baldwin's money, rather—was where his clothes had been and with it his work card as Jack Gillespie and his few personal articles. By them someone had laid out a fresh pair of walking shorts and new sneakers, in his size.

He noted, with almost shocking surprise, that someone had been able to serve him thus without waking him.

He put on his shorts and shoes and went out. Thalia and her companion had left while he dressed. No one was about and he found the dining room empty, but three places were set, including his own of supper, and hot dishes and facilities were on the sideboard. He selected baked ham and hot rolls, fried four eggs, poured coffee. Twenty minutes later, warmly replenished and still alone, he stepped out on the veranda.

It was a beautiful day. He was drinking it in and eyeing with friendly interest a desert lark when a young woman came around the side of the hoouse. She was dressed much as he was, allowing for difference in sex, and she was comely, though not annoyingly so. "Good morning," he said.

She stopped, put her hands on her hips, and looked him up and down. "Well!" she said. "Why doesn't somebody tell me these things?"

Then she added. "Are you married?"

"No."

"I'm shopping around. Object: matrimony. Let's get acquainted."

"I'm a hard man to marry. I've been avoiding it for years."

Robert A. Heinlein

"They're all hard to marry," she said bitterly. "There's a new colt down at the corral. Come on."

They went. The colt's name was War Conqueror of Baldwin; hers was Gail. After proper protocol with mare and son they left. "Unless you have pressing engagements," said Gail, "now is a salubrious time to go swimming."

"If salubrious means what I think it does, yes."

The spot was shaded by cottonwoods, the bottom was sandy; for a while he felt like a boy again, with all such matters as lies and nova effects and death and violence away in some improbable, remote dimension. After a long while he pulled himself up on the bank and said, "Gail, what does 'tsumaeq' mean?"

"Come again?" she answered. "I had water in my ear."

He repeated all of the conversation he had heard. She looked incredulous, then laughed. "You didn't hear that, Joe, you just didn't." She added. "You got the 'New Jersey' part right."

"But I did."

"Say it again."

He did so, more carefully, and giving a fair imitation of the speakers' accents.

Gail chortled. "I got the gist of it that time. That Thalia; someday some strong man is going to wring her neck."

"But what does it mean?"

Gail gave him a long, sidewise look. "If you ever find out, I really will marry you, in spite of your protests."

Some one was whisting from the hill top. "Joe! Joe Greene—the boss wants you."

"Gotta go," he said to Gail. "G'bye."

"See you later," she corrected him.

Baldwin was waiting in a study as comfortable as himself. "Hi, Joe," he greeted him. "Grab a seatful of chair. They been treating you right?"

"Yes, indeed. Do you always set as good a table as I've enjoyed so far?"

Baldwin patted his middle. "How do you think I came by my nickname?"

"Kettle Belly, I'd like a lot of explanations."

"Joe, I'm right sorry you lost your job. If I'd had my druthers, it wouldn't have been the way it was."

"Are you working with Mrs. Keithley?"

"No. I'm against her."

"I'd like to believe that, but I've no reason to—yet. What were you doing where I found you?"

"They had grabbed me—Mrs. Keithley and her boys."

"They just happened to grab you—and just happened to stuff you in the same cell with me—and you just happened to know about the films I was supposed to be guarding—and you just happened to have a double deck of cards in your pocket? Now, really!"

"If I hadn't had the cards, we would have found some other way to talk," Kettle Belly said mildly. "Wouldn't we, now?"

"Yes. Granted."

"I didn't mean to suggest that the set up was an accident. We had you covered from Moon Base; when you were grabbed—or rather as soon as you let them suck you into the New Age, I saw to it that they grabbed me too; I figured I might have a chance to lend you a hand, once I was inside." He added, "I kinda let them think that I was an FBS man, too."

"I see. Then it was just luck that they locked us up together."

"Not luck," Kettle Belly objected. "Luck is a bonus that follows careful planning—it's never free. There was a computable probability that they would put us together in hopes of finding out what they wanted to know. We hit the jackpot because we paid for the chance. If we hadn't, I would have had to crush out of the cell and look for you—but I had to be inside to do it."

"Who is Mrs. Keithley?"

"Other than what she is publicly, I take it. She is the queen bee—or the black widow—of a gang. 'Gang' is a poor word—power group, maybe. One of the several such groups, more or less tied together where their interests don't cross. Between them they divvy up the country for whatever they want like two cats splitting a gopher."

Gilead nodded; he knew that Baldwin meant, though he had not known that the enormously respected Mrs. Keithley was in such matters—not until his nose had been rubbed in the fact. "And what are you, Kettle Belly?"

"Now, Joe—I like you and I'm truly sorry you're in a jam. You led wrong a couple of times and I was obliged to trump, as the stakes were high. See here, I feel that I owe you something; what do you say to this: we'll fix you up with a brand-new personality, vacuum tight—even new fingerprints if you want them. Pick any spot on the globe you like and any occupation; we'll supply all the money you need to start over—or money enough to retire and play with the cuties the rest of your life. What do you say?"

"No." There was no hesitation.

"You've no close relatives, no intimate friends. Think about it. I can't put you back in your job; this is the best I can do."

"I've thought about it. The devil with the job, I want to finish my case! You're the key to it."

"Reconsider, Joe. This is your chance to get out of affairs of state and lead a normal, happy life."

" 'Happy.' he says!"

"Well, safe, anyhow. If you insist on going further your life expectancy becomes extremely problematical."

"I don't recall ever having tried to play safe."

"You're the doctor. Joe. In that case—" A speaker on Baldwin's desk uttered: "oenɪ ʀ ʰɒg rylp."

Baldwin answered, "nʊ," and sauntered quickly to the fireplace. An early-morning fire still smouldered in it. He grasped the mantel piece, pulled it toward him. The entire masonry assembly, hearth, mantel, and grate, came toward him, leaving an arch in the wall. "Duck downstairs, Joe," he said. "It's a raid."

"A real priest's hole!"

"Yeah, corny, ain't it? This joint has more bolt holes than a rabbit's nest—and booby-trapped, too. Too many gadgets if you ask me." He went back to his desk, opened a drawer, removed three film spools and dropped them in a pocket.

Gilead was about to go down the staircase; seeing the spools, he stopped. "Go ahead, Joe." Baldwin said urgently. "You're covered and outnumbered. With this raid showing up we wouldn't have time to fiddle; we'ud just have to kill you."

They stopped in a room well underground, another study much like the one above, though lacking sunlight and view. Baldwin said something in the odd language to the mike on the desk, was answered. Gilead experimented with the idea that the lingo might be reversed English, discarded the notion.

"As I was saying," Baldwin went on, "if you are dead set on knowing all the answers—"

"Just a moment. What about this raid?"

"Just the government boys. They won't be rough and not too thorough. Ma Garver can handle them. We won't have to hurt anybody as long as they don't use penetration radar."

Gilead smiled wryly at the disparagement of his own former service. "And if they do?"

"That gimmick over there squeals like a pig, if it's touched by penetration frequencies. Even then we're safe against anything short of an A-bomb. They won't do that; they want the films, not a hole in the ground. Which reminds me—here, catch."

Gilead found himself suddenly in possession of the films which were at the root of the matter. He unspooled a few frames and made certain that they were indeed the right films. He sat still and considered how he might get off this limb and back to the ground without dropping the eggs. The speaker again uttered something; Baldwin did not answer it but said, "We won't be down here long."

"Bonn seems to have decided to check my report." Some of his—former—comrades were upstairs. If he did Baldwin in, could he locate the inside control for the door?

"Bonn is a poor sort. He'll check me—but not too thoroughly; I'm rich. He won't check Mrs. Keithley at all; she's too rich. He thinks with his political ambitions instead of his head. His late predecessor was a better man—he was one of us."

Gilead's tentative plans underwent an abrupt reversal. His oath had been to a government; his personal loyalty had been given to his former boss. "Prove that last remark and I shall be much interested."

"No, you'll come to learn that it's true—if you still insist on knowing the answers. Through checking those films, Joe? Toss 'em back."

Gilead did not do so. "I suppose you have made copies in any case?"

"Wasn't necessary; I looked at them. Don't get ideas, Joe; you're washed up with the FBS, even if you brought the films and my head back on a platter. You slugged your boss—remember?"

Gilead remembered that he had not told Baldwin so. He began to believe that Baldwin did have men inside the FBS, whether his late bureau chief had been one of them or not.

"I would at least be allowed to resign with a clear record. I know Bonn—officially he would be happy to forget it." He was simply stalling for time, waiting for Baldwin to offer an opening.

"Chuck them back, Joe. I don't want to rassle. One of us might get killed—both of us, if you won the first round. You can't prove your case, because I can prove I was home teasing the cat. I sold 'copters to two very respectable citizens at the exact time you would claim I was somewhere else." He listened again to the speaker, answered it in the same gibberish.

Gilead's mind evaluated his own tactical situation to the same answer that Baldwin had expressed. Not being given to wishful thinking he at once tossed the films to Baldwin.

"Thanks, Joe." He went to a small oubliette set in the wall, switched it to full power, put the films in the hopper, waited a few seconds, and switched it off. "Good riddance to bad rubbish."

Gilead permitted his eyebrows to climb. "Kettle Belly, you've managed to surprise me."

"How?"

"I thought you wanted to keep the nova effect as a means to power."

"Nuts! Scalping a man is a hell of a poor way to cure him of dandruff. Joe, how much do you know about the nova effect?"

"Not much. I know it's a sort of atom bomb powerful enough to scare the pants off anybody who gets to thinking about it."

"It's not a bomb. It's not a weapon. It's a means of destroying a planet and everything on it completely—by turning that planet into a nova. If that's a weapon, military or political, then I'm Samson and you're Delilah.

"But I'm not Samson," he went on, "and I don't propose to pull down the Temple—nor let anybody else do so. There are moral lice around who would do just that, if anybody tried to keep them from having their own way. Mrs. Keithley is one such. Your boyfriend Bonn is another such, if only he had the guts and the savvy—which he ain't. I'm bent on frustrating such people. What do you know about ballistics, Joe?"

"Grammar school stuff."

"Inexcusable ignorance." The speaker sounded again; he answered it without breaking his flow. "The problem of three bodies still lacks a neat general solution, but there are several special solutions—the asteroids that chase Jupiter in Jupiter's own orbit at the sixty degree position, for example. And there's the straight-line solution—you've heard of the asteroid 'Earth-Anti'?"

"That's the chunk of rock that is always on the other side of the Sun, where we never see it."

"That's right—only it ain't there any more. It's been novaed."

Gilead, normally immune to surprise, had been subjected to one too many. "Huh? I thought this nova effect was theory?"

"Nope. If you had had time to scan through the films you would have seen pictures of it. It's a plutonium, lithium, and heavy water deal, with some flourishes we won't discuss. It adds up to the match that can set afire a world. It did—a little world flared up and was gone.

"Nobody saw it happen. No one on Earth *could* see it, for it was behind the Sun. It couldn't have been seen from Moon Colony; the Sun still blanked it off from there—visualize the geometry. All that ever saw it were a battery of cameras in a robot ship. All who knew about it were the scientists who rigged it—and *all* of them were with us, except the director. If *he* had been, too, you would never have been in this mix up."

"Dr. Finnley?"

"Yep. A nice guy, but a mind like a pretzel. A 'political' scientist, second-rate ability. He doesn't matter; our boys will ride herd on him until he's pensioned off. But we couldn't keep him from reporting and sending the films down. So I had to grab 'em and destroy them."

"Why didn't you simply save them? All other considerations aside, they are unique in science."

"The human race doesn't need that bit of science, not this millenium. I saved all that mattered, Joe—in my head."

"You *are* your cousin Hartley, aren't you?"

"Of course. But I'm also Kettle Belly Baldwin, and several other guys."

"You can be Lady Godiva, for all of me."

"As Hartley, I was entitled to those films, Joe. It was my project. I instigated it, through my boys."

"I never credited Finnley with it. I'm not a physicist, but he obviously isn't up to it."

"Sure, sure. I was attempting to prove that an artificial nova could not be created; the political—the *racial*—importance of establishing the point is obvious. It backfired on me—so we had to go into emergency action."

"Perhaps you should have left well enough alone."

"No. It's better to know the worst; now we can be alert for it, divert research away from it." The speaker growled again; Baldwin went on, "There may be a divine destiny, Joe, unlikely as it seems, that makes really dangerous secrets too difficult to be broached until intelligence reaches the point where it can cope with them—*if* said intelligence has the will and the good intentions. Ma Garver says to come up now.''

They headed for the stairs. ''I'm surprised that you leave it up to an old gal like Ma to take charge curing an emergency.''

''She's competent, I assure you. But I *was* running things—you heard me.''

''Oh.''

They settled down again in the above-surface study. ''I give you one more chance to back out, Joe. It doesn't matter that you know all about the films, since they are gone and you can't prove anything—but beyond that—you realize that if you come in with us, are told what is going on, you will be killed deader than a duck at the first suspicious move?''

Gilead did; he knew in fact that he was already beyond the point of no return. With the destruction of the films went his last chance of rehabilitating his former main *persona*. This gave him no worry; the matter was done. He had become aware that from the time he had admitted that he understood the first message this man had offered him concealed in a double deck of cards he had no longer been a free actor, his moves had been constrained by moves made by Baldwin. Yet there was no help for it; his future lay here or nowhere.

''I know it; go ahead.''

''I know what your mental reservations are, Joe; you are simply accepting risk; not promising loyalty.''

''Yes—but why are you considering taking a chance on me?''

Baldwin was more serious in manner than he usually allowed himself to be. ''You're an able man, Joe. You have the savvy and the moral courage to do what is reasonable in an odd situation rather than what is conventional.''

''That's why you want me?''

''Partly that. Partly because I like the way you catch on to a new card game.'' He grinned. ''And even partly because Gail likes the way you behave with a colt.''

''Gail? What's she got to do with it?''

''She reported on you to me about five minutes ago, during the raid.''

''Hmm—go ahead.''

''You've been warned.'' For a moment Baldwin looked almost sheepish. ''I want you to take what I say next at its face value, Joe—don't laugh.''

''Okay.''

''You asked what I was. I'm sort of the executive secretary of this branch of an organization of supermen.''

''I thought so.''

''Eh? How long have you known?''

''Things added up. The card game, your reaction time. I knew it when you destroyed the films.''

''Joe, what is a superman?''

Gilead did not answer.

"Very well, let's check the term," Baldwin went on. "It's been overused and misused and beat up until it is mostly comic connotations. I used it for shock value and I didn't shock you. The term 'supermen' has come to have a fairy tale meaning, conjuring up pictures of x-ray eyes, odd sense organs, double hearts, uncuttable skin, steel muscles—an adolescent's dream of the dragon-killing hero. Tripe, of course. Joe, what is a *man*? What is man that makes him more than an animal? Settle that and we'll take a crack at defining a superman—or New Man, *homo novis,* who must displace *homo sapiens*—*is* displacing him—because he is better able to survive than is homo sap. I'm not trying to define myself, I'll leave it up to my associates and the inexorable processes of time as to whether or not I am a superman, a member of the new species of man—same test to apply to you."

"*Me?*"

"You. You show disturbing symptoms of being *homo novis*, Joe, in a sloppy, ignorant, untrained fashion. Not likely, but you just might be one of the breed. Now—what is man? What is the one thing he can do better than animals which is so strong a survival factor that it outweighs all the things that animals of one sort or another can do much better than he can?"

"He can think."

"I fed you that answer; no prize for it. Okay, you pass yourself off as a man; let's see you do something. What is the one possible conceivable factor—or factors, if you prefer—which the hypothetical superman could have, by mutation or magic or any means, and which could be added to this advantage which man already has and which has enabled him to dominate this planet against the unceasing opposition of a million other species of fauna? Some factor that would make the domination of man by his successor, as inevitable as your domination over a hound dog? Think, Joe. What is the *necessary* direction of evolution to the next dominant species?"

Gilead engaged in contemplation for what was for him a long time. There were so many lovely attributes that a man might have; to be able to see both like a telescope and microscope, to see the insides of things, to see throughout the spectrum, to have hearing of the same order, to be immune to disease, to grow a new arm or leg, to fly through the air without bothering with silly gadgets like helicopters or jets, to walk unharmed the ocean bottom, to work without tiring—

Yet the eagle could fly and he was nearly extinct, even though his eyesight was better than man's. A dog has better smell and hearing; seals swim better, balance better, and furthermore can store oxygen. Rats can survive where men would starve or die of hardship; they are smart and pesky hard to kill. Rats could—

Wait! Could tougher, smarter rats displace man? No, it just wasn't in them; too small a brain.

"To be able to think better," Gilead answered almost instantly.

"Hand the man a cigar! Supermen are superthinkers; anything else is a side issue. I'll allow the possibility of supersomethings which might exterminate or dominate mankind other than by outsmarting him in his own racket—thought. But I deny that it is possible for a *man* to conceive in discrete terms what such a super-something would be or how this something would win out. New Man will beat out homo sap in homo sap's own specialty—rational thought, the ability to recognize data, store them, integrate them, evaluate correctly the result, and arrive at a correct decision. That is how man got to be champion; the creature who can do it better is the coming champion. Sure, there are other survival factors, good health, good sense organs, fast reflexes, but they aren't even comparable, as the long, rough history of mankind has proved over and over—Marat in his bath, Roosevelt in his wheelchair, Caesar with his epilepsy and his bad stomach, Nelson with one eye and one arm, blind Milton; when the chips are down it's *brain* that wins, not the body's tools."

"Stop a moment," said Gilead. "How about E.S.P.?"

Baldwin shrugged. "I'm not sneering at extra-sensory perception any more than I would at exceptional eyesight—E.S.P. is not in the same league with the ability to think correctly. E.S.P. is a grab bag name for the means other than the known sense organs by which the brain may gather data—but the trick that pays off with first prize is to make use of that data, to *reason* about it. If you would like a telepathic hook-up to Shanghai, I can arrange it; we've got operators at both ends—but you can get whatever data you might happen to need from Shanghai by phone with less trouble, less chance of a bad connection, and less danger of somebody listening in. Telepaths can't pick up a radio message; it's not the same wave band."

"What wave band is it?"

"Later, later. You've got a lot to learn."

"I wasn't thinking especially of telepathy. I was thinking of all parapsychological phenomena."

"Same reasoning. Apportation would be nice, if telekinetics had gotten that far—which it ain't. But a pick-up truck moves things handily enough. Television in the hands of an intelligent man counts for more than clairvoyance in a moron. Quit wasting my time, Joe."

"Sorry."

"We defined thinking as integrating data and arriving at correct answers. Look around you. Most people do that stunt just well enough to get to the corner store and back without breaking a leg. If the average man thinks at all, he does silly things like generalizing from a single datum. He uses one-valued logics. If he is exceptionally bright, he may use two-valued, 'either-or' logic to arrive at his wrong answers. If he is hungry, hurt, or personally interested in the answer, he can't use any sort of logic and will discard an observed fact as blithely as he will stake his life on a piece of wishful thinking. He uses the technical miracles created by superior men without wonder nor surprise, as a kitten accepts a bowl of milk. Far from aspiring to higher reasoning, he is not even aware that high reasoning exists. He classes his own mental process as being of the same sort as the genius of an Einstein. Man is not a rational animal; he is a rationalizing animal.

Robert A. Heinlein

"For explanations of a universe that confuses him he seizes onto numerology, astrology, hysterical religions, and other fancy ways to go crazy. Having accepted such glorified nonsense, facts make no impression on him, even if at the cost of his own life. Joe, one of the hardest things to believe is the abysmal depth of human stupidity.

"That is why there is always room at the top, why a man with just a *leetle* more on the ball can so easily become governor, millionaire, or college president—and why homo sap is sure to be displaced by New Man, because there is so much room for improvement and evolution never stops.

"Here and there among ordinary men is a rare individual who really thinks, can and does use logic in at least one field—he's often as stupid as the rest outside his study or laboratory—but he can think, if he's not disturbed or sick or frightened. This rare individual is responsible for *all* the progress made by the race; the others reluctantly adopt his results. Much as the ordinary man dislikes and distrusts and persecutes the process of thinking he is forced to accept the results occasionally, because thinking is efficient compared with his own maunderings. He may still plant his corn in the dark of the Moon but he will plant better corn developed by better men than he.

"Still rarer is the man who thinks habitually, who applies reason, rather than habit pattern, to all his activity. Unless he masques himself, his is a dangerous life; he is regarded as queer, untrustworthy, subversive of public morals; he is a pink monkey among brown monkeys—a fatal mistake. Unless the pink monkey can dye himself brown before he is caught.

"The brown monkey's instinct to kill is correct; such men are dangerous to all monkey customs.

"Rarest of all is the man who can and does reason at all times, quickly, accurately, inclusively, despite hope or fear or bodily distress, without egocentric bias or thalamic disturbance, with correct memory, with clear distinction between fact, assumption, and non-fact. Such men exist, Joe; they are "New Man'—human in all respects, indistinguishable in appearance or under the scalpel from homo sap, yet as unlike him in action as the Sun is unlike a single candle."

Gilead said, "Are you that sort?"

"You will continue to form your own opinions."

"And you think I may be, too?"

"Could be. I'll have more data in a few days."

Gilead laughed until the tears came. "Kettle Belly, if I'm the future hope of the race, they had better send in the second team quick. Sure I'm brighter than most of the jerks I run into, but, as you say, the competition isn't stiff. But I haven't any sublime aspirations. I've got as lecherous an eye as the next man. I enjoy wasting time over a glass of beer. I just don't *feel* like a superman."

"Speaking of beer, let's have some." Baldwin got up and obtained two cans of the brew. "Remember that Mowgli felt like a wolf. Being a New Man does not divorce you from human sympathies and pleasures. There have been New Men all through history; I doubt if most of them suspected that their difference entitled them to call themselves a different breed. Then they went ahead and bred with the daughters of men, diffusing their talents through the racial organism, preventing them from effectuating until chance brought the genetic factors together again."

"Then I take it that New Man is not a special mutation?"

"Huh? Who isn't a mutation, Joe? All of us are a collection of millions of mutations. Around the globe hundreds of mutations have taken place in our human germ plasm while we have been sitting here. No, homo novis didn't come about because great grandfather stood too close to a cyclotron; homo novis was not even a separate breed until he became aware of himself, organized, and decided to hang on to what his genes had handed him. You could mix New Man back into the race today and lose him; he's merely a variation becoming a species. A million years from now is another matter; I venture to predict that New Man, of that year and model, won't be able to interbreed with homo sap—no viable offspring."

"You don't expect present man—homo sapiens—to disappear?"

"Not necessarily. The dog adapted to man. Probably more dogs now than in umpteen B.C.—and better fed."

"And man would be New Man's dog."

"Again not necessarily. Consider the cat."

"The idea is to skim the cream of the race's germ plasm and keep it biologically separate until the two races are permanently distinct. You chaps sound like a bunch of stinkers, Kettle Belly."

"Monkey talk."

"Perhaps. The new race would necessarily run things—"

"Do you expect New Man to decide grave matters by counting common man's runny noses?"

"No, that was my point. Postulating such a new race, the result is inevitable. Kettle Belly, I confess to a monkey prejudice in favor of democracy, human dignity, and freedom. It goes beyond logic; it is the kind of a world I like. In my job I have jungled with the outcasts of society, shared their slumgullion. Stupid they may be, bad they are not—I have no wish to see them become domestic animals.

For the first time the big man showed concern. His *persona* as "King of the Kopters," master merchandiser, slipped away; he sat in brooding majesty, a lonely and unhappy figure. "I know, Joe. They are of us; their little dignities, their nobilities, are not lessened by their sorry state. Yet it must be."

"Why? New Man will come—granted. But why hurry the process?"

"Ask yourself." He swept a hand toward the oubliette. "Ten minutes ago you and I saved this planet, all our race. It's the hour of the knife. Someone must be on guard if the race is to live; there is no one but us. To guard effectively we New Men must be organized, must never fumble any crisis like this—and must increase our numbers. We are few now, Joe; as the crises increase, we must increase to meet them. Eventually—and it's a dead race with time—we must take over and make certain that baby never plays with matches."

He stopped and brooded. "I confess to that same affection for democracy, Joe. But it's like yearning for the Santa Claus you believed in as a child. For a hundred and fifty years or so democracy, or something like it, could flourish safely. The issues were such as to be settled without disaster by the votes of common men, befogged and ignorant as they were. But now, if the race is simply to stay alive, political decisions depend on real knowledge of such things as nuclear physics, planetary ecology, genetic theory, even system mechanics. They aren't up to it, Joe. With goodness and more will than they possess less than one in a thousand could stay awake over one page of nuclear physics; they can't learn what they must know."

Gilead brushed it aside. "It's up to us to brief them. Their hearts are all right; tell them the score—they'll come down with the right answers."

"No, Joe. We've tried it; it does not work. As you say, most of them are good, the way a dog can be noble and good. Yet there are bad ones—Mrs. Keithley and company and more like her. Reason is poor propaganda when opposed by the yammering, unceasing lies of shrewd and evil and self-serving men. The little man has no way to judge and the shoddy lies are packaged more attractively. There is no way to offer color to a colorblind man, nor is there any way for us to give the man of imperfect brain the canny skill to distinguish a lie from a truth."

"No, Joe. The gulf between us and them is narrow, but it is very deep. We cannot close it."

"I wish," said Gilead, "that you wouldn't class me with your 'New Man'; I feel more at home on the other side."

"You will decide for yourself which side you are one, as each of us has done."

Gilead forced a change in subject. Ordinarily immune to thalamic disturbance this issue upset him; his brain followed Baldwin's argument and assured him that it was true; his inclinations fought it. He was confronted with the sharpest of all tragedy; two equally noble and valid rights, utterly opposed. "What do you people do, aside from stealing films?"

"Mmm—many things." Baldwin relaxed, looked again like a jovial sharp businessman. "Where a push here and a touch there will keep things from going to pot, we apply the pressure, by many and devious means. And we scout for suitable material and bring it into the fold when we can—we've had our eye on you for ten years."

"So?"

"Yep. This is a prime enterpirse. Through public data we eliminate all but about one tenth of one per cent; that thousandth individual we watch. And then there are our horticultural societies." He grinned.

"Finish your joke."

"We weed people."

"Sorry, I'm slow today."

"Joe, didn't you ever feel a yen to wipe out some evil, obscene, rotten jerk who infected everything he touched, yet was immune to legal action? We treat them as cancers; we excise them from the body social. We keep a 'Better Dead' list; when a man is clearly morally bankrupt we close his account at the first opportunity.''

Gilead smiled. "If you were sure what you were doing, it could be fun."

"We are always sure, though our methods would be no good in a monkey law court. Take Mrs. Keithley—is there doubt in your mind?"

"None."

"Why don't you have her indicted? Don't bother to answer. For example, two weeks from tonight there will be giant powwow of the new, rejuvenated, bigger-and-better-than-ever Ku Klux Klan on a mountain top down Carolina way. When the fun is at its height, when they are mouthing obscenities, working each other up to the pogrom spirit, an act of God is going to wipe out the whole kit and kaboodle. Very sad.''

"Could I get in on that?"

"You aren't even a cadet as yet." Baldwin went on. "There is the project to increase our numbers, but that is a thousand-year program; you'd need a perpetual calendar to check it. More important is keeping matches away from baby. Joe, it's been eighty-five years since we beheaded the last commissar: have you wondered why so little basic progress in science has been made in that time?"

"Eh? There have been a lot of changes."

"Minor adaptions—some spectacular, almost none of them basic. Of course there was very little progress made under communism; a totalitarian political religion is incompatible with free investigation. Let me digress: the communist interregnum was responsible for the New Man getting together and organizing. Most New Men are scientists, for obvious reasons. When the commissars started ruling on natural laws by political criteria—Lysenko-ism and similar nonsense—it did not sit well; a lot of us went underground.

"I'll skip the details. It brought us together, gave us practice in underground activity, and gave a backlog of new research, carried out underground. Some of it was obviously dangerous; we decided to hang onto it for a while. Since then such secret knowledge has grown. For we never give out an item until it has been scrutinized for social hazards. Since much of it *is* dangerous and since very few indeed outside our organization are capable of real original thinking, basic science has been almost at a—public!—standstill.

"We hadn't expected to have to do it that way. We helped to see to it that the new constitution was liberal and—we thought—workable. But the new Republic turned out to be an even poorer thing than the old. The evil ethic of communism had corrupted, even after the form was gone. We held off. Now we know that we must hold off until we can revise the whole society.''

"Kettle Belly," Joe said slowly. "you speak as if you had been on the spot. How old are you?"

"I'll tell you when you are the age I am now. A man has lived long enough when he no longer longs to live. I ain't there yet. Joe, I must have your answer, or this must be continued in our next."

"You had it at the beginning—but, see here, Kettle Belly, there is one job I want promised to me."

"Which is?"

"I want to kill Mrs. Keithley."

"Keep your pants on. When you're trained, and if she's still alive then, you'll be used for that purpose—"

"Thanks!"

"—provided you are the proper tool for it." Baldwin turned toward the mike, called out, "Gail!" and added one word in the strange tongue.

Gail showed up promptly. "Joe," said Baldwin, "when this young lady gets through with you, you will be able to sing, whistle, chew gum, play chess, hold your breath, and fly a kite simultaneously—and all this while riding a bicycle under water. Take him, sis, he's all yours."

Gail rubbed her hands. "Oh, boy!"

"First we must teach you to see and to hear, then to remember, then to speak, and then to think."

Joe looked at her. "What's this I'm doing with my mouth at this moment?"

"It's not talking, it's a sort of grunting. Furthermore English is not structurally suited to thinking. Shut up and listen."

In their underground classroom Gail had available several types of apparatus to record and manipulate light and sound. She commenced throwing groups of figures on a screen, in flashes. "What was it, Joe?"

"Nine-six-oh-seven-two—That was as far as I got."

"It was up there a full thousandth of a second. Why did you get only the left hand side of the group?"

"That's all the farther I had read."

"Look at *all* of it. Don't make an effort of will; just look at it." She flashed another number.

Joe's memory was naturally good; his intelligence was high—just how high he did not yet know. Unconvinced that the drill was useful, he relaxed and played along. Soon he was beginning to grasp a nine-digit array as a single *gestalt;* Gail reduced the flash time.

"What is this magic lantern gimmick?" he inquired.

"It's a Renshaw tachistoscope. Back to work."

Around World War II Dr. Samuel Renshaw at the Ohio State University was proving that most people are about one-fifth efficient in using their capacities to see, hear, taste, feel and remember. His research was swallowed in the morass of communist pseudoscience that obtained after World War III, but, after his death, his findings were preserved underground. Gail did not expose Gilead to the odd language he had heard until he had been rather thoroughly Renshawed.

However, from the time of his interview with Baldwin the other persons at the ranch used it in his presence. Sometimes someone—usually Ma Garver—would translate, sometimes not. He was flattered to feel accepted, but gravelled to know that it was at the lowest cadetship. He was a child among adults.

Gail started teaching him to hear by speaking to him single words from the odd language, requiring him to repeat them back. "No, Joe. Watch." This time when she spoke the word it appeared on the screen in sound analysis, by a means basically like one long used to show the deaf-and-dumb their speech mistakes. "Now you try it."

He did, the two arrays hung side by side. "How's that, teacher?" he said triumphantly.

"Terrible, by several decimal places. You held the final guttural too long—" She pointed. "—the middle vowel was formed with your tongue too high and you pitched it too low and you failed to let the pitch rise. And six other things. You couldn't possibly have been understood. I heard what you said, but it was gibberish. Try again. And don't call me 'teacher.' "

"Yes, ma'am," he answered solemnly.

She shifted the controls; he tried again. This time his analysis array was laid down on top of hers; where the two matched, they cancelled. Where they did not match, his errors stood out in contrasting colors. The screen looked like a sun burst.

"Try again, Joe." She repeated the word without letting it affect the display.

"Confound it, if you would tell me what the words mean instead of treating me the way Milton treated his daughters about Latin, I could remember them easier."

She shrugged. "I can't, Joe. You must learn to hear and to speak first. Speedtalk is a flexible language; the same word is not likely to recur. This practice word means: 'The far horizons draw no nearer.' That's not much help is it?"

The definition seemed improbable, but he was learning not to doubt her. He was not used to women who were always two jumps ahead of him. He ordinarily felt sorry for the poor little helpless cuddly creatures; this one he often wanted to slug. He wondered if this response were what the romancers meant by "love"; he decided that it couldn't be.

"Try again, Joe." Speedtalk was a structurally different speech from any the race had ever used. Long before, Ogden and Richards had shown that eight hundred and fifty words were sufficient vocabulary to express anything that could be expressed by "normal" human vocabularies, with the aid of a handful of special words—a hundred odd—for each special field, such as horse racing or ballistics. About the same time phoneticians had analyzed all human tongues into about a hundred-odd sounds, represented by the letters of a general phonetic alphabet.

On these two propositions Speedtalk was based.

To be sure, the phonetic alphabet was much less in number than the words in Basic English. But the letters representing sound in the phonetic alphabet were each capable of variation several different ways—length, stress, pitch, rising, falling. The more trained an ear was the larger the number of possible variations; there was no limit to variations, but, without much refinement of accepted phonetic practice, it was possible to establish a one-to-one relationship with Basic English so that *one phonetic symbol* was equivalent to an entire word in a "normal" language, one Speedtalk word was equal to an entire sentence. The language consequently was learned by letter units rather than by word units—but each word was spoken and listened to as a single structured gestalt.

But Speedtalk was not "shorthand" Basic English. "Normal" languages, having their roots in days of superstition and ignorance, have in them inherently and unescapably wrong structures of mistaken ideas about the universe. One can think logically in English only by extreme effort, so bad it is as a mental tool. For example, the verb "to be" in English has twenty-one distinct meanings, *every single one of which is false-to-fact.*

A symbolic structure, invented instead of accepted without question, can be made similar in structure to the real-world to which it refers. The structure of Speedtalk did *not* contain the hidden errors of English; it was structured as much like the real world as the New Men could make it. For example, it did not contain the unreal distinction between nouns and verbs found in most other languages. The world—the continuum known to science and including all human activity—does not contain "noun things" and "verb things"; it contains space-time events and relationships between them. The advantage for achieving truth, or something more nearly like truth, was similar to the advantage of keeping account books in Arabic numerals rather than Roman.

All other languages made scientific, multi-valued logic almost impossible to achieve; in Speedtalk it was as difficult *not* to be logical. Compare the pellucid Boolean logic with the obscurities of the Aristotelean logic it supplanted.

Paradoxes are verbal, do not exist in the real world—and Speedtalk did not have such built into it. Who shaves the Spanish Barber? Answer: follow him around and see. In the syntax of Speedtalk the paradox of the Spanish Barber could not even be expressed, save as a self-evident error.

But Joe Greene-Gilead-Briggs could not learn it until he had learned to hear, by learning to speak. He slaved away; the screen continued to remain lighted with his errors.

Came finally a time when Joe's pronunciation of a sentenceword blanked out Gail's sample; the screen turned dark. He felt more triumph over that than anything he could remember.

His delight was short. By a circuit Gail had thoughtfully added some days earlier the machine answered with a flourish of trumpets, loud applause, and then added in a cooing voice, "Mama's *good* boy!"

He turned to her. "Woman, you spoke of matrimony. If you ever do manage to marry me, I'll beat you."

"I haven't made up my mind about you yet," she answered evenly. "Now try this word, Joe—"

Baldwin showed up that evening, called him aside. "Joe! C'mere. Listen, lover boy, you keep your animal nature out of your work, or I'll have to find you a new teacher.''

"But—"

"You heard me. Take her swimming, take her riding, after hours you are on your own. Work time—strictly business. I've got plans for you; I want you to get smarted up.''

"She complained about me?''

"Don't be silly. It's my business to know what's going on.''

"Hmm. Kettle Belly, what is this shopping-for-a-husband she kids about? Is she serious, or is it just intended to rattle me?''

"Ask her. Not that it matters, as you won't have any choice if she means it. She has the calm persistence of the law of gravitation.''

"Ouch! I had had the impression that the 'New Men' did not bother with marriage and such like, as you put it, 'monkey customs.' ''

"Some do, some don't. Me, I've been married quite a piece, but I mind a mousy little member of our lodge who has had nine kids by nine fathers—all wonderful genius-plus kids. On the other hand I can point out one with eleven kids—Thalia Wagner—who has never so much as looked at another man. Geniuses make their own rules in such matters, Joe; they always have. Here are some established statistical facts about genius, as shown by Armatoe's work—''

He ticked them off. "Geniuses are usually long lived. They are not modest, not honestly so. They have infinite capacity for taking pains. They are emotionally indifferent to accepted codes of morals—they make their own rules. You seem to have the stigmata, by the way.''

"Thanks for nothing. Maybe I should have a new teacher; is there is anyone else available who can do it?''

"*Any* of us can do it, just as anybody handy teaches a baby to talk. She's actually a biochemist, when she has time for it.''

"When she has time?''

"Be careful of that kid, son. Her real profession is the same as yours—honorable hatchet man. She's killed upwards of three hundred people.'' Kettle Belly grinned. "If you want to switch teachers, just drop me a wink.''

Gilead-Greene hastily changed the subject. "You were speaking of work for me: how about Mrs. Keithley? Is she still alive?''

"Yes, blast her.''

"Remember, I've got dibs on her.''

"You may have to go to the Moon to get her. She's reported to be building a vacation home there. Old age seems to be telling on her; you had better get on with your homework if you want a crack at her.'' Moon Colony even then was a center of geriatrics for the rich. The low gravity was easy on their hearts, made them feel young—and possibly extended their lives.

"Okay, I will.''

Instead of asking for a new teacher Joe took a highly polished apple to their next session. Gail ate it, leaving him very little core, and put him harder to work than ever. While perfecting his hearing and pronunciation, she started him on the basic thousand-letter vocabulary by forcing him to start to talk simple three and four-letter sentences, and by answering him in difference word-sentences using the same phonetic letters. Some of the vowel and consonant sequences were very difficult to pronounce.

Master them he did. He had been used to doing most things easier than could those around him; now he was in very fast company. He stretched himself and began to achieve part of his own large latent capacity. When he began to catch some of the dinner-table conversation and to reply in simple Speedtalk—being forbidden by Gail to answer in English—she started him on the ancillary vocabularies.

An economical language cannot be limited to a thousand words; although almost every idea can be expressed somehow in a short vocabulary, higher orders of abstraction are convenient. For technical words Speedtalk employed an open expansion of sixty of the thousand-odd phonetic letters. They were the letters ordinarily used as numerals; by preceding a number with a letter used for no other purpose, the symbol was designated as having a word value.

New Men numbered to the base sixty-three times four times five, a convenient, easily factored system, most economical, i.e., the symbol "100" identified the number described in English as thirty-six hundred—yet permitting quick, in-the-head translation from common notation to Speedtalk figures and vice versa.

By using these figures, each prefaced by the indicator—a voiceless Welsh or Burmese "1"—a pool of 215,999 words (one less than the cube of sixty) were available for specialized meaning without using more than four letters including the indicator. Most of them could be pronounced as one syllable. These had not the stark simplicity of basic Speedtalk; nevertheless words such as "icthyophagous" and "constitutionality" were thus compressed to monosyllables. Such shortcuts can best be appreciated by anyone who has heard a long speech in Cantonese translated into a short speech in English. Yet English is not the most terse of "normal" languages—and expanded Speedtalk is many times more economical than the briefest of "normal" tongues.

By adding one more letter (sixty to the fourth power) just short of thirteen *million* words could be added if needed—and most of them could still be pronounced as one syllable.

When Joe discovered that Gail expected him to learn a couple of hundred thousand new words in a matter of days, he balked. "Damn it, Fancy Pants, I am not a superman. I'm in here by mistake."

"Your opinion is worthless; I think you can do it. Now listen."

"Suppose I flunk; does that put me safely off your list of possible victims?"

"If you flunk, I wouldn't have you on toast. Instead I'd tear your head off and stuff it down your throat. But you won't flunk; I *know*. However," she added, "I'm not sure you would be a satisfactory husband; you argue too much."

He made a brief and bitter remark in Speedtalk; she answered with one word which described his shortcomings in detail. They got to work.

Joe was mistaken; he learned the expanded vocabulary as fast as he heard it. He had a latent eidetic memory; the Renshawing process now enabled him to use it fully. And his mental processes, always fast, had become faster than he knew.

The ability to learn Speedtalk at all is proof of super-normal intelligence; the *use* of it by such intelligence renders that mind efficient. Even before World War II Alfred Korzybski had shown that human thought was performed, when done efficiently, only in symbols; the notion of "pure" thought, free of abstracted speech symbols, was merely fantasy. The brain was so constructed as to work without symbols only on the animal level; to speak of "reasoning" without symbols was to speak nonsense.

Speedtalk did not merely speed up communication—by its structures it made thought more logical; by its economy it made thought processes enormously faster, since it takes almost as long to *think* a word as it does to speak it.

Korzybski's monumental work went fallow during the communist interregnum; *Das Kapital* is a childish piece of work, when analyzed by semantics, so the politburo suppressed semantics—and replaced it by *ersatz* under the same name, as Lysenkoism replaced the science of genetics.

Having Speedtalk to help him learn *more* Speedtalk, Joe learned very rapidly. The Renshawing had continued; he was now able to grasp a gestalt or configuration in many senses at once, grasp it, remember it, reason about it with great speed.

Living time is not calendar time; a man's life is the thought that flows through his brain. Any man capable of learning Speedtalk had an association time at least three times as fast as an ordinary man. Speedtalk itself enabled him to manipulate symbols approximately seven times as fast as English symbols could be manipulated. Seven times three is twenty-one; a New Man had an *effective* lifetime of at least *sixteen hundred years*, reckoned in flow of ideas.

They had time to become encyclopedic synthesists, something denied any ordinary man by the straitjacket of his sort of time.

When Joe had learned to talk, to read and write and cipher, Gail turned him over to others for his real education. But before she checked him out she played him several dirty tricks.

For three days she forbade him to eat. When it was evident that he could think and keep his temper despite low bloodsugar count, despite hunger reflex, she added sleeplessness and pain—intense, long, continued, and varied pain. She tried subtly to goad him into irrational action; he remained bedrock steady, his mind clicking away at any assigned task as dependably as an electronic computer.

"Who's not a superman?" she asked at the end of their last session.

"Yes, teacher."

"Come here, lug." She grabbed him by the ears, kissed him soundly. "So long." He did not see her again for many weeks.

His tutor in E.S.P. was an ineffectual-looking little man who had taken the protective coloration of the name Weems. Joe was not very good at producing E.S.P. phenomena. Clairvoyance he did not appear to have. He was better at precognition, but he did not improve with practice. He was best at telekinesis; he could have made a soft living with dice. But, as Kettle Belly had pointed out, from affecting the roll of dice to moving tons of freight was quite a gap—and one possibly not worth bridging.

"It may have other uses, however," Weems had said softly, lapsing into English. "Consider what might be done if one could influence the probability that a neutron would reach a particular nucleus—or change the statistical probability in a mass."

Gilead let it ride; it was an outrageous thought.

At telepathy he was erratic to exasperation. He called the Rhine cards once without a miss, then had poor scores for three weeks. More highly structured communication seemed quite beyond him, until one day without apparent cause but during an attempt to call the cards by telepathy, he found himself hooked in with Weems for all of ten seconds—time enough for a thousand words of Speedtalk standards.

—it comes out as speech!

—why not? thought is speech.

—how do we do it?

—if we knew it would not be so unreliable. as it is, some can do it by volition, some by accident, and some never seem to be able to do it. we do know this: while thought may not be of the physical world in any fashion we can now define and manipulate, it is similar to events in continuum in its quantal nature. You are now studying the extension of the quantum concept to all features of the continuum, you know the chronon, the mensum, and the viton, as quanta, as well as the action units of quanta such as the photon. the continuum has not only structure but texture in all its features. The least unit of thought we term the psychon.

—define it. put salt on its tail.

—some day, some day. I can tell you this: the fastest possible rate of thought is one psychon per chronon; this is a basic, universal constant.

—how close do we come to that?

—less than sixty-to-the-minus-third-power of the possibility.

—!!!!!!

—better creatures than ourselves will follow us. We pick pebbles at a boundless ocean.

—what can we do to improve it?

—gather our pebbles with serene minds.

Gilead paused for a long split second of thought. *—can psychons be destroyed?*

—vitons may be transferred. psychons are—

The connection was suddenly destroyed. "As I was saying," Weems went on quietly, "psychons are as yet beyond our comprehension in many respects. Theory indicates that they may not be destroyed, that thought, like action, is persistent. Whether or not such theory, if true, means that personal identity is also persistent must remain an open question. See the daily papers—a few hundred years from now—or a few hundred thousand." He stood up.

"I'm anxious to try tomorrow's session, Doc," Gilead-Greene almost bubbled. "Maybe—"

"I'm finished with you."

"But, Doctor Weems that connection was clear as a phone hook-up. Perhaps tomorrow—"

"We have established that your talent is erratic. We have no way to train it to dependability. Time is too short to waste, mine and yours." Lapsing suddenly into English, he added, "No."

Gilead left.

During his training in other fields Joe was exposed to many things best described as impressive gadgets. There was an integrating pantograph, a factory-in-a-box, which the New Men planned to turn over to ordinary men as soon as the social system was no longer dominated by economic wolves. It could and did reproduce almost any prototype placed on its stage, requiring thereto only materials and power. Its power came from a little nucleonics motor the size of Joe's thumb; its theory played hob with conventional notions of entropy. One put in "sausage"; one got out "pig."

Latent in it was the shape of an economic system as different from the current one as the assembly-line economy differed from the family-shop system—and in such a system lay possibilities of human freedom and dignity missing for centuries, if they had ever existed.

In the meantime New Men rarely bought more than one of anything—a pattern. Or they made a pattern.

Another useful but hardly wonderful gadget was a dictaphone-typewriter-printing-press combination. The machine's analyzers recognized each of the thousand-odd phonetic symbols; there was a typebar for each sound. It produced one or many copies. Much of Gilead's education came from pages printed by this gadget, saving the precious time of others.

The arrangement, classification, and accessibility of knowledge remains in all ages the most pressing problem. With the New Men, complete and organized memory licked most of the problem and rendered record keeping, most reading and writing—and most especially the time-destroying trouble of rereading—unnecessary. the autoscriber gadget, combined with a "librarian" machine that could "hear" that portion of Speedtalk built into it as a filing system, covered most of the rest of the problem. New Men were not cluttered with endless bits of paper. They *never* wrote memoranda.

The area under the ranch was crowded with technological wonders, all newer than next week. Incredibly tiny manipulators for micrurgy of all sorts, surgical, chemical, biological manipulation, oddities of cybernetics only slightly less complex than the human brain—the list is too long to describe. Joe did not study all of them; an

Robert A. Heinlein

encyclopedic synthesist is concerned with structured shapes of knowledge; he cannot, even with Speedtalk, study details in every field.

Early in his education, when it was clear that he had had the potential to finish the course, plastic surgery was started to give him a new identity and basic appearance. His height was reduced by three inches; his skull was somewhat changed; his complexion was permanently darkened. Gail picked the facial appearance he was given; he did not object. He rather liked it; it seemed to fit his new inner personality.

With a new face, a new brain, and a new outlook, he was almost in fact a new man. Before he had been a natural genius; now he was a *trained* genius.

"Joe, how about some riding?"

"Suits."

"I want to give War Conqueror some gentle exercise. He's responding to the saddle; I don't want him to forget."

"Right with you."

Kettle Belly and Gilead-Greene rode out from the ranch buildings. Baldwin let the young horse settle to a walk and began to talk. "I figure you are about ready for work, son." Even in Speedtalk Kettle Belly's speech retained his own flavor.

"I suppose so, but I still have those mental reservations."

"Not sure we are on the side of the angels?"

"I'm sure you mean to be. It's evident that the organization selects for good will and humane intentions quite as carefully as for ability. I wasn't sure at one time—"

"Yes?"

"That candidate who came here about six months ago, the one who broke his neck in a riding accident."

"Oh, yes! Very sad."

"Very opportune, you mean, Kettle Belly."

"Damn it, Joe, if a bad apple gets in this far, we can't let him out." Baldwin reverted to English for swearing purposes; he maintained that it had "more juice."

"I know it. That's why I'm sure about the quality of our people."

"So it's 'our people' now?"

"Yes. But I'm not sure we are on the right track."

"What's your notion of the right track?"

"We should come out of hiding and teach the ordinary man what he can learn of what we know. He could learn a lot of it and could use it. Properly briefed and trained, he could run his affairs pretty well. He would gladly kick out the no-goods who ride on his shoulders, if only he knew how. We could show him. That would be more to the point than this business of spot assassination, now and then, here and there—mind you, I don't object to killing any man who merits killing; I simply say it's inefficient. No doubt we would have to continue to guard against such crises as the one that brought you and me together, but, in the main, people could run their own affairs if we would just stop pretending that we are so scared we can't mix with people, come out of our hole, and lend a hand.''

Baldwin reined up. "Don't say that I don't mix with the common people, Joe; I sell used 'copters for a living. You can't get any commoner. And don't imply that my heart is not with them. We are not like them, but we are tied to them by the strongest bond of all, each and every one, sickening with the same certainly fatal disease—we are alive.

"As for our killings, you don't understand the principles of assassination as a political weapon. Read—'' He named a Speedtalk library designation. "If I were knocked off, our organization wouldn't even hiccup, but organizations for bad purposes are different. They are personal empires; if you pick the time and the method, you can destroy such an organization by killing one man—the parts that remain will be almost harmless until assimilated by another leader—then you kill *him*. It is not inefficient; it's quite efficient, if planned with the brain and not with the emotions.

"As for keeping ourselves separate, we are about like the U-235 in U-238, not effective unless separated out. There have been potential New Men in every generation, but they were spread too thin.

"As for keeping our existence secret, it is utterly necessary if we are to survive and increase. There is nothing so dangerous as being the Chosen People—and in the minority. One group was persecuted for two thousand years merely for making the claim.''

He again shifted to English to swear. "Damn it, Joe, face up to it. this world is run the way my great aunt Susie flies a 'copter. Speedtalk or no Speedtalk, common man *can't* learn to cope with modern problems. No use to talk about the unused potential of his brain, he has not got the *will* to learn what he would have to know. We can't fit him out with new genes, so we have to lead him by the hand to keep him from killing himself—and us. We can give him personal liberty, we can give him autonomy in most things, we can give him a great measure of personal dignity—and we will, because we believe that individual freedom, at all levels, is the direction of evolution, of maximum survival value. But we can't let him fiddle with issues of racial life and death; he ain't up to it.

"No help for it. Each shape of society develops its own ethic. We are shaping this the way we are inexorably forced to, by the logic of events. We *think* we are shaping it toward survival.''

"Are we?" mused Greene-Gilead.

"Remains to be seen. Survivors survive. We'll know—Wup! Meeting's adjourned.''

The radio on Baldwin's pommel was shrilling his personal emergency call. He listened, then spoke one sharp word in Speedtalk. "Back to the house, Joe!" He wheeled and was away. Joe's mount came of less selected stock; he was forced to follow.

Baldwin sent for Joe soon after he got back. Joe went in; Gail was already there.

Robert A. Heinlein

Baldwin's face was without expression. He said in English, "I've work for you, Joe, work you won't have any doubt about. Mrs. Keithley."

"Good."

"Not good." Baldwin shifted to Speedtalk. "We have been caught flat-footed. Either the second set of films was never destroyed, or there was a third set. We do not know; the man who could tell us is dead. But Mrs. Keithley obtained a set and has been using them.

"This is the situation. The 'fuse' of the nova effect has been installed in the New Age hotel. It has been sealed off and can be triggered only by radio signal from the Moon—her signal. The 'fuse' has been rigged so that any attempt to break in, as long as the firing circuit is still armed, will trigger it and set it off. Even an attempt to examine it by penetration wavelengths will set it off. Speaking as a physicist, it is my considered opinion that *no* plan for tackling the 'Nova' fuse bomb itself will work unless the arming circuit is first broken on the Moon and that no attempt should be made to get a fuse before then, because of extreme danger to the entire planet.

"The arming circuit and the radio relay to the Earthside trigger is located on the Moon in a building inside her private dome. The triggering control she keeps with her. From the same control she can disarm the arming circuit temporarily; it is a combination dead-man switch and time-clock arrangement. It can be set to disarm for a maximum of twelve hours, and let her sleep, or possibly to permit her to order rearrangements. Unless it is switched off any attempt to enter the building in which the arming circuit is housed will also trigger the 'Nova' bomb circuit. While it is disarmed, the housing on the Moon may be broached by force but this will set off alarms which will warn her to rearm and then to trigger at once. The set up is such that the following sequence of events must take place:

"First, she must be killed, and the circuit disarmed.

"Second, the building housing the arming circuit and radio relay to the trigger must be broken open and the circuits destroyed *before* the time clock can rearm and trigger. This must be done with speed, not only because of guards, but because her surviving lieutenants will attempt to seize power by possessing themselves of the controls.

"Third, as soon as word is received on Earth that the arming circuit is destroyed, the New Age will be attacked in force and the 'Nova' bomb destroyed.

"Fourth, as soon as the bomb is destroyed, a general roundup must be made of all persons technically capable of setting up the 'Nova' effect from plans. This alert must be maintained until it is certain that no plans remain in existence, including the third set of films, and further established by hypno that no competent person possess sufficient knowledge to set it up without plans. This alert may compromise our secret status; the risk must be taken.

"Any questions?"

"Kettle Belly," said Joe. "Doesn't she know that if the Earth becomes a nova, the Moon will be swallowed up in the disaster?"

"Crater walls shield her dome from line-of-sight with Earth; apparently she believes she is safe. Evil is essentially stupid, Joe; despite her brilliance, she believes what she wishes to believe. Or it may be that she is willing to risk her own death against the tempting prize of absolute power. Her plan is to proclaim power with some pious nonsense about being high priestess of peace—a euphemism for Empress of Earth. It is a typical paranoid deviation; the proof of the craziness lies in the fact that the physical arrangements make it certain—if we do not intervene—that Earth will be destroyed automatically a few hours after her death; a thing that could happen any time—and a compelling reason for all speed. No one has ever quite managed to conquer all of Earth, not even the commissars. Apparently she wishes not only to conquer it, but wants to destroy it after she is gone, lest anyone else ever manage to do so again. Any more questions?''

He went on, ''The plan is this:

''You two will go to the Moon to become domestic servants to Mr. and Mrs. Alexander Copley, a rich, elderly couple living at the Elysian Rest Homes, Moon Colony. They are of us. Shortly they will decide to return to Earth; you two will decide to remain, you like it. You will advertise, offering to work for anyone who will post your return bond. About this time Mrs. Keithley will have lost through circumstances that will be arranged, two or more of her servants; she will probably hire you, since domestic service is the scarcest commodity on the Moon. If not, a variation will be arranged for you.

''When you are inside her dome, you'll maneuver yourselves into positions to carry out your assignments. When both of you are so placed, you will carry out procedures one and two with speed.

''A person named McGinty, already inside her dome, will help you in communication. He is not one of us but is our agent, a telepath. His ability does not extend past that. Your communication hook up will probably be, Gail to McGinty by telepathy, McGinty to Joe by concealed radio.''

Joe glanced at Gail; it was the first that he had known that she was a telepath. Baldwin went on, ''Gail will kill Mrs. Keithley; Joe will break into the housing and destroy the circuits. Are you ready to go?''

Joe was about to suggest swapping the assignments when Gail answered, ''Ready''; he echoed her.

''Good. Joe, you will carry your assumed I.Q. at aboout 85, Gail at 95; she will appear to be the dominant member of a married couple—'' Gail grinned at Joe. ''—but you, Joe, will be in charge. Your personalities and histories are now being made up and will be ready with your identifications. Let me say again that the greatest of speed is necessary; government security forces here may attempt a fool-hardy attack on the New Age hotel. We shall prevent or delay such efforts, but act with speed. Good luck.''

Operation Black Widow, first phase, went off as planned. Eleven days later Joe and Gail were inside Mrs. Keithley's dome on the moon and sharing a room in the servants' quarters. Gail glanced around when first they entered it and said in Speedtalk, "Now you'll have to marry me; I'm compromised."

"Shut that up, idiot! Some one might hear you."

"Pooh! They'd just think I had asthma. Don't you think it's noble of me, Joe, to sacrifice my girlish reputation for home and country?"

"What reputation?"

"Come closer so I can slug you."

Even the servants' quarter was luxurious. The dome was a sybarite's dream. The floor of it was gardened in real beauty save where Mrs. Keithley's mansion stood. Opposite it, across a little lake—certainly the only lake on the Moon—was the building housing the circuits; it was disguised as a little Doric Grecian shrine.

The dome itself was edge-lighted fifteen hours out of each twenty-four, shutting out the black sky and the harsh stars. At "night" the lighting was gradually withdrawn.

McGinty was a gardener and obviously enjoyed his work. Gail established contact with him, got out of him what little he knew. Joe left him alone save for contacts in character.

There was a staff of over two hundred, having its own social hierarchy, from engineers for dome and equipment, Mrs. Keithley's private pilot, and so on down to gardeners' helpers. Joe and Gail were midway, being inside servants. Gail made herself popular as the harmlessly flirtatious but always helpful and sympathetic wife of a meek and older husband. She had been a beauty parlor operator, so it seemed, before she "married" and had great skill in massaging aching backs and stiff necks, relieving headaches and inducing sleep. She was always ready to demonstrate.

Her duties as a maid had not yet brought her into close contact with their employer. Joe, however, had acquired the job of removing all potted plants to the "outdoors" during "night"; Mrs. Keithley, according to Mr. James, the butler, believed that plants should be outdoors at "night." Joe was thus in a position to get outside the house when the dome was dark; he had already reached the point where the night guard at the Grecian temple would sometimes get Joe to "jigger" for him while the guard snatched a forbidden cigarette.

McGinty had been able to supply one more important fact: in addition to the guard at the temple building, and the locks and armor plate of the building itself, the arming circuit was booby-trapped. Even if it were inoperative as an arming circuit for the 'Nova' bomb on Earth, it itself would blow up if tampered with. Gail and Joe discussed it in their room. Gail sitting on his lap like an affectionate wife, her lips close to his left ear. "Perhaps you could wreck it from the door, without exposing yourself."

"I've got to be sure. There is certainly some way of switching that gimmick off. She has to provide for possible repairs or replacements."

"Where would it be?"

"Just one place that matches the pattern of the rest of her planning. Right under her hand, along with the disarming switch and the trigger switch." He rubbed his other ear; it contained his short-range radio hook-up to McGinty and itched almost constantly.

"Hmm—then there's just one thing to be done; I'll have to wring it out of her before I kill her."

"We'll see."

Just before dinner the following "evening" she found him in their room. "It worked, Joe, it worked!"

"What worked?"

"She fell for the bait. She heard from her secretary about my skill as a masseuse; I was ordered up for a demonstration this afternoon. Now I am under strict instructions to come to her tonight and rub her to sleep."

"It's tonight, then."

McGinty waited in his room, behind a locked door. Joe stalled in the back hall, spinning out endlessly a dull tale to Mr. James.

A voice in his ear said, "She's in *her* room now."

"—and that's how my brother got married to two women at once," Joe concluded. "Sheer bad luck. I better get these plants outside before the missus happens to ask about 'em."

"I suppose you had. Goodnight."

"Goodnight, Mr. James." He picked up two of the pots and waddled out.

He put them down outside and heard, "She says she's started to massage. She's spotted the radio switching unit; it's on the belt that the old gal keeps at her bedside table when she's not wearing it."

"Tell her to kill her and grab it."

"She says she wants to make her tell how to unswitch the booby-trap gimmick first."

"Tell her not to delay."

Suddenly, inside his head, clear and sweet as a bell as if they were her own spoken tones, he heard her. —*Joe, I can hear you, can you hear me?*

—*yes, yes!* Aloud he added, "*Stand by the phones anyhow, Mac.*"

—*it won't be long. I have her in intense pain; she'll crack soon.*

—*hurt her plenty!* He began to run toward the temple building. —*Gail, are you still shopping for a husband?*

—*I've found him.*

—*marry me and I'll beat you every Saturday night.*

—*the man who can beat me hasn't been born.*

—*I'd like to try.* He slowed down before he came near the guard's station. "Hi, Jim!"

—*it's a deal.*

"Well, if it taint Joey boy! Got a match?"

284   Robert A. Heinlein

"Here." He reached out a hand—then, as the guard fell, he eased him to the ground and made sure that he would stay out. —*Gail! It's got to be now!*

The voice in his head came back in great consternation:

—*Joe! She was too touch, she wouldn't crack. She's dead!*

—*good! get that belt, break the arming circuit, then see what else you find. I'm going to break in.*

He went toward the door of the temple.

—*it's disarmed, Joe. I could spot it; it has a time set on it. I can't tell about the others; they aren't marked and they all look alike.*

He took from his pocket a small item provided by Baldwin's careful planning. —*twist them all from where they are to the other way. You'll probably hit it.*

—*oh, Joe, I hope so!*

He had placed the item against the lock; the metal around it turned red and now was melting away. An alarm clanged somewhere.

Gail's voice came again in his head; there was urgency in it but no fear: —*Joe! they're beating on the door. I'm trapped.*

—*McGinty! be our witness!* He went on: —*I, Joseph, take thee, Gail, to be my lawfully wedded wife—*

He was answered in tranquil rhythm:—*I, Gail, take thee, Joseph, to be my lawfully wedded husband—*

—*to have and to hold,* he went on.

—*to have and to hold, my beloved!*

—*for better, for worse—*

—*for better, for worse—* Her voice in his head was singing.

—*till death do us part, I've got it open, darling; I am going in.*

—*till death do us part! They are breaking down the bedroom door, Joseph my dearest.*

—*hang on! I'm almost through here.*

—*they have broken it down, Joe. They are coming toward me. Good-bye my darling! I am very happy.* Abruptly her "voice" stopped.

He was facing the box that housed the disarming circuit, alarms clanging in his ears; he took from his pocket another gadget and tried it.

The blast that shattered the box caught him full in the chest.

The letters on the metal marker read:

TO THE MEMORY OF
MR. AND MRS. JOSEPH GREENE
WHO, NEAR THIS SPOT,
DIED FOR ALL THEIR FELLOW MEN ■

ABOUT THE EDITOR

Stanley Schmidt has
a varied background,
including formal training
and professional experience
as a physicist. One of the
last writers developed
by the legendary John W. Campbell, he was
a frequent contributor to
Analog for ten years
before becoming its editor in 1978.

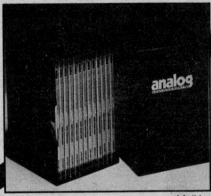